"WE CAN'T SEE EACH OTHER
IN LONDON."

"Do you have a wife?" she asked, steeling herself for an answer she wouldn't like.

"Good God, no!" he exclaimed, his expression horrified. "But we come from separate worlds. They must remain that way."

"Why?" She moved toward him.

"Jesus, Lady Kiri!" He bolted from his chair and retreated as if she were wielding her new dagger. "You are not making it easy to do the right thing!"

"Call me Kiri." She smiled with wicked delight at seeing how she affected him. Apparently she had inherited some of the family allure. "I am not interested in making this easy for you. What I want is to know if this . . . means anything." She cornered him by the window and raised her face for a kiss, resting her hands lightly on his arms.

"Damnation!" Swearing, he dropped his flask and drew her hard against him.

Fire flared again, the flames fanned by the fact that they wore only thin nightwear. She felt his bones and muscles and . . . more. Much more.

Books by Mary Jo Putney

The Lost Lords series:

Loving a Lost Lord
Never Less Than a Lady
Nowhere Near Respectable

One Perfect Rose
The Bargain

Published by Kensington Publishing Corporation

Nowhere Near Respectable

THE
LOST LORDS

MARY JO PUTNEY

ZEBRA BOOKS
KENSINGTON PUBLISHING CORP.

http://www.kensingtonbooks.com

ZEBRA BOOKS are published by

Kensington Publishing Corp.
119 West 40th Street
New York, NY 10018

All Kensington titles, imprints and distributed lines are available at special quantity discounts for bulk purchases for sales promotion, premiums, fund-raising, educational or institutional use.

Special book excerpts or customized printings can also be created to fit specific needs. For details, write or phone the office of the Kensington Special Sales Manager: Attn. Special Sales Department. Kensington Publishing Corp., 119 West 40th Street, New York, NY 10018. Phone: 1-800-221-2647.

Zebra and the Z logo Reg. U.S. Pat. & TM Off.

ISBN-13: 978-1-4201-1722-6
ISBN-10: 1-4201-1722-X

First Printing: May 2011
10 9 8 7 6 5 4 3 2 1

Printed in the United States of America

In memory of two splendid and much-loved curmudgeons:

*Kate Duffy, truly justifying the title of the
"Julia Child of romance."
And my editor, though not for anywhere
near long enough.*

*And to:
Larry Krause, publisher, author, idealist, and
mineral maven, and one of those rare folk
who always live by their principles.*

ACKNOWLEDGMENTS

To the Cauldron, my talented and equally crazed brainstorming buddies.

And to the Muses, my ever-supportive wailing wall.

Prologue

London, early November 1812

The death notice in the London newspapers was small, but it attracted considerable attention. Three of Mad Mac Mackenzie's gambling friends met at the club and raised their glasses to him. "At least he cheated the hangman," one said respectfully. They raised their glasses again to that.

Several society ladies sighed with regret, perhaps wiping away a tear or two of genuine sorrow. What a waste of virile, albeit annoying, manhood.

A man who had claimed to be Mackenzie's friend swore and crushed the newspaper with one agonized fist.

His legitimate half brother, Will Masterson, learned the news in Portugal some days later. He grieved without tears—and wondered if his maddening brother was really dead.

Mackenzie's old schoolmistress and surrogate mother, Lady Agnes Westerfield, closed her eyes and wept. Trust Mad Mac to get it wrong. The young should not be allowed to die before their elders. It was damnably unfair.

Mac frowned as he read his obituary, and hoped his brother, Will, didn't see it. As he set the newspaper aside, he also hoped he didn't have to stay dead for long.

Dying was bad for business.

Chapter 1

Kent, late October 1812

She left with a chime of laughter, sweeping up the skirts of her riding habit and darting down the long corridor before the golden young man could finish his proposal. But when she reached the door at the end, she paused to glance over her shoulder, her expression mischievous.

The Honorable Godfrey Hitchcock smiled, blond and confident in the sunshine that had appeared after days of rain. "We shall talk later, Lady Kiri. And I shall finish what I started to ask you."

Kiri Lawford gave him the swift smile that always left men breathless, then slipped through the door. Once she was out of his sight, she slowed down, her expression thoughtful. Godfrey was charming, the most appealing suitor she'd had since her family had come to London a year before.

But did she really want to marry him?

She liked that Godfrey had joined her for this late afternoon ride even though they risked being late for dinner. She hadn't wanted to waste the rare sunshine after being trapped indoors ever since arriving at Grimes Hall for this house party. He was a first-rate rider who'd kept up with her as they galloped headlong over the hills of Kent.

Officially Kiri was only one of a number of guests at the party. But everyone understood that she was there to meet Godfrey's family while they became better acquainted in a relaxed setting. Kiri's mother had planned to come, but their household had been full of measles, so she'd remained in London.

Luckily Kiri had been staying at Ashton House with her brother and hadn't been exposed to illness. That allowed her to travel down to Kent with an older couple who were attending the house party.

The visit was going well. The Hitchcocks looked Kiri over with a thoroughness that suggested they thought she'd soon be part of the family. She found them pleasant enough, in a cool English way.

It would not be a brilliant match, since Godfrey was only the third son of a baron while Kiri was a duke's daughter. But she liked him very well. In the year since her family arrived from India, she'd found no eligible men she liked better.

Godfrey hadn't treated her like an exotic foreign slut unworthy of respect. He also kissed very nicely, which was surely a good trait in a husband, and his touch of rebelliousness matched her own. But was that a strong enough basis for marriage?

Kiri's mother came of royal Hindu blood, and despite her gentleness, she'd defied tradition to twice marry Englishmen. Both had been love matches. Kiri's father, the sixth Duke of Ashton, had died before she was born, but she had seen the love between Lakshmi and her second husband, John Stillwell. Her stepfather had been a famous general in India, and he was the only father she'd ever known. A good father, too, who treated his stepdaughter exactly the same as his own two children.

Godfrey was amusing and good company, but compared to General Stillwell, he seemed rather short on substance. Of course, most men were. Though her brother Adam measured up to the general rather well. So did most of Adam's intriguing friends, now that she thought about it. A pity they all treated her like a little sister.

But perhaps she wasn't being fair to Godfrey. They simply weren't well enough acquainted for her to know if he had hidden depths. She must accept the offer made by his mother, Lady Norland, who'd suggested Kiri stay on for another week after the formal house party ended.

Wondering if her parents would be able to come down if she stayed longer, Kiri decided to stop by Lady Norland's morning room. Her hostess would probably be there if she hadn't gone up to dress for dinner, so Kiri could ask to extend her visit. Surely another week in Godfrey's company would clarify whether they would suit.

The countess's morning room was cozy and attractive, and she spent a good deal of her time there with her female friends. Kiri quietly opened the door, then paused, seeing that Lady Norland was chatting with her sister, Lady Shrimpton. Lounging on a sofa with their backs to the door, the sisters didn't see Kiri.

Kiri could talk to her hostess later. She was on the verge of withdrawing when Lady Shrimpton said, "Is Godfrey really going to marry that Kiri creature?"

Kiri froze at the sneering tone. What on earth . . . ?

"It's looking likely," Lady Norland replied. "She seems quite smitten. What girl could resist a man so handsome and charming?"

"I'm surprised you and Norland would allow such a match," her sister said disapprovingly. "I wouldn't let one of my boys marry a half-breed foreigner. Such a bold, vulgar creature! I've seen the lures she casts out. Why, men sniff around her like hounds. Godfrey won't know if his children are his own."

Kiri's hand pressed to her chest as her heart pounded with shock. Her brother Adam had experienced dangerous disapproval of his mixed blood, but Kiri had been treated with more tolerance because she was a mere female, not an English duke. While some members of society disapproved of her heritage, they were usually discreet about it. She had never heard such malice directed at her.

"The chit is half English and her stepfather is General Stillwell, so she should have some sense of proper conduct." Lady Norland sounded as if she wasn't quite sure about that. "What matters is that she's a duke's daughter and will have a very generous dowry. Godfrey is expensive, and he won't find a richer wife than this one. If she foists other men's brats on him—well, he has two older brothers and they both have sons, so her blood will never taint the title."

"A good dowry does compensate for much," Lady Shrimpton said. "But you'll have to socialize with that dreadful little mother of hers. A heathen, and so dark!"

"Lady Kiri is less dark, and her dowry is golden!" Lady Norland laughed. "I suppose I mustn't give her mother the cut direct, but believe me, there will be little social intercourse between that family and ours despite the presence of General Stillwell."

Kiri's vision darkened as a red, killing rage possessed her. How *dare* they speak that way about her mother, who was the wisest, gentlest, kindest woman Kiri had ever known! She was a true lady by any standard. Kiri wanted to mangle both of those horrible women with her bare hands. She yearned to crush their sneers and bigotry.

She could, too. As a girl, she'd been fascinated by tales of ancient Hindu warrior queens, so she'd insisted on joining her male Hindu cousins to study the traditional Indian art of fighting called Kalarippayattu. Kiri had been one of the best students in the class, and now she burned to use her skills on those evil females.

But it would be very bad form to kill her hostess. Nor should she murder Godfrey, the lying, deceitful fortune hunter. As she turned and headed blindly to her room, she felt ill at the knowledge that she'd considered *marrying* the man! She wiped her fist across her mouth as if she could rub off the memory of his kisses.

Almost as infuriating as the slurs against her mother were the horrible claims that Kiri was a slut who cast out lures to men. She had been raised in military camps among men, and she enjoyed their company. From the time she was old enough to walk, General Stillwell's subordinates had teased and talked and taught her riding, hunting, and shooting. When she grew up, young officers sometimes fell desperately in love with her. Of *course* she was no shy English miss who was afraid of all men outside her family!

She could not stay in this house for another day, or even another hour. She entered her bedroom with relief. She would borrow a Norland horse and ride cross country to Dover, a busy port where she could easily get a coach back to London.

Hands shaking and buttons popping, she jerked off the expensive new riding habit she'd worn on her daily rides with Godfrey. She had made an effort to be an English lady in all ways, but no longer.

Free of the yards of fabric, she dug into her wardrobe for the well-worn divided riding skirt she'd brought from India. The skirt made it possible to ride astride, and she'd thought she might wear it here.

The buff-colored twill of the divided skirt settled into place with welcome familiarity. As she donned a tailored navy jacket, she glanced at herself in the wardrobe mirror.

Dark hair, vivid green eyes, above average height even for an English girl. Her complexion was darker than the average Briton, but not startlingly so.

This was the true Kiri Lawford—a daughter of the empire, half English and half Hindu and proud of both heritages. In a sari and with a bindi on her brow, she would look almost entirely Indian, just as in a riding habit she looked almost entirely English.

But never fully one or the other. She could not change that about herself. Nor did she want to. *Especially* not to please spiteful cats like Lady Norland and her sister.

She could carry little on horseback, so she scanned the room to see if there was anything she must take besides her money. She'd brought some of her finest outfits, but she wouldn't stay here merely to protect her wardrobe.

She wrapped her jewelry in a change of linen, then an Indian shawl. Tucked in a leather pouch, the bundle would pack unobtrusively behind her saddle.

Much as she wanted to storm out of the house, she had been too well raised to leave without a word. She must write a note to the woman she'd traveled down with, which would be easy. Also a note to Godfrey, which would not be easy, but she couldn't bring herself to address Lady Norland directly. She sat at the desk, wanting to rage at him. But mere paper could not contain her fury.

She settled for scrawling, *You must find another fortune to hunt. Please send my belongings to Ashton House.* She deliberately specified her brother's ducal mansion. Though these people might consider her a slut, by God, she was a high-born slut.

Since Kiri's maid had been trapped in the measles quarantine, she'd been assigned a Norland girl of small skill and less personality. Kiri left a generous vail for the girl's service, then swept from the room.

Luckily she didn't see any of the Hitchcocks or other

houseguests on her way downstairs and out to the stables. She knew which horse she wanted—Chieftain, a splendid blood bay gelding belonging to Godfrey's oldest brother, George Hitchcock. George, the pompous heir to the title, married to a bland blonde and with two sturdily English, towheaded sons. He didn't deserve so fine a horse. She'd been longing to ride it.

The stables were quiet and she guessed that the grooms were eating their supper. No matter, she'd made friends with Chieftain during the past week. She paused over which saddle to use.

Godfrey's was a good size, but using anything of his would make her skin crawl, so she chose anonymous tack. It took her only a few minutes to saddle Chieftain and walk him out of the stable. She swung onto the horse as easily as any man, turned Chieftain toward Dover, and left Grimes Hall forever.

Chapter 2

A good thing Kiri had her anger to keep her warm, she thought acidly, or she'd be shivering. The late October night fell quickly as the sky clouded up, and the temperature dropped like a stone. Though Chieftain was a splendid mount, progress was slow because the ground was muddy from several days of rain. The track she was following north to Dover twisted up and down through the rugged hills, which slowed her even more.

But Dover was only a few miles farther. She couldn't miss it as long as she followed this track, which paralleled the coast. She would spend the night in an inn—a nice, warm inn—and take a coach back to London in the morning. It would be interesting to ride a public coach instead of a luxurious private carriage. She liked new experiences, even if they were likely to be uncomfortable.

The track descended a hill in a narrow cut that was barely wide enough for a horse and rider. A good thing she was in relatively safe England rather than India, where bands of dacoits might lie in wait.

She was contemplating a roaring fireplace when she rounded a bend and found herself face-to-face with a pack train of heavily laden ponies heading upland. What the devil . . . ? It took a moment for Kiri to sort out the jumble of rough-looking men, ponies, and tightly shielded lanterns.

Smugglers! As soon as the thought crossed her mind, she tried to pull Chieftain around so they could escape, but the free traders had also recovered from their surprise. "Get 'im!" a sharp voice bellowed. "Can't let a stranger see us!"

A smuggler lunged at Kiri. She slashed her riding crop across his face while applying her heels to Chieftain. But more men grabbed her and the track was so narrow the horse couldn't turn quickly. She kicked two men away, slashed others with her whip, but before she could win free, the sharp voice shouted, "Jed, use yer bird net!"

A weighted, malodorous net flew through the air and dropped over her, entangling arms and legs. As she struggled to free herself, her assailants dragged her from her horse. She slammed to the ground with bruising force and exploded into furious Hindi curses.

A redheaded trader grabbed her and exclaimed, "Jesus, it's a bloody woman!"

"Wearing trousers and riding astride?" another said skeptically.

"I know a tit when I feel one!"

A lean man with a long, morose face approached and knelt beside Kiri. Her hat had come off, and in the narrow beam of a lantern, her face was clearly visible. "'Tis a woman, right enough," he said in the leader's voice. "Or rather a girl. She was babbling in some foreign language. Do you speak English, gal?"

"Better than you do!" She tried to knee him in the groin but was too trapped by the net to manage it.

"In those trousers, Captain Hawk, she's mebbe a whore," a smuggler remarked.

"I'm no whore!" Kiri cursed them again, this time in

English and using the filthiest language a little girl could learn in an army cantonment.

"Mebbe not be a whore, but she sure ain't no lady," a man said rather admiringly.

"Gag and blindfold her," Hawk said tersely. "Then tie her up and toss her over her saddle. Howard, Jed, take her down to the cave and make sure she don't get away. Mac the Knife is coming tonight, so make him welcome if he arrives before we get back. We'll figure out what to do with 'er then."

"I already know what to do to her, Captain," a man said with a lewd chuckle.

"We'll have none of that," Hawk said as he admired Chieftain. "This horse is worth a pretty penny, so the girl might be valuable, too."

"We need to be careful," the heavyset man warned. "If her people are too important, asking for ransom might bring a troop of soldiers out here looking for us. Safer to roger her, then toss her off a boat with a few rocks for weight."

Kiri stiffened. If they learned she was sister to a duke, they might be so afraid of consequences they'd kill her out of hand. She unobtrusively used her right thumb to turn her ring so the diamonds were underneath and only a plain band showed on top. "I'm neither rich nor important, so no need to murder me."

"You talk like money." The captain's eyes narrowed. "What's your name?"

She thought quickly for a name close to her own. "Carrie Ford."

"Some Fords over in Deal," a man volunteered. "She don't look like one of 'em."

Stick to the truth when possible. She said, "I'm from London, not Deal."

"Where did you get your fancy horse?" Hawk asked.

Her mouth twisted. "I stole him to get away from a man who lied to me." Which had the advantage of being true.

The smugglers laughed. "Sounds like she's our kind of woman," one said.

"Could be she's lying." Hawk scowled. "We'll figure that out later. For now, truss 'er up and don't damage her. We need to be moving."

Despite Kiri's furious struggles, the smugglers were able to peel the net off her upper body and tie her wrists with a length of thin, hard line. She wanted to scream with frustration because she couldn't free herself to fight properly. She should have been carrying a knife, but she had wanted to be genteel for the wretched Norland house party.

Howard, the heavyset man, tried to gag her with a filthy square of cloth. "You swine!" she snarled before biting his fingers.

"Bitch!" He slapped her cheek and tied the gag painfully tight, but she had the satisfaction of seeing that she'd drawn blood.

After her bite, the free traders handled her with wary efficiency. Jed, the wiry redhead, blindfolded her. Trussed like a goose, she was draped over Chieftain's saddle and tied to the horse.

It was a gut-wrenchingly uncomfortable way to travel, especially since she could see nothing. Using her hearing and other senses, she knew that she was being taken downward on a path so narrow that sometimes her feet brushed a rough stone wall.

Kiri was perilously close to throwing up before the horse halted and she was untied and pulled from the saddle. She staggered, but a hard hand caught her elbow. "Since there's nothing for her to see but rock," Jed's voice said, "I'm taking off the blindfold so she can walk down on her own."

Even though it was night, having the blindfold taken

off gave her some sense of her surroundings and cleared her head. They stood in a sheltered pocket surrounded by boulders on all sides. One end was fenced off for a crude paddock that held a couple of ponies munching on a mound of hay.

Looking wary, Jed tried to remove Chieftain's saddle, and got nipped for his efforts. Rubbing at the rapidly forming bruise on his forearm, he growled, "Then you can just stay in your tack and be uncomfortable, horse."

Chieftain entered the paddock willingly since hay awaited. He was a fine animal, so Kiri hoped one of the other runners knew how to care for horses. Not that she blamed Jed for being afraid. Chieftain was a large, high-spirited aristocrat among horses, and he obviously had little patience with peasants.

Jed took her arm and led the way to a path hidden between two boulders. Unable to use her hands, she might have fallen if he hadn't kept hold of her. No chance of escape with Howard just behind them.

The path flattened out to a ledge that led to the narrow entrance of a sea cave. A path split from the ledge down to a sliver of shingle beach. There was just enough light for her to see several boats moored out in the small natural harbor. The free traders' fleet—fish by day, brandy by night. It was a good hideout that excise ships sailing along the coast would have trouble finding.

Jed led her into the cave, which broadened into a surprisingly large chamber. Kiri estimated that it was almost as large as the ballroom at Ashton House.

Once they were inside and away from the entrance, Jed lit a lantern that illuminated much of the cavern. Alcoves were stacked with contraband, particularly wine and spirits in small, easily carried casks. She'd heard that smuggled spirits were so concentrated that large amounts would kill a man. They had to be diluted before being served.

There were oilskin-wrapped bales that probably contained tea and tobacco. Other packages might have been bolts of fabric and lace and other luxury goods. She couldn't even guess at how much the merchandise was worth. Surely a lot.

Kiri was marched to the far end of the cavern. Before she realized what Howard was doing, he snapped a manacle around her left wrist. Despite her fury at being tethered to the wall like a beast, she held still while he cut her wrist bonds. The rope had been tied with a sailor's skill and it was cutting cruelly into her wrists.

She was massaging the grooves left by the rope when Howard put a heavy hand on her breast and squeezed. Outraged, she jerked back and kicked hard at his groin.

She didn't connect dead center, but her riding boot hit close enough that Howard screamed and fell backward, clutching himself. "You *bitch!*" Bent over and gasping with pain, he raised his knife. "You'll be sorry for that!"

"Can't blame the chit for not wanting to be groped." Jed put a restraining hand on the other man's arm. "The captain will know what to do with her. Start a fire while I get the fixin's for a kettle of bumbo. The lads will want a hot drink when they get back."

Grumbling, Howard obeyed, and within a few minutes the two men were sitting by a fire and taking turns swigging from a bottle of gin. Kiri could smell the sharp scent of juniper clear across the cavern.

The gin kept Howard quiet while Jed prepared the bumbo, which required him to suspend a large kettle of water over the fire, Then he added sugar, a lemon, and a pinch of nutmeg. Smuggling must be profitable to afford the ingredients.

The nutmeg and lemon put a pleasant scent in the air while the smoke disappeared into crevices in the ceiling. Kiri guessed that when the flavored water was hot, it would be combined with rum or some other spirit. Kiri wouldn't mind a tankard of it herself—she was horribly thirsty, and cold as well.

Since she could do nothing about thirst or cold, she sat with her back against the wall and drew her knees up. Resting her wrists in her lap, she investigated the manacle. Cave damp had put rust on the surface of the metal, but it was still solid.

Or was it? She twisted at the metal circlet with her left hand, and had a sense that the manacle was more rusted than her captors realized. If the metal was weakened just a little bit more, she might be able to wrench the manacle open.

On her right hand, she wore the ring her parents had given her on her eighteenth birthday. Elegant rather than vulgar, the ring was set with seven small, perfect diamonds in a line across the top, tapering in size from the largest in the middle down to slightly smaller stones. Diamonds were very hard, and a line of them were like a saw. If she could groove the rusting metal, she might be able to twist and break the manacle.

She began to scrape the diamonds across the rustiest section, glad the surf covered up the rasping sound. The element of surprise would help her get past Jed and Howard if she could free herself before the other runners returned. Once she was on Chieftain, she'd be halfway to Dover before they figured out what happened.

The diamonds scratched into the metal, but progress was painfully slow. She was still tethered when the other smugglers returned. They were in high spirits from safely landing and moving so much valuable merchandise. Even if she could break free, she'd have to get past the whole gang of them to escape.

Quickly Kiri rested her hands in her lap when Hawk

came over to examine her, fingers of her right hand resting on the manacle. "What to do with you?" he muttered.

Howard gave a bark of laughter. "Careful, Cap'n, she kicks as well as bites. Like a horse, she needs to be broken to saddle. I'm willin' to ride her."

"We're smugglers, not criminals," Hawk said tersely. "A pity she ain't a local gal who could be trusted to keep her mouth shut about us."

"Worry about 'er later, Hawk." One of the men brought his captain a steaming tankard of bumbo. "'Tis time to celebrate a good run."

Hawk turned away from Kiri. "Send a draft up to Swann since he's waiting above for Mac. He deserves a bit of warmth."

Kiri watched uneasily. Most of the smugglers would be family men and not prone to murder. But drink could make even sensible men violent, and Howard and perhaps others might kill in cold blood. Grimly she returned to working on the manacle. She had to do something, or she'd go mad.

Time passed, the runners got drunker—and then the devil from hell swept into the cave.

Chapter 3

Shock jolted down Kiri's spine before she realized the newcomer was only a large man with a torch-bearing smuggler behind him. The sweeping folds of a dark great-coat and the wildly flaring flames were what made him look like the devil arriving to claim Faust.

He stepped into the light, doffing a hat to reveal a handsome face that looked as if it was seldom troubled by deep thought. "Greetings," he said in an easy voice that filled the cavern. "How are my favorite free traders?"

Staccato exclamations greeted his appearance. "It's Mackenzie!"

"Aye, Mac the Knife himself!"

"I bet you say that to all the smugglers, you silver-tongued devil!"

"Where ye been, ye rogue?"

"Pull up a rock and join us, Mac!"

"Sorry I'm late," Mackenzie said cheerfully. "I spotted a troop of excisemen and didn't think you'd want me to lead them here." He shook hands with the captain. "Could you bring in all I ordered?"

"We were a cask short of the hock, but everything else

is on its way." Hawk poured wine into a glass. "Taste this claret. 'Tis a new vintage, but mighty fine."

Mackenzie accepted a glass and swallowed thoughtfully, judging the wine. "Excellent. I'll want some of this next time around." He held out his glass for a refill.

"Here's your special French tobacco." Hawk handed over a packet. "Smells nice, but no tobacco is worth what you pay me for smuggling this in."

Mackenzie sniffed the packet appreciatively before tucking it inside his greatcoat. "Worth every penny. A moment, please . . ." He reached into a different pocket and pulled out two canvas pouches, one large, one small. They clanked when he handed them over. "This for the tobacco. This for the wine and spirits wending their way to London."

"'Tis a pleasure doing business with you," the captain said with a rare smile. Kiri noticed he didn't count the money. Mackenzie must be a regular and trusted customer.

Though the newcomer was large, good-looking, and well dressed, that wasn't why everyone in the cave watched him. The word *charisma* flitted through Kiri's mind. She'd had a brief flirtation with a Cambridge student who claimed Kiri was charismatic because her beauty compelled all attention whenever she entered a room. Charisma was a personal magnetism that drew others close, he'd explained. It gave leaders the power to inspire their followers.

Then he'd presented her with a poem written in Greek, which was sweet of him, and concealed the fact that he was probably a bad poet. Calling Kiri charismatic was mere flattery, but Mackenzie was the real thing. All the runners, even the angry Howard, brightened when the newcomer acknowledged them with a glance or a smile.

Mackenzie was savoring his claret when his gaze

reached Kiri. "Who's the wench?" he asked as he moved in her direction.

Hawk, Howard, and Jed moved with him. "Trouble," the captain said dryly. "She rode into us when we were moving the goods. Had to take her captive. I'm not sure what to do with her. Maybe see how much her family will pay to get her back."

"They'd be fools to pay a shilling," Howard growled. "She needs taming, and I'm going to be first in line."

Jed laughed. "A good thing her kick was a little off or you'd not be able."

Coarse banter ensued among the smugglers, but Mackenzie ignored them and went down on one knee to study Kiri more closely. She stared back with narrowed eyes.

The man looked a little familiar, though she was sure she'd never met him. Despite his air of genial frivolity, he moved with the feral alertness of a soldier. One who knew how to kill. But she didn't sense mad-dog violence.

"If looks could kill, we'd all be dead," he said with amusement. "She might be handsome under that gag. Is it necessary?"

"Had to gag her because her filthy tongue was embarrassin' us," Hawk said morosely. "Swears like a drunken sailor."

The smugglers found that hilarious, and a roar of laughter filled the cavern. Kiri was chilled by the recognition that they were getting to the drunken state where they didn't care about consequences for their actions.

"What are you going to do with her?" Mackenzie asked.

"Not sure. She's probably worth something to someone, but I don't know who." The captain scowled. "She ain't the cooperative sort."

"Bites like a wildcat and kicks like a bloody mule," Howard muttered.

"She has spirit," Hawk agreed. "The sort to march off

to the excisemen and persuade them out to hunt us down. She must have a pretty fair idea where this hideout is, too. Damned if I know what to do with her."

"Tie rocks to her and drop her in the Channel," Howard said.

Kiri glared at the man with murderous rage. She had meant these men no harm. Though she didn't approve of smuggling, she knew that it was accepted and almost respectable in this area. She'd not have interfered.

But she no longer felt neutral. Given the way they'd treated her, she wanted to do just what the captain feared: bring the law down on these filthy kidnappers. Though she would pass on that in return for the opportunity to kill Howard with her bare hands.

"Says she stole her fancy horse, but I'm thinkin' she comes from money," Hawk continued. "Her clothes are strange but not cheap."

"Sellin' her back to her family would cause trouble," Howard argued. "Better to use her and lose her."

"That would be a waste of a tasty morsel." Mackenzie's gaze was still on Kiri, but coolly unreadable. "What's her name? Maybe I can tell you how valuable she is."

"Says she's Carrie Ford, but she could be lyin'," the captain said with a frown. "Know any rich Ford families?"

"No, but maybe if you take off the gag she'll say more now that she's had time to evaluate the situation."

"Careful she don't bite you," Jed said.

"Or kick you in the bollocks," Howard added. "She's trouble for sure."

"Trouble is my middle name." Mackenzie caught Kiri's gaze. "If I take off the gag, will you promise not to damage me or injure the delicate sensibilities of our companions with your language?"

She wanted to kick the lurking smile off his handsome

face. But even more, she wanted to be free of the filthy, choking gag, so she nodded.

Mackenzie leaned forward and reached around her head to untie the gag. She gulped a deep breath, grateful for the air.

"That was really cutting into your face." For a moment he cupped her face in his hands, and his warm touch almost unraveled her. Kiri wanted to turn her face into his palm and weep at the nearest thing to kindness she'd experienced since her capture.

But she could not afford to weaken. Burying her emotions, she said, "Thank you." Her eyes narrowed. "In gratitude for untying me, you have until the count of three to move out of biting and kicking range. One . . . two . . ."

"You really are quite a handsome wench," he said admiringly as he moved a safe distance away. "Your name is Carrie Ford?" He handed her his half-empty wineglass.

She took a swallow of wine, grateful for the moisture and for the taste that washed away the grime of the gag. "Call me what you will."

"Very well, wench." His gaze still on Kiri, Mackenzie said, "I'll buy her off you, Hawk, and offer my personal assurance that she'll keep silent about this little episode."

Hawk looked startled, then interested. "How much?"

Mac considered. "I have fifty gold guineas on me. I should think that would do."

It was a small fortune, and an unexpected bonus for the night's work. The captain's eyes narrowed speculatively. "She might be worth more to her family."

"Perhaps," Mackenzie agreed. "But finding her people could be difficult and perhaps dangerous." He pulled another bag from an inside pocket and tossed it in one hand. It jingled alluringly. "Cash in hand, and no trouble for you."

Hawk scratched his stubbled jaw thoughtfully. "That

sounds like a good bargain to me." He glanced at his men, who were listening raptly. "What say you?"

The nods and "ayes" of agreement were interrupted when Howard said belligerently, "*I* don't agree! I want the bitch, and I'll challenge this London sharper for the right to have her."

"Then we won't get our guineas!" someone complained.

"I'll pay fifty guineas for her myself!" Howard retorted.

"You have that kind of money?" someone asked with surprise.

Howard stared at Kiri with hot, angry eyes. "I can come up with . . . thirty guineas now, and I'll pay the rest out of my share of future profits."

Kiri tried to hide her fear. Maybe she should be flattered Howard was willing to spend his savings and pawn his future for her—but not when she knew she wouldn't survive his ownership.

Some of the runners looked troubled, but others found the business highly entertaining. "Sure, we'll wait for part of her price," one said drunkenly. "But when you're through with her, you have to share."

"She won't look so pretty then," Howard said. "What will it be, Mackenzie—guns or knives? Or will you withdraw your offer since I saw her first?"

"I'll take your challenge, but really, nothing so deadly as guns or knives. I greatly dislike the sight of blood. Particularly my own." Mackenzie pondered. "You gave the challenge, so I pick the weapons. I choose cards."

Howard smiled, showing bad teeth. "Then I'll have her, because I'm the best damned cardplayer in Kent."

"Even good players are subject to the gods of chance." Mackenzie reached into another pocket. "I have a new pack of cards here. You may check them before we start. What shall we play?"

Howard frowned as he shuffled through the cards. "Brag is my game."

"Very well. Best of three, and may the goddess of chance decide."

Howard squared up the cards. "With my skill, I don't bloody need luck."

Brag had different versions, so the contestants negotiated the rules while a battered card table and two stools were set by the fire. The smugglers began placing bets on the outcome, with Howard strongly favored.

The two men settled at the table and Howard handed the shuffled cards to his opponent, who shuffled again. "So we're playing for the right to purchase the lady," Mackenzie mused. "The most amusing stakes I've had for donkey's years."

Kiri wished that he was less amused and more serious about winning the match. The scene could have come from *Dante's Inferno,* with steam from the great kettle curling ominously through the air and smugglers crowded around to watch the play, avid faces lit by lantern and firelight.

Mouth tight, Kiri continued scratching at her shackle with her ring. There was so much racket, no one could hear, and finally she was making progress. Soon she might be able to twist off the shackle and escape past the drunken men before they realized.

If that couldn't be done, she prayed to all Christian and Hindu gods that Mackenzie would win. He was an unknown quantity, but he had to be less brutal than Howard. Certainly he was a lot cleaner. She would also have a much better chance of escaping from one man than from two dozen.

The opponents were silhouetted against the fire, Howard intent and wolfish, Mackenzie handsome, elegant, and casual to a fault. The progress of the game could be followed by the groans and exclamations of approval uttered by the onlookers.

The men seemed well matched. Given how devoted most English gentlemen were to gaming, she guessed Mackenzie was a good player. But she was very afraid that Howard was better. She bit her lip when she realized that the match had reached its climax.

"Three of a kind, Mackenzie!" Howard said gloatingly as he spread his cards out. "It'll take a bloody miracle for you to beat that!"

"It appears you're right," Mackenzie said, to Kiri's dismay. "But let's see what the goddess of fortune has given me. . . ."

The audience hushed as tension built. The cards slapped flatly onto the table against the more distant whoosh of the waves. Nerves at the breaking point, Kiri continued scraping at the manacle even though her fingers were cramping and her hands were numb with fatigue. She was close, so close . . .

As a gasp of surprise rose from the onlookers, Mackenzie said with mild pleasure, "Fancy that. I also have three of a kind, and mine are all natural, without using a wild card. The match and the lady are mine."

"No, damn it!" Howard leaped to his feet, knocking the board to the floor. "You cheated, you filthy cardsharp!"

Mackenzie stood but remained calm. "I cheated? Pray tell me how."

Howard hesitated. "I'm not sure, but you did something, and by God, you won't get away with it!" He swung at his opponent, who effortlessly dodged Howard's fist.

Fighting exploded on all sides as if sparks had fallen into black powder. Howard lunged after Mackenzie, who was remarkably adept at avoiding his opponent's blows. Their partisans attacked each other, apparently fighting for the pure pleasure of it.

The kettle of steaming water pitched over, extinguishing the fire. As bodies crashed back and forth, the three lanterns were knocked out one by one. Only a couple of embers illuminated the suffocating blackness.

This was Kiri's chance. She wrenched ferociously at the manacle and managed to break the ring of metal. She twisted again to open it farther, and was free.

Scrambling to her feet, she headed toward the entrance as quickly as she could, swinging wide around the still raging brawl. The fighting proved impossible to avoid entirely, though. A man who smelled of rum careened into Kiri. She tripped him and he fell with a bellow.

A stride later she collided with a beefier man. When she tried to slide away, he seized her. She slammed her elbow into his gut. Swearing, he kept hold of her arm.

She sensed rather than saw him raise his right arm. Guessing he had a knife, she managed to catch his wrist and twist it backward. He howled with pain and released her.

Moving on instinct, she ripped the knife from his loosened grip. Glad to have a weapon in her hand, she headed toward the cave's entrance again. Now that she was armed, nothing and no one would prevent her escape.

Chapter 4

While dodging Howard, Mackenzie deftly upended the kettle to extinguish the fire, then overturned a lantern. No need to put out the others—the battling smugglers managed to do that without his aid.

Under cover of the choking darkness, he headed for the girl, hoping that collisions with brawlers wouldn't disorient him. The stone wall was closer than he thought, and his outstretched hands banged into it. He felt along the rough stone surface, sure he must be close to where she was tethered.

He couldn't find the blasted girl. Was he that far off course?

No, his sweeping right hand rattled the chain. He followed the links down—and she wasn't there. How the devil . . . ?

The manacle had been broken and twisted. Miss Carrie Ford was even more formidable than he'd realized. He spun and headed toward the cave entrance, hoping she hadn't become caught up in the fighting.

A man shouted, "The wench is escaping!"

"Get her!" Howard bellowed.

As voices were raised in question or confusion, Mac

reached the cave's exit. He found the girl by her scent. He'd noticed earlier that she wore an alluring perfume that reminded him of lilacs and subtle spices. Giving thanks that she was safe, he wrapped a protective arm around her shoulder . . .

. . . and found himself falling to the floor when she hooked an ankle around his leg and jerked. He grabbed at her reflexively and they fell together with him on top.

She made a vicious attempt to knee him in the groin. Immobilizing her with his weight, he hissed in her ear, "Stop trying to unman me when I'm rescuing you!"

She stopped fighting. "Then let go so we can get the devil out of here!"

He promptly released her and they both scrambled to their feet. He tossed the pouch containing the fifty guineas into the cave, then followed her out the exit passage.

Outside it was pouring rain, but the night seemed light compared to the darkness of the cave. At least now it was possible to see the general shape of his surroundings.

Ahead of him, Kiri ran recklessly along the ledge, then scampered up the rocky path ahead like a crazed mountain goat. Mackenzie grinned as he matched her speed. The girl must have been frightened by her captivity, but she hadn't let fear paralyze her. Which was good, since it wouldn't be long until Howard and maybe some of the other smugglers came after them.

Rain made the path dangerously slippery. Kiri had almost reached the small clearing that contained the paddock when she lost her footing and fell, sliding toward the edge that would drop her to the rocks below. Barely in time, Mac anchored himself on a gnarled bush with one hand and made a frantic grab at the girl.

The force of his sweeping arm jerked her back to safety against the cliff wall. For a moment they stood frozen, warm bodies pressed together against the cold, wet stone.

Intoxicating lilacs and spice and woman jolted through him with an intensity that made him forget that drunken, furious smugglers were after them.

His trance was broken when she snapped, "Let go of me, you oaf!"

Jerking free, Kiri raced up the path again. He reached the clearing a few steps behind her. He could hear her panting as she stood at the paddock gate, and he guessed that she was calming herself so as not to upset the animals inside.

Before he reached her, she opened the gate and moved in among the shaggy ponies. A tall riding hack with a white blaze made a whuffling sound and ambled toward her. She began crooning soft words and captured the horse easily. Mac was glad to see that the beast was saddled and ready to ride. That didn't speak well for the smugglers' care for horses, but it was convenient now.

Since Mac had expected his visit to be short, his horse was also saddled, so they could get away quickly. Because of the threatening rain, he'd rolled up a spare cloak and fastened it behind César's saddle. He retrieved the cloak and shook it out, then took it to his warrior maiden as she led her horse out of the paddock. "Here, lass."

She whirled around, a knife glinting in her hand. "Keep away!"

"Put that thing down," he said mildly. "I'm offering this cloak so you won't freeze to death."

"Sorry." She didn't sound as if she meant it, but the knife disappeared and she accepted the cloak. "My thanks."

Mackenzie thought he heard a faint chattering of teeth as she wrapped the garment around herself. On most females, the cloak would drag on the ground, but this one was tall enough that the fabric swirled around her ankles.

"Need a hand in mounting?" he asked.

She glanced up at the large horse. "Yes," she said grudgingly.

The lass didn't waste words, and her tone was icier than the night. She planted a riding boot on his linked hands and vaulted into the saddle. He watched in admiration, wondering if other women might adopt split skirts like hers. Ignoring him, Kiri put her heels to her mount and headed up the slanting trail with a skill that suggested she'd been put on horseback directly from the cradle.

Shaking his head with amusement, Mac shooed a couple of friendly ponies back so he could latch the gate, then mounted César. The darkness and rain slowed Kiri down, so she wasn't far ahead of him. When he reached the top of the track, he found her halted and scanning the stormy night while the cloak billowed around her.

Guessing she had no idea which way to go, Mackenzie pulled up next to her. "Dover is several treacherous miles, there are no villages nearby, and the rain is going sideways, so we'd better take shelter," he remarked. "I know a comfortable barn that's about half an hour away. Farther than the smugglers are likely to follow."

Her face was a pale oval against the dark fabric. She asked, "Might they do that?"

"I left the fifty-guinea purchase price, which will mollify most of them." Mac remembered Howard's furious expression. "But Howard might be drunk and angry enough to pursue us, and maybe he can persuade some of his friends to come along. Better to put some distance between us and them."

"There is no 'us,' Mr. Mackenzie," she said icily. "I have every intention of distancing myself from you as well. I most certainly will not share a barn with you."

"There is a gale blowing off the Channel," he pointed out. "Shall we continue this discussion undercover?"

She looked up into the rain, shivering. After a long

pause, she said, "Your word as a gentleman that you won't trouble me in this barn of yours?"

"I give my word that I won't harm you, but if I'm not a gentleman, my word is worthless. You must trust your instincts."

"It's hard to be afraid of a man who admits to laziness and a distaste for the sight of his own blood," she said with a sigh. "I'm tired enough to take my chances with your uncertain honor. That and my knife should keep me safe."

"Never fear, I'm harmless," he said in his most guileless manner. "Women are a lot of work even when they're willing. Why would I want an unwilling one?"

She snorted. "Very well, but remember that I am armed, Mr. Mackenzie."

It wasn't the most gracious agreement Mac had ever heard, but it would do. He set César in motion in the right direction—and the warrior maiden followed.

Mackenzie's barn was isolated, with no other farm buildings visible. Kiri pulled up beside it gratefully. She was wet and exhausted and any shelter would do. Hard to remember that she'd started this day with hot chocolate and fresh bread served in a comfortable bedroom at Grimes Hall.

Her unwelcome companion dismounted and opened the wide doors so she could lead Chieftain into the barn. "There will be hay inside," he said. "Burrowing in should help warm you up. I'll rub your horse down for you."

She dismounted creakily, aching in every muscle. "I take care of my own mount."

"Spoken like a true horsewoman," he said with approval. "I'll see if I can get a fire going. There's no one close enough to see."

Wondering where he'd find dry wood, she removed

Chieftain's saddle and blanket. As the horse munched on a pile of hay, she used handfuls of the dried grasses to wipe him down.

When she finished one side of the horse and moved around to the other, she was surprised to see Mackenzie striking sparks into a nest of tinder. It caught immediately, and the flames showed a stack of kindling and cut wood piled nearby.

"Convenient to have firewood here," she said as smoke wound out the door, which he'd left ajar. "Do your smuggler friends use this barn for storing goods?"

"Sometimes, which explains the wood. But they're not friends of mine." He slipped his tinderbox back into his greatcoat. "Merely business associates."

"Drinking is your business?"

"I have an establishment that requires high-quality wine and spirits." With the fire going well, he stood and began rubbing down his horse. "Buying directly from Captain Hawk ensures quality."

"Practical, if not exactly legal." She looked over Chieftain's back to study Mackenzie's rangy, ill-favored mount. "That's a remarkably ugly horse."

"César might be jeered at in Rotten Row, but I've never met his equal for endurance." Mackenzie patted the horse's neck. "I traded a pouch of tobacco for him in Portugal. He was such an ugly colt that he was about to be turned into horse stew. We were both lucky that day."

Kiri found his obvious affection for his horse rather endearing. Chieftain was far more handsome, though.

The barn had several empty box stalls—convenient for storing casks of claret—so after Kiri had groomed Chieftain, she led him into a stall and made sure he had hay and water. Then she settled down by the fire. In the flickering light, she examined the knife she'd stolen. It was a sleek, well-made weapon, small enough to go into an arm or leg sheath. The handle was elaborately etched and the short blade had a businesslike edge.

She was testing the balance when Mackenzie joined her at the fire. He eyed the blade, which happened to be pointing at him. "Is that a warning to keep my distance?"

"Perhaps." She turned the knife, watching the reflections on the blade. "Why should I trust you?"

"I'm not the one who captured you and chained you in a cave."

Her eyes narrowed. "True, but you didn't seem upset to see what your 'business associates' had done!"

His brows arched. "Would it have helped if I'd cried out in horror, 'You brutes! Release that young lady right now!'"

She looked down at the knife, thinking that he was distractingly handsome now that she could see him clearly. "They would have laughed in your face, and possibly chained you up next to me. If you'd tried to free me yourself, you would have been stopped immediately."

"Exactly. One must know one's audience," he said. "If not for Howard, buying your freedom might have worked, but since he didn't want to let you go, I had to come up with another approach. Playing cards for your fate amused them."

She shivered. "Clever, but you might easily have lost. Even winning, the beastly Howard accused you of cheating."

"He's beastly, but not stupid," Mackenzie said, amused. "I *was* cheating."

She gasped, shocked by his casual admission of dishonorable behavior. "You cheat at cards?"

"When necessary," Mackenzie replied. "You wouldn't have wanted me to lose, would you?"

She knew her eyes must be as wide as saucers. "No, but . . . you're a gentleman, and that is not respectable behavior."

"I am not a gentleman," he said with a laugh. "In fact,

I'm nowhere near respectable, which makes life easier than if I was a gentleman."

Having spent her life surrounded by highly honorable gentlemen, Kiri was fascinated to meet a man so cheerfully dishonorable. "How come Howard didn't notice that you'd marked the cards when you pulled that deck out?"

"Because that deck *wasn't* marked. It was new, just as I said. But the matching deck that I palmed had marked cards. After I won and Howard became difficult, I kicked over the kettle and one of the lanterns to confuse the situation enough for us to escape."

She couldn't quite suppress her choke of laughter. "I was glad you won, because I knew you'd be easier to escape from than a gang of smugglers."

"In the morning the storm should have passed and I'll put you on the road to Dover. You can escape me then." He pulled a flask from another internal pocket. "Have some brandy. It will help warm you up."

The flask was warm from Mackenzie's body. Kiri sipped cautiously and discovered that it contained a powerful but smooth French cognac. "The brandy you buy from the smugglers is first-class."

"Nothing but the best for my customers." He reached into another inside pocket and pulled out an irregularly shaped packet wrapped in cloth. "If you're hungry, here's some cheese to test your knife on."

This time she didn't even try to stop herself from smiling. "You've pulled out money, cards, drink, and now food. How many pockets does that greatcoat have?"

"Many." He produced two bread rolls from inside his coat, then pulled two thin pieces of kindling from the woodpile. "I'm going to toast my cheese. Care to join me?"

Hot food. Realizing she was ravenous, she sliced the cheese into several chunks and handed half to him. "I'll cut the bread rolls so they can be toasted as well."

"Excellent thought." He passed the rolls so she could slice them. "That's a handsome knife. You didn't have time to pull it out when you were captured?"

"I didn't have it then." She held the knife on her palm so he could see it more clearly. "I took this from a smuggler who tried to stab me when I was escaping."

Mackenzie looked appalled. "I'm not sure which is worse—knowing you could have been stabbed, or knowing that you might have stabbed me. The mere thought of my blood being spilled makes me feel faint."

She laughed. "So far, I'm glad I didn't stab you."

Half her roll was toasted, so she removed the bread and stuck the cheese on the sharp end of the stick. When the pale lump of cheddar began to melt and smell delicious, she smeared it onto her toasted bread and took a bite.

The tangy bite of the melted cheese contrasted exquisitely with the crisp toast in a symphony of texture and flavor. She gave a soft moan of pleasure. "It's *ambrosia!*"

He took a bite of his own toasted bread and cheese, savoring it. "Nectar of the gods indeed. Nothing like cold, rain, hunger, and fear for one's life to make even the simplest of meals taste divine."

"I'm definitely glad I didn't knife you," Kiri decided. "If I'd done that, I wouldn't have had food, drink, and shelter."

"I have my uses." He started toasting his other piece of bread. "How did a very competent young lady like you fall into the smugglers' hands?"

She sighed, remembering what had brought her to the wrong place at the wrong time. "I was visiting in the country and by accident overheard something that was—very distressing. I left for Dover immediately with the intention of catching a coach home from there. But I blundered into the smugglers moving their goods and they feared I'd give them away. If Chieftain and I had had running room, I could have escaped, but we didn't. A bird net was thrown over me before I could get away."

"Bad luck," he said sympathetically. "You borrowed the horse to ride to Dover?"

"A stickler might say I stole it," she admitted. "But I was so *furious!* If I'd stayed, I might have hurt someone. So I took Chieftain. I'll send him back from Dover."

"I have no trouble believing you might damage someone," he said with a lazy, admiring smile that did strange things to her insides. "But if you hadn't overheard that conversation, I wouldn't have met you. I'm selfish enough to be glad our paths crossed."

"So am I, since I might not have escaped without your help."

"How did you break the manacle? Was it rusted through?"

"There was some rust." She held up her right hand and the diamonds flashed in the firelight. "I also used the stones in this ring to scrape the metal until I could break it."

"You really are the most amazing female," he said with warm admiration.

She dropped her gaze, feeling shy. "I'll see you're paid back after I return to London."

His lips curved in a smile. "I can think of another payment that would do."

Her hand tensed on her knife. If he thought that she would lie with him . . . !

"Not what you're thinking, my warrior maiden," he said with a grin. "But I would certainly enjoy a kiss."

Chapter 5

Carrie Ford did not react to his request with the outrage of a virgin, nor with the sensual assessment of an experienced woman. Instead, her eyes narrowed like a cat's and she studied him as if he was an intriguing artifact of uncertain origin. "A kiss might be interesting." She stabbed the knife down through the hay beside her. "But only one."

"Then I shall try to make it a good one." He slid over until they were sitting side by side, his thigh pressing against hers.

He cupped her cheek with one hand. "Your eyes are the most remarkable shade of green," he murmured, thinking it was only right that they were as unique as the rest of her. "Like the finest emeralds."

Her brows arched in surprise. "And your eyes are two different colors. Brown and a misty blue-gray. How very odd."

"It has been said that my eyes are a good expression of my generally odd self," he said, thinking it was pure pleasure to study Carrie at close range.

When he first saw her, she'd been gagged and furious, but now that she was relaxed, she was a striking beauty. Her shining dark hair had come loose to fall over her shoulders in extravagant waves. He brushed her hair back and caught a whiff of her scent. "Lilacs and spice," he said. "Feminine but with bite."

She laughed. "You understand perfume."

"Perfume is easier to understand than women." Certainly he wanted to understand this woman, whose fine features had a faintly exotic cast. His fingers drifted down her throat, butterfly light. Her exquisite complexion had the warmth of Devonshire cream rather than the pale milk of a fashionable blonde. "You look entirely edible."

"Perhaps you need more bread and cheese." Her tone was demure, but her green eyes sparked with amusement.

He touched his lips to hers, prepared to savor gently. She leaned into the kiss with innocent interest. Then her lips opened under his. Pure fire blazed between them. The sensual shock raced through every vein, raw and urgent.

He drew her closer until her breasts were pressed into his chest. Her hands came to rest on his waist, her fingernails biting through his coat like tiger claws.

"Dear God, Carrie," he said hoarsely, his hands kneading her back. "You are even more extraordinary than I realized."

She gulped for breath, her lips parted in irresistible invitation. "You are definitely to be preferred to Howard."

"I should hope so!" He kissed her again, and she did not point out that he'd already had his kiss. His pulse was pounding and so was hers. Lilacs and spice and the sweet, fresh scent of crushed hay.

He realized that they were lying on their sides in the hay, his knee between hers and his hand on her breast. Their hips were pulsing together as if trying to dissolve the fabric that separated them so they could be fully joined. "This isn't wise," she whispered in a voice balanced between desire and doubt.

"You are entirely right." Yet he didn't want to stop.

Hoping she had more sense than he did, he said hoarsely, "Tell me to stop, Carrie. Or hit me. Not too hard, but hard enough to restore some common sense."

"Actually, my name is Kiri, not Carrie," she said with a choke of laughter. "I didn't want the smugglers to know my real identity."

"No matter," he said distractedly. "You are beautiful under any name. . . ."

Wait. *Kiri*.

He'd only heard that name once. He gasped and released her as if she were a burning coal. "My God—Kiri! You must be Lady Kiri Lawford. Ashton's sister." Damnation, he should have guessed when he saw her green eyes. She and her brother looked very alike.

"You know my brother?" she said, pleased, as she pulled his head down again.

For dizzy moments he forgot why he should not be doing this. It took sharp nails on the back of his neck to bring him back to his senses.

Summoning all his will, he rolled onto his back, staring up at the beams as he gasped for breath. "If I touch you again, just stick the knife into me. It will be quicker than waiting till Ashton breaks me into very small pieces."

She pushed herself up on one elbow and stared down at him. "What on earth are you talking about? Adam is the best and kindest of brothers."

"He is also one of the most dangerous men in England if he's offended," Mac said gloomily. "And he would be very offended indeed if he knew I was halfway to seducing his sister in a haystack."

"He is indeed very skilled at bare-hands fighting," she agreed. "But I have not known him to be easily offended. And this is not seduction, but just very fine kissing. Are we not allowed to celebrate a narrow escape?"

"We are *not!*" Mac sat up, thinking she was more

innocent than he'd realized if she didn't recognize mutual seduction. A few minutes more and all thoughts of wisdom would have been gone beyond recall. "We have to leave now. The rain has slowed."

Kiri was looking at him as if he'd run mad. "You and my brother are enemies?"

"No, but that doesn't mean he would approve of me kissing you." Much less anything more intimate than kissing. "I knew Ashton at school. He was a couple of years ahead of me."

"Ah, the Westerfield Academy, for young men of good breeding and bad behavior," she said with amusement. "So you *are* a gentleman. Much more of one than the despicable man I actually considered marrying. I do not see the problem here."

He caught her gaze, trying to impress her with the fact that he was serious. "Most of the Westerfield students are indeed gentlemen. A fair number of them have exalted titles, like Ashton's. But not me. I am the bastard son of an actress, I was cashiered from the army, and I own a gambling and dinner club. Your stepfather, General Stillwell, would horsewhip me on sight."

He rose and offered his hand to help her up. "If we leave now, we should be able to reach the Westerfield Academy in an hour or so."

"I thought you moved like an army man." She frowned as she came to her feet. "It's true the general would not like knowing you were cashiered. Why?"

"It's complicated." Not only complicated, but a sordid tale he wouldn't tell to a young woman who, despite her fire and courage, had led a fairly sheltered life.

She brushed hay from her skirt. "Why do we need to go to Lady Agnes?"

"To protect your reputation. You have high rank, Lady

Kiri. There will always be people looking for ways to smear your name."

"Because of my mixed blood?" she asked bluntly.

"Yes," he replied, equally blunt. "You will always be held to a higher standard. There are many who disapprove of those who are different." It was hard for him to imagine how anyone could disapprove of a female as remarkable and beautiful as Kiri Lawford, but he knew enough of the world to recognize that she would be a target for the jealous and the narrow-minded.

Her mouth twisted. "I've noticed that disapproval."

He wondered what had caused that expression. "With luck, the world won't learn you were kidnapped. But just in case, it will be best if you spend the rest of the night under the irreproachable protection of Lady Agnes."

"Lady Agnes has the soul of a rebel," Kiri pointed out. "How will staying with her save my delicate reputation?"

"She's the daughter and sister of a duke and widely respected, so she is considered a charming eccentric, not a rebel." He draped the cloak over Kiri's shoulders. *Lilacs and spice and woman.* He drew a deep breath, then continued, "So yes, staying with her will shield you from possible consequences."

"Then why didn't you take me to Westerfield Manor to begin with?"

"It was an hour more riding on a wicked ugly night. Also, the fewer people who saw you, the better. Knowing who you are changes the situation." He waved toward the door. "The rain has stopped, so another hour on horseback won't be quite so unpleasant."

She pulled the hood over her dark hair. "I thought you looked familiar when I saw you in the cave. Have I met you in passing in my brother's house?"

He shook his head. "I'm not a part of what is called

good society. But you would have met Lord Masterson, my half brother. There's a strong resemblance between us."

"Of course! Will Masterson. He's a lovely fellow." Her gaze raked Mac. "Your personalities are very different."

He grinned. "That's probably an insult, but you're right. Will is sober, reliable, and honorable. Not at all like me."

"But you are both kind," she said softly.

"Will certainly is." Mac ignored the disquieting compliment. "If not for his kindness, Lord only knows where I'd have ended up. Probably Newgate Prison."

"For cheating at cards?"

"There are so many ways to end in Newgate." He led her horse from its box stall and started to saddle it. "After my mother died, I could have been left in a parish workhouse, but her maid sent me to my father. Will took a fancy to me and wouldn't let me be sent away. The Masterson heir needed a good education, but our father didn't want the by-blow to accompany Will to Eton. Hence, Lady Agnes."

Kiri checked her saddle and cinch. "From what Lady Agnes's other Lost Lords tell me, you were better off with her anyhow."

"Without question. And you'll be better off with her, too."

Kiri made a face. "Honesty compels me to agree."

He grinned. "Comfort yourself with the knowledge that you'll have a bed and even a hot bath if you want it."

As he saddled César, she said, "Tell me about your gambling and dinner club."

He hesitated. But since she knew his name, she'd have no trouble finding out about the club when she returned to London. "Damian's, and I hope you've never heard of it. My club is no place for a young lady."

"Of course I've heard of it!" she exclaimed. "Damian's

is very fashionable. How can you be unrespectable if the prince regent patronizes your club?"

"The prince is hardly a model of respectability." Mac opened the door to the cool, windswept night. A quarter moon rode high in the sky, casting a silvery light over the fields. He turned to stamp out the fire. "Apart from that, I'm only one step above a servant. Not only illegitimate and cashiered, but I'm in *trade*."

"They say Damian's has the best chef in London, and gentlemen can take ladies there to dine," Kiri said as they led the horses out.

"My chef is indeed extraordinary, but only very fast ladies enter my doors," he said repressively. "A fair number of them aren't even ladies."

"Your masquerades are famous." She set a foot in his linked hands and swung into the saddle.

For a brief, paralyzed moment all he could think of was *lilac, spice, woman*. The bloody female was dangerous.

"Or infamous," he said when his brain cleared.

She looked down at him thoughtfully. "I see why you need the very finest illegal beverages. Where does the club's name came from?"

"My first name is Damian." He closed the door to the barn and mounted César.

She chuckled. "It's true you don't look like a George or a Robert. But Damian?"

"Remember my mother was an actress. She had dramatic tastes." He set his horse to a trot and headed for the Westerfield Academy. He needed to get far, far away from the dangerously delightful Lady Kiri Lawford.

Chapter 6

Kiri watched in disbelief as Mackenzie hurled a pebble at one of Westerfield Manor's upper windows. "This is how one communicates with the most noble and respectable Lady Agnes Westerfield, who is supposed to save my reputation?"

"Don't forget that she is also eccentric and a schoolmistress. I am not the first to wake her this way." He threw another pebble. "This is one of those occasions when it's best not to rouse the whole household."

He was selecting a third pebble when the casement windows above swung open and a soft but penetrating voice said, "Which of my young rascals is this?"

"Damian Mackenzie, Lady Agnes." His voice was also pitched to avoid waking other sleepers. "I have a young lady whose reputation needs salvaging."

The headmistress's voice was more amused than shocked. "If she's with you, Mr. Mackenzie, her reputation is already shredded beyond repair. I'll meet you at the door."

"This way." As the windows closed, Mackenzie took Kiri's arm and guided her toward a small side door near the back corner of the wing.

Kiri wondered whether he took her arm because he

guessed she was exhausted to the point of keeling over. In the spacious stables where they'd left their mounts, she'd been ready to grab a horse blanket and roll up in the hay.

He'd been right not to head to the school earlier, though. It had been a hard ride even under a clear night sky. In the rain, it would have been abysmal.

The door opened, revealing Lady Agnes holding a lamp. She was as tall as Kiri, with a floor-length scarlet robe and a thick braid falling over her shoulder. As her guests entered, she exclaimed, "Lady Kiri! How did you fall in with this rogue?"

For a paralyzed moment, Kiri wasn't sure how much to say. Though she had met the headmistress briefly in her brother's house, she didn't really know the woman.

But Adam trusted Lady Agnes completely, so Kiri could, too. "I was captured by smugglers, and Mr. Mackenzie helped me escape. For propriety's sake, he thought it best to come here."

Lady Agnes laughed. "Propriety, Mac? That could ruin your reputation. But come along in. Shall I take you to the kitchen for food, or a bedroom for rest?"

"The bedroom, please," Kiri replied. "With a washbasin, if possible."

"It looks like you had a very muddy ride," the headmistress agreed. "What about you, Mac?"

"I could use some food, Lady Agnes."

"Then I shall meet you in the kitchen after I have settled Lady Kiri." Lady Agnes lit a candle for Mackenzie, then turned and gestured for Kiri to come with her.

As Kiri went up the stairs, she said, "You seem so matter-of-fact, Lady Agnes. Does this sort of thing happen often?"

"Various forms of mayhem arrive with some regularity." The older woman chuckled. "Having been a surrogate mother to a generation of high-spirited, rebellious boys has made me very hard to shock."

Kiri would love to know what Mackenzie had been like as a boy, but she was too tired to ask. Lady Agnes's obvious affection spoke well for the man, though.

"Since Westerfield is on the road to Dover, I usually have a guest room or two ready just in case. I'll get a pitcher of water from my bedroom." The headmistress retrieved the pitcher, then took Kiri into a bedroom that was well furnished if not lavish. If Kiri hadn't been so muddy, she would have dropped facedown on the coverlet.

Lady Agnes set the pitcher on the washstand and lit the fire laid in the fireplace. "Hot water would take time and delay your rest, so I assume cold will do?"

"That will be lovely." Kiri sighed. "This morning started in such a normal fashion. I had no idea what the day would bring."

"Someday you'll tell this story to your grandchildren and it will seem like a jolly adventure. But it will take time to see the day like that." The older woman smiled. "You'll find clean nightclothes in the wardrobe. Sleep well, Lady Kiri. Tomorrow you'll find the world a new normal."

Lady Agnes left, closing the door behind her. Numbly Kiri undressed, hanging Mackenzie's damp cloak and her muddied skirt over chair backs by the fire. With luck, they would dry overnight. Both badly needed brushing to be presentable.

After a quick wash, she pulled on the nightgown. It was short on her, but no matter. She crawled in the bed and pulled the covers over her head. The mattress seemed the most comfortable she'd ever slept on, probably because every muscle ached.

Yet despite her fatigue, her mind was spinning. Kiri had enjoyed occasional kisses from her more attractive suitors.

She'd enjoyed Godfrey's quite a lot. That was a good part of the reason she had considered marrying him.

But the unrespectable Damian Mackenzie was in an entirely different class. Even now, thinking of their embrace sent liquid heat flowing through her. Was that because he was more experienced? A worldly man who surely had his choice of worldly mistresses?

Or was there some vital, unexpected connection between the two of them, like blending rose and frankincense to create more than the sum of the parts? Given how dazed Mackenzie looked after their kissing session, she was inclined to think there might be something special between them. The only way to be sure was by more kissing, but that might be hard to arrange since they would go their separate ways in the morning.

If anything was to be done, it must be tonight.

Mac was halfway through a platter of sliced ham and cheese when Lady Agnes joined him in the kitchen. She waved him to stay seated when he started to rise. "Don't interrupt your midnight supper. You look as if you need sustenance." She took a chair on the other side of the scrubbed pine table. "Unless you are drinking two glasses of that very fine claret you provide, one of those drinks must be for me."

"Perspicacious as always, Lady A." He handed her the glass. "Keeping you in wine and spirits is a small price to pay for the sanctuary you provide when needed."

She sipped the claret with pleasure. "Will tonight's misadventure damage your relationship with your smuggler friends?"

"I'm too good a customer. After they sleep off their bumbo, the only one who will still be angry is the unpleasant fellow who wanted to rape and murder Lady Kiri."

Lady Agnes winced at the thought. "You've often called here unexpectedly, but never with a damsel in distress in tow. And Ashton's sister, no less!"

"I didn't know who she was until later, but she was obviously a young lady in need of help." He thought of how she'd broken the shackle and fought through the cave. "Though she might have managed to escape on her own. She's amazingly intrepid."

"Well, she is Ashton's sister, and they resemble each other greatly. Like him, she's an expert in Kalarippayattu." Lady Agnes took a piece of cheese from the platter. "Her mother's family has a very old tradition of retaining a Kalarippayattu master to teach the sons of the family. And the daughters, if they're interested."

"So Lady Kiri learned from the same master who taught Ashton. That explains a great deal." Mac grinned. "She almost crippled me for life before I convinced her I was trying to help. She makes me think of the stories of ancient Hindu warrior queens that Ashton would sometimes tell late at night."

"Kiri is a direct descendant of those warrior queens," Lady Agnes said seriously. "One reason her family moved to England was so the girls could find British husbands, but there aren't many men who can fully appreciate Kiri's unique qualities."

Of course a beautiful young woman with a good dowry would be in the market for a husband. Perfectly logical, but Mac found that his food had lost its savor. He wrapped the slab of ham in cheesecloth and returned it to the pantry. "I'm for bed now, Lady Agnes. My usual room?"

She nodded. "Move quietly. It's right next to Lady Kiri's since those were the only guest rooms made up."

With a candle in one hand, he bent to give her a one-armed hug. "Thanks for always being here, Lady A."

She hugged him back. "And my thanks to you for keeping my life from becoming dull, Mac."

"You never lack for excitement running the school," he said with a laugh.

He had just about enough energy to make it up the steps and into the sanctuary of his usual room. Because of his disreputable activities, he ended up here with some regularity. It was always good to see Lady Agnes, even though she was not enthusiastic about his dealings with smugglers. She knew they were necessary, though.

He lit the waiting fire, then stripped down to shirt and drawers, adding the gray wool banyan that hung in the wardrobe. Then he sat in the comfortably worn wing chair by the fire, stretched out his legs, and tried to settle his mind.

He'd always lived a complicated life that ran along the ragged edge of the beau monde. The friends he'd made here at Westerfield were true, and they would have welcomed him into their social world. Others would not have been so charitable. Since he'd started life without wealth, a title, or even legitimate birth, he preferred to live in a less rarified social stratum where he could be accepted as he was.

He didn't miss attending boring routs and other *ton* events, but he'd be lying if he didn't envy his legitimate friends the security of knowing they belonged. Life was interesting on the edge, but sometimes . . . tiring.

Thinking he needed some brandy, he collected his flask, managing to knock over a wooden chair on his way back to the fire. He hadn't drunk enough to be that clumsy, so it must be fatigue. Yet still he watched the flickering flames, reluctant to go to bed.

He knew who and what he was. But he was human enough to regret what could never be his.

Chapter 7

Kiri was pulled from deep sleep by a muffled bang in the next room. It took her a moment to remember where she was. Ah, yes, insult, horse theft, smugglers, kidnapping, escape—and Damian Mackenzie. The man she'd been ready to knife, who had transformed into a protector and ally.

The sky was still dark and she sensed that she hadn't slept long. Someone, probably Mackenzie, had dropped something or banged into the furniture to wake her.

Mackenzie. Damian. Knowing he was in the next room, probably stripping off his clothing, sent a wave of heat through her body.

She was a normal female who had always admired attractive males. But though she enjoyed hugging and kissing, she hadn't realized the power of passion. She wanted to walk into his room and rip off any clothes that covered that powerful body and wrap herself around him. The thought was equally exciting and alarming.

She bit her lip. Decent females did not do such things, and despite Kiri's rebellious streak, she was decent. Or at least, she had been raised well. But she couldn't let the most appealing man she'd ever met ride away, never to be seen again.

Mackenzie had made it clear that a great and impassable social chasm divided them. She agreed it was great, but impassable? That she was less sure of.

If the gap between them was to be bridged, she would have to make the first move. And tonight might be the only chance she would have, despite her fatigue and the staggering impropriety of what she must do.

Her heart accelerated with anxiety. It would be . . . hard to bear if he laughed at her overtures. No, he wouldn't be cruel, but he might very well reject her politely. He must meet endless numbers of attractive, experienced women. Why would he want to involve himself with an inexperienced mixed-blood female?

And yet—there had been that blazing reaction when they came together. She was sure such passion was rare.

Whether passion was enough remained to be seen. Reminding herself that she was a daughter of warrior queens, she rose and lit a candle from the fireplace. She donned a robe as a gesture to propriety. Candle in one hand, she left her room and tapped on the door of the next room. She held her breath, hoping he was awake still.

Almost as much, she hoped that he wasn't.

Her tentative knock was met with a low-voiced invitation to enter. She drew a deep breath and opened the door.

Mackenzie sat by the fire, his face weary and his long legs stretched out in front of him. He also wore a robe that was too short as he sipped from his silver brandy flask. As firelight sculpted his strong features, he was far more handsome than was safe.

He looked up—and choked on his brandy. After a brief coughing fit, he gave her a ferocious glare. "You're supposed to be sleeping the sleep of the innocent, Lady Kiri."

She closed the door behind her. "Not as innocent tonight as I was last night."

He looked uncomfortable. "I'm sorry for kissing you."

She raised her chin. "I'm not sorry."

"Very well, I'm not sorry, either," he said wryly. "But I shouldn't have done it."

"Perhaps not." She wouldn't be standing here with bare, cold feet if not for that kiss. "But what's done can't be undone. You . . . intrigue me, Mr. Mackenzie. I would like to see you again in London."

His amusement died. "The feeling is mutual, Lady Kiri. But no, we can't see each other in London."

"Do you have a wife?" she asked, steeling herself for an answer she wouldn't like.

"Good God, no!" he exclaimed, his expression horrified. "But we come from separate worlds. They must remain that way."

"Why?" She moved toward him. She was descended not only from warrior queens, but great beauties who were famously alluring. A war had been fought for the right to marry one of her great-great-grandmothers. Summoning all the ancestral sensuality she could imagine, she imagined herself beautiful. Desirable.

"Jesus, Lady Kiri!" He bolted from his chair and retreated as if she were wielding her new dagger. "You are not making it easy to do the right thing!"

"Call me Kiri." She smiled with wicked delight at seeing how she affected him. Apparently she had inherited some of the family allure. "I am not interested in making this easy for you. What I want is to know if this . . . means anything." She cornered him by the window and raised her face for a kiss, resting her hands lightly on his arms.

"Damnation!" Swearing, he dropped his flask and drew her hard against him.

Fire flared again, the flames fanned by the fact that they

wore only thin nightwear. She felt his bones and muscles and . . . more. Much more.

His mouth was hungry, giving no quarter. Her fear dissolved, leaving only desire and soaring excitement. She hadn't imagined this fierce rightness. It was real, more real than anything she'd ever experienced. . . .

Mac's wits fled as Kiri melted against him with shocking intimacy. She was intoxicating, as irresistible as air to a drowning man. He inhaled her fierce, lovely essence as he caressed her sweetly curving body. The bed was only a few feet away. . . .

No! He'd always prided himself on his control, but it took every last shred of discipline to put his hands on her shoulders and shove her an arm's length away. She swayed, staring at him with huge, vulnerable green eyes. "What's wrong?"

He wasn't sure whether to laugh or howl. Dropping his hands, he said, "You are sent by the devil to tempt me for my sins, Lady Kiri."

She bit her lip. "Why can't I be reward instead of temptation? Or are your sins so great they are beyond forgiveness?"

"Many people do not forgive easily." He stalked out of touching distance as he thought of all the things he'd done that he wished he hadn't. Sorting through his past, he said, "The best I can say for myself is that I've never killed a man without good reason, nor lain with a woman I didn't genuinely like."

Her dark brows drew together. "Men sleep with women they don't like?"

She really was essentially innocent despite her fiery nature. "Sometimes," he said dryly. "As do women on occasion. Lust is not the same as friendship or caring."

She thought about that. "I would think that lust is enhanced by caring."

He tried not to be distracted by her elegant bare feet. "It is. That's why I only choose women I care about."

She tilted her head to one side, her dark, silky hair sliding over her shoulders. "To me, the . . . the attraction between us seems rare and special and not to be wasted, but I have little experience. Am I wrong? Is such powerful desire common?"

"It is indeed rare," he said, knowing only the truth would do. "But passion is pain, not pleasure, if there is no honorable channel for it. To my regret, that is the case here." He regretted it *hugely.* "Our mutual attraction can be no more than a bright, passing moment."

Her lush lips tightened. "I am not convinced there can be nothing between us."

"A major drawback of passion is that it melts the brain," he said sharply. "There are only two possibilities, Lady Kiri. Do you wish to have an affair? A well-bred virgin who did that would ruin her life. Courtship? Your entire family would rise up as one to drive me from your door—and they would be right to do so."

"I just don't see an impassable social gulf." Her brow furrowed. "Yes, you are in trade, but you are not a rag-picker or fishmonger. Your father was a lord and you went to school with my brother. You look and talk like a gentleman. Can't we meet and dance at a ball? Ride together in the park?"

Mac shook his head. "Your brother is an important reason why this must end tonight. I respect him too much to want to hurt him or you. Not to mention that Ashton once saved me from being beaten to death by an aristocratic bad loser and his cronies." He caught her gaze, needing to convince her he was right. "The ability to feel passion is a gift, Lady Kiri. What you feel for me you can also feel for another man who will be the honorable partner you deserve. Wait for him."

"Can't we even be friends?" she asked quietly.

If her aim was as good with a dagger as it was with words, any man she confronted would be dead. When he was sure his voice would be level, he said, "I wish that was possible. But given the force of the attraction between us—no, Lady Kiri, we cannot be friends. No one would believe there was nothing more between us. And they'd be right, because I would never be able to keep my hands off you."

His words made her pale, but after a long moment, she inclined her head with graceful acceptance. "Then I thank you for your honesty, Damian Mackenzie. As I thank you for your aid in escaping the smugglers. Sleep well."

"I will be gone by the time you rise tomorrow morning." He hesitated, then added, "It has been a pleasure meeting you."

"A pleasure and an education." She gave him a ghost of a smile. "A pity that you are honorable but not respectable. I would have preferred it the other way around."

He almost laughed. "Be gone, you minx. A week from now you'll thank me for my forbearance."

Her smile faded. "I wish I was sure of that." Then she was gone.

He fought a desperate desire to go after her, bring her back to his room and his bed. Not only because she was beautiful and utterly desirable, but for the wit and strength and vitality that lit up any room she entered. He'd never met a woman like her.

A beautiful woman, not his.

Chapter 8

Kiri managed to fall asleep after leaving Mackenzie's room but her dreams were full of smugglers and threatening knives and intoxicating kisses. Not restful.

She woke to the shrieks of the young and energetic and guessed that the school playing fields were behind the manor. Though Kiri felt neither young nor energetic, she made herself get up to face the day. She discovered that a silent maid had entered, removed her skirt and cloak, and returned them brushed and wearable.

Impulsively Kiri picked up the cloak and buried her face against the heavy, dark folds. Mackenzie's scent was in the fabric, triggering a vivid image of broad, powerful shoulders and his impish, multicolored eyes. After she'd stopped thinking of him as a possible threat, she'd loved being in his company. Fierce desire coupled with liking was a dangerously potent combination.

Yet he had been right that they had no future, damn him. She wasn't about to take him as either lover or husband. It might be different if circumstances allowed a proper courtship, where they would have time to further their acquaintance. Instead, she must be grateful for his restraint.

With a sigh, Kiri laid the cloak down. If it were an expensive garment, she would return it. But it was a simple wool cloak such as might be owned by any working man, and rather worn to boot. Unless Mackenzie asked for the cloak back, she would keep it as a memento of their bright, passing moment.

The maid had also left a pitcher of water that was still warm. As Kiri was washing, a young maid peeked in the door, then entered when she saw that the guest had risen. "Now that you're awake, miss, can I help you dress?"

"I can manage my clothes, but I'd be very grateful for some breakfast."

"Down the stairs and to the left," the girl said promptly. "I'll tell Lady Agnes so she can meet you in the family dining room."

The maid bobbed a curtsey and was gone before Kiri could say that she didn't want to interrupt her hostess's work. Reminding herself that Lady Agnes was unlikely to do anything she didn't want to do, Kiri finished dressing and headed downstairs.

She weighed her situation. The intriguing Damian Mackenzie was gone from her life, the Honorable Godfrey Hitchcock was not to be thought of, and she hadn't a single marital prospect that interested her. But she was alive and well and breakfast awaited. She was more fortunate than not, so she should not be in such low spirits.

Her spirits began lifting as soon as she saw the covered dishes and steaming pot of tea waiting in the family dining room. Kiri served herself eggs, bacon, beans, toast, and an extra large serving of kedgeree. She'd made a good start on her meal when Lady Agnes joined her.

"How are you this morning, Lady Kiri?" The older woman smiled. "Apart from ravenous."

Kiri rose politely. "Ravenous indeed. Mr. Mackenzie shared some bread and cheese with me, but this is the first

proper meal I've had since yesterday morning." She took
her seat again at Lady Agnes's gesture. "I'm very well, and
grateful that nothing worse happened to me. I assume Mr.
Mackenzie has already left for London?"

"He has." Lady Agnes poured herself tea and took the
chair opposite her guest. "My question wasn't polite small
talk, Lady Kiri. Being kidnapped by a gang of smugglers
had to have been terrifying." She took a thoughtful sip of
tea. "When I was traveling in India, we were attacked by
a band of dacoits. Several men were badly wounded and
a guard was killed. It was a very . . . unsettling experience." Lady Agnes smiled with wry self-mockery. "I was
known as the Mad Fearless Englishwoman, but for some
months after the attack, I was rather less fearless than my
reputation."

Kiri looked down at her plate, remembering her fear
and her fury at her helplessness. "You're right. It was . . .
unsettling." The sort of experience that forever changed
one's view of the world. "Terrifying, in fact."

"Terror is a rational response to danger," the headmistress said. "But if it gives you nightmares, don't be
afraid to ask for help. I'm never more than a letter away."

"Thank you." Kiri studied the other woman's face, wondering how old she was. Not really that old. In her fifties,
perhaps. "I see why your lost lordlings adore you."

Lady Agnes laughed. "I adore them, too. Most have an
odd kick in their gallop, but they're good boys. They just
need extra attention and acceptance." Her voice became
businesslike. "I gather your horse must be returned somewhere?"

"Grimes Hall."

"I'll see to it. My carriage is waiting to take you back to
London. I'll send a maid with you for propriety's sake."

"Thank you! I was expecting to travel back to London

on a public coach," Kiri said. "You're very generous to an uninvited guest."

"Any friend of Mackenzie's is welcome here," the older woman said.

"I'm not his friend," Kiri said wryly. "I'm a damsel in distress who was lucky enough to be rescued by him."

"Friendship grows swiftly in dramatic circumstances," Lady Agnes observed.

Kiri wondered if that was a quiet warning not to become overattached to Damian Mackenzie. Lord, had Mackenzie told his old headmistress that Kiri had invaded his bedroom? Surely not. Better to talk about the horse. "After I say good-bye to Chieftain, I'll be ready to leave. He's a fine mount."

"He'll be home by the end of the day," Lady Agnes promised as she stood and offered her hand. "I'm glad we've had a chance to become better acquainted, Lady Kiri. We'll meet again in London, I'm sure."

Since she had virtually nothing to pack except the pouch that held her jewelry, she walked out to the stables when she finished her breakfast. Chieftain looked content, if tired. He delicately lapped sugar from her palm when she offered a chunk, then nuzzled her shoulder in hopes of more.

As she stroked the horse's glossy neck, she thought about her unexpected adventure. Running away from Grimes Hall might have been reckless, but it made sense given what she'd overheard. If she'd stayed, she might have broken someone's neck. She had a history of being reckless, with the saving grace that she was as good at getting out of trouble as she was at getting into it.

But recklessness had dissolved into pure madness once Mackenzie kissed her. What had she been *thinking?* By the cold light of day, her behavior with Mackenzie had moved beyond reckless into mad folly.

She hadn't been thinking at all, simply reveling in that bright, fierce passion. Consequences be damned, she'd cared only for the moment. If not for Mackenzie's hard-won restraint, they would have become lovers. Which might have been wonderful, but the potential for disaster had been very, very high.

She gave Chieftain a last pat, then pivoted and headed out to where the coach waited in front of Westerfield Manor. Under normal circumstances, she and Mackenzie would never have met. The likelihood was that they'd never meet again.

But if they did meet—well, next time she would think through what consequences she was willing to face before she behaved like a damned fool.

Within half an hour, Kiri was on the road home in Lady Agnes's plush carriage. The maid who accompanied her was a quiet older woman who worked on mending when the roads were smooth enough. Kiri spent much of the journey gazing out the carriage window at the vividly green landscape.

The events of the previous day seemed almost dream-like. Lady Norland's sneering words still stung, but not as much. Kiri guessed that the Hitchcock family would be more upset at losing a horse than a mixed-blood heiress.

She was lucky to be going home with no damage to her person or her reputation. But she couldn't stop thinking about Mackenzie. If he wasn't owner of a scandalous gambling club, perhaps courtship would be possible.

But given his business, any kind of involvement with him would risk not only her own reputation, but that of her family. Her younger half brother and sister, Thomas and Lucia Stillwell, were mixed blood, like her, and Lucia was close to marriageable age. Anything Kiri did would reflect on them, and on her mother.

Why could logic be so compelling, yet leave her feeling so empty?

By the time Mac arrived home in London, he was weary to the bone. He'd been unable to sleep after Kiri Lawford visited him, so he'd left Westerfield Manor at dawn. He wrote Lady Agnes a quick note thanking her for taking them in, saying he must return to London immediately and that he knew she would take good care of Lady Kiri. All true, if cowardly. He wondered if Kiri had slept any better than he.

Mac checked in with his manager, Jean-Claude Baptiste, to be sure no disaster had occurred at Damian's during his absence. Baptiste laughed and sent him home, which was easy since Mac lived next door to the club.

He was making up for two-and-a-half days without sleep when stealthy footsteps jarred him out of blessed unconsciousness. Mac came awake with a dagger in his hand, his gaze scanning the room for possible threat. He relaxed back into his pillows. "Oh, it's you, Kirkland. You shouldn't sneak up on me like that."

His old friend Kirkland said with mild indignation, "I sneak very well and didn't think I'd wake you. But since I did, where is my most precious tobacco?"

Mac covered a yawn. By the light, it was nearing dusk and he'd have to be up soon anyhow. "Upper inside right pocket of my greatcoat."

Kirkland found the coat where Mac had dropped it over a chair and located the fat pouch of French tobacco. He opened the packet and sifted through the fragrant dried leaves. After a minute, he said, "Eureka."

He pulled a small tube the same brown as the tobacco

from the pouch. A quick twist removed one end and he extracted a whisper-thin piece of paper. Kirkland scanned the precise, tiny lettering with a frown.

"Bad news?" Mac swung his legs from the bed, feeling like a rumpled mess.

"About as expected. I'll read through this more carefully later." Kirkland wrapped tube and paper in a handkerchief and tucked it away.

"Anything on Wyndham?" Mac always asked about their long-lost schoolmate, who'd been in France when the Peace of Amiens ended and hadn't been heard of since.

Mac always asked, and Kirkland, as always, said, "No. Though my informant said he'd heard a rumor of a captive Englishman who might fit Wyndham's description. More information is being sought."

Mac refused to let himself feel hope. There had been other false trails over the years. "If one of these leads ever turns out to be real, what then?"

"We get him out," Kirkland said flatly. "Rescue from France would be difficult, but it's a challenge I'd take in a heartbeat."

"You'd have plenty of help." Mac crossed to his washstand and splashed water in his face to clear his head. Energetic and wickedly funny, Wyndham had been popular with the other Westerfield students. His disappearance ached even all these years later.

It would be easier if his fate was certain. Realistically, Mac knew Wyndham must be dead. The Peace of Amiens had ended abruptly and every Englishman in France between eighteen and sixty had been interned. Wyndham would have fought that, and probably resistance had cost him his life. Yet without confirmation of his death, hope never quite died.

"I trust your visit to the smugglers was uneventful?" Kirkland asked.

"Actually, no. They'd captured a young lady who had the bad luck to ride into one of their pack trains." Mac felt his raspy chin and reached for his shaving kit. The owner of Damian's must always look elegant and impeccably groomed. "The captive turned out to be Lady Kiri Lawford."

"Good God!" Kirkland sat bolt upright. "Is she all right?"

"Lady Kiri is fine." Mac lathered the shaving brush and smoothed the lather over his lower face. "She was well on her way to escaping on her own when I appeared on the scene. With modest help from me, she got away and I escorted her to Lady Agnes."

Kirkland relaxed. "That's good news. If Lady Agnes is involved, I assume the matter can be covered up. Kiri doesn't need more social black marks against her name."

"Does she have some now?" Mac asked, more interested than he should be. "I'd not met her before, so I have no idea how she's regarded."

"Duke's daughter, good. Dowry, excellent. Hindu blood, regrettable," Kirkland said succinctly. "The male half of society appreciates that she's a beauty, while many women, especially mothers of girls who are also seeking husbands, think there's something distinctly vulgar about being *quite* so beautiful."

Mac laughed. "She doesn't seem the sort to hide her light under a barrel."

"She isn't." Kirkland filled his pipe with some of the newly smuggled French tobacco. "Not only is she as intelligent as she is lovely, but she's more outgoing than Ashton. Though her manners are lovely and entirely British, she's considered very forward in some circles." He frowned. "I suspect there are also men who regard her as a dark-haired temptress who will welcome their attentions."

Mac tugged four times at the bellpull, his signal for a pot of coffee and sandwiches, then opened his straight razor and set to work. "I assume she's looking for a husband. Or has she found one already?"

"Not yet. It would help if she was as soft-spoken and self-effacing as her mother, but that's not Lady Kiri." Kirkland grinned. "Any man with half a brain in his head will realize that she is a high holy handful."

To spare himself a cut throat, Mac lifted the razor away as he remembered what a very lovely handful Kiri was. After a deep breath, he resumed shaving. "If the wrong sort of man sniffs around her and her dowry, I'm sure Ashton and General Stillwell will run him off."

"I believe that has happened a time or two. I doubt there's a girl in London who has more formidable guardians."

That was good, Mac told himself. Lady Kiri was vivid, unique. She deserved devoted male protectors who would keep men like Mac away from her.

He was glad she was so well guarded. That would save Mac from his lower self, and that was good.

Wasn't it?

Chapter 9

Since measles might still be rampaging through her parents' house, Kiri had the carriage take her to Ashton House. Her brother's London residence was so vast that she could wander for days without being in the way. It was Kiri's second home, and she'd become great friends with both Adam and Mariah.

The butler greeted her fondly. "So good to see you back in London, Lady Kiri. The duchess is out, but if you would like to see your brother, he's in his study."

"I always like to see my brother, Holmes," she said breezily. She was carrying Mackenzie's cloak and should have given it to the butler, but—she didn't want to let go of it. She was an idiot.

She tapped at the door of the ducal study, entering when Adam called permission. He glanced up from his desk, then stood and gave his slow smile. "Kiri. What an unexpected pleasure. How did your visit to the home of the prospective husband go?"

She had intended a lighthearted comment about how they'd decided they wouldn't suit, but to her shock, she dissolved into tears. "Oh, *Adam!*"

Her brother closed the space between them and

enveloped her in his arms. He was only average height, not much taller than Kiri, but his strength and kindness made him a safe port in an emotional storm.

Growing up, she'd known she had an older brother who was a duke on the other side of the world. She had day-dreamed about her mother's lost son, wondering if they would ever meet. But she hadn't realized that a big brother could give her so much friendship, comfort, and wise advice.

He patted her back as she buried her face in his shoulder. "I gather things didn't work out well?"

"An understatement." She forced her tears to stop as Adam led her to his deep-cushioned leather sofa. "I overheard Godfrey's mother telling her sister that my dowry made me acceptable as wife to a younger son, but barely. They said I was vulgar and cast out lures and always had men sniffing around me. And they were *awful* about Mother!"

Adam gave her his handkerchief as he swore under his breath. "I had hoped you would never run into that degree of prejudice, but I suppose it was inevitable."

Kiri blotted her tears. "Lady Norland was always rather cool, but I thought she was just concerned for her son's happiness. I had no idea how much she despised me."

"Inferior people often despise those who are different," Adam said calmly. "It's the only way they can feel superior."

That surprised a watery chuckle from Kiri. "I expect you're right. But it was still lowering to find that I was a vulgar creature tolerated only for my dowry. Perhaps you shouldn't be too generous in the portion you intend to give me."

"Nonsense," her brother said. "You are as much the sixth duke's child as I am, so you are entitled to a dowry equal to your rank. Money does draw fortune hunters, but you have good sense." He gave a glinting smile. "And a protective family that will need to be convinced that a prospective suitor is worthy of you."

She was reminded of Mackenzie's comment that her brother was one of the most dangerous men in England. She tended to forget that since he was amazingly even-tempered and very fond of the family he had only just discovered. But Mackenzie was right: The Duke of Ashton was not a man to cross. "Such protection is a mixed blessing," she said wryly. "Your standards may be too high. What if you and the general don't agree with me on the subject of worthiness?"

He grinned. "Then we negotiate. Time tends to cure unfortunate infatuations, while finding the strength of true feeling."

That sounded reasonable. In a fortnight, she'd have largely forgotten Mackenzie. But for now . . .

She saw that she'd dropped Mackenzie's cloak near the door when she started crying, and had to restrain herself from rushing over to pick it up. "There's more to the story than being insulted by Lady Norland and her equally dreadful sister. I was so furious that I immediately took the best horse in the stables so I could ride to Dover and book a coach to London. But it was late in the day when I started, night fell, and I ran into a group of smugglers moving illegal goods."

Adam became very still. "And . . . ?"

"I was kidnapped and taken to their hideout on the coast. They were drinking and wondering what they might do to me when one of their London clients showed up and helped me get away. Interestingly, he was an old schoolmate of yours."

Adam grinned. "Let me guess. Damian Mackenzie?"

She frowned. "It can't be good for Mackenzie if everyone in London knows he deals in smuggled goods."

"I doubt anyone has proof of that. It's more a matter of knowing he couldn't possibly serve such excellent wines and spirits if he weren't dealing with contraband," Adam explained. "But you needn't worry about him too much. Most of the top politicians and diplomats in London go to Damian's regularly and will happily overlook the source of their drink because they enjoy the place."

She hoped Adam was right. Editing the events of the night, she said, "Mackenzie escorted me to the Westerfield Academy as fast as he could and handed me over to Lady Agnes. Would my reputation be hopelessly tarnished by the mere fact of having spent several hours riding with him? He seemed a gentleman."

"He's Will Masterson's brother, so he's basically sound, but the club is very fashionable and not entirely respectable," Adam observed. "It was good of him to take you to Lady Agnes, then quietly disappear so he wouldn't tarnish your reputation."

"Lady Agnes seems to think well of him," Kiri said a little defensively.

"She loves all her old boys, for which I'm deeply grateful." Adam's brows drew together. "Are you going to tell your parents what happened?"

She hesitated. "I don't like to be deceitful, but I don't want them to be upset. Mother will feel hurt by what I overheard, and the general will want to go down to Grimes Manor to crack heads. Perhaps it's best if I just tell them that I decided Godfrey wouldn't do, so I left quickly rather than cause awkwardness."

"A version of the truth is usually best," Adam agreed. "I think the measles quarantine will be lifted in a day or two, but it's best if you stay here for tonight at least."

"You are the *best* of brothers!" she said soulfully.

Adam laughed. "You and Thomas know each other so

well that it's harder to be admiring, so I haven't much competition for the title."

The door opened, and two beautiful blondes wearing similar shades of spring green entered the room. The Duchess of Ashton and her identical twin sister had returned from an expedition. Kiri rose and gave her sister-in-law a hug. "Every time I see you, it's easier to tell you and Sarah apart."

Mariah laughed and patted her swelling abdomen. "I keep looking at Sarah and reminding myself that someday, I might once again look as slim and lovely as she does."

"When that day comes, you won't need to nap as much, either," Sarah Clarke-Townsend said firmly. "Adam, Mariah was dozing in the carriage on the way home. She needs to go upstairs and rest. "

"That's not necessary!" Mariah said with exasperation. "Everyone fusses so. Bearing children is perfectly natural. Kiri, I need someone to argue on my side!"

"It won't be me," Kiri said with a grin. "Having children is natural, and so is being fatigued by the process. Resign yourself to being pampered, Your Grace."

"And if you refuse to be pampered, I shall carry you upstairs against your will," Adam said with a mischievous gleam in his eyes. "I'd rather enjoy that."

Laughing, Mariah took her husband's arm and let him escort her from the room. When they were gone, Sarah said with a sigh, "Is it terribly wicked of me to be so envious of my sister for having a wonderful, doting husband?"

"If so, I'm wicked, too." Kiri felt a twinge that made her think of the dratted Mackenzie. "There are other good men around. It just takes time to find the right one."

Sarah's eyes shadowed. Kiri remembered that the other girl had been betrothed, and her intended had died before they could marry. Wanting a distraction, Kiri pulled the bell cord. "Let's have tea. You must also be tired if you've been shopping."

"Excellent thought." As Sarah sat on the leather sofa, she glanced curiously at Mackenzie's cloak, which still lay on the floor.

Kiri retrieved the garment and folded it over the back of the chair. After ordering a tea tray when a footman entered, she said, "I noticed that the orange notes are starting to dominate in the perfume I made for you. Is it time to go back to the mixing bowl?"

Sarah sniffed her wrist. "You're right, it is smelling more orangelike as I wear it longer. You have the most amazing nose. I rather like this, actually, at least for day wear, but if you have the time, would you be willing to come up with a richer, more alluring version for evening?"

"I'd love to. Every woman should have a wardrobe of perfumes that fit different moods. It's interesting how this scent is different on you than on Mariah." Kiri surrendered to curiosity. "Speaking of identical twins—this is an appalling question and feel free to ignore it if you don't want to answer. But I've wondered. Given how much you and Mariah resemble each other, are you a little bit in love with Adam?"

Sarah looked startled, and certainly distracted from any memories of her lost love. "Not in the least. Or rather, I love him, but as a brother. He's wonderful, and he and Mariah suit splendidly, but he doesn't make my heart beat faster."

"That's fortunate." The tea tray arrived, so Kiri poured for them.

Sarah sipped her tea thoughtfully. "Mariah and I look very much alike and we have many similarities, including the way we choose the same colors for the same occasions." Sarah gestured at her light green morning gown, almost exactly the same shade as her sister wore that day.

"But since we were raised apart, we grew in our own separate ways. Mariah has that bright charm that dazzles everyone who sees her. Since Adam is reserved, they balance each other beautifully."

"If balance is your ideal relationship," Kiri said, intrigued, "what does that mean for the kind of husband you would like?"

"Mariah was raised rather irregularly and was always having to adapt to new circumstances, so she loves that Adam is so solid and reliable," Sarah explained. "I, on the other hand, had the most calm and respectable of upbringings and have a rather mousy temperament, so I find myself drawn to men who are a little wild." She made a face. "I suspect this is not a good thing."

"You're not mousy!" Kiri exclaimed. "But I see you've thought seriously about the subject. I'm still trying to decide what kind of man would suit me best."

Sarah helped herself to a ginger cake. "Since you're still looking, I gather that you decided Godfrey Hitchcock won't suit?"

"Most definitely not." Kiri's voice was edged.

Sarah frowned. "What happened?" When Kiri hesitated, Sarah said, "If something dreadful happened and you told Adam, he'll tell Mariah, and she'll tell me, so you might as well tell me directly."

Kiri laughed. "You're right. As long as you don't tell anyone else."

"I won't," Sarah assured her. "Your story will end with me."

Knowing Sarah's word was good, Kiri gave a terse summary of why she had bolted from Grimes Manor, and what had happened later. The other girl listened raptly.

When Kiri finished, Sarah said wistfully, "Imagine being rescued by Damian Mackenzie himself! I've been hearing about his club ever since it opened three years ago. It's the most fashionable evening spot in London." She consumed an almond cake in two bites. "The masquerades at Damian's are famous. The last one of the year is two nights from now. I'd love to go, but my mother would be horrified."

"So would mine." Kiri paused with her teacup halfway to her mouth as inspiration struck. "I just had the most wonderful idea! We could go to the masquerade together. I must repay the money Mackenzie spent on buying my freedom, and we can take the opportunity to see the club." She also needed to see the man in his normal world if she was to get over him.

Sarah's eyes widened with shock. "I couldn't possibly do such a thing!"

"Of course you can. Damian's is on Pall Mall near royalty and the best other clubs, not in some horrid waterfront stew," Kiri said persuasively. "With a domino to cover head and body and a mask over half our faces, no one will recognize us. We'll leave before the unmasking."

"Going there secretly would be dreadfully wicked." The other girl bit her lip. "I *long* to be wicked! But how would it be done?"

"While we're both of age and can do as we choose, it would be better to go undiscovered." Kiri pondered. "Since I'm staying here for the next several days, why not say you want to stay as well to keep me company?"

"That would work! With Mariah increasing, she and Adam usually withdraw to their quarters not long after dinner. We could leave after they retire."

"I'll ask Murphy, the head groom, to drive us to the club and wait. I think I can persuade him not to give us away until later."

Sarah frowned. "Would he risk his job if he helps us?"

Kiri shook her head. "No, Adam trusts Murphy's judgment. He's guaranteed Murphy employment for life for his aid in the past."

"That's all right, then. We can tell Adam and Mariah the next day. I doubt they'll tell our parents."

"The next question is where to get dominos. I don't have one." Kiri glanced ruefully at her divided skirt, which needed more than a good brushing to look proper. "Since I ran off from Kent without my baggage and I can't get clothing from home until the measles pass, I can't go in society unless I'm completely covered by a domino."

"I can borrow my parents' dominos. Since you're tall, you can wear my father's." Sarah was beaming. "This will be such an adventure!"

Kiri made a face, thinking of Lady Agnes's words. "I have discovered that adventures aren't much fun when they're happening."

"Being kidnapped by ruffians would be too much of an adventure," the other girl agreed. "Attending a masquerade at a racy but safe club is a proper size adventure. Apart from perhaps a gentleman stealing a kiss, what could go wrong?"

Kiri could think of a number of things that might go wrong, but surely Sarah was right in this case. She'd repay Mackenzie, banish his lingering image from her imagination, and have an amusing evening.

Racy, but safe.

Chapter 10

Kiri peeked into her wardrobe to enjoy the sight of her domino. All had gone according to plan, with Sarah coming to stay and bringing her parents' dominos in her baggage. Tonight was the night of the masquerade, and they were both brimming with excitement. A nice, safe adventure, and for Kiri, a legitimate reason to see Mackenzie.

Needing to think of something else, Kiri settled at her desk to write letters. Her industry was interrupted by a tap at the door. She called permission to enter, and the butler, Holmes, appeared.

"There is a gentleman here to see you, Lady Kiri. He won't give his name, but he appears most respectable." There was a note of disapproval in the butler's voice at the visitor's refusal to identify himself. "He is in the small receiving room."

Kiri's heart leaped. Mackenzie! Had he spent the past two days thinking about her as she'd been thinking about him? More likely he just wanted his money back. Keeping her voice even, she said, "I believe I know his identity, so I shall see him."

Before going down, she glanced regretfully in the mirror. Her hair was neat, but her limited wardrobe meant that she was wearing a plain green morning gown that she'd left at Ashton House before she went down to Kent.

Reminding herself that Mackenzie had seen her look worse, she descended the stairs. Trying not to look too eager, she swept into the receiving room—and found the Honorable Godfrey Hitchcock, who looked so blond and handsome that she remembered why she'd considered marrying him.

Kiri froze, torn between snarling Hindi curses and stalking out. She had one hand on the doorknob and was on the verge of escape when Godfrey exclaimed, "Please, Lady Kiri! Tell me what I did wrong!" He drew a step closer. "I thought we were reaching an understanding. Then you were gone, leaving me a note to hunt another fortune. Yes, my portion is not the equal of yours, but I'm no pauper, and we both knew that. What changed? If I offended you in some way, give me a chance to correct my error!"

She didn't leave, but her voice was cold when she said, "You came all the way from Kent to say that?"

"You requested that your baggage be sent here, so I decided to deliver it myself. It's being unloaded from my carriage now." Godfrey's blue eyes were worried. "But I also needed to talk to you. I want very much to understand what happened."

He was either a magnificent liar, or genuinely unaware of his mother's views, though it was hard to believe the latter. "I decided we would not suit, so staying longer would be awkward," Kiri said. "It seemed simplest to leave."

"So awkward that you commandeered a horse and rode off in late afternoon with a storm coming?" He shook his head, unconvinced. "We'd had such an enjoyable day. I was ready to offer for you, and you seemed willing to listen. But even if you decided to say no, I'm sure you could refuse me so gently that there would be no awkwardness. Instead, you ran off as if pursued by demons."

She sighed, thinking he was more perceptive than she'd given him credit for. "Do you truly want to know? I doubt the knowledge will make you happy."

"I am not happy now," he said tightly. "If you explain, at least I will understand."

"Very well. After our ride, I stopped by the morning room to tell your mother that I would accept her invitation to stay longer," Kiri said. "I was considering your offer, but thought we needed to spend more time together."

"Surely she didn't withdraw her invitation for you to stay longer," Godfrey said, puzzled. "She was most hopeful that you would accept me."

"Because of my dowry," Kiri said bitterly. "I was about to enter the morning room when I overheard your mother conversing with your aunt, Lady Shrimpton. They said . . ." She hesitated, feeling the painful words in her viscera.

"They said what?"

Kiri took a deep breath. "That I was a vulgar foreign slut barely redeemed by my dowry. Good enough for an expensive younger son. Such a mercy that your older brothers had sons so future Lord Norlands wouldn't be tainted by my Hindu blood."

Godfrey gasped, but Kiri continued inexorably, "That was bad enough, but what they said about my mother was . . . unforgivable. I knew I had to leave immediately, or I would start smashing china. Civility was not possible. Now do you understand?"

Godfrey looked ill. "I can't believe my mother would say such things!"

"Can you really not believe it?" Kiri said in a hard voice.

He started to speak, then shook his head. "She is . . . very old-fashioned in many ways. Very proud of the family bloodlines. But I thought she liked you. You are a beautiful, vibrant girl who can charm the stones from the fields. Your lineage is better than mine, and naturally a good dowry is appreciated." He swallowed hard. "Perhaps because I wanted her to welcome you into our family, I didn't see anything else."

"She would welcome my dowry. No doubt she would have been civil to me until the day she became angry, or drank too much sherry, and explained how much she despised me." Kiri turned back to the door. "I regret telling you this, but you did ask."

"Don't leave yet," he pleaded. "I swear that I do not share my mother's prejudice. Will you try to believe that?"

She remembered the very enjoyable kisses they'd shared. Was he free of prejudice, or was it that he desired her enough to overlook her heritage? Some of both, perhaps. Even he probably didn't know for sure. "I accept your word," she said, wanting to end the unpleasant scene. "Now there is nothing left to be said. Good-bye, Godfrey."

"So the sins of my mother are to be visited on me?" There was real pain in his eyes. "It is me you would marry, not my mother. We need have nothing to do with her."

He was sincere, she thought, but when she looked at Godfrey, she saw a boy, not a man. In the last days, she'd realized that she wanted a man. "A marriage joins families almost as much as it joins a man and a woman. I will not marry into a family that doesn't want me, nor do I wish for you to be estranged from your own mother." She held out a hand. "Go in peace, Godfrey."

He held her hand, squeezing it for a long moment before releasing her. "Thank you for your honesty and graciousness, Lady Kiri. I'm sorry you were hurt by my mother's narrow-mindedness."

She shrugged. "I'm grateful that the countess's true feelings were revealed before it was too late."

He sighed, but inclined his head in agreement before he left. It was only a matter of time until he found a nice blond English girl who would suit his family. Kiri returned to her room and found a maid unpacking the luggage Godfrey had delivered.

Kiri smiled wryly. At least she now had more clothes to wear.

Sarah gasped as she stared up at the glittering dome that arched over the club's ballroom. "Damian's is everything I've heard, and more!"

Kiri agreed. Even for someone who had experienced sumptuous Hindu temples, Mackenzie's club was dazzling. The ballroom was a great circular chamber topped by the flamboyantly painted dome and lit by a vast, sparkling gas chandelier. Kiri had seen some of the new gas streetlights, but this was the first gaslit building she'd been in.

The masquerade was in full swing and the ballroom was crowded with laughing, chattering guests. Some treated the dominos as cloaks that swept back over their shoulders to show off rich garments and jewels. Others, like Kiri and Sarah, concealed themselves in the voluminous hooded dominos and half masks.

Sarah had tied back her hair so no bright curls could hint at her identity. Kiri wore a divided skirt and boots. The boots were barely visible below the hem of her black domino, but combined with her height, she could be thought male. The two of them looked like a couple, which was preferable to appearing like two females on the prowl.

After entering the ballroom, they took positions by one curving wall while they studied the scene. Arched doorways led to connecting chambers that were used for gaming or refreshments. Kiri tapped her foot to the music, played by musicians on a balcony above. The music, like everything in Damian's, was top quality.

Men dressed in black evening wear, masked but without dominos, circulated through the rooms carrying trays of champagne glasses. All were strong-looking fellows. Kiri guessed their jobs included preventing unpleasantness as well as serving champagne.

Was one of them Mackenzie? She didn't think so. None had quite the right build, or the right way of moving. Though perhaps she was fooling herself to think she would recognize Mackenzie in this crowd of masqueraders.

A gentleman approached them and made a sweeping bow in front of Sarah. In a young, playful voice, he asked, "Will you dance with me, fair lady?"

He sounded like a boy down from Oxford and as delighted by the occasion as Kiri and Sarah. Not a threat. Sarah glanced at Kiri, who gave a nod.

They had discussed this in advance. Sarah's domino was dark blue rather than the more usual black, her mask glittered with sequins, and she carried a whistle to blow if she ran into trouble. The sound would bring Kiri running, and perhaps offer a chance to use her Kalarippayattu. Or else the knife she'd taken from the smuggler, which was now tucked into a sheath on her forearm.

She doubted weapons would be needed, though, given how well run this masquerade was. A few couples shared heated kisses, but she saw nothing else untoward.

They'd arranged to meet in the entrance foyer a quarter hour before midnight so they could leave before the unmasking. Murphy, the Ashton groom, had raised his brows when Kiri asked if he would bring them to Damian's, but he said they'd be safe here. He would have the closed carriage at the door just before midnight.

And if they didn't come out by midnight, Murphy said

he'd come in and get them. He would, too. As a former soldier, he was a good protector for their night out.

With Sarah happily dancing with her mystery man, Kiri began to explore, looking for Mackenzie while admiring her extravagant surroundings. The scene wasn't too different from a grand ball in a private home, but the masks and dominos made a difference. The atmosphere held breathless mystery because anyone might be here. Handsome strangers, or friends transformed into strangers. Great lords, wicked ladies—or respectable ladies like Sarah Clarke-Townsend, who yearned for a bit of naughtiness.

Three rooms led off the ballroom, two for gambling and the other equipped with a massive buffet and supper tables. When she entered the left-hand gaming room, a black-clad servant approached to offer her champagne. She accepted a flute with thanks, lowering her voice to make her gender ambiguous.

Sipping slowly, Kiri continued to stroll, absorbing the atmosphere with all her senses. In particular, she used her sense of smell. She had the fragrance equivalent of perfect pitch in music, which was a great asset to a perfumer. She could recognize and identify complex scents, and usually duplicate them in her laboratory.

On occasions like this, she'd learned to block out the usual scents, which might have been overpowering otherwise. But she enjoyed trying to identify the fragrances worn by the other guests. It was easy to pick out the common perfumes, like eau de Cologne and French violet and Hungary water.

More challenging was to discern the subtle shifts that occurred from wearing the perfumes. For example, on some people Hungary water shifted toward lavender or mint. On others, the citrus notes were more pronounced.

She wrinkled her nose when she passed a woman who smelled of rancid chypre. Some poor unfortunates really shouldn't wear perfume at all because something about their bodies turned even the finest fragrances sour.

As she entered the dining room, another guest bumped into her, spilling a glass of champagne onto Kiri. "I'm so sorry!" The speaker's voice was that of a well-bred but flustered girl. She wore a purple domino so dark it was almost black. Though her perfume was a custom blend of expensive ingredients, it was clumsily composed and too heavy for a young girl. Perhaps she'd borrowed her mother's perfume.

"No matter," Kiri said in her normal voice, thinking a female voice would be less alarming to her. "A little spilled champagne won't show on a black domino."

"You are gracious." The girl's eyes sparkled even behind her mask. "Isn't this all wonderfully exciting? I like that I can talk to someone without being introduced!"

"It feels very free," Kiri agreed. "This is my first visit to Damian's."

"Mine, too!" The girl seemed delighted to have found a fellow newcomer.

Kiri was glad Damian's was safe, because the girl seemed so naive that she might fall into trouble in a less well-regulated environment. They chatted a few more minutes, then went their separate ways, Kiri to check on Sarah, with the girl in the purple domino out to acquire more champagne and sample the lobster patties.

Kiri looked for Sarah, and saw that her friend was laughing as she danced, clearly having a good time. Still no sign of Mackenzie. Kiri had hoped to hand over the heavy pouch of gold guineas slung under her domino. Even more than repaying her debt, she wanted to satisfy her curiosity.

But first she had to find the blasted man.

Chapter 11

Mac drifted through the crowd, enjoying the season's last masquerade as well as watching and listening to ensure that nothing happened to disturb the peace. Damian's was one of the few public places in London where well-born men and women could dance, drink, and gamble together. He would not allow anything to happen that might drive the females away, since they were what made Damian's more than just another club.

He scanned the ballroom, looking for his manager, Jean-Claude Baptiste. Lean and dark, Baptiste had fled France and the Terror as a youth, and his years in London had left him with only a faint French accent. Dressed in black evening clothes and a mask, he was easy to find. He was speaking with his friend, Lord Fendall, a most fashionable gentleman who was a regular, and profitable, habitué of Damian's.

Anonymous in his domino, Mac went unrecognized until he was standing right next to Baptiste. Pitching his voice to be heard through the happy clamor of the crowd, Mac asked, "Any problems?"

Baptiste startled violently. "If I perish of a heart spasm,

it will be your fault, *mon ami*. No problems, other than more guests than expected."

"But of course," Fendall said with a lazy smile. "Since this is Damian's last masquerade ball until spring, we must absorb every morsel of pleasure."

"Every last morsel of lobster patty is going fast, too," Mac said.

"More are being brought from the kitchen," Baptiste said. "And extra wine and spirits are being brought from the cellar. A good thing the new shipment arrived today."

"What about the footmen?" Mac asked. "These aren't all our usual staff."

"I invited several struggling actors, promising them free food and drink at the least, and payment for their time if I needed them to work." Baptiste nodded at the nearest man in black with his tray of champagne. "All have been pressed into service."

"Good thinking." Mac had been lucky the day he'd hired Baptiste. The Frenchman was an excellent manager, and he'd taken much of the routine work off Mac's shoulders. "I'll take another swing through the gambling rooms."

Baptiste nodded and they moved off in different directions. Mac listened to fragments of conversation, but heard only the usual flirtations and comments on the entertainment and the recent redecorating.

Mac spent most of his time at masquerades monitoring the different gambling tables. Troublemakers generally stayed away from Damian's, but Mac knew from experience that masks and dominos increased the opportunities for mischief.

He was almost through his circuit and thinking of trying the buffet when a table in the back of the second gambling room caught his eye. Two players were engaged in piquet and the atmosphere was so tense that Mac could almost see the air thrumming above the table. He strolled over, his experienced gaze analyzing the situation.

One player's hood had fallen back, revealing fair hair and a sweaty brow. From the sections of face that were visible, he was young and frightened. His opponent was expertly dealing more cards, and several notes were on his side of the table, each probably an IOU for more money won from his young opponent.

Mac's eyes narrowed as he studied the man's hands and the expert card-handling skills. Identity confirmed by a small scar on the back of the man's hand, he stepped up to the table. "Good evening, Digby. How thoughtful of you to give this young gentleman a lesson in cardsharping." He laid a casual-seeming hand on Digby's shoulder, his fingers biting in painfully. "Did Digby mention that he was seeking to educate you?"

The young man looked up, desperate hope showing through the eyeholes of his mask. "No. No, he didn't. Are you saying this isn't a real game?"

"The lesson is more effective if the fear is real," Mac said jovially as he scooped up the IOUs. He read the scrawled signature on the top one. "Wait here a few minutes, Mr. Beaton. I'll tell you more about our educational program after I talk to Mr. Digby."

The boy nodded, dazed by his good fortune, while Digby muttered a filthy curse under his breath as Mac's grip forced him to rise. Mac draped a casual arm around the other man's shoulder as he steered them toward a side door.

"Such language!" Mac said. "I don't want to see the ladies offended." He grinned when that produced an even filthier curse, but in such a low voice that no one other than Mac could hear it.

Once they left the gambling room for a service corridor, Mac asked silkily, "When I banned you from Damian's,

Mr. Digby, was I insufficiently clear? Did I say anything to suggest that masquerade nights were an exception?"

Digby flung off Mac's arm with a growl. "Someone is going to relieve that boy of his money, and it might as well be me!"

"Perhaps, but it won't happen at Damian's." Mac frowned as he ushered Digby along the corridor. "It's not actually a bad idea to hold classes in cardsharping for innocent lads from the country. It would teach them what to watch out for. The more intelligent will learn to guard their purses better."

"Others will just learn how to cheat," Digby grumbled.

"Then you will be well matched." They reached the outside door. Mac put a hand on the other man's wrist and twisted. "Consider this a final warning. Appear here again in any guise, and you'll find there's a reason I'm called Mac the Knife."

Digby jerked away. "Don't worry, I won't sully your precious club again!" He removed his mask, revealing a ferretlike face.

"How fortunate that we are in agreement." Mac held the door until Digby left, then locked it behind the man.

Now it was time to deal with Digby's idiot victim. Mac found young George Beaton still at the table and clutching an empty glass of champagne.

Mac took the chair Digby had occupied, asking mildly, "Whatever possessed you to gamble so deeply with a stranger at a masquerade? Even if you knew your opponent, it's impossible to read faces properly through masks, which makes it easier to lose."

The visible part of the boy's face reddened. "It started out as a friendly game."

Mac pulled the crumpled vowels from his pocket and leafed through, whistling softly as he totaled up the numbers. "It didn't stay friendly for long."

He studied what he could see of the boy's face. "Are you Alfred Beaton's son?" When the boy nodded, Mac said, "I heard that he died recently. My condolences."

After young Beaton muttered thanks, Mac held up the collection of IOUs. "Would he be proud of you for this?"

The face that had been red now turned white. Mac continued relentlessly. "I'm guessing these couldn't be paid without mortgaging the family estate. You have younger sisters, don't you? And a newly widowed mother? Will they enjoy living in a hovel if you gamble away their home? I hope your sisters will enjoy being governesses since they might never be able to marry if your gaming deprives them of their portions."

"I didn't mean any harm!"

Mac sighed. "Gamesters never do. And somehow, it's never their fault when they devastate their families. It was the cards, or the dice, or Lady Luck."

"I was foolish, I admit it." Beaton stared at the IOUs Mac held. "I will not be such a fool again. Will you return my vowels to me?"

Mac decided the lesson needed reinforcement. "I'm going to keep them for —hmm, three years. If you gamble so recklessly again, I will hear sooner or later, and then I will produce these IOUs for the world to see. You will stand revealed as a dishonorable fool trying to gamble with money you've already lost."

"That will ruin my reputation!"

"As opposed to ruining everyone you love?" Mac said dryly. "Has it occurred to you that it might be wiser to stop gambling?"

"Everyone gambles," Beaton said defensively. "My father visited Damian's whenever he was in London."

"And he never lost more than he could afford." Mac guessed that tonight's escapade had something to do with the boy's loss of his father and wanting to prove himself a man. "If you feel gambling is necessary for your social life, I will tell you how to play without ruining yourself. It's the method your father used."

Beaton's brows drew together. "How can I do that?"

"Decide how much you can afford to spend on an evening's entertainment. Ten pounds? Fifty? Surely no more than that. Carry that with you in cash, and don't gamble anything beyond that. As long as you win, you can play as long as you want.

"But when you've lost the stake you brought, the game is *over*. Write no IOUs, make no promises." Mac glanced at Beaton's empty champagne glass. "And take no more than two drinks in the course of your gaming, even if it lasts all night."

"You're talking chicken stakes!" the boy exclaimed. "I'll be a laughingstock to my friends."

"Perhaps you need new friends. Those who urge you to ruin yourself for their entertainment are not worthy of the term." Mac brandished the vowels. "And if you forget yourself and lose a fortune for real, I will be happy to ruin your reputation."

"You're blackmailing me," Beaton said, more in amazement than in anger.

"Indeed I am," Mac said cheerfully. "Is it working?"

Beaton drew a deep breath. "I . . . I believe it is. I never felt so sick in my life as when I realized how much I'd lost." He swallowed, his Adam's apple bobbing. "I understand now why men kill themselves after losing everything. But I kept playing because the only solution I could see was winning it all back."

"Not the best strategy, particularly when facing a Captain Sharp."

"Was he cheating?"

Mac picked up the cards and expertly shuffled through, noting that several were sanded. "Yes. But even if he hadn't been, he probably would have won because of his skill. No matter how good a cardplayer is, someone is always better. Or luckier."

Beaton smiled crookedly. "You have succeeded in your lesson. I will no longer let myself be guided by those who don't have my true interests at heart. I assume you're Damian Mackenzie himself? My thanks for taking the time to haul me out of the hole I'd dug, and beat me soundly about the ears."

"Metaphorically speaking. It's bad business to physically beat guests without a really good reason. Go and enjoy the buffet. It will leave you in a better mood than the gambling." Mac inclined his head and left. Enormous sums were won and lost at Damian's, but Mac not would allow underage fools to fall into disaster. At least this lad might have actually learned his lesson.

He paused by the door of the ballroom to scan the dancing couples. He liked seeing his guests enjoying themselves, and he liked dancing. Perhaps after the unmasking, he'd have a dance or two if all continued smoothly.

A figure swathed in black paused beside him, also studying the dancers. Mac froze as sensation blazed through him, going right to his viscera. *Blooming lilacs and subtle spices and irresistible woman.*

Without conscious thought, he wrapped an arm around her waist and drew her hard against him so her back was pressed into his chest. She was slim and strong as a panther under the concealing folds of fabric. Blood running rampant through his veins, he whispered into her ear, "What mischief brings you here tonight, Lady Kiri?"

Chapter 12

Kiri stiffened when Mackenzie appeared from nowhere and pulled her against his hard, unyielding body. She felt heat from her shoulder blades to her derriere. She didn't know if she should break away or lean back into him. Choosing neither, she said with matching softness, "I'm here to return the fifty guineas I owe you, Mr. Mackenzie."

"It wasn't a loan, Lady Kiri," he said, startled. "I did what any man would. I didn't expect to be repaid."

"Perhaps not. But I do not wish to be in your debt, and fifty guineas is a substantial sum. Or are you too proud to accept money from a woman?"

"I'm never proud where money is concerned." He released her, his chuckle a warm breath against her ear. "But you shouldn't hand over such a sum in public. We can go to my office, where I have a strongbox."

A firm hand on her elbow, he guided her across the left-hand gambling room and through a door unobtrusively tucked into the paneling. On the other side was a long corridor lit by small gas sconces. Closing the door reduced the talking and music to a muted roar so they could speak normally.

"The gas lighting is impressive," Kiri remarked as she

looked down the corridor. "My brother is considering having it installed in Ashton House. I shall encourage him."

"The light is stronger and steadier than any candle or lamp. Since Pall Mall was the first street in London to get gas lighting, I arranged to have it installed here at the same time." Hand still on her arm, he guided her down the corridor, which was just wide enough for two. "Did you come alone?"

She shook her head. "I have a companion, and we will have highly reliable transportation home when we leave the club."

He gave a twisted smile. "Ironic that I expend great effort to make this club safe for all comers, yet I find myself worrying about such a very capable young lady."

"There is no need to concern yourself with me," she said tartly.

They turned into a left-hand corridor, then again to the right. "You have a maze of passages here," she said as they walked toward the back of the building.

He tugged off his mask. "The club was created from three separate buildings. Lots of corridors, not much logic. That door on the right is my office."

Instead of entering, he gazed at her intently. Then he raised one hand and pulled off her mask, his hand a feather caress on her hair. The air between them rose to simmering point. "When we were in the barn, I collected a nonmonetary reward," he said huskily. "But since you're repaying my money, I must give back what I took."

He drew her into his arms and returned her kiss with interest.

Oh, *damnation!* Kiri thought helplessly as her mouth opened eagerly under his. The blazing reaction she'd had when they first met wasn't a fluke. She wanted to sink into him, talk to him, laugh with him, and the attraction was as much mental as physical.

But he was a man of the world who had surely desired many women. And acted on that, or he wouldn't be so very skilled at dissolving her wits. Or at finding sensitive places and teasing her tongue and rubbing her back so that she melted into him.

She forced herself to remember that some of London's most celebrated beauties were his regular guests, including married women ripe for dalliance. That recognition gave her the willpower to say breathlessly, "Kiss returned in full measure." She broke away from his embrace. "Once I return the money, our accounts are in balance."

He stared at her for a long, tense moment before opening the door to his office. She stepped in and was startled to see a dark-haired man standing over the desk as he examined a portfolio of papers. She had a swift impression of alertness and danger.

The man looked up, his expression instantly changing to amiable warmth. Good Lord, it was her brother's school friend, Lord Kirkland! A wealthy Scottish shipping merchant, Kirkland visited London regularly and called on Adam and Mariah when he was in Town. She'd always found Kirkland courteous, amusing, and rather enigmatic. She had not thought of him as dangerous.

He bowed elegantly. "Lady Kiri. I suppose I shouldn't ask why you're here." He smiled, the tanned skin crinkling around his eyes. "Mackenzie told me the story of your adventure, in case you were wondering."

"I was," she admitted as she offered her hand. "I am here to repay a debt, but I also wished to see the dazzling Damian's of which I've heard."

"I hope you're enjoying your visit?"

"Oh, yes," she assured him. "The club lives up to its reputation."

"I didn't think you'd be here tonight, Kirkland," Mackenzie remarked as he moved a framed satirical sketch, revealing a wall safe with a sophisticated-looking lock.

"Something came up that I need to discuss with you," Kirkland explained. "Just a small matter of business." His words were light, but his eyes were serious.

"It's not generally known," Mackenzie said as he unlocked the safe, "but Kirkland and I are partners in Damian's."

Kirkland shrugged. "Mac does all the work. I helped with the boring financing, and a profitable investment the club has been."

Mackenzie grinned. "Money may seem boring, but it was essential."

Reminded of money, Kiri unbuttoned her domino so she could reach the pouch containing the guineas. As she handed the money over, she said formally, "Mr. Mackenzie, my thanks for your courage and willingness to cheat at cards."

He laughed as he accepted the money, but as his fingertips brushed hers, she felt a tingle like a small electric shock. It would be so much *easier* if the attraction had only been a result of their shared adventure! But there was more to it than that. She felt—connected to him in some way. Keeping her voice light, she asked, "Aren't you going to count to see if it's the full fifty guineas?"

Mackenzie's brows arched. "You'd be more likely to overpay than to underpay." He tossed the pouch thoughtfully. "But given my vast experience of handling money, I'd say this is exactly fifty guineas."

He was damnably perceptive. She'd thought of putting more money in the pouch but didn't know how to price what he'd done for her. "Since my business is done, I shall leave you two gentlemen." When Mackenzie moved to join her, she raised a hand. "No need, Mr. Mackenzie. I can find my way back. It's almost time for me to collect my companion and leave."

"I'm glad to see that you recovered from the kidnapping," he said politely, but his eyes showed a wary longing that matched hers. At least she wasn't the only one who was disturbed by this unwelcome attraction.

Kiri opened the office door, wondering what intense, manly things would be discussed when she was out of earshot. As she stepped out, her eye was caught by movement to her right, near the end of the corridor where it intersected another.

She turned to look, then sucked in her breath, shocked. Five masked men were dragging off a smaller figure—who wore a dark purple domino.

"Mackenzie! Kirkland!" she said sharply. "A woman is being attacked!"

She raced down the corridor. As she ran, she undid the last button on her domino and let it fall away to free herself from the enveloping folds of fabric. Behind her, she heard Mackenzie and Kirkland emerging from the office to follow her.

The attackers and their victim disappeared down the cross corridor to the right. When she reached the intersection, she saw that the short passage ended in a door that led to the alley behind the club. The kidnappers were almost at the door, and this close, Kiri confirmed that their victim was the girl she'd talked to earlier.

The struggling girl's mask had been ripped off and a heavy hand was clamped over her mouth. Why would five men capture an innocent girl? A drunken bet? Desire for gang rape?

Though she couldn't stop five men by herself, she could slow them for critical seconds until Mackenzie and Kirkland arrived. With warrior exhilaration, she attacked with a banshee wail, using her Kalarippayattu to confuse and disorient the kidnappers.

The men turned, startled by her cry. She leaped into a flying kick, the toe of her riding boot smashing between the legs of the last man in the group. "Thug!" she spat.

He shrieked horribly and folded to the floor, clutching himself. Giving thanks she'd worn a riding skirt and boots, she pulled out the neat little knife she'd taken from a smuggler. When she stabbed the next man, he howled and retreated, the knife so deeply buried in the muscle of his left arm that the handle was wrenched from her hand.

"Out *now!*" a tall man barked in a voice of authority. He seemed to be the leader, and he had the kidnapped girl beside the outside door.

There was no time to waste retrieving the knife when the other men were on the verge of dragging their captive out of the building. Kiri rushed the kidnappers—and found herself looking down the barrel of a pistol held by the largest, most threatening of the men.

Since the corridor offered no place to hide, she began zigzagging and praying that he'd miss when he shot. He smiled nastily and took aim.

A boom echoed through the corridor and the big man's face disintegrated into smashed bone and blood. A pistol ball had struck dead center. His weapon fired harmlessly into the wall as he collapsed.

Kiri glanced back and saw Kirkland standing at the intersection with a smoking pistol in his hand, his face icily calm as he reloaded. Mackenzie had caught up with the other kidnappers and was using his fists with the ruthless professionalism of a boxer.

The leader reached for the doorknob, his other hand locked on the girl's upper arm. Kiri caught up with him and kicked the arm holding his captive.

Swearing, he lost his grip. Kiri wrapped an arm around

the girl's waist and dragged her away. The leader lunged toward them to retrieve his captive. "No, damn you! You're too valuable a pigeon to fly away!"

Something about him said that he was expensive and fashionable. Kiri jabbed him in the throat with stiffened fingers.

He made a gagging sound. Furious defeat in his pale, angry eyes, he wrenched the door open and half fell outside. Two of his men crowded out behind him.

Mackenzie thundered up as the kidnappers escaped. "Bloody bastards!" he swore as he followed them into the dark alley. "They'll not get away with this!"

As the door slammed shut behind him, Kiri kept a firm arm around the shaking girl. "Are you all right?"

The girl nodded, tears on her cheeks despite her valiant efforts to control them. Though she was attractive, she wasn't such a raving beauty as to drive men mad. And she looked very, very young. "They . . . they didn't hurt me."

Kirkland joined them, pistol pointing toward the floor. "At least we stopped them before they . . ."

His voice fell into stunned silence as he stared at the girl in the purple domino. He sank down on one knee, his head bowed. "Your Royal Highness. Thank God you are safe."

Your Royal Highness? Kiri stared at the girl with shock, then sudden paralyzed understanding.

They had just rescued Princess Charlotte, only legitimate daughter of the prince regent, and the heiress of England.

Chapter 13

Kiri had never met Princess Charlotte, since the girl was only sixteen and led a famously sheltered life. But she had the look of the royal House of Hanover. She was above-average height, fair haired, and full figured.

More to the point, Kirkland seemed to have no doubt of her identity. Since the princess looked as if she could now stand on her own, Kiri released her and curtsied deeply. "Your Royal Highness, forgive me if my behavior lacked decorum."

"I owe you thanks for your efforts on my behalf." Charlotte's light blue eyes brightened. "I didn't know a woman could fight like that!"

"I was trained in an ancient Hindu martial art," Kiri explained as she straightened. Her heart was pounding from the fight and this astonishing meeting. "But without Lord Kirkland and Mr. Mackenzie, we both would have been in trouble."

The princess's gaze went to the bloody corpse of the man Kirkland had shot. Another man lay facedown on the floor. He was unconscious and blood pooled around him, but he was still breathing. Kiri thought he might be the kidnapper she'd stabbed in the arm, but couldn't bear to look to see if her knife was still in him.

Charlotte's face paled at the sight of the bodies and she began to sway unsteadily. Kiri caught her arm. "I'll take Her Highness to the office. Is there any brandy there?"

"In the cabinet. After you've given her some, pull the bell cord hard three times. That will bring two guards." Kirkland radiated rigidly controlled shock. "The princess must be taken home safely. How did you travel to the club, Kiri?"

"Sarah Clarke-Townsend and I came together, driven by Adam's head groom."

"Send one of the guards to find Sarah and bring her to the office. The other guard can locate Murphy's carriage and have him bring it down the alley on the side of the building. You and Sarah can escort the princess home with Murphy and the guards for protection." Kirkland studied the fallen men with a flinty gaze. "I'll see if I can learn anything about these fellows and their purpose."

It was a relief to turn into the main corridor, out of sight of the blood and bodies. Kiri guided the princess toward the office, supporting part of the girl's weight. She retrieved the domino she'd dropped, chilled by the realization that this must not have been a random attack. The five men had recognized the princess and deliberately kidnapped her. But why? And how had they known where to find her?

After they entered the office, she guided Charlotte to the most comfortable chair. "I imagine you came here for a bit of adventure, and this is more than you bargained for."

Charlotte smiled crookedly. "I am treated as a child and not allowed to go into society, but Damian's is said to be safe. I live in Warwick House, quite near here, so after my governess and the rest of my household retired, I slipped out with a domino and mask I'd borrowed from my mother."

"You walked over alone?" Kiri tried not to sound appalled.

"No one accosted me." The princess looked wistful. "It was so exciting to be out on my own instead of living in a cage. Once I reached Damian's, I thought I was safe. I was having a lovely time. Then a man in one of the gaming parlors said, 'Your Highness?' I looked around, of course, forgetting that no one should know. That man and several others drew around me so no one could see when the leader grabbed me and put a hand over my mouth. They whisked me from the gaming room into a corridor. I struggled, but had no chance against them all. If not for you . . ." She shuddered.

"Time for that brandy." Kiri opened a likely looking cabinet and found spirits and glasses. Picking the bottle with a silver collar that said "Cognac," she poured a generous dose and handed it to the princess. "Best drink slowly. I'm sure it's powerful."

Charlotte sipped cautiously, choked a little, sipped some more. "You were right, but it's most invigorating."

Kiri poured another glass. "With your permission?" Not waiting for a reply, she took a swallow, grateful for the electrifying burn as it rolled down her throat. "Like you, I've had more adventure than I expected."

Charlotte emptied her glass and held it out for more. "Pray introduce yourself and my other brave rescuers."

Kicking herself for such an elementary failing, Kiri replied, "I am Lady Kiri Lawford, sister of the Duke of Ashton."

Charlotte's gaze sharpened. "So you're half Hindu, as he is? No wonder you are so beautiful and know exotic fighting skills!" She looked envious.

Kiri blushed. "Thank you, Your Majesty. The two men are Lord Kirkland, who recognized you, and Mr. Mackenzie, owner of Damian's." She pulled hard at the bell cord, then sat down and concentrated on her brandy. "Before the guards arrive, you may wish to don your mask."

Charlotte did so immediately. "If this becomes known, there will be a frightful scandal, won't there?"

"A scandal, and public outrage on your behalf." Kiri hesitated, wondering if the princess was so shielded that she didn't know her own position. "You are immensely popular with the public, Your Highness. Far more so than your father."

Charlotte's face lit up. "Really?"

"Really." The girl's happiness about her popularity hurt Kiri's heart. Her parents, the prince regent and his German cousin, Caroline of Brunswick, should never have married. They loathed each other and had separated not long after Charlotte's birth. Too many of their conflicts had played out with their hapless daughter as a pawn.

The two guards arrived quickly, both of them tall, brawny men dressed in black evening wear. Kiri recognized them as footmen who'd served champagne in the public rooms. They looked intelligent as well as strong. "Lord Kirkland wishes for one of you to locate a particular carriage with a driver named Murphy." She described the small, shabby vehicle they'd used rather than one with the Ashton crest.

"Yes, miss," one of the men said. He bobbed his head and left the room.

Kiri turned to the other footman, who had the battered features of a former boxer. "Your task is to locate one of the guests and bring her here. She is petite, wearing a dark blue domino, and with gold sequins sparkling on her mask."

He frowned. "She is unlikely to come away with a stranger."

Realizing he was right, Kiri said, "Say the message is from Mumtaz."

After he left, Charlotte asked, "What is Mumtaz?"

"Mumtaz Mahal was the most beloved wife of a great Moghul ruler, Shah Jahan," Kiri explained. "He was devastated by her death in childbirth. He built the Taj Majal in her memory, and it is surely the most beautiful tomb in the world."

Charlotte's eyes rounded. "What a romantic story!"

"I think it would be more romantic if they'd lived happily together to a great age," Kiri said dryly. "Because Mumtaz was the object of great love and devotion, I used the name for the perfume I created for Miss Clarke-Townsend."

"You make perfumes?" The princess's gaze approached hero worship. "You do so many interesting things!"

"The women in my mother's family have a long tradition of making perfume," Kiri said. "In India, many of the scents are from incense, so I find great pleasure in exploring the floral essences of Europe."

She almost offered to demonstrate how perfumes were made, but stopped herself. Charlotte wasn't allowed many visitors, and Kiri wouldn't be one of them. After tonight, the princess might be locked up in the Tower of London by her father.

Her glass was empty, so she set it aside. "I'm concerned about Mr. Mackenzie, who went outside in pursuit of the kidnappers. I hope he has returned safely. Will you be all right if I leave you for a few minutes? I'll be within calling distance."

Charlotte extended her brandy glass again. "With more cognac, I shall be fine."

Kiri raised the decanter, but cautioned, "Much more and you probably won't feel fine in the morning!"

"You cannot imagine how much I long for dissipation!" Charlotte declared with a slightly intoxicated gleam in her eyes.

She sounded like Sarah. Well-born girls were hedged in dreadfully, and royal princesses most of all.

After pouring more brandy for Charlotte, Kiri left the office and walked swiftly to the scene of carnage in the cross corridor. Kirkland knelt by one of the kidnappers, his expression grim as he closed the man's eyes. The other man lay on his side, his ruined face invisible, for which Kiri was grateful. "Mr. Mackenzie hasn't returned?"

"Not yet, but don't worry," Kirkland said reassuringly. "Mac is very good at taking care of himself."

"I hope you're right." She looked away from the fallen men, the brandy roiling in her stomach. "This fellow was still breathing when we went into the office. He was mortally wounded?"

Kirkland's expression shuttered. "Yes, but I did manage to learn a few things from him before he died."

Kiri wondered queasily if the second man might still be alive if Kirkland hadn't needed to get information from him. But she didn't really want to know. Tonight had made it clear that her brother's charming friend had a ruthless streak. If his questioning had hastened the kidnapper's end, well, the man had surely deserved it.

Kirkland lifted a knife from the floor. "This was in his arm. Yours?"

She nodded. "I took it from a smuggler and brought it tonight in case a weapon might be needed. I didn't really expect trouble, though."

Kirkland wiped the blade carefully on the dead man's coat, then offered her the knife hilt-first. "It's a good weapon."

She regarded it uncertainly. "He didn't die of my stab wound, did he?"

"No," he said reassuringly. "But you slowed him down and evened the odds. Even if you don't wish to carry the knife again, you should keep it as a memento of your bravery. Without you, Princess Charlotte would have vanished without a trace."

"But why?" Kiri accepted the knife, which looked mercifully clean, though she'd boil it in a kettle before she carried it in the future. She pulled up her sleeve so she could return the knife to the sheath on her arm.

The exit door a few feet away opened and Mackenzie reentered the building. He looked tired and exasperated, but his expression changed when he saw her bared arm. "The evening has just taken a turn for the better."

Blushing but not displeased, she slid the knife into the sheath and pulled down the loose sleeve. "The villains escaped?"

He frowned and rubbed at his left forearm. "They had a coach waiting. One big enough for all five men and the girl as well if they'd been successful. I almost captured one, but all three turned on me and it was too much."

Kirkland rose, his expression grave. "The girl they were trying to kidnap is Princess Charlotte."

Mackenzie stared. "*The* Princess Charlotte? The prince regent's daughter?"

Kirkland nodded. "The very one. And steady now, Mac. Your arm is bleeding."

Mackenzie stared at the dripping blood. "It's . . . nothing." He swallowed hard. "Just a scratch."

Then he crashed unconscious to the floor.

Chapter 14

"Mackenzie!" Lady Kiri's rich, musical voice. Swift footsteps. Lilacs and spice, the rustle of fabric as she knelt beside him. "He's been injured!"

As Mac's wits emerged from dizzy darkness, he wondered wryly if there was anything worse for male vanity than passing out cold at the sight of his own blood in front of a pretty girl he wanted to impress.

He pushed the humiliation aside. There would be time for that later. He was so weak he couldn't open his eyes, much less climb up from the cold floor where he sprawled. But he could hear and smell. The ability to speak would return soon.

"The injury probably isn't serious." That was Kirkland, calm as usual, though with a thread of worry in his voice. He knelt on Mac's other side and performed an examination with competent hands.

After a minute or two of poking and prodding, Kirkland said, "His arm was slashed, but that's all, I think." He improvised a bandage and began wrapping Mac's limp left arm. "Mackenzie has always reacted badly to seeing his blood spilled."

Lady Kiri was going to laugh, Mac was sure of it. He

wished he was completely unconscious so he wouldn't have to hear.

Instead, she said thoughtfully, "An army surgeon in India once told me that fainting at the sight of blood isn't that uncommon. Often it's the biggest, strongest men who go down." A smooth hand rested on his forehead.

Mac attempted speech and managed a raspy whisper. "What a comforting thought." With effort, he was able to open his eyes. Kiri removed her hand but she still leaned over him, her lovely face concerned but not panicky. Just the right amount of concern. Female hysterics would have been too much.

Female . . . Princess Charlotte . . . Good God! He struggled to a sitting position. "The royal princess was here and almost kidnapped? Is she unharmed?"

"She's fine. In a few minutes Lady Kiri and Miss Clarke-Townsend will escort her back to Warwick House," Kirkland said. "They'll use the anonymous Ashton carriage they arrived in. A couple of house guards will go along."

Mac rubbed his forehead, trying to put the pieces together. "Damnation. Now that I know whom they were trying to kidnap, it makes sense," he muttered. "The French were behind this, and they'll try again."

Kirkland became very still. "That confirms what I learned from one of the men here before he died."

Driven by urgency, Mac got to his feet, bracing his hand on the wall as he tried to figure out what needed to be done. His gaze went to the two bodies lying on the floor. One was a big, brawny fellow, the other shorter and slighter in build. Both were expensively dressed in black evening wear.

Voices sounded in the main corridor. Kiri lifted her head. "Sarah has arrived at the office. She and I will take the princess home now."

"Wait!" Mac frowned as he considered a plan. "Surely Miss Clarke-Townsend is a sufficient chaperone? Please stay so we can talk, Lady Kiri. We'll make sure you get home safely." His gaze went to the fallen men. "And . . . don't mention me. As far as you know, I'm still pursuing the kidnappers through the night."

Kirkland regarded him thoughtfully. "What do you have in mind?"

"Maybe nothing, but I won't know until we've talked." After the others left, Mac scowled at the bodies of the dead men and wondered if his plan was necessary. He hoped not—but he had a bad feeling about the night's events.

When Kiri reached the office, she found Charlotte describing the kidnapping attempt to Sarah, who listened with horrified fascination. Now that the danger had passed and Charlotte was safe and the beneficiary of two stiff brandies, she was enjoying herself. This was probably the most excitement she'd ever had. Kiri hoped the princess hadn't had so much fun that she eluded her guardians again in the future.

When she entered the room, Kiri said, "Your Highness, it's time to return you home, before your absence is noted. Sarah, will you escort her? Lord Kirkland and I have some business to discuss."

Sarah got to her feet and offered Kirkland her hand. Like Kiri, she'd seen him regularly at Ashton House. "I shouldn't leave without Kiri, Lord Kirkland."

"I will personally return her to Ashton House," Kirkland promised.

When Sarah glanced at her, Kiri said, "I'll be fine. You take the princess home."

"Very well," Sarah said doubtfully. "But come to my room and let me know you're back, no matter how late it is."

"I will." Kiri curtsied to Princess Charlotte. "I hope we have the opportunity to meet again, Your Highness."

Charlotte looked wistful. "They can't keep me caged forever. I shall look forward to the day when we meet publicly, Lady Kiri."

The princess and Sarah left, followed by the two capable-looking guards who had located Sarah and the carriage. When they were gone, Kiri asked Kirkland, "Do you have any idea what Mr. Mackenzie might intend?"

"I could hazard a guess, but better to wait and see what he has to say." Kirkland headed for the door. "I'll tell him he can come to the office without being seen."

After he left, Kiri sank wearily into a chair. She'd acquired bumps and bruises while fighting with the kidnappers, and she was starting to feel them.

When the two men entered the office. Mackenzie looked more serious than she would have thought possible, while Kirkland was downright grim. She opened the cabinet again. "Brandy for both? Or something different?"

"I'll take some Scotch whiskey," Mackenzie said. "Kirkland can absorb endless amounts of brandy."

When Kiri glanced at Kirkland, he smiled faintly. "I'm not denying it."

Kiri poured whiskey for Mackenzie, brandy for Kirkland, and claret for herself because it wouldn't be wise for her to drink more spirits. When they were all seated, she asked, "Why do you both look so fierce even though the kidnapping was prevented? And why did you wish to talk with me, Mr. Mackenzie?"

"We need to know more, Lady Kiri," he replied. "You were closest to the kidnappers. Can you describe them?"

She frowned as she tried to remember. "It happened so quickly and they were all masked. The leader was fairly tall, with light brown hair that was receding a little. He struck me as a gentleman and perhaps a bit of a dandy."

Mackenzie nodded. "There was something about the way he moved that was familiar. He's probably been in Damian's before. Did you notice anything else?"

"He wore a cologne made by Les Heures, a very expensive shop in St. James," Kiri replied. "It's called Alejandro. Perfumes change on the body as they're worn, and I'd probably recognize his scent if we meet again."

The men stared at her. "You can do that?" Mackenzie asked.

She nodded. "It's not impossible that the cologne would react in the same way on a different man, but Alejandro costs the earth, so it's not common. With few wearers, it's unlikely the cologne would change in exactly the same way on anyone else."

Since the men still looked dubious, she rose and moved next to Kirkland. "Your scent is Imperial water and brandy and secrets." She looked into his startled eyes. "The Imperial water has shifted to emphasize the cloves in the blend."

He stared at her. "What do secrets smell like?"

"Dark. Deep. Like the bottom of the sea where strange things lurk." She smiled. "Imperial water contributes to that lighthearted-gentleman image you like the world to see. One's superficial scent can change from hour to hour or even moment to moment, but there is an individual essence that is always there, as distinctive as one's voice."

"You are unnerving, Lady Kiri," he said, his eyes narrowing.

"Kirkland is already considering how he can use your ability," Mackenzie said.

She laughed as she turned to Mackenzie. His individual scent she knew intimately, and she'd recognize it anywhere. But for the sake of her demonstration, she kept to what was easily described. "I smell a whiff of rosemary—from soap, I think." Their gazes locked. She was mesmerized by his multicolored eyes. The blue eye looked more blue-gray tonight. "You are rosemary, blood, whiskey, and trouble."

"I didn't know trouble had a scent," he said uneasily.

"It smells like hot spices that intrigue the nose but sear the tongue."

"I have no idea what that means." He drew a deep breath, breaking the connection between them. "Of course, trouble is my middle name."

"That's not a joke," Kirkland added. "Damian T. Mackenzie. Trouble really *is* his middle name."

Kiri blinked. "How very prescient of your parents."

Mackenzie ignored that. "What can you tell of the other kidnappers?"

She returned to her chair and closed her eyes while she thought. "One was dark-haired and smelled . . . French? A lover of garlic who wore Hungary water. The other one was very solid, like a boxer. He smelled like a working man not overfond of bathing." Opening her eyes, she said, "I'm sorry I can't think of more. Perhaps I'll remember something later. What did you gentlemen learn?"

"The solid working man fought like a professional boxer," Mackenzie said. "Stronger with his left fist than the right. I'll recognize his style if I see it again."

"The man I shot in the face might also have been a boxer," Kirkland said. "There was something familiar about the way he moved. I'll try to remember his name. Anything else?"

"When I chased the other three outside, they talked among each other in French," Mackenzie replied. "The kidnapping attempt wasn't random. It's part of a far-reaching plot, though I don't know any of the details. But they intend to try again."

"What could the French want with a sixteen-year-old girl?" Kiri asked.

"To some extent this is guesswork," Kirkland replied,

his brow furrowed. "But between what Mac heard and the information the wounded kidnapper told me before he died, it appears that these plotters hope that if the French take Princess Charlotte hostage, Britain might become willing to make peace with France to ensure her safe return."

Kiri choked on her claret. "Surely they don't think we'd surrender!"

"Not surrender. Make peace," Kirkland said. "Napoleon's troops have taken a beating on the Peninsula this year. About three years ago, he would have welcomed peace. He had secret talks with our prime minister, though they came to naught."

"So Napoleon might welcome a treaty where Britain would cease hostilities in return for a complete French withdrawal from Spain and Portugal," Mackenzie said thoughtfully. "Naturally, France would retain its other conquered territories."

"In other words, keeping much of Europe." Kiri shook her head. "I can't believe Napoleon is stupid enough to think this will work. Even assuming Britain agreed, I'm sure France's other enemies won't tamely accept French conquests."

"No, but Britain has been the most consistent and successful of Napoleon's opponents," Kirkland said. "With us out of the equation, the emperor would be in a better position to bargain or battle with his other foes."

"The plot might not come from Bonaparte himself." Mackenzie stared broodingly into his whiskey. "Assassination doesn't seem his style. My guess is that an ambitious underling hopes to bring off a coup to improve his own position."

"Is there any chance that capturing the princess would work?" Kiri asked. "Charlotte is very popular with the public. With the king and the prince regent both in poor health, she could inherit the throne at any time."

"Many people don't support the war, but the government is committed to defeating Napoleon," Kirkland said slowly. "Even if the concept is foolish, the plotters were serious and they seemed well prepared. They might succeed next time."

"Or accidentally get the princess killed in the process," Mackenzie said.

Kiri shuddered at the thought of such a fate for that eager, tragic young girl. "She must be protected."

"The princess's residence, Warwick House, is not secure," Kirkland said. "Plus, the plotters must have an informant inside her own household. That person might have given Princess Charlotte the idea of attending the masquerade at Damian's. At the least, the kidnappers were notified when she slipped out to come to the club tonight, and what color domino she'd be wearing."

"There's a good chance that someone here at Damian's was also in league with them," Mackenzie said, his eyes cold. "Not only did the kidnappers avoid the security guards, but they knew their way around the building as no outsider could. That's how they came so close to succeeding."

Kiri caught her breath. "So you don't know whom to trust. If there's a traitor in the princess's household, he might be able to let kidnappers into Warwick House itself."

Kirkland nodded. "She will have to move to a safer place. Probably Windsor Castle, with the king and queen and her aunts. She doesn't like staying there, but it's much better protected than Warwick House."

Kiri absently pulled her dagger from the arm sheath, turning it restlessly as she thought. Not looking up, she said, "I suspect that the two of you are engaged in secret matters. Such as spying?"

Kirkland said repressively, "Some matters are best not discussed."

Mackenzie shook his head. "Better to tell Lady Kiri more and satisfy her curiosity, or she might tumble into trouble trying to learn more."

"You're very perceptive," Kiri said wryly. "My curiosity has indeed been roused, and it's a dangerous quality."

Bowing to the inevitable, Kirkland said, "As you know, I have a large merchant fleet. Over the years, my ships began to carry information as well as goods. I have become something of a specialist in transmitting and interpreting military intelligence."

Mackenzie took over. "He does the serious work. I'm only a courier. One reason we started Damian's was to give me an excuse to deal with smugglers who make regular trips to France. That allows messages to move between Kirkland and British agents on the Continent. I picked up a message the night I met you."

"Mackenzie underrates his value," Kirkland said. "Not only did he devise the smuggler route for passing messages, but he's made Damian's such a fashionable club that diplomats and government officials are regular customers. Sometimes they say more than they should when under the influence of drink and gambling fever."

"And the genial host is always moving around the club, addressing problems, listening, and perhaps hearing useful information," Kiri said, amused. "Take care, Mr. Mackenzie. If your activities become known, people might consider you a hero instead of a mere charming rogue."

He looked embarrassed. "I'm not sure which is worse."

As Kiri started to return the dagger to its sheath, Mackenzie said, "That's the dagger you took from one of the smugglers, isn't it? Now that I see it more clearly, the design reminds me of another I saw once. May I?"

Kiri handed the weapon to him hilt-first. "This little toy

is as pretty as it is dangerous. It might be Turkish, but that's only a guess."

Mac studied the elaborately chased hilt. Then he took the knife in both hands and twisted hard. When nothing happened, he twisted in the opposite direction, and the hilt separated into two pieces along what had looked like a decorative line. Inside was a cavity containing a tightly rolled piece of paper.

Kiri gasped. "I had no idea there was a secret chamber!"

Mackenzie unrolled the paper and scanned the tiny script. "This looks like a French code. What do you think, Kirkland?"

His friend studied the neat rows of letters. "You're right, and it's a code I've worked with before. Your merry band of smugglers are a busy lot. Give me a moment and perhaps I can decipher some of it."

Mackenzie sniffed at the chamber in the hilt. "There's a trace of fragrance here. Can you identify it, Lady Kiri?" He handed her both parts of the dagger.

She closed her eyes to concentrate on the scent. "It's very faint. I might be able to tell more from the paper."

Kirkland handed over the message. She rolled it tight again and sniffed. Her eyes snapped open. "The cologne is Alejandro, and the scent is *exactly* the same as the leader of the kidnappers."

Mackenzie gave a low whistle. "If your bloodhound nose is correct, the kidnappers are also using Hawk's band of smugglers as a conduit to and from France. Do you think the leader was in the cave when we were there?"

Kiri thought back to the night she was captured. During the time she'd been chained to the wall, she'd observed the smugglers carefully, though most didn't get close enough that she could smell them. Not that she would have wanted to, since they were a fishy lot. "It's possible, but I didn't see or smell anyone who smelled or moved like the leader. You were the only man I met who seemed like a gentleman."

"The fellow probably wasn't there," Mac said. "I wonder which of the smugglers is his courier. Most are loyal Englishmen, but some would do anything for money."

Kirkland had reclaimed the message and scrutinized it closely before he swore, "Damnation! My apologies for the language, Lady Kiri. This is a much larger plot than we realized. Not only do they want to kidnap Princess Charlotte—they also aim to assassinate the prince regent and as many of his brothers as possible."

Kiri gasped. "That would throw Britain into chaos!"

Mackenzie looked as shocked as Kiri felt. "The king mad, the prince regent and the royal dukes dead, the heiress to the throne a prisoner in France—it's unimaginable."

"Even the plotters can't predict what would happen if they achieve all their goals," Kirkland said grimly. "But there would be chaos. They may hope to bring down the Tory government. The Whigs have always have been less supportive of the war."

"They're fools," Mackenzie said flatly. "If they succeed in their assault on the royal family, everyone in Britain will rise up to attack France. Small children will throw stones and grannies will wield canes and skillets. The war won't end until Paris has fallen and Napoleon is in chains."

"They don't understand British stubbornness," Kirkland said. "But while they may be fools in their policy, that doesn't mean they can't be successful in striking down the prince regent and some of the royal dukes. They must be stopped."

"You'll need to throw every man you have after the plotters." Mackenzie sighed. "I think it best if I die."

Chapter 15

Kiri stared at Mac, appalled. "I hope you don't mean that literally."

"I don't, but it might be best if the world thinks I was killed here tonight." He grimaced. "That's why I stayed out of sight until we could talk. The man who was shot in the face is pretty close to my size and build, and dressed in a similar way. If you identified him as me, Kirkland, no one would doubt it."

"Probably not," Kirkland agreed, frowning. "But why pretend you're dead?"

"I foolishly swore at the kidnappers in French, so they must know I heard what they said about getting Princess Charlotte another time. If they think I'm dead, they'll feel safer. Enough shots were fired to make it believable that I was hit."

"But they'll be missing the man who was killed," Kiri pointed out. "Won't they realize that it wasn't you who died, but their man?"

"My guess is that the boxers will disappear into the London stews, and the leader won't know who died and who ran away," Mackenzie explained. "If I change my identity, I can go to places where Damian Mackenzie would be far too noticeable."

"You're a well-known figure in London," Kiri agreed, not liking the idea of him dead even if it was pretend. "Those eyes of yours are an instant identification."

"My mother was an actress, and I'm good at disguise." Mackenzie added more whiskey to his glass. "The lead kidnapper looked like a gentleman and a gambler, and at least one of his men might be a professional boxer. There is a decent chance of finding them at gambling hells, boxing matches, or other sporting venues."

Kiri could imagine him swaggering through rough places, ready to take down any other man there, but she doubted he'd have much luck finding the plotters. He hadn't seen enough of them.

An idea struck her, as alarming as it was fascinating. She turned it around, thinking hard. Yes, she wanted to do this. "You need my help. It doesn't sound as if you can identify any of those men by sight since they were masked and you got only a quick glimpse of them. I need to be with you because I saw them better, and I can provide much better identification by their scents."

Mac stared at her, his expression horrified. "You couldn't possibly go to the places where I'll be searching!"

Amused by his reaction, she asked, "Why not?"

"Because you're a *lady!*" he retorted. "Most of the establishments I'll be searching are neither safe nor savory."

"Surely you noticed that I'm not unskilled at taking care of myself," she said reasonably. "If you and I are together, we'll both be safer than either of us would be alone. And having me could be the difference between success and wasted time."

Before Mackenzie could protest further, Kirkland said thoughtfully, "Her ability could be useful. At the moment, we have very little to go on."

"Her family would forbid it!" Mackenzie exclaimed. "Ashton and General Stillwell are both very protective."

So was Mackenzie, apparently. "I'm of legal age," Kiri pointed out. "They may disapprove, but they can't stop me."

"You'd stand out like a swan in a chicken coop," Mackenzie said.

Kiri thought fondly of Sergeant O'Neil, the general's regimental sergeant major. She'd learned so much from him. She'd also observed the camp followers to be found around any army. It took only a moment for her to shift her posture from lady to slut, the rounding of her spine and the looseness of her knees suggesting coarseness and vulgarity. "You think I can't look like an Irish bit o' muslin?" she said in a perfect Irish accent.

Mac stared. "Where on earth did you learn to act and sound like a Dublin doxy?"

"Remember that I was raised in army cantonments in India, and many of the soldiers were Irishmen." She grinned wickedly. "They liked my dark hair and green eyes. Said I looked a proper colleen. I spent a good bit of time with the enlisted men and learned many interesting things."

"And General Stillwell allowed this?" Kirkland asked with fascination.

She straightened into an innocent young lady again. "My father was a very busy man. How could he possibly know where I was at all times?"

"If he'd had any sense, he would have locked you in your room until you were twenty-five," Mackenzie growled. "Better yet, fifty."

"Lady Kiri wouldn't be anywhere near as interesting if he'd done that." Kirkland studied Kiri with cool calculation in his eyes. "She has a better chance of identifying the kidnappers than you or I do, Mac."

Mackenzie plowed his fingers through his hair with a

sigh of exasperation. "Maybe the theory is sound, but I can't imagine Lady Kiri waltzing out of Ashton House to accompany me to different stews every night."

"Adam and Mariah are going to his country seat soon, and my family will go with them," Kiri said. "I can stay quietly in London and anyone who cares about my whereabouts would assume I'd gone to Ralston Abbey with everyone else."

"I have a house on Exeter Street, near Covent Garden, that's available for associates of mine who need a quiet refuge," Kirkland said. "You could both stay there, since you also will need a place to go to ground, Mac."

Mackenzie stared at Kiri, even more appalled. "We can't possibly stay under the same roof! If that became known, she'd be ruined forever."

"You worry about my reputation more than I do," Kiri said tartly. "Surely the fates of Britain and the royal family are more important than that."

"You wouldn't be alone in the house," Kirkland added. "Besides the couple who take care of the house, Cassandra is staying there. I'm going to ask her to remain in London and help us locate the plotters. So Lady Kiri will be adequately chaperoned."

"Cassandra is an amazing agent, but . . . a chaperone?" Mackenzie said in such an incredulous way that Kiri immediately wanted to meet the woman.

"Her presence would settle any question of propriety if the situation became known," Kirkland said. "And increase Kiri's protection."

Mackenzie's snort demonstrated his opinion of that. Catching Kiri's gaze, he said vehemently, "This will be a dangerous investigation, Lady Kiri. It's not a game or an adventure. You risk a great deal, up to and including your life. Unless you truly think you can help catch these villains, you should abstain. Because of who and what you are, Kirkland and I and others will try to protect you, which increases our risk. Are you sure you want to ask that of us?"

Kiri's amusement vanished. The thought of Mackenzie getting himself killed in her defense made her heart clench. But instead of changing her resolve, it stirred her temper. "Why is it only men who are allowed to take risks for the greater good? I am not a china doll to be set on a shelf and forgotten! I may be able to help, and you gentlemen are going to need all the help you can get."

"She's right," Kirkland said. "We need to work fast and well. Lady Kiri is beautiful and well born, but she also has a warrior heart and a very valuable skill."

With a sigh, Mackenzie surrendered. "I suppose you're right, but I don't have to like it." He got to his feet while directing a scowl toward Kiri. "I sincerely hope that General Stillwell locks you in your room, but I suppose that won't happen. Will you at least discuss this with your family? Maybe one of them will be more persuasive than I."

"Of course I'll discuss it with them." Though they wouldn't change her mind.

"I'll be off, then. Kirkland, will you let Will know he shouldn't believe the obituaries? An officer serving in Spain doesn't need distractions."

"I'll send him a circumspect note," Kirkland promised. "What are your plans for faking your death?"

"I'll move the bodies out into the alley behind the building," Mackenzie said. "Then I'll arrange them to look like they killed each other."

"After you do that, you'll need to go to ground quickly." Kirkland produced a key from an inside pocket. "You know where to find the house. Here's a key."

Mackenzie grinned. "I've stayed at Exeter Street before. Did you think I wouldn't have had a spare key made?"

Kirkland laughed and pocketed the key again. "How remiss of me not to realize."

Tonight's adventure was over, and Kiri realized that she was exhausted. "I think I have reached my limit of amazement for now." She covered a yawn. "May I have that escort home? I'll need all my strength to persuade my parents that I'm needed by king, princess, and country."

"If you were always an obedient daughter, you wouldn't be here tonight," Mackenzie said dryly.

"True." Kiri smiled mischievously. "But I try not to alarm them more than is absolutely necessary."

"I'll summon a carriage now." Kirkland also stood. "Mac, I'll see you at Exeter Street. When you see Cassandra, tell her about this plot. She might have some good thoughts on the matter."

"She always has thoughts." After Kirkland left the office, Mackenzie opened his hidden safe to collect the fifty guineas he'd put there earlier. Turning to Kiri, he said, "If you'll excuse me, I must go and rearrange some bodies."

Kiri grimaced as she stood. "That will be grisly. Will you be all right?"

"Do you mean will I pass out again?" His lips twisted. "I won't enjoy it, but other people's blood doesn't bother me anywhere near as much as my own."

Yet he lingered, his gaze on Kiri. He looked as if he was torn between fleeing or kissing her. Kiri would welcome the kiss, though it would be foolish beyond belief to encourage this unruly attraction, especially when they might share a roof for a time.

"I'll leave before I get us both into trouble," he said. "Kirkland will keep you informed."

"Take care." She extended one hand. "I shouldn't like you to be more dead than you are now."

He took her hand between both of his, his clasp warm

and protective. "No need to worry. I have demonstrated repeatedly that I'm difficult for the ungodly to kill."

"The ungodly only have to get it right once, Mr. Mackenzie."

"You truly are one of a kind, Lady Kiri," he said wryly. "There's no need to be concerned for me tonight. I live in the building next door, and there's a private entrance to a room that has everything I need to change my identity. By the time I leave for Exeter Street, only someone who knows me very well indeed might recognize me."

"If you don't change your scent, I'll know who you are," she said, eyes glinting.

"The only noses that can compare with yours belong to bloodhounds." He smiled. "And your nose is much prettier."

She bit her lip, perilously close to losing her control. "You'd best be going. The longer you're here, the greater the chance you'll be seen."

"Right. Leave. *Now.*" His hands tightened on hers. "Before I do something that I shouldn't. Yes. I'm leaving now."

She said shakily, "Mr. Mackenzie. You're still holding my hand."

"So I am." Instead of letting go, he raised her hand and pressed his lips to the back of her fingers. Releasing her with reluctance, he added, "I trust that the next occasion when we meet will be less dramatic. Take care, my warrior maiden."

He closed the door quietly behind him, and was gone.

Chapter 16

Kiri knotted her hand into a fist, as if she could hold on to the feel of his mouth. She was staring at the door when Kirkland returned. "Your carriage awaits, Lady Kiri."

Feeling vastly tired, she collected her domino and followed him from the office. He led her to a side entrance where a carriage stood outside the door. On the box was one of Damian's capable black-clad guards.

As Kirkland helped Kiri into the carriage, she said, "You don't need to escort me personally, Lord Kirkland. I'm sure your driver can be relied on to get me home, and I imagine you have much to keep you busy at the club tonight."

He swung into the carriage and took the facing seat. "I promised Miss Clarke-Townsend I'd personally bring you home." And he was not a man to break his promises. "Do you want me present when you discuss what you'll be doing with your family?"

"An ally?" she said wryly. "I'll need one. I'll speak to Adam at breakfast if he's available. Your presence would add an air of gravitas to the discussion."

"I'll stop by then."

As the carriage rattled into motion, she studied Kirkland in the dim light. He was a remarkably handsome man, and he had more interesting edges than she'd realized. Yet when he touched her, it was like being touched by—her brothers. It was Mackenzie who turned her brain to steaming gruel.

With a quiet sigh, she settled back into her leather seat. Life would be easy if she and Kirkland fell in love. He was wealthy, well born, and one of her brother's best friends. A marriage between them would be welcomed by everyone.

There was something to be said for arranged marriages, she realized. Relying on attraction and love was much more untidy. It made women long for unsuitable men who had nothing to commend them but intelligence, humor, ravishing attractiveness. . . .

Getting a firm grip on her wandering mind, she asked, "Do you think we can stop the plotters before they assassinate members of the royal family? Most of the royal dukes are as useless as they are expensive, but Princess Charlotte offers hope for the future."

"If she goes to Windsor, I think she'll be safe," Kirkland said. "Her father and uncles are in more danger because they are out and about Town. They're also a stubborn lot and might refuse to believe they're in danger. All we can do is our best. While this conspiracy is well organized, there can't be a huge number of people involved."

"I assume that you will be tracing the plotters by all possible means." Kiri tried to make out Kirkland's austere features. "How did you become involved in the spying trade? The challenge of matching wits? The desire to contribute?"

"All of those things, I suppose." He sighed. "Someone needs to do this work."

"But why you?"

After a long silence, he said, "Mostly it was an accident.

Have you heard Ashton or another Westerfield student mention Wyndham?"

"The classmate lost when the Peace of Amiens ended? He haunts you all."

Kirkland gave a faint, humorless smile. "He's the ghost who may or may not be dead. Wyndham was exuberant and very likable. Wild, but no malice in him. Before going to France, he organized a reunion of Westerfield students for when he returned. After leaving Lady Agnes, we'd all gone in different directions, and we looked forward to getting together again. Students from the two classes following were also invited since the school was so small we all knew each other well."

"But Wyndham never returned," she said softly.

"France was in chaos when the truce ended." He hesitated, and Kiri guessed that he was deciding how much to tell her.

He continued, "Because of my family shipping connections, I made inquiries to see if I could trace Wyndham in France. Though I wasn't successful, I found other information that might interest the foreign office."

"And one thing led to another," Kiri murmured.

"After I passed on what I'd learned, I was told there would be much joy in Whitehall if I continued to provide information." He shrugged, a movement more felt than seen in the darkness. "Of such chances are lives changed."

"But you never learned Wyndham's fate."

"No." After a long silence, he added, "Perhaps someday."

Kiri heard in his voice that he didn't believe he'd ever find out what happened to his friend. But he'd never give up.

She decided she would much rather have Kirkland as a friend than an enemy.

* * *

Kiri entered Ashton House on feather feet, glad the household slept, since she was too weary for explanations. But she'd promised to notify Sarah when she returned, so she tapped on her friend's door.

Sarah flung open the door almost instantly. She was dressed for bed, but didn't look as if she'd been sleeping. Expression relieved, she gestured for Kiri to enter. "Thank heaven you're back! I've been kicking myself for leaving you behind."

"Truly, there was no danger," Kiri said as she closed the door behind her. "Lord Kirkland just wanted to know anything I'd observed useful about the kidnappers. Were you able to return Princess Charlotte without causing an uproar?"

Sarah nodded. "She has a clever private route in and out of Warwick House. Did you know that her windows look straight into Carlton House? Her father can glare right at her, if he bothers."

"Even if she returned to her bed unnoticed, the kidnapping is going to change her life." On the ride home, Kiri had thought about how much to tell Sarah. Enough to explain the kidnapping, but no more. "Kirkland has reason to believe the French were behind the attempt to capture the princess. And that they'll try again."

Sarah gasped. "How dreadful! Will she be removed to a safer place?"

"Probably. Windsor Castle, most likely. She should be safe there."

"I hope so. Now that I've met her, I like her. Despite the horrible way she's been caught between her parents and grandparents, she has a sweet nature and generous heart."

"I hope she has a good head as well, since she may well become Queen of England someday." Kiri smothered a yawn. "I'm for bed now."

"So am I, now that you're home safe." Sarah wrinkled

her nose. "I think that's enough adventuring for me for quite some time to come."

For Kiri, the adventure was just beginning.

Mac artfully arranged the two bodies in the back alley, doing his best to make the larger man look like the late Damian Mackenzie. Then he walked the short distance along the alley to the gate that led into his house's walled back garden.

The main connection between house and garden was a pair of French doors in the center of the building, but there was also an unobtrusive entrance near the right corner of the back wall. It opened into a room originally intended for tools and storage. Because it could be entered from either house or garden, Mac had installed very good locks on both doors and turned the room into his headquarters for nefarious activities.

Mac had enjoyed watching his actress mother change her appearance, and his favorite game as a boy was disguising himself to look like someone else. Perhaps it had been a way to escape his own less than satisfactory identity.

Though he'd grown more comfortable in his own skin, his work with Kirkland sometimes required that he look like a laborer or sailor or coachman if he wanted to move about London without being recognized. He had clothing and accessories to change his appearance anywhere from a fop to a ragpicker.

It would be convenient if he were average height and build. But he'd learned a few tricks to make his height and build less noticeable. One was donning a padded vest that made him look shorter and bulkier. His hair was an unmemorable shade of medium brown. It would do for tonight, but he collected a pouch of dye so he could make the color darker and duller.

Then he covered his brown eye with a patch. Eye patches were common and drew little attention, and the patch obscured his distinctively different eyes. The uncovered eye was changeable, shifting from blue to gray and even green depending on what he was wearing. It was a useful trait for a chameleon.

He put on coaching garments since they were comfortably worn and good enough quality to show that he was a respectable man of his trade. The boots were also comfortable, but he'd had the soles shaped in a way that subtly altered his walk.

Like all his coats, the multi-caped coaching garment had plenty of pockets inside and out. He added a wad of banknotes to the fifty guineas repaid by Lady Kiri. Though he had a bank account in a false name that he could access if necessary, nothing beat cash for bribes or buying his way out of trouble.

After stashing several weapons around his person and packing a bag with other essentials, he was ready to go. He had several false identities at hand, and he decided on Daniels, a name enough like Damian's to be easy to answer to.

As he locked the door and the gate behind him, he wondered if Lady Kiri Lawford would be able to identify him. Probably, since he hadn't drenched himself in cologne to change the way he smelled.

His thoughts were wry as he made his way through the darkness. Though his mission was to protect the royal family, if he had to choose between saving Princess Charlotte and saving Kiri Lawford—king, princess, and country could go hang.

"My lord. You must come quickly." The black-garbed footman was pale as he addressed Kirkland. "There are two dead men behind the building, and I think they came out of the club."

"Damnation!" Kirkland pushed away from his desk and stood. After taking Lady Kiri home, he'd returned to the club office to wait for someone to find the bodies. He recognized the footman as a regular employee called Borden. "How did you find them?"

"I was taking a quick break from the ballroom. I thought the back alley would be a good place to relax for a few minutes." Borden drew a shuddering breath. "I found . . . them."

"Not very relaxing." Kirkland strode down the hall beside the footman. "Have you notified Mackenzie? If the bodies belong to regulars, he will recognize them."

"Sir . . ." The footman was so pale he seemed on the verge of fainting. "I'm afraid . . . Mr. Mackenzie . . ." He swallowed hard. "I thought it best to check the office, and found you."

"Come along, then," Kirkland said briskly. He saw no traces of blood to reveal where the two men had died. Mac had done a good job of cleaning the corridor.

Borden had left a lantern by the back door, and he lifted it to light their way into the back alley. The bodies were only a few feet away. One clasped a gun; the other had dropped a weapon by his side.

"It looks like they killed each other," Kirkland said. "Maybe they had an argument over cards and decided to settle it directly rather than a formal duel. Any idea who they might be?"

"Sir . . . ," Borden whispered. "Look closer at the big one."

Kirkland obeyed, trying to act exactly as he would if this scene was unexpected. He stepped closer to the large man with the ruined face, whose head was turned away from them. The fellow had brown hair similar in length and color to Mac's.

Borden lowered the lantern, and the light picked up a flash of gold on the dead man's left hand. Kirkland looked, and his heart clenched with shock. "Dear God!"

No. It wasn't possible. He'd *seen* Mac alive and well less than an hour ago!

Stomach knotted, he knelt by the body. The pistol gripped by the dead hand looked like Mac's, and the engraved ring . . .

He lifted the limp hand to study the family crest engraved into the gold. The design showed the Masterson arms, with a black onyx bar slashing diagonally across. It was the bar sinister, the traditional mark of illegitimacy.

"This is Mackenzie's ring," he said, his throat tight. "It was a gift from his brother, Lord Masterson." Mac had enjoyed the blatant proclamation of his bastardy, since it came from Will Masterson. They'd both laughed over the ring.

"I . . . I was hoping I was wrong," Borden said, his voice on the edge of tears. "Mr. Mackenzie—he saved my life, sir. I was in trouble and on the edge of being shipped to Botany Bay when he took me in and gave me a job. I can't believe he's dead."

Borden's words cleared Kirkland's paralysis. Of course Mac would have known his ring was perfect identification. That harrowing instant when Kirkland believed his friend really was dead had also produced a damned convincing reaction.

"Bring Baptiste and a couple of other men and a pair of blankets so the bodies can be covered. And send someone for a magistrate." Knowing Mac would want the ring back and not stolen by a casual thief, Kirkland tugged it off the cold hand. "Lord Masterson will want this."

Borden went back inside, clearly glad to get away from the death scene. Wearily Kirkland got to his feet. Mac was alive and well for now, and should be able to return to his life soon. But there were others whom Kirkland had sent to their doom, and that knowledge weighed heavily on a night like this.

His friend Wyndham had been one of them.

Within five minutes, Baptiste rushed from the building, accompanied by his friend Lord Fendall and two strong footmen with blankets. "Kirkland! Tell me it is not true!" Baptiste cried frantically.

"I'm afraid it is." Kirkland opened his hand to show the ring. "Mackenzie was shot in the face and is . . . not easily recognized. But I took this from his finger."

Baptiste stared at the ring with horror. "No. *No!* Mackenzie can't be dead!" His gaze strayed to the broad, powerful body as the footmen covered it with a blanket. The club manager made a choking sound and turned away to retch, steadying himself against the wall with a shaking hand.

Fendall moved close to Kirkland. "What happened?" he asked in a low voice, as if the dead might be disturbed.

"My guess is that Mackenzie interrupted a thief and was killed trying to stop him." Kirkland shook his head. "We'll probably never know for sure."

"Such a great pity," Fendall said with regret. He turned away from the bodies. "You are waiting for the magistrates?"

Kirkland nodded. "I thought it was best not to move anything until they arrive."

Baptiste turned from the wall and wiped his mouth with a handkerchief. He was still pale, but he'd managed to collect himself. "It seems impossible that Mackenzie is gone. He seemed—indestructible."

Kirkland nodded, his own nerves still shaken.

"The club," Baptiste said hesitantly. "Damian's. What will become of it? Will Lord Masterson, the army brother, inherit?"

Life goes on. Baptiste might be upset at the loss of his friend and employer, but he was understandably concerned for his job.

"No, Mackenzie and I were partners with right of survivorship. If one of us died, the other inherits." Kirkland stared at the blanket-covered body, thinking how easily it could have been Mackenzie in truth. "Neither of us expected . . . this."

Baptiste shook his head sorrowfully. "To think he was killed by a common thief! Better to have let the villain escape than to lose his own life in the pursuit."

"A damned shame we can't tell the future," Kirkland agreed. "For now, nothing changes. Continue to run the club as you always have." He shook his head. "But Damian's will not be the same without Mac."

Baptiste nodded in silent agreement. "Never. But . . . if you decide to sell the business, will you give me a chance to buy?"

Kirkland nodded. "You've earned that right. But for now, carry on."

In the silence that followed, he wondered how long it would be before Mac could return to his proper place.

Chapter 17

Kiri went to bed, but her spinning mind interfered with sleep. She was yawning when she went down to the breakfast room. Adam was there already, browsing a newspaper while he finished his meal.

He rose with a smile when she entered. "Good morning, Kiri. You look like you had a restless night."

She gave him a quick sisterly kiss. "I did. Is Mariah sleeping late? She's usually appallingly awake at this hour."

"She decided to take advantage of her delicate condition to have breakfast in bed. Sarah is joining her." He grinned. "I heard giggles as I left, so I don't expect either of them to come down anytime soon."

As he resumed his seat, Kiri said, "Soon she'll be brimming with energy. At least, so says Lady Julia. So convenient that Mariah's best friend is a midwife." Kiri poured herself a cup of fragrant, hot coffee from one of the silver pots, since she needed something stronger than tea this morning. "I live in fear that you shall tire of my company and toss me into the streets of Mayfair."

"Never," he laughed. "I came late to the status of paterfamilias, and I won't weary of it soon. I'm looking forward to having everyone at Ralston Hall next week." He poured himself more tea. "General Stillwell sent a note yesterday. He's discovered that an estate near Ralston will be coming up for sale. As you know, he's been thinking of buying a place in the country. He'll look Blythe Manor over on this visit."

"It's certainly a cheerful name! The location sounds perfect. We would be close, but not underfoot. We can make up for time lost when we were all on opposite sides of the world." As she scooped kedgeree and eggs from silver warming pans, she wondered if this was a good time to tell her brother that she wouldn't be traveling to Ralston with the rest of her family.

Before she could decide, the door to the breakfast parlor opened to admit her parents. Lakshmi was dressed in English style, petite and dark and stunning, while the general looked exactly like what he was: a tall, handsome man with an air of command who was still fit enough to ride all day and half the night if necessary.

Abandoning her plate, Kiri swooped across the room and fell into her mother's embrace, thinking how much had happened since she'd last seen her. "Oh, Mama, how lovely that you've been released from your imprisonment!"

"It has been almost a month since I saw you. Far too long." Lakshmi Lawford Stillwell, dowager Duchess of Ashton, though she never used the title, had laughing green eyes and seemed far too young to be the mother of grown children. She was also quite possibly the wisest, kindest mother in the world, and hugging her made Kiri feel better.

"My turn," Adam ordered. "I haven't seen her for a month, either."

Kiri turned to the general while her brother embraced Lakshmi. "I'm glad you are finally free from quarantine," Adam said. "Are Thomas and Lucia with you?"

"They have recovered from the measles, but they tire

easily. I thought it best they stay home," Lakshmi replied in her musical voice. "You may call on them if you like."

"I shall like." Adam shook the general's hand. "Have you come for breakfast?"

"We've eaten," the general said as he hugged Kiri, "but I wouldn't say no to tea and a couple of those cinnamon buns I see on the sideboard."

As Adam seated his mother and stepfather, Kiri poured their tea and set the cinnamon buns between them. Ashton House had no shortage of servants, but Kiri liked the hominess of having only family in the breakfast room.

Returning to her own meal, Kiri ate quietly while the others chatted. With brother and parents present, it was a perfect time to talk to them all at once.

But how did one interrupt a conversation to say, "By the way, last night I slipped out to an alarmingly fashionable club and helped foil a royal kidnapping, and I intend to move to a house in a bad neighborhood so I can live with dangerous strangers and dress like a doxy and go to gambling hells and sniff men to see if they're French conspirators?"

It would not be an easy discussion to initiate.

She was trying to find the right words when the door opened again, this time admitting Lord Kirkland, who looked as contained as always despite his busy night. Adam met his friend with a smile and an outstretched hand. "Has my breakfast room become London's fashionable gathering spot?"

"So it appears." Kirkland glanced about the room, his gaze holding Kiri's briefly. "Lady Kiri, Mrs. Stillwell, General Stillwell."

Kiri felt cowardly relief that she would have Kirkland's support for the upcoming discussion. After he poured himself coffee, he sat at the table opposite the general and

Lakshmi. "I'm glad you're all here, since I have something important to discuss concerning Lady Kiri."

The general looked startled but pleased. "You want to marry my little girl? She'll be a handful, but you won't be sorry."

Lakshmi and Adam also looked startled, but that was nothing compared to the shock on Kirkland's face. "Good God, no!" he exclaimed.

Realizing too late how insulting that sounded, he said hastily, "Lady Kiri is beautiful, charming, skilled, and resourceful, but I have no romantic intentions toward her. It is because of her skills that Britain needs her." His gaze flicked to Kiri. "Do you wish to tell them the whole story?"

As all eyes turned to her, Kiri collected herself, glad that she sounded composed. "I've had an adventurous week," she said to her parents. "Rather than try to write about what happened, I preferred to wait until I could tell you in person."

Of course she'd rather have said nothing about the smugglers, but that was no longer possible since her kidnapping led directly to Damian's. Briefly she described how she'd left Grimes Hall after overhearing the discussion about her dowry. The bigotry she didn't mention, though a shadow in her mother's expression suggested that Lakshmi understood some of what wasn't said.

As expected, the general exploded when Kiri told of being captured by smugglers, instinctively reaching for weapons he wasn't carrying. As Lakshmi put a hand on his arm, Kiri said quickly, "As you see, I am here and unharmed. Please let me continue."

Adam winced. "There's more?"

"I'm afraid so." She kept the description of her visit to Damian's succinct, following Kirkland's policy of saying no more than necessary. Sarah she didn't mention at all. Her brother and parents showed varying degrees of surprise and disapproval that turned to shock when she mentioned Princess Charlotte. Kiri finished, "Because I had a chance to scent the kidnappers, Lord Kirkland says my aid will be valuable in finding the conspirators before they can do great damage."

From Adam's expression, she guessed that he knew something about his friend's covert activities. Warily he asked, "What form would this aid take?"

"Instead of going to Ralston Abbey, I will stay in London and visit establishments where the conspirators might be found," she said, trying to sound as if such activities were perfectly normal. "I will use my ability to recognize scents to attempt to locate the kidnappers. If found, they might lead us to their fellow conspirators."

Before she could say more, the general leaped to his feet and slammed his hand on the table, rattling the teacups. "Gambling hells and rookeries? I forbid it!"

Clenching her hands, Kiri said, "I am of age, sir. You can't prevent me."

"I can damn well tie you up and carry you to Ralston Abbey and lock you in one of the monk's cells!" Under his outrage, she saw fear.

In a voice that was quieter but edged, Adam said, "Surely you have other means to locate conspirators, Kirkland. My sister should not have to do such dangerous work."

"Her ability to recognize scents is unique," Kirkland replied. "I swear that she will be well protected. She would stay in a house of mine that contains several trained agents, and she would not go anywhere hazardous without a bodyguard."

"No matter how many guards there are, you can't guarantee her safety!" the general snapped. "Even if she isn't hurt, what about her reputation?"

For the first time, Lakshmi spoke. "You forget of whom

you speak, John. Kiri is no frail hothouse flower. She is a warrior and a descendant of warriors, raised in an army household and taught of duty and honor. If she is needed, how can she refuse?"

The general look shocked. "Won't you worry about what might happen if she puts herself into danger?"

"Of course I will worry, but life comes with no guarantees," Lakshmi said quietly. "If the measles had been severe, we might have lost Thomas or Lucia or both. Kiri might go with us to the country and break her neck riding." She gestured at Kiri. "Look at her. She is eager to do this work no one else can do, both to serve and to test herself in a matter of great significance. Would you deny her that opportunity? You cannot." She gave a fleeting smile. "Even if you want to."

The room was utterly silent for the space of a dozen heartbeats. Leave it to Lakshmi to understand her unruly daughter. Kiri broke the silence by saying brightly, "Now that *that's* settled, would anyone like more tea?"

The others laughed, easing the tension. Except for the general, who watched Kiri with brooding misery.

"Papa," she said softly, deliberately using her childhood name for him. "I once heard of a young man who came from a family of vicars. He was very clever and his family had great plans for him. Oxford, a good living, perhaps someday he'd even become a bishop.

"But the boy was mad to be a soldier, and he resisted all attempts to guide him for his own good. He organized the neighborhood lads into armies and led them to war. He practiced cavalry maneuvers with his old pony. He mastered Latin only so he could read Caesar's war commentaries in the original language. To his parents' regret, he never became a bishop. But he became a very fine and honored general, didn't he?"

Her stepfather exhaled roughly. "Very well, my dear,

I surrender. It's not right to try to force one's child against his or her nature. You were not born to spend your days in embroidery and watercolors. But if you must do this, be careful! These are treacherous waters you're entering."

She got up and rounded the table to give him a hug. "I'll be very careful indeed, Papa. And I'm going to be surrounded by people determined to keep me safe."

"Sir," Adam said, "I can assure you that Kirkland has a great deal of experience in these matters, and he's well respected at the highest levels of government. He also has excellent people working with him. I trust him to see that Kiri is as safe as humanly possible." His cool gaze implied that Kiri would be safe, or *else*.

The general asked, "How soon must Kiri begin this?"

"As soon as possible," Kirkland replied. "Today, even."

Lakshmi sighed. "Will you come home to see your brother and sister before embarking on your mission?"

Today! Kiri's heart leaped with anticipation. "Of course. I want to see them, and I must do some packing as well."

Kirkland looked wary. "Not too many clothes. Almost anything you own will stand out where you will be staying."

"I understand that. But I do want to bring some of my perfume-making materials, since they might be useful."

Kirkland looked as if he wanted to ask how, but since he'd proclaimed her his expert on scents, he refrained. "Shall I collect you at your parents' home at four o'clock this afternoon?"

After a swift calculation, Kiri nodded. "I can go home now if you're ready," she said to her parents.

They agreed and a maid was dispatched to pack Kiri's belongings. After Kiri took her leave of Mariah and Sarah, she left Ashton House with her parents.

She had a strange, unsettled feeling that was a mix of alarm and excitement. She was fairly confident that she'd

be able to stay alive. But she knew in her bones that this
mission marked a turning point in her life.

In the quiet after the Stillwells and Lady Kiri left, Kirkland said to Ashton, "I must be off also. I have much to do."

"I can imagine." Ashton was watching with unsettling
intensity. "Was recruiting my sister really the only
choice?"

"No. But it was the best choice," Kirkland said honestly.
"She's very capable, and she may make the difference between success and failure in stopping this assassination plot."

"Are you bringing in Rob Carmichael as part of your
team?"

"Of course."

"That's comforting. He's the best." Ashton looked every
inch a powerful duke as he lifted a newspaper he'd glanced
at as the others were leaving. A bold headline proclaimed
NOTED CLUB OWNER KILLED IN ROBBERY ATTEMPT. Other
newspapers had similar headlines. The murder of someone
so well known in the fashionable world would be a subject
of shocked discussion in many houses across the city and
the nation.

Ashton continued, "A great pity that Mackenzie was a
victim of your conspirators." There was a question in his voice.

Kirkland hesitated from the habit of secrecy, but devil
take it, this was Ashton, one of his oldest and most trusted
friends. "You shouldn't always believe what you read in
the newspapers."

Then he turned and left Ashton House, praying that
nothing would go wrong and injure those who trusted him.

Chapter 18

Night fell early in November, and it was nearly dark as the small, nondescript hackney carriage made its way to 11 Exeter Street. Kiri watched out her window as the streets became narrower and shabbier. Kirkland said, "It's not too late to change your mind, Lady Kiri."

She turned and asked curiously, "If I decided to go home, what would you do to catch the conspirators?"

"The same as we're doing now, only with longer odds of success. In my trade, we work with what we have. If enough good people are working on the problem, eventually there is a breakthrough." After a long pause, he added in a low voice, "Sometimes that comes too late."

It was easier to be a soldier than a spy, she decided. More straightforward. "Could you tell me who else will be staying at your house? Mackenzie, of course. Did you mention a couple who take care of the house?"

"Yes, Mr. and Mrs. Powell. They're very capable and completely discreet. If you need anything, ask one of them."

"What about my chaperone, Cassandra?"

He laughed a little. "I don't usually think of her as a chaperone. She's one of my best agents and recently back from France. She stays in Exeter Street whenever she's in London. If she wishes you to know more than that, she'll tell you."

The hackney stopped in front of a sizable town house. "It's larger than I expected," Kiri observed.

"This was a fashionable neighborhood once. The *ton* has moved west, but the well-built houses remain. Most are broken up into flats or rooms to let. Number 11 is considered to be a boardinghouse since people come and go." Kirkland opened the door and climbed down, then turned to give her a hand out. "I do hope you don't come to regret your courage in joining this particular mission."

"I doubt I shall." Kiri took his hand and climbed from the hackney. His touch still felt brotherly, not that there was anything wrong with brotherly. "I don't usually look back. When I make foolish decisions, I file the consequences under lessons learned and tell myself not to be stupid in the same way again."

He laughed. "You're a remarkably wise young woman."

"My grandmother said I was an old soul, but she was biased. If I was really an old soul, I wouldn't make as many mistakes in the first place," Kiri said candidly.

"If you weren't a duke's daughter, I'd recruit you as an agent in a finger snap," he said with conviction. "Now come inside and meet your companions for the next little while. It's best not to use your own name. Mackenzie said you told the smuggler that you were Carrie Ford. Will that do?"

"It sounds delightfully average." As she climbed the steps, she said thoughtfully, "It will be interesting not to be Lady Kiri Lawford."

"Perhaps, but you'll be glad to go back to her when this mission is done." Kirkland opened the door with a key. "Our own problems have the virtue of familiarity."

He ushered her into the front hall. The table and two

chairs that flanked it were modest and the picture above was an unremarkable watercolor of the Thames, but the area was spanking clean. A middle-age man and woman appeared, followed by a hulking man who looked like a servant. Kirkland said, "Miss Ford, meet Mr. and Mrs. Powell. She and her husband will take good care of you."

Mrs. Powell was short and plump, with shrewd blue eyes and an imperturbable expression. "Welcome, Miss Ford. Our lodgers mostly look after themselves, but I clean the rooms once a week and his lordship has arranged for you to take your meals here. You're also welcome to make tea in the kitchen whenever you wish."

"I know I shall be very comfortable, Mrs. Powell." As for Mr. Powell . . . Kiri asked, "Would that be Sergeant Powell, retired?"

He grinned. "'Tis that obvious, Miss Ford?"

"A lucky guess," she said, returning his smile.

Mrs. Powell said, "Daniels, bring in Miss Ford's baggage and take it to the back room on the second floor."

The servant bobbed his head and moved toward the door with stolid steps. As he moved past Kiri, she caught his scent. After a startled moment, she whirled and said, "Good evening, Mr. Daniels. Haven't we met before?"

The fellow wore an eye patch, but the other eye sparkled with amusement. It was Mackenzie, looking older and wider and very unlike the dashing club owner. "Doubt it, miss," he said in a voice subtly different from his usual speech. "I'd've surely remembered such a fine lady as yourself." His visible eye closed in a slow wink before he shuffled outside to get her luggage.

As Kiri grinned, Kirkland offered his hand. "You can trust all the residents of this house, Miss Ford. Good luck and good hunting."

"I'll do my best." She cocked her head. "Am I now an official British agent?"

"Indeed you are." His gaze was sober. "Be careful. I don't want to face your brother if something happens to you."

"I'll try to spare you that," she promised.

Then Kirkland was gone, and Kiri was on her own. She must succeed or fail on her own merits, not because she was the general's daughter or of royal Hindu blood, or the daughter of an English duke. The prospect was . . . exhilarating.

Mackenzie had already left most of Kiri's bags in her room, so she unpacked. The room was simple, but pleasant. Medium size, very clean, a comfortable bed, and a frayed but warm carpet on the floor.

As she placed folded garments into the clothespress, Kiri realized how carefully thought-out the house was. There was no grandeur that might attract unwelcome attention in a poor neighborhood.

But the modest furnishings were well made and included everything a guest might need, including a screen in one corner, a washstand, a desk, and writing materials. There were even a couple of books, one a King James Bible. Kirkland had created a refuge for agents who might be exhausted or emotionally frayed from their work. The house offered uncomplicated welcome.

Kiri's heart jumped when a knock sounded on the door. Mackenzie with the last of her luggage? But when she opened the door, she found a woman so neutral in appearance that she didn't need a crowd to disappear into.

The newcomer looked a few years older than Kiri, probably under thirty, though it was hard to tell. Medium height, medium brown hair, a well-worn calico gown in shades of tan, and unremarkable blue eyes. The perfect appearance for an agent.

Guessing the newcomer's identity, Kiri said, "You must be Cassandra. Welcome to my humble abode."

"Call me Cassie." She moved soundlessly into the room. "You are Kiri, known as Carrie, and I'm supposed to offer guidance and try to keep you from serious trouble."

They eyed each other like cats. "Cassie and Carrie," Kiri remarked. "This could become complicated. Do I pass the test?"

The other woman sighed. "You can't do this kind of work. You may be wearing a gown with a simple cut, but your demeanor says you're an aristocrat and rich."

Kiri looked more closely and realized that Cassandra's eyes weren't unremarkable. The blue depths went all the way down to hell. Sobered by that recognition, Kiri said, "I'm still Lady Kiri. I can do better."

"I hope so," Cassie said pessimistically. "Can you act like a poor Londoner?"

Kiri slipped into her East End accent. "Aye, that I can. Be there any rag shops around where I can buy me a wardrobe?"

Cassie's brows shot up. "Your accent is good," she admitted, "but that's not enough. You move like a woman who is beautiful, confident, and knows that all eyes will turn when you enter a room. That's all very well for Lady Kiri, but you'll stand out like a horse in a cow shed in this neighborhood."

Kiri had worked hard to develop that demeanor because living with the general had taught her the value of confidence. Looking fearful or weak brought out the jackals in some situations, including London drawing rooms. When she first arrived in England, she'd decided it was better to be despised for brashness than weakness.

She closed her eyes and suppressed the knowledge that she was an aristocrat and a general's daughter. Instead, she conjured up moments such as Lady Norland's sneers at her mixed-blood heritage. Kiri's mother might be a princess and a Brahmin, her father and brother English dukes, but Carrie Ford was a mongrel who belonged nowhere.

Her only gifts were a quick wit, enough prettiness to catch a man's eye, and fierce determination to survive in a hard world. She had learned early to be attractive, but not to look too available. To pretend confidence to keep the jackals away.

And Carrie was as real as Kiri. Opening her eyes and softening her posture, she said, "Who sez a gel like me can't have a fine gown? Got it for six bob at a rag shop, cut out the bloodstains, and made it fit. Glad you think it makes me look rich and well born. Maybe I should raise me prices." She swished her hips like a camp follower looking for business. "A gel's gotta use what she's got while it's fresh enough for a good price."

After a moment of astonishment, Cassie laughed. "You have unexpected talents. I should have known Mackenzie wouldn't foist an amateur on me. But you do need a different wardrobe. There's a good shop in the next street that will still be open, if you're not too tired to go over now."

"I'm not tired at all." Kiri thought of the vulnerable royal princess, who wouldn't be safe until the conspirators were caught. "The sooner I start, the better."

Another knock at the door. This time it was Mackenzie carrying a small leather-covered trunk. He had the worn air of a tired servant. As practice, Kiri made sure her voice was noncommittal when she said, "Please put that on the table, Daniels."

As he obeyed, Cassie said tartly, "Everyone knows who you are, Mackenzie, so you might as well straighten up. Did you come up with anything useful today?"

Mackenzie grinned and his posture changed to that of a former officer. "Carmichael and I have been making lists of the most likely hells and sporting houses, based on what little we know of the kidnappers."

Carrie's brows arched. "That's a large task."

"Which is why we're reducing the possibilities." He set the box on the desk.

"Does your list include Les Heures perfume shop?" Seeing his blank expression, Kiri added, "That's the shop in St. James that makes the cologne worn by the leader of the kidnappers. Since it's the one thing we know, it's a good place to start."

"An expensive shop won't reveal who buys their products," Mackenzie warned.

"Perhaps not, but it's worth trying. Tomorrow morning." She smiled. "Come dressed as my faithful footman."

He tugged his forelock like a farm laborer. "Yes, my lady."

"Carrie or Kiri, but not 'my lady.'"

"She's right," Cassandra said. "You know better, Mac. We must live the roles we're playing."

"I stand corrected." He tapped the leather box he'd brought in. "What's inside, Carrie? It clinks. A portable liquor cabinet? You're too young for such dissipation."

"Too young, and far too wise," she replied as she unbuckled the lid. "This is my traveling perfume case." Flipping up the lid, she removed a square of padding to reveal rows of vials packed neatly into racks. "The women in my mother's family have been perfumers since the world egg hatched. We have a lot more material and equipment in our workroom at home, but I wanted something easily transportable."

"Why did you bring it here?" Cassie asked, her brows furrowed.

"Since my well-educated nose got me recruited for this mission, I thought it might be useful. And if not— well, I like playing with my perfumes."

Mackenzie was frowning over what she'd said earlier. "What is the world egg?"

"A Hindu creation myth," she explained. "My mother's family says 'since the world egg hatched' to indicate a very long time."

Though Adam didn't use the phrase, she realized. Kiri had spent most of her life in India and was comfortable with her Hindu self. Adam, as a very young duke who had to prove how very English he could be, had denied half of his own history. He was still learning to balance the two sides of his heritage.

Cassie was studying the vials with interest. "May I open a bottle?"

"By all means." Kiri indicated the top row. "These are base mixtures that I've developed as a foundation for a perfume. This group contains essences that can be added to a base," she indicated the middle row. "The bottom row is finished perfumes that I particularly like. The one you're picking up is called Spring Flowers."

Cassie pulled out the stopper and sniffed cautiously, then smiled with a sweet pleasure that made her look much younger. "It really is like a garden in spring!" She carefully plugged the bottle and picked up another from the top row. After sniffing, her nostrils flared. "This is too intense. Musky."

"That's because you have a base mixture. It's not a finished perfume yet," Kiri explained. "Many perfumers just combine similar scents to intensify them. I like more complex fragrances. My specialty is blending unique perfumes that fit a woman's personality. Of course, it also has to wear well on the woman, so experimentation is required. Rather like tuning a violin to find the perfect, true notes."

Cassie picked up a bottle with essence of roses, exhaling wistfully after she smelled it. "Would you be able to make a perfume just for me?"

"I'll be happy to, but I'll need to know you better." Kiri studied the other woman thoughtfully. "You have many secrets, many layers of character. I imagine that is usual in your trade. The right perfume for you would reflect that."

Cassie's expression blanked and she stoppered the rose essence. "Better that you not seek to know more. Come, I'll take you to the rag shop."

"I'll go, too," Mackenzie said. "To carry your purchases home, like a footman."

"I'm unlikely to need that much help," Kiri pointed out. "I'm buying the most basic of wardrobes."

"Maybe you'll need protection between here and there."

Cassie snorted. "If I thought you were deliberately insulting my abilities to protect, Mackenzie, you'd pay for that remark."

His mobile features changed to a mask of fear. "No, no! No insult intended!" His face relaxed into a smile. "Mostly I want to come because I'm bored."

"That's a reason I can understand," Kiri said.

"Very well," Cassie agreed. "Come along, but try to stay out of mischief."

Mackenzie switched to a wounded expression. "Would I cause trouble?"

"Trouble is your middle name!" Kiri and Cassie said the words in unison, then looked at each other and laughed.

"Maybe I'll change my middle name," Mackenzie said as he ushered the two of them out of Kiri's room. "T for Thaddeus, perhaps. Or Tarquin. Or Tancred. Or . . ."

"Trouble is the most suitable," Kiri said, her eyes dancing. Mackenzie's presence wouldn't be required tonight. But she was sinfully pleased that he was with them.

The rag shop was small and badly lit, and so stuffed with secondhand clothing that it resembled Aladdin's cave.

As Kiri tried to make sense of the jumble, Cassie called, "Customers, Mrs. B.! I've brought you a lass who needs pretty much everything."

A rustling sound from the back heralded the appearance of a wiry old lady with an unlit clay pipe clamped between her teeth. "That you, Cassie? Aye, and this must be your lass." She stopped by Kiri and pinched Kiri's left sleeve, rubbing the fabric between thumb and forefinger. "Very nice. Want to trade it in? I'll give you at least two gowns in return, maybe more, depending on what you pick."

Kiri thought of herself as adaptable, but the idea of wearing one of those unwashed garments out of the shop made her twitch. "First I'll look at what you got. Me old mum made this for me just before she died, and I'm right fond of it."

The pipe in the old lady's mouth twitched. "Anything else she made that you might be willing to sell?"

Kiri saw a satiric glint in Cassie's eyes, and realized that the other woman wanted to see how Kiri managed life and business outside the beau monde. She shook her head dolefully. "Haven't anything else my mum made. I just ran away from my man with only the clothes on my back. That's why I'm here." She reached into her pocket and pulled out a gold guinea. "I have this to spend. How much can I buy with a guinea?"

As the proprietress's eyes gleamed, Mackenzie held up a green satin gown. "Try on this. You'd look good in it."

"If you think I'm looking for another man, Daniels," Kiri said saucily, "your loft is to let. I need everyday clothes, not some trumpery gown that's been worn by a woman no better than she should be."

"Go ahead," he said coaxingly. "You'll look mighty fine in green silk. I'll take you to a play."

"If you insist," Kiri said with a show of mock reluctance. They were flirting in the guise of poor Londoners, which kept a safe distance between them. Carrie Ford could behave in ways Kiri Lawford wouldn't. This could become interesting.

"Is there a place where I can try this on, Mrs. B.? I don't want Danny Boy here to get ideas if I try this in front of him." She fluttered her lashes at Mackenzie as she collected the green dress, her fingertips trailing over his wrist. He tried to catch her hand, but she slid away, saying, "Cassie, will you help me?"

"Back here in the corner." Mrs. B. led the way back to a small area created by hanging old draperies. Very little light penetrated from the main shop, and there was just about room for Kiri and Cassie. Mrs. B. withdrew and began a raucous flirtation with Mackenzie, who responded the same way.

"How am I doing?" Kiri asked Cassie in an undertone as the other woman helped her out of her gown.

"Well enough, but it's only been five minutes." Cassie worked with brisk efficiency. "Mrs. B. has good stock, but I warn you, she's a tough bargainer."

"I'll try not to be too easy a mark." After the green silk gown was laced up, Kiri stared down at her very bare chest. "If this was cut any lower, my navel would show."

Cassie chuckled. "It's a gown that will allow you to get close to gambling men when you visit a hell. How good are you at defending your virtue?"

Kiri frowned, recognizing a new problem. "Too good. If I'm not careful, I might break bones. Maybe you can teach me some gentler means of discouraging unruly men."

Cassie looked surprised, then intrigued. "We'll talk about this later." She glanced at her own more modest figure. "I've never had to fight for my virtue as hard as you'll have to. But now it's time to emerge and dazzle your aspiring suitor."

Another trait the women in her family had had since the

world egg hatched was an ability to turn their allure on and off. Looking as provocative as she knew how, Kiri returned to the main space.

Mackenzie stared at her and a muscle in his jaw jerked. "If you don't buy that, I'll buy it for you."

She smiled sweetly, wondering how much of his reaction was real and how much was the game they were playing. "And have you think I owe you something? I'm no such fool!" She smoothed the silk of the skirt. There were a few snags in the fabric and a small stain, but it was certainly a dramatic gown, and it suited her, in a sluttish way. "I need other kinds of clothes more than I need anything like this."

Mackenzie looked mournful. "Maybe you'll change your mind."

Maybe she would. But for now, it was more fun to tease Mackenzie.

In the end, Kiri left Mrs. B.'s with the green silk gown, a golden evening gown that wasn't quite as sluttish as the green one, a morning gown, and several other garments. Her bargaining ability left Mackenzie and Cassie wide-eyed with amazement.

When Kiri had squeezed every last ha'penny out of her guinea, she piled her folded purchases into Mackenzie's arms. "Make yourself useful, Danny Boy, or you won't see that green gown on me again."

"Yes, Miss Ford," he said meekly, but his visible eye danced with amusement.

When the three of them were halfway home, Cassie asked, "Where did you learn to bargain like that? I thought Mrs. B. would weep before you were done with her."

"She enjoyed it as much as I did." Kiri grinned. "As

for where I learned—there is no training ground like an Eastern bazaar."

The others laughed, and she sensed that Cassie was less doubtful about Kiri's ability to do this work. She had passed her first test.

Chapter 19

Mac doubted that Kiri would wear the green silk gown for their expedition to Les Heures, but a man could hope. His first reaction was disappointment when she floated down the stairs to join him dressed in black.

His second reaction was paralysis. She wore an elegant black mourning outfit she'd brought with her. He guessed it should have a fichu tucked into the bodice for modesty's sake. But the fichu was missing, revealing enough of her magnificent figure to ensure that any man breathing would lust after her, and feel guilty for doing so.

Her deep mourning bonnet had yards of black veil that drifted around her head and shoulders. The veil blurred her features and created a tragic, haunted beauty while making her hard to identify. *Breathe, Mackenzie, breathe.*

When his brain began functioning again, he said, "You look like you just stepped out of a Gothic novel. The Wanton Widow."

"Splendid!" She lifted a black lace fan and wafted it gently. "I was aiming for grieving but toothsome widow, hoping that a combination of sympathy and lechery might loosen some information."

"Those poor devils at Les Heures haven't a chance," he said with conviction.

"I hope not." Kiri pulled a black armband from her reticule and tied it around his arm. "My servants must also be in mourning, of course. A really high-priced footman wouldn't have an eye patch, but it's a nice touch that you matched it to your gray livery."

"I loathe powdered wigs, but details make all the difference when one is pretending to be someone else." He ushered her outside to the waiting carriage.

Kirkland kept several vehicles in Town. One was an eye-catching coach with his arms painted on the door, another was the shabby hire carriage used when anonymity was preferred. The carriage Mac had borrowed today was expensive but with no markings that made it memorable. It would not look out of place in fashionable St. James Street.

Mac nodded to the driver, one of Kirkland's men, and handed Kiri into the carriage. After flipping up the steps and closing the door, he took his position on the back step of the vehicle. It would be much more amusing to ride inside with the lady, but he was a servant. He needed the reminder of the social distance between them in the real world, because his brain tended to work badly around her.

When they reached Les Heures, Mac helped Kiri from the carriage. She handed him a folded piece of paper and said under her breath, "Be prepared to take notes."

Notes? Obediently he said, "Yes, milady."

In his most formal footman fashion, he held open the shop door and she swept through, a grand lady assuming that where she led, her servant would follow. Under her black veil, she looked imperious and vulnerable, and older than her actual years.

Les Heures was richly scented and quietly luxurious. Behind the counter was a well-dressed man of mature years. He came to immediate attention when Kiri entered, Mac in her wake.

Voice sultry, Kiri said to the salesman, "Good day, sir. I am told that you sell the finest fragrances in London?"

"Indeed we do. I am Mr. Woodhull. And you are Lady . . ." His voice trailed off with a question.

Kiri waved her hand to silence him. "Please, no names, Mr. Woodhull, though no doubt you recognize me. It is not entirely proper for me to be shopping for something so frivolous as scent when my dear husband is barely cold in his grave."

Mac admired the pretty little catch in her voice. The devastated widow, bravely carrying on.

She continued, "I find that beautiful fragrances help keep melancholia at bay."

"You are not alone, milady," Woodhull said in an unctuous voice. "Others have said exactly the same thing to me. It is your *duty* to use anything that will help you maintain your strength at such a difficult time."

"So very true," she said with warm gratitude. "What do you consider your finest perfume?"

He pursed his lips thoughtfully. "For you, milady, I suggest Royal Violets." He unlocked a glass-fronted case and brought out a handsome little bottle with a gold-leaf pattern incised in it. "This is the same scent cherished by the Empress Josephine."

Kiri breathed a happy sigh. "Lovely. Let me test it." She slowly peeled off her left glove, exposing her creamy skin in a luxurious contrast to the black glove.

Mr. Woodhull watched in fascination. Mac was just as fascinated, and also amused. Removing the glove revealed a plain gold wedding band that supported Kiri's status as widow. She also understood the necessity of proper details.

Gracefully Kiri extended her hand to Mr. Woodhull,

palm up. "Will you place a touch of Royal Violets right over the pulse?"

Swallowing hard, he obeyed. She raised her wrist and delicately sniffed the perfume through her veil. "How very fine. But not only violets, I think. There's a touch of carnation, and I believe lily of the valley?"

His brows lifted. "Your ladyship has superior perception."

Her long black lashes fluttered modestly, easily visible despite the veil. "I should like to try several others if you will."

Mr. Woodhull was willing. Several more bottles were removed from the locked case, applied in different places on her left forearm, then discussed. Not only was Kiri demonstrating her knowledge of perfumes, but she was making the man sweat with suppressed lust. Mac would have laughed except that he was equally enthralled.

Finally Kiri chose a perfume, paying an eye-popping price with more gold guineas. Mac was wondering how any of this would help them find the chief kidnapper when she leaned in to Mr. Woodhull and said with breathy confidentiality, "There is another matter I wish to discuss. I believe you make the cologne called Alejandro?"

"Indeed we do. It's the finest fragrance for gentlemen made anywhere, if I do say so." He made an attempt to look into her eyes rather than at her décolletage. "Was it the choice of your late, lamented husband?"

"He preferred Eau de Cologne, which is a fine scent, though rather too common." She looked regretful. "Might I try Alejandro to see if the scent is as I remember it?"

"Of course, milady." He opened a different case and brought out a bottle. Again Kiri extended her slim wrist and he applied a touch of scent.

She closed her eyes as she lifted her wrist and inhaled

reverently. "Ah, yes, this is what I remember. I'll take a bottle."

"Of course, milady." Mr. Woodhull collected a price that was even higher than what she'd paid for the bottle of Royal Violets. As he wrapped the cologne in a heavy parchment, he asked, "Is this a gift?"

"It's . . . hard to explain." Kiri cast her eyes down bashfully as she tucked the wrapped bottle in her reticule next to the Royal Violets. "I met a gentleman under rather difficult circumstances. He was so kind to me in my grief. I would like to find him and thank him for his kindness, but we were interrupted before I could learn his name. I thought he was wearing Alejandro, and now that is confirmed."

"You're certain it was Alejandro?" Mr. Woodhull asked.

Kiri's brows arched delicately. "I do not make mistakes about scents, sir."

"No, no, of course you don't," he said hastily. "Your ability to identify scents is the equal of a professional perfumer. You are buying the cologne to remember his kindness? Scent works very powerfully on memory."

"Actually, I hope to locate the gentleman. Since Alejandro is so rare and expensive, you surely have only a handful of regular buyers. There can be no harm in mentioning who they are." She smiled enchantingly.

Mr. Woodhull frowned, torn between professional discretion and desire to please the lady. "I don't know that it would be proper for me to reveal the names of customers."

"How can a man's cologne be considered a private matter when it's worn in public for all the world to appreciate?" Kiri pointed out.

"That's true," he said uncertainly. "But the number of customers is large enough that it would be difficult to list them all. Can you describe the gentleman?"

"He was quite tall"—Kiri indicated a height with her

hand—"well built, with broad shoulders and a fine figure. Early middle years, I think, with medium brown hair that was thinning just a little."

"That narrows the possibilities a bit," Mr. Woodhull agreed. Reluctant but unable to resist Kiri's great, hopeful eyes, he pulled a ledger from a drawer. Even across the room, Mac could read the script that spelled out "Alejandro" on the leather cover.

Kiri moved so that Woodhull was looking in her direction, leaving Mac free to pull out the paper and pencil she'd given him. Mr. Woodhull paged through the book. "Let's see, who fits your description? Perhaps Lord Hargreave. Or Mr. Sheraton. Or Captain Hawley. Or perhaps . . ."

As he listed names, Kiri listened intently and Mac jotted them down. After mentioning a dozen or so, the perfumer closed the ledger. "That's the lot, milady. As you said, there are only a handful of men who use Alejandro, and fewer still who might be the gentleman you seek."

"You have been so *very* kind!" Kiri leaned forward and brushed a light kiss on his cheek through her veil. "You have my deepest gratitude."

Mr. Woodhull beamed, but there was a rueful light in his eyes. A perfumer must be glad for a swift kiss, while the mystery man, if Kiri found him, would receive much more of her attention and person. "I am glad to be of service, milady."

Giving one last radiant smile, Kiri turned and headed for the door of the shop. Mac held it open, then followed her into the street, every inch the proper footman.

Kirkland's carriage waited only a short distance down the street. When they reached it, Mac helped Kiri into the carriage. Then properness vanished as he told the coachman, "Exeter Street, please," and climbed inside to sit opposite her.

Kiri grinned at him as she tossed the veil back from her

face. "That went rather well. But shouldn't you be on the outside of the carriage?"

"Having spent a couple of hours being respectable, I feel the need to revert to my usual behavior." He glanced out the window, afraid to look at her in such close quarters. Unfortunately, not looking at her ravishing person made him intensely aware of the delicious rainbow of scents that wafted around her. He took a deep, slow breath. "Why were those perfumes so insanely expensive?"

"The ingredients are very costly, but it's also necessary to pay the rent and ensure the perfumers a fine profit," she replied. "Les Heures caters to people who think the more expensive a perfume is, the better it must be. The Alejandro isn't bad, but the Royal Violets is rather boring. I'll play with it to make it better."

"Why did you buy them?" It was conspicuous to be staring out the window when they were talking, so he tried to gaze in her general direction without looking *at* her. "Apart from the fact that spending lots of money makes a shopkeeper happy."

"That was part of it, but I thought it would be useful if everyone involved in this hunt had a chance to learn what Alejandro smells like." She rustled in her reticule and produced the bottle, then handed it across the carriage. "It's distinctive enough that most people should be able to recognize the scent even if they don't notice the subtle variations on different wearers."

He unstopped the bottle and took a whiff. "It seems like a combination of musk and something sharp. Can't say as I like it." He put the stopper back and returned it.

"You have a good nose." She returned it to her reticule. "But it's distinctive, masculine, and smells expensive, which pleases some men. Did you recognize any of the names he listed?"

"Most of them have visited Damian's at one time or

another." He frowned. "I wish I'd had a closer look at the fellow. I saw enough to confirm your general description, but not enough to recognize which of my customers he might be."

"Perhaps Kirkland will have some thoughts when he sees the list." Humor sounded in her voice. "Why won't you look at me? Are you appalled at my flirtatiousness? It's my job to get information, after all."

Mac felt like grinding his teeth together. "I half expected you to pull Woodhull down behind the counter and give him an experience he'd never forget."

"It was rather fun to flirt without consequences," she said thoughtfully.

"*Without consequences?*" He finally allowed himself to look at her, darkly alluring as Lilith, every inch of her lush body an incentive to sin. He yanked down the shades on both windows, then turned and pulled Kiri into a fierce, carnal kiss.

He had been prepared for the enticing taste of her mouth and the soft pressure of her lips. He was *not* prepared for her to flow forward into his arms as she kissed him back. Her mouth opened in invitation and her arms slid around his neck. Mac's pulse began to hammer, driving out all rational thought.

Somehow she was on his lap, her knees bracketing his. They ground together, their bodies as urgent as their mouths. Common sense wasn't even a distant memory. All he could think of was Kiri—brave and irresistible, and more than a little wicked.

His hand slid up her left leg under her skirt, cupping the perfect curve of her derriere. "Dear God," he groaned. "Kiri . . ."

He crushed her in his arms as he convulsed into shattering pleasure, and the horrified recognition of his madness. *Dear God.* He loosened his grip enough for her to breathe and buried his face in her silky, scented hair. The black bonnet and her hairpins had gone astray. His powdered wig had fallen off at some point, too.

Panting, she said, "Was that what I think it was?"

He made an effort to collect himself. "I'm afraid so. My deepest apologies, Lady Kiri. I haven't behaved so badly since I was a boy."

"Not half as sorry as I am!" Wild-eyed, she lifted her head and bit him on the shoulder. Hard. "You are driving me mad, Mackenzie!"

"That's entirely mutual." Her feverish expression showed that she was as aroused as he was, and it was his damned fault for starting something he shouldn't have done. "Let me make amends."

Keeping one arm around her shoulders, he shifted her onto the seat beside him and bent into another kiss while his hand slid up the curve of her calf, over her knee, to the smooth, firm flesh of her thigh. Her mouth was hungry and her knees opened invitingly. He took his time, caressing ever higher as her breathing roughened. Sweet, silky moisture and heat, her gasp when he first touched her intimately . . .

She cried out, the sound lost in his mouth as he brought her to culmination with only a few gentle strokes. When her body stilled, he held her close, soothing and silently cursing himself for being a dishonorable fool.

They clung to each other, bodies damp and entangled. There was utter silence within the carriage, leaving space for the sounds of the city. Carriages, a street vendor calling the price of his oysters, a dray driver shouting filthy insults. But inside the coach was silence, except for gradually slowing breath.

Having Kiri in his arms was happiness greater than any he'd ever dreamed. He understood now what she'd said about each person having an individual scent, because even under the layers of perfume and sweat, he was aware of an essence of Kiri that in the future he'd never forget. She smelled of strength and humor and mischief.

Yet twined with happiness was despair. He never should have allowed such intimacy between them. It made him long for more while bitterly aware that he'd already taken too much.

Voice husky, Kiri whispered, "Explain to me why something that feels so right is supposed to be wrong."

"Passion lies outside of right and wrong. It exists to keep the human race going." He sighed and stroked his fingers through the darkly shining cascade of her hair, which fell almost to her waist. "But society had reasons why passion can't be freely indulged. Good reasons, most of which have to do with the protection of women and children. Since we live in society, those rules can't be disregarded."

"And here I thought you broke rules all the time," she said wryly.

"Some rules. Not the ones that cause harm to others." He brushed her hair back, revealing the fine curve of her cheek. "Especially not others whom I care about."

"So you care about me?"

Her wistfulness went to his heart. "How could I not? You're as remarkable as you are beautiful." His lips twisted. "If I didn't care, I would have behaved much better."

"I'm glad you didn't behave." She raised her head from his shoulder, and even in the dim carriage, he could see the green burn of her eyes. "You're right that social laws are ignored at one's peril. But we have this moment in time when we are both outside our lives, and I intend to take advantage of it." Her eyes turned mischievous. "And of you."

He laughed, even more enchanted by her mixture of worldliness and naïveté. Growing up in the middle of an army and having a curious mind had given her experience far beyond that of most young ladies of her class. She had the pure fire of youth that had not yet been seriously tarnished by injustice and regret.

She also had the arrogance that came with high birth and the belief that she was above consequences if she broke society's rules. That could . . . cause problems. They came from different worlds that touched now only by chance.

Reminding himself of that, he said, "This time is precious, but I'm determined not to take advantage of you, and I'll do my damnedest not to let you take advantage of me."

He caught her around the waist and moved her to the seat on the other side of the carriage, where he should have left her in the first place. "We'd better make ourselves as presentable as possible since we must be nearing Exeter Street."

She raised the blinds. "Lord, we both look disgraceful. As if we've been doing exactly what we've been doing. Do you see any of my hairpins on the floor?"

She looked magnificent, not disgraceful, but even in the irregular world of Exeter Street, they must maintain some decorum. He scrounged on the floor and managed to find several hairpins. "Is this enough? I know you had more, but I can't find them."

"These will suffice." She expertly pinned back her heavy hair, smoothed down her wrinkled gown, then donned her bonnet and drew the veil across her face. One would have to look closely to see the subtle signs of disorder.

Wishing he had a veil himself, he retrieved the powdered wig from the floor and settled it down again. "Do I look like a proper footman, or a tipsy gentleman of an earlier generation?"

"Not much can be done about the fact that livery is

old-fashioned. But the wig can be fixed." She leaned across the carriage and straightened the hairpiece with meticulous care. Her face was only inches from his. "There. Much better."

Their gazes met, and he wondered if he showed as much yearning as she did. Very gently he leaned forward and touched his lips to hers in a sweet, regretful kiss. "It would be better if we'd never met," he murmured, savoring her warmth and delicacy. "But I can't be sorry we have, selfish though that is."

"I'm not sorry, either." She sat back against the seat with a sigh. "Unlike you, I don't regret my selfishness. Sometimes selfishness is exactly the right thing to do."

He blinked, then burst into laughter. "My brother Will says that Ashton is both Christian and Hindu, but you, my warrior maid, are pure pagan."

She gave him a slow, wicked smile. "And all the better for it."

Chapter 20

By the time they reached Exeter Street, Mackenzie had transformed himself into the perfect blank-faced footman. Kiri hoped her acting was equally good as he handed her out of the carriage and escorted her into the house.

As soon as they were inside, Mackenzie pulled off the powdered wig, and formality with it. "I hate this thing. It's like wearing a dead animal on my head."

Kiri's tension eased with a smile. "A rabbit? Or perhaps a ferret?"

"More like a badger. Coarse." Turning serious, he said, "Now that we have those names, I'll send a note to Kirkland to set up a meeting with him and Cassie."

Kiri concentrated on removing her bonnet, which gave her an excuse to look away from Mackenzie. He'd always been damnably attractive, and the more intimate they became, the more irresistible she found him. "What is Cassie's part in this?"

"She's half French and spends much of her time in France, so she'll visit some of the clubs and taverns that cater to French émigrés."

"She'll go alone?" Kiri was willing to frequent dens of

iniquity, but even with her fighting skills, she wouldn't go to such places on her own without a life-or-death reason.

"She'll have a male companion, probably Rob Carmichael. He's mainly a Bow Street Runner, but he also works with Kirkland and his French is excellent."

"Another student from the Westerfield Academy, no doubt."

Though Kiri meant the comment as a joke, Mackenzie chuckled. "Yes, in fact. We're a far-flung lot. Even if we weren't particular friends while in school, there's a general level of trust among Lady Agnes's Lost Lords."

Kiri moved toward the stairs. "And trust is vital for this particular mission."

"Even more vital than usual." He frowned. "Under other circumstances, my club manager, Baptiste, would be a good escort for Cassie because he really is French, with many connections in the émigré community. I've trusted him with my business for years. But given the attempted kidnapping, I don't dare trust anyone who works at Damian's."

"I saw Baptiste at the masquerade." Kiri had been looking for Mackenzie without success, but it was easy to spot the well-dressed manager who kept a watchful eye on the activities. "He must be upset by your death."

"Kirkland said he was so shocked he became sick." Mackenzie's expression lightened. "As soon as he started to recover, Baptiste told Kirkland that if the club is sold, he wanted a chance to make an offer. A practical race, the French."

Kiri paused with her hand on the newel post at the base of the stairs. "Could he be a secret Bonapartist who helped the kidnappers?"

"I thought of that," Mackenzie said slowly. "But if so, he's one of London's great actors. He's always despised the revolution and the emperor. Half his family died during the Reign of Terror, and he barely got out alive."

Her brow furrowed. "If you find Damian's a fertile place for collecting indiscreet conversation, he might also."

Mackenzie frowned as he thought. She liked that he considered what she said instead of dismissing her as a mere female. "In theory, yes, but I know Baptiste very well. When Bonaparte is mentioned, his hatred is visceral. You can see it in his body."

Since he knew the Frenchman and Kiri didn't, she accepted his opinion. In his business, Mackenzie had to be a keen judge of people. "Let me know the time of our strategy session. If you give me the list of names, I'll make copies."

"That's a good idea." He returned her pencil and the paper he'd written the names on. She headed up the staircase, refusing to look back at him. If she did, she wouldn't want to leave.

As she neared her room, she saw that she was being shadowed by a shy-looking tabby cat. The tabby was sleek and well fed, so she must be the kitchen cat. Kiri liked cats, so she held her door open and stood back.

Watching Kiri warily, the cat darted past her into the bedroom, then leaped onto the bed and proceeded to turn several times before settling down at the foot. "I see I won't have to sleep alone," Kiri said. "Thanks for that, Puss."

Green eyes opened in a flat stare, then closed. Kiri got the impression that the cat was a habitué of the room, and not about to let a human disturb her routine.

Drained by the events of the morning, Kiri folded onto the wooden chair. She didn't want to think of what she'd felt in Mackenzie's arms, but she could think of nothing else. His touch, his warmth, his strength. A shiver burned through her, overwhelming her determination to be wise.

Mackenzie was right that passion existed apart from social rules. She had a rebellious streak, but her family would not welcome a gambler of dubious reputation as a member. In particular, the general would be appalled that she would even talk to a man who'd been cashiered from the army.

She might be willing to fight her family over an unsuitable man, but she couldn't do anything that might reflect badly on them. Particularly not something that would diminish the choices for her younger, shyer, better behaved sister. She and Lucia teased each other regularly, but they were close. Kiri had adored her younger sister from the day she was born. She adored Thomas, too, though she'd never embarrass them both by saying such a thing aloud.

Lucia and Thomas were both Stillwells, sane and practical. But Adam was her full brother, and even though they'd been raised on opposite sides of the world, they shared a streak of romanticism that must come from their father, who had briefly been the Duke of Ashton. He'd hated the idea so much that he'd died of a fever so he wouldn't have to leave India. At least, that was Adam's theory.

If she would be the only person to suffer consequences, she'd hurl herself into Mackenzie's arms. Which was exactly what she'd done when he kissed her in the carriage. If she'd shown a grain of sense, they would have gone no further than the kiss.

But her yearning hunger for him had overwhelmed her and pushed them into a deeper layer of involvement. A pity she didn't have only herself to think of.

But she had a family she loved and didn't want to disgrace. Even so, control would be hard. It helped that Mackenzie didn't seem the marrying kind. She believed that he did care for her. But she also believed that he'd cared for many women in his life. That didn't mean he'd wanted to marry any of them, or he would have done so.

For a man like Damian Mackenzie, marriage would just be an unwelcome, not to mention unnecessary, distraction. When he wanted a woman, he had no shortage to choose from. If he ever did take a wife, he'd probably choose an actress who was as flamboyant and unrespectable as he was.

But Kiri had been serious about taking advantage of this brief time out of time. For a few days or weeks, they were joined in a mutual mission and living under the same roof. She'd be no worse off if a few more rules were broken.

If she had only a few weeks, she would make the best of them.

"Kirkland said he might be late, and we should start eating without him," Mackenzie informed Kiri, Cass, and Rob Carmichael, the Bow Street Runner. The Runner was tall, lean, and contained, a little like Kirkland but with more visible edges. Kiri decided that if they met in a dark alley, she wanted him to be on her side.

The strategy meeting took place over a supper of thick fish and vegetable stew and fresh bread prepared by Mrs. Powell. By mutual consent, they concentrated on the meal rather than talking business. Having spent the afternoon in her room, Kiri had an appetite and was finishing her second bowl of stew by the time Kirkland arrived.

He greeted them tersely. "I'm glad you had a chance to eat before I ruined your appetites. This afternoon there was an assassination attempt on the prince regent."

Kiri gasped. The regent might be self-indulgent and extravagant, but he was still the ruler of England. "Was the prince killed or injured?"

"He escaped unharmed, though he was understandably upset. He's taking this conspiracy a lot more seriously now." Kirkland looked bleak. "But one of my men was badly injured protecting the regent."

"Who?" Carmichael asked sharply. "And how badly?"

"Edmund Stevenson. The surgeon thinks his arm can be saved."

"Poor devil," Carmichael muttered. "A good thing he was there."

Mackenzie asked, "Did you catch the assassin?"

"There were three. Two escaped, the third was shot by Stevenson. He seemed to be a Frenchman."

"Do you want me to look at the body?" Cassie asked. "I might recognize him."

"I hope you do." Kirkland frowned. "I hate to ask this of you, Kiri. Could you come with Cassie and me after supper to see if he might be one of the kidnappers you saw at the club?"

If Cassie could identify dead bodies, so could Kiri. "Of course."

"If you've finished eating, we can go right now," Kirkland said.

Cassie gave him a gimlet stare. "Sit down and eat, Kirkland. Starvation won't make your brain work better."

Kirkland started to protest, then smiled tiredly. "You're right." He accepted the bowl of stew that Cassie dished up for him.

As Kirkland dug into the food like a man who'd skipped too many meals, Mackenzie said, "We have other business as well."

He gave Kiri a warm, private smile. "Remember how Lady Kiri identified the cologne worn by the leader of the kidnappers? This morning we went to the shop that makes it, and she charmed the proprietor into giving her a list of customers who use that scent and fit the general description of our quarry."

Kirkland looked up from his food with approval. "You're a born agent, Kiri."

She laughed. "It's good to know that my troublemaking qualities have their uses." She produced tiny bottles containing a couple of drops of Alejandro each. "There's no guarantee that our man will be wearing this at any given moment, but it's one more element to the description."

As the others sniffed at the scent bottles, Kirkland said, "I want to see the names he gave you."

"I made copies of the list this afternoon." Kiri passed the sheets to each of the others. "I met several of these men in society, but I can't say much about them."

"At least five of them are French, or have strong ties to the émigré community," Cassie contributed.

Kirkland scanned the list. "Merritt has been in the West Indies since spring, Palmer is in the navy and seldom in England, Lord Wellston is an Irish peer who rarely crosses the Irish Sea." He pulled out a pencil and made notes by the names.

"Most of these fellows have come to Damian's often enough for me to recognize them," Mackenzie said. "I know who I'd suspect first, but that would be guesswork."

"A man who runs a gambling house is going to be better at guessing than most," Kirkland said. "Who of these men would you consider most suspicious?"

Mackenzie listed them, and for the next hour, they all talked back and forth, each person contributing what knowledge or insights they had. By the time they finished, the list had been narrowed down to six men who seemed the most likely.

Sir Wilbur Wilks. George Burdett. Jacques Masson. Lord Fendall. Comte Vasseur. Paul Clement. Kiri drew little stars by those names on her list. "Of course, none of them might be guilty," she murmured.

"This is how investigations are done. Piece by piece, until a pattern begins to form." Carmichael smiled. "It's not a job for impatient people."

Kirkland pushed his chair from the table. "The next piece of the pattern to consider is the late and unlamented assassin. Are you ready, Kiri?"

"Lead on, Lord Kirkland." Kiri controlled her expression. It was gentlemanly of him to be concerned for her tender sensibilities, but she'd rather be in the same category as Cassie: ready for anything.

The dead assassin lay on a stained table in a cold room by the river. Kiri did her best to turn off her nose so she wouldn't be overwhelmed by multiple odors in the old building. As they crossed the ill-lit room to look at the corpse, Mackenzie murmured, "Steady, lass."

She was grateful for his warm hand on her waist, and hoped none of the others were aware of her nervousness. Telling herself she could do this, she moved to one side of the table while Cassie went to the other.

The corpse looked peaceful enough, with a blanket drawn up to his neck. He seemed to be average height or a little below. Thin. Scrawny, even.

Mackenzie lifted a lantern high so light fell on the assassin's face "Do you recognize him?"

Kiri studied the lined face, trying to imagine it partially covered with a mask. He looked to be about forty, but might appear older than his years if he'd lived a hard life. She frowned as a memory was triggered. "The man at the club had a scar on his left cheek running from here to here." She indicated with her finger. "I just remembered that."

"What about you, Cassie?" Kirkland asked.

"I recognize him." Cassie stood on the other side of the table, her gaze intent. "I've seen him at some of the French taverns. His name is Hervé. He's one of those disreputable sorts who lurks around the émigré community in London. I've heard that he was in Napoleon's army until he deserted."

"In other words, Hervé was the sort who could be hired for criminal activities like assassination." Kirkland said.

"Exactly. I will make some inquiries." Cassie gave a very French shrug. "That might give us an idea who hired him."

"If no one has any other comments . . ." Kirkland drew the blanket over Hervé's head. "Then now, ladies and gentlemen, it's time for us to hunt."

Chapter 21

Thinking herself into the role of a dim doxy, Kiri floated down the steps to join Mackenzie for their first foray into London's shadier night places. One hand glided down the railing while the other caught up the skirt of the scandalous green silk gown. She wore a quantity of cheap jewelry to mitigate the lowness of her neckline—and one of her own personal perfume blends. Not lilacs. Tonight she wore a less innocent scent.

She also carried a folding fan. Cassie had shown her the places to jab a folded fan into impertinent males if she needed to defend herself.

Mackenzie waited at the foot of the stairs, his gaze riveted on Kiri. She saw him swallow hard before asking in a Lancashire accent, "Are you ready for your first den of iniquity, Carrie, my lass?"

"Indeed I am, Danny Boy," she said with an Irish lilt as she studied Mackenzie. He was dressed with foppish vulgarity, his skin tanned like a man who spent too much time in the sun. The eye patch covered his blue eye, leaving the brown one to match his coloring. He had gray in his hair and padding around his middle to make him look heavier. Even a close acquaintance would have trouble recognizing him.

They had worked out their roles earlier. He was Daniel Mackey, a prosperous mill owner from near Manchester, in London for business and pleasure. She was Carrie Ford, his mistress. He was a provincial, but a shrewd one. Kiri would be a giggling doxy with a short attention span. She could do that very well.

She tapped his arm coquettishly with her folded fan. "This is my first time in London and you're a man of the world, so I expect you to show a lass a good time."

"I'll do my best." He helped her into her cloak, since the fog had risen after they'd viewed the dead Frenchman. "I hope you're a night owl, because the places we'll be visiting don't get lively until midnight or after."

"I'm more an owl than a lark." She took his arm and they left the house. Outside a shabby hackney waited, mist swirling around it. She glanced toward the driver's box as Mackenzie handed her in.

"One of Kirkland's men," he explained. "Absolutely trustworthy, and good assistance if there's trouble."

After he settled beside her and the vehicle started moving, Kiri said, "Now that the time has come, I feel like I'm looking for a needle in three haystacks. And the needle might not be in any of them. What if our man isn't in a gambling mood, or is too busy for amusement, or patronizes different hells? Or he ran out of Alejandro and doesn't want to pay a small fortune for another bottle?"

"All our efforts could be wasted," Mackenzie said, his voice uncharacteristically sober. "In this kind of work, a great deal of effort is expended in eliminating possibilities. But if the haystacks aren't sifted, there's no chance at all of success." He took hold of her hand. "And if we aren't lucky . . . there are still compensations."

She laughed softly, lacing her fingers through his. "There are indeed."

As the hackney turned into the Strand, he said, "There's another haystack I've been thinking about. Could you identify the smuggler you took the knife from?"

Kiri thought back to the skirmish in the pitch-black cave. An impression of size, a rank, fishy scent, a rasp of voice. "I'm not sure. It happened so fast, and there wasn't anything that defined him, since his cologne was Eau de Fish. Would it be safe to go back? We left under something of a cloud."

He laughed. "Delicately put. The day after I returned to London, I wrote Hawk to see if I and my business were still welcome. Loosely translated, his reply said that most of the smugglers thought the dustup was quite jolly, they liked the bonus payment for the wench, and I was a valued customer. As long as I could deliver on my promise to keep Miss Ford from leading troops to the hideout, all was forgiven."

"I doubt Howard would agree with that last part," she said dryly.

"Probably not, but he's only one man. We'd be safe if we visited the hideout under Hawk's protection." The carriage stopped in front of a nondescript building on Jermyn Street. A small brass plate by the door read JOHNSON'S.

Mackenzie climbed out and flipped down the steps. "If we need to travel down to Kent, would you be willing, or have you had your fill of smugglers?"

She suppressed a shiver at her memory of being captured and chained to the wall. "How would they react to seeing me again? My presence might set them off."

"Cassie could disguise you so you won't be recognized. You could go as a young male." He grinned. "Though your figure would need a lot of binding. I'll understand if you'd rather not go after another needle in a fish-scented haystack."

Kiri was ruefully aware that all anyone need do was suggest she was too weak or fearful to do something, and she immediately became determined to do it. "I'll go."

"Good lass." His large hand at the back of her waist, he guided her past a pair of beefy, sharp-eyed guards and into the building. She much preferred having him as her escort rather than her servant.

Inside was a foyer that opened to a large gambling room with a variety of card games and a roulette wheel. The setting and clientele were less fashionable than Damian's, with patrons of the middling sort. There were a few women, some playing cards, the younger and flashier ones companions like Kiri.

A sharp-eyed gentleman approached and bowed. "Good evening. I'm Mr. Johnson. Have I had the pleasure of entertaining you before?"

"Nay, I'm just down from the North for a bit. Mackey's my name." Mackenzie laid on the Manchester accent and didn't introduce Kiri.

Having looked Mackenzie over and decided he was respectable, Mr. Johnson welcomed them to the establishment. He invited them to enjoy a glass of wine, then moved away to greet another guest.

Kiri unfastened her cloak and let Mackenzie take it from her shoulders, his fingers trailing tantalizingly over her nape. She gave a shiver of pleasure as heads swiveled in her direction. "You were right that this gown would attract notice."

She heard a growling sound come from her escort. "I have a strong desire to flatten every man who is staring at you," he muttered.

She settled into her role with a throaty chuckle. "Just remember who's taking me home." She fluttered her lashes and saw answering humor—and desire—in his eyes. Good. She would use that later.

For the next couple of hours, Mackenzie played at different tables, not spending long at any. His play was unremarkable, with bets neither large nor small. Kiri noticed that his winnings were also unremarkable, with him gaining a bit, losing some, winning a bit more. She guessed he was using his skills to avoid standing out.

Kiri spent her time wandering about, sipping wine very slowly. As Mackenzie played at the different tables, she was able to study his opponents. After that, she flirted with gentlemen who were taking breaks from the play.

The flirtation netted her a hissed threat from another female who thought Kiri was poaching on her man. Kiri purred back, "Don't worry, duck, I've got me a good man of my own. No need to steal another."

She moved away, her hips swaying provocatively. After a spell watching dice being cast at the hazard table, she joined Mackenzie, who was now playing whist. The club was getting busier, but she hadn't smelled even a trace of Alejandro. Hungary water was widely used, but not by any men who might be kidnappers.

She was returning from a visit to the ladies' retiring room when a drunken gamester cornered her in the corridor. "You're the prettiest thing here, sweeting," he said with sloppy admiration. "Give me a kiss?"

She laughed and tried to sidle away. "I don't give away my kisses, sir."

"Then call it a sample, because I might be willing to pay your price after I taste the goods." He moved in quickly, pinning her against the wall as he tried to find her lips.

Gagging from his whiskey-tainted breath, Kiri gave him a hard jab in the ribs with her fan, but he was so drunk he barely noticed. When one meaty paw clamped onto her breast, her temper flared and she almost smashed her knee into his groin.

Before she could emasculate the drunk, he flew backward with a squawk. Mackenzie had the back of the drunk's collar. In a voice that would have frozen a more sober man solid, he snapped, "Keep your hands off the lady."

The drunk just blinked at him. "She ain't no lady," he said reproachfully. "As sweet a piece of mutton as I've ever seen. Jus' wanted to get to know her better."

Mackenzie made a disgusted sound and tossed the drunk into the opposite wall. The fellow slid to the floor with an "Oof!"

Mackenzie kicked the drunk in the ribs, not with bone-shattering force, but hard enough to leave bruises. "The lady is mine. Be grateful I didn't let her destroy your chance of future children."

"Jus' telling her how pretty she was," the drunk said petulantly.

Mackenzie kicked the drunk's ribs harder. "*Mine!*" He turned to Kiri and offered his arm. "Time to leave, lass?"

A little shaken, she nodded. "After we collect my cloak." She gave the drunk a contemptuous glance. "I can use some fresh air."

They returned to the main room. If anyone had noticed the altercation, it wasn't considered significant enough to react. Mackenzie reclaimed her cloak, setting it around her shoulders as if she were a glass princess.

She pulled the garment tight when they stepped outdoors. The night air had become even colder and the sky was spitting rain.

As they waited for their carriage, he asked, "Had enough for one night?"

She took a deep breath. "I'm ready for another establishment. I knew there would be men like that drunk. The hard part was remembering not to hurt him too badly."

"You're a stalwart lass." The carriage arrived and he handed her in. After giving an address to the driver, Mackenzie joined her inside and wrapped an arm around her shoulders. "Did you spot anyone suspicious?"

She nestled close to his warm body. "There were several who used Hungary water, but none that looked like the kidnappers. Did you learn anything interesting?"

He shook his head. "It would be the sheerest luck to learn anything so soon. We could spend weeks or even months visiting such places and discover nothing. Or we could find our villain at the next stop."

"I haven't the temperament for spying," she decided. "Patience is so singularly absent from my nature."

"I'm much the same," Mackenzie admitted. "But I'll help Kirkland when needed. It isn't always clear if spying is useful, but stopping an assassination matters."

"What's the name of this next place?"

"The Captain's Club. It's a hell, not a proper club, but it draws a number of past and present military men. There will be fewer women."

"So I'll have less chance of getting my eyes scratched out."

"I have the utmost faith that you will win any catfights," he said with warm confidence. "Unless you take on Cassie. That would be even odds."

She laughed. "You keep a close eye on me, don't you? You appeared rather quickly when that drunk got out of hand."

"My first duty is to keep you safe. All else is secondary."

"Thank you." She took his hand, comforted by the knowledge that they were a team. "More of this tomorrow?"

"Yes, we'll visit a gambling hell in a woman's house. Madame Blanche runs her establishment more like a private house party than a club, so there's dancing and decent food as well as gaming. You'll need Cassie's help for a thorough disguise." He frowned. "At some point, we might need to go to a boxing match if that's where the third surviving kidnapper is to be found."

"That would be interesting. I've never seen a regular boxing match," she said. "Only fights between soldiers where there were no rules."

"The fact that regular matches follow Broughton's rules doesn't mean they aren't bloody," he warned.

No matter. She and Mackenzie would be safe together.

The Captain's Club was smaller, and as Mackenzie had said, there were only a couple of other women present. The gaming salon was quiet, the only sounds murmured comments on the play and the flat slap of cards on green baize tabletops.

The host came to greet them. "I'm Mr. Smythe," he said hospitably. "Welcome to the Captain's Club. What would you like to play tonight?"

"Good evening to you, sir," Mackenzie said in his robust northern accent. "I'm Dan Mackey, and I'm in the mood for ombre."

"You're in luck. An ombre table is just starting, and there's room for one more player." Smythe led them to a round table toward the back with four men sitting around it. "Gentlemen, Mr. Mackey will join you. Mr. Mackey, meet Lieutenant Hardy, Major Welsh, Captain Swinnerton, and Mr. Reed."

Beside Kiri, Mackenzie turned to stone. She guessed that he knew one of the men well and feared being recognized. For a moment, she thought he would announce he preferred to play at a different table.

But the other players barely glanced up from their cards and drinks to acknowledge his presence. Mac, the newcomer, was a civilian and a northerner and of no interest to them. He was also very well disguised. Overcoming his doubts, Mackenzie sat down to play.

As cards were dealt, Kiri wandered around the table to check the players' scents. No Alejandro, one man wore Jockey Club, and two wore Guard's Bouquet. The fourth wasn't wearing cologne but smelled strongly of horse.

After she passed his chair, Swinnerton, the Jockey Club man, glared at her and snapped at Mackenzie, "Keep control of your doxy if you don't want her accused of spying on other men's cards."

Kiri gave him a look of innocent outrage. "I'd not do that!"

Mackenzie pulled an empty chair from the table next to him, and patted the seat. "Sit here, lass." He gave her a besotted smile. "Bring me luck." He'd thickened his accent and raised the pitch of his voice, she noticed.

Kiri obeyed with a doxyish pout. The table was small, which gave her an excuse to sit so closely that her thigh pressed against Mac's. With no conversation other than that required by the game, Kiri had plenty of time to survey the other players in the club. Though she wasn't close enough to check scents, she saw no one the right size and shape and movement to have been among the kidnappers.

Eventually her gaze came to rest on Swinnerton, who sat opposite. Her interest quickened as she studied him more closely. He was a hard-edged man currently softened by the half-empty bottle of brandy in front of him. Though he wasn't wearing Alejandro, his build and manner reminded her of the leader of the kidnappers. Could he be their quarry? A man didn't have to wear the same cologne every day.

As a new hand was dealt, Lieutenant Hardy said casually, "Swinnerton, did you hear how the owner of Damian's was killed the other night? They say he went after a thief and was shot for his pains."

Kiri's attention sharpened, and Mackenzie's thigh tensed, though his expression didn't change. It must be strange to hear men discussing one's alleged death.

His tension increased even more when Swinnerton said, "No loss, Hardy. That bastard Mackenzie was cashiered from the army, you know. Good riddance to him."

"I hadn't heard that." Hardy fanned the cards in his hand, a frown showing that he wasn't pleased with them. "I met Mackenzie a time or two at his club. Seemed a pleasant enough chap. What was he cashiered for?"

Face like granite, Swinnerton said, "He raped and murdered the wife of a fellow officer."

Chapter 22

The harsh statement triggered a sharp intake of breath around the table. A horrified voice exclaimed, "The devil you say!"

Mac froze, his heart pounding. It was sheer damned bad luck to be put at a table with Rupert Swinnerton. Even so, he hadn't expected this horror to be tossed casually into the middle of a card game. Though perhaps he should have. Mackenzie's reported death made him news.

Even more than three years later, Swinnerton wasn't saying that he was the man whose wife had been murdered. The story didn't reflect well on either of them.

As all eyes, including Kiri's, went to Swinnerton, Hardy asked in a shocked voice, "If that's true, how come he wasn't hanged?"

"The murder took place in Portugal. Easier to hush up a crime in a distant country at war," Swinnerton said bitterly. "Mackenzie was a Masterson family bastard. His half brother and some other fancy friend got the charges dropped in return for shipping him home and forfeiture of his commission."

"So maybe being shot was justice catching up with him," Major Welsh murmured as he played a card.

"Justice, or the husband of the woman he dishonored," Mr. Reed said grimly. "If Mackenzie had done that to my wife, he would have been a dead man much sooner."

"It's hard to believe the murder of an officer's wife could be hushed up," Hardy said, his brows furrowed. "Maybe the story was distorted in the telling?"

Swinnerton shook his head. "I heard it from an officer who was right there and saw it all firsthand. A nasty business. The woman was having an affair with Mackenzie, so her husband didn't have much desire to blare the news to the heavens."

"One can see why not." Welsh shook his head. "The poor devil. To lose his wife in such a ghastly way, and then be denied justice! I assume Mackenzie was rushed out of Portugal before the husband could challenge him to a duel."

Before Swinnerton could answer, Reed said impatiently, "A very sad business, but enough. We're here to play cards."

Though the talk died down, Mac was still shaken to the marrow. Ombre, a Spanish game that relied more on tactics than luck, was one of his favorites, but now he could barely see the cards.

A strong female hand squeezed his thigh and Kiri purred into his ear, "I'm getting sleepy, darling. Ready to go home to bed?"

When she licked the edge of his ear teasingly, he almost jumped out of his skin, but she had given him a good excuse to leave. The game was ending, so he said, "Since my lady is tired, I shall withdraw, gentlemen. My thanks for the play, and good night."

The others said good night with knowing expressions and some envy as they looked at Kiri. As Mac walked away with her, she took hold of his arm adoringly and gave her hips some extra sway. None of the men present would remember her face, since they'd been staring at other parts of her person.

Knowing Kiri would ask about Swinnerton's story, Mac draped her cloak over her shoulders and led her out to the waiting hackney. Once they were inside and the carriage was heading home, she asked mildly, "What really happened?"

"Didn't you hear?" he said, voice brittle. "I raped and killed the wife of a fellow officer and barely escaped a well-deserved hanging."

"Rubbish! You're a protector, not a rapist and murderer." In the darkness, her hand closed over his. His fingers convulsively tightened around hers.

"But I have killed," he said bleakly, the weight of every mistake he'd ever made bearing down on him. "Too often."

"Of course you have killed. That's what soldiers do," she said calmly. "And there are other sorts of war that aren't conducted on the battlefield, like our search for assassins. But rape and murder a helpless woman? Never."

"Thank you." He closed his eyes, intensely grateful for her belief. "It was appalling to be accused of such a ghastly crime. Worse yet that some people believed it."

"What happened?" she asked softly.

"Harriet Swinnerton was the woman murdered, and she was the wife of Rupert Swinnerton, who told the story."

Kiri caught her breath. "You served with him?"

"Barely. When I first joined the army, I served under Alex Randall. After we were sent to Portugal, I transferred to a different company that needed a junior officer. Though Swinnerton was a lieutenant and my superior, I very seldom saw him. He was usually busy carrying on his affairs." Mac sighed. "I did my duty, but I wasn't much of a soldier, Kiri. I only joined because my father offered to buy me a commission to set me up in the world. It's more than some men do for their bastards."

"And you might have enjoyed fighting," she observed. "It's not as if you were suited to the vicarage."

He almost laughed. "So very true. Actual combat was—interesting. One feels very alive. Terrified and exalted and challenged. But battle is a small part of a soldier's life, and the rest—well, I hated the rules, the restrictions, the orders from fools."

"Like Swinnerton?"

"He was not only a fool, but a brutal fool. Rumor said that he'd had to marry Harriet after seducing her. There was certainly no love lost between them. They both were notorious for affairs." He shook his head, still unable to believe his stupidity. "I knew it was a mistake to become involved with her, but I did it anyhow."

"Did you love her?" Kiri asked softly.

Even three years later, he wasn't sure of the answer. "A little, I think. She was beautiful and angry. But she also had a fragile quality that made me want to take care of her. I was lonely, and when she made advances, I didn't walk away as a wiser man would have." She had been very beautiful, after all, and a very skilled lover.

"She sounds rather tragic," Kiri said. "How did she die?"

Every moment of that night was engraved in his memories. "I visited her at her lodgings. Swinnerton was away and it seemed safe enough. She was restless that night, and as I was about to leave, she suddenly demanded that I run away with her."

"Were you tempted?" In the faint light through the carriage window, Kiri's profile was intent and lovely.

"Not in the least. I'd been thinking of ending the affair, and her suggestion made me decide it was time. She wasn't in love with me. She just wanted to leave Portugal. That would have ruined both of us." His mouth twisted. "But if I'd said yes, she might be alive today."

"Why do you think that?"

"She was furious with me, raging and throwing vases and threatening to tell her husband that I tried to force myself on her. That made it a lot easier to leave and to know I'd done the right thing."

"So she was alive when you left."

"Very much so." He took a deep breath, hating to speak of what came next. "Then Swinnerton unexpectedly arrived home late that night, and all hell broke loose. He said he found Harriet and her Portuguese maid brutally beaten and near death."

Kiri sucked her breath in sharply, but Mac kept going, wanting to get through it as quickly as possible. "Swinnerton claimed Harriet was still alive when he found her, and that with her dying breath, she accused me of raping her and beating her and the maid."

"Dear God," Kiri whispered, her hand tightening on his with bruising force. "Do you suppose Swinnerton learned of the affair and this was his revenge on both of you?"

He nodded. "I think Harriet was so furious that she told him about me, and maybe her other affairs as well, and he went berserk," Mac said. "After she was dead, Swinnerton used her so-called dying accusation to justify a drumhead court-martial the next morning. I was convicted and sentenced to be flogged, then hung by the neck until dead, dead, dead."

Kiri shivered. "How did you escape the gallows?"

"Alex Randall and my brother, Will. My sergeant sent a message to Will, who went haring off to Lord Wellington while Randall swooped into our camp to find out what was going on." Mac smiled humorlessly. "If Swinnerton hadn't been so keen to see me flogged, I'd have been dead before Randall arrived. Instead, I was able to argue my innocence to Randall and tell him what I thought really happened."

"Thank God he got there in time and believed you!" she said vehemently.

"And that he's Randall." Mac shook his head in wonder. "He stood in front of the building where they'd locked me up and said he didn't believe I was guilty, and that if they tried to hang me on hearsay evidence, they'd have to go through him."

"I've seen enough of Randall to believe that he could stare down a whole company of infantrymen," Kiri said with awe. "How did Swinnerton react?"

"He was screaming and threatening Randall when Wellington and Will galloped into the camp. While Wellington ordered everyone to stand down and tell him what happened, Will found a witness to the beatings. The maid had been badly injured, but she survived and was able to talk. She testified that Harriet and I had been having an affair, but when I left that night, her mistress was well and unhurt."

"Could she identify the real killer?"

"She said she didn't see the man clearly, but she was pretty sure he was short and Portuguese," he said dryly. "A thief, surely."

"You think she recognized Swinnerton, but she didn't dare say that?"

"That's my theory, but I could be wrong. There was no more evidence against him than against me. There was no blood on him, but his quarters weren't searched, so he could have changed his clothing before raising the alarm." Mac's lips thinned. "Another theory being tossed around was that I'd been sleeping with the maid as well as the mistress, so she lied to protect me."

"Why would she lie to protect a man who murdered her mistress and almost killed her?" Kiri asked. "That makes no sense."

"Such matters have nothing to do with sense," he said even more dryly. "Lord Wellington ruled that a British officer couldn't be executed without evidence. Even if Harriet had claimed it was me, any woman so injured might have been raving, while the woman who survived said definitely that I wasn't the murderer.

"After dismissing the charges, Wellington strongly suggested I sell out of the army and return to England with all due haste. So I did." He couldn't have done it without his brother's help. Will was only a couple of years older, but he'd always been the protective big brother.

"A wise move. Even though you were never charged, it would have been impossible to continue serving in the same regiment."

"I was glad to get back to London, though I had no idea what I'd do. Then Kirkland came calling and suggested a different career." The idea of doing useful work instead of being the Mastersons' disgraceful bastard had been irresistible. He'd turned out to be a much better gaming-house proprietor and informant than he'd been a soldier.

"I suppose Harriet's murder is still unsolved?"

"Officially. The incident wrecked two careers. Swinnerton wasn't well liked, so plenty of suspicion fell on him as well me. His family bought him an exchange into a West Indies regiment so he could get away from the worst of the scandal."

"That's a punishment in itself, given the amount of disease there," Kiri said. "He looked rather yellow under his tan. He may have sold out for health reasons."

"I hadn't heard he was back in London, so he probably returned recently." Mac grimaced. "I wasn't sorry to leave the army. But any other way would have been better."

"I'm sorry you had to endure that." Kiri turned and rested her head on his shoulder and slid her free arm around his waist. A warm and wonderful armful of woman. She continued, "Rupert Swinnerton sounds like a monster. He also might be one of the kidnappers."

Mac came sharply alert. "Was he wearing Alejandro?"

"No, but he does resemble the chief kidnapper. More than anyone else we've seen tonight."

"How sure are you that he's our quarry?"

"I'm not positive," she warned. "But I think he should be watched closely."

Mac considered what he knew of Swinnerton. The man was cold as a snake, and in the army, he'd learned skills useful to assassins. "I'm trying not to be biased here. But I think Rupert Swinnerton is capable of anything."

"I do hope he's guilty," Kiri said wistfully. "He was quite unpleasant."

"So we've accomplished something tonight after all. A good start to our investigation." Glad for some progress and grateful for Kiri's understanding, Mac bent his head to kiss her. His lips landed on the smooth curve of her cheek.

She turned into the kiss, and thanks transformed to passion. The green silk dress had been driving him mad since the first time Kiri put it on, and now he wanted nothing more than to get her out of it. Her breasts—so full, so perfect. Her scent, the essence of Kiri, was enhanced by an exotic perfume that drove reason straight out of his head.

Her knee slid between his and her hands roved as much as his. It was a shock when the hackney creaked to a halt. They had reached 11 Exeter Street.

Body throbbing, Mac broke the embrace. "What is it about carriage rides?" he panted. "Good sense goes out the window when I travel with you."

"It's perfectly logical," she said with a choke of laughter. "In a carriage, we're close and alone. Whenever that happens, we want to pounce on each other."

"You do logic very well." He cradled her head against his shoulder tenderly. "You're really good at pouncing, too."

"It comes from watching cats." Her hand slid between his legs and cupped him with paralyzing accuracy. "Having reached this point, the logical thing is to go up to my room and make mad, passionate love."

Chapter 23

Kiri's words blazed a direct line from Mac's brain to his groin. Every muscle in his body clenched while he fought to regain control. They were in a *hackney*, for God's sake! In front of their temporary home. They really must alight and go inside.

He had a swift image of them making love right here and now and the whole lightweight vehicle shaking madly. The humor of that cleared his wits a little.

"We are going to exit from this hackney and leave madness behind us," he said firmly. "We will go inside and retire to our separate bedrooms and separately sleep the sleep of the just." Except he'd lie awake all night from frustrated lust so intense that his good right hand would be unable to fully relieve it.

"Don't be absurd," she said tartly as she straightened her garments and felt around for her bonnet. "We may have no future, but we have a present. We desire each other, and we are living outside our normal lives. For as long as this investigation lasts, we can do as we wish without social censure."

Needing to drown that tempting vision, he threw the

door open and jumped to the street. This time he didn't offer his hand to help her out since he didn't dare touch her, and she was certainly capable of climbing from a carriage on her own.

She proved that she could, and ruined his good intentions by taking his arm. Wordlessly they climbed the steps and he unlocked the door. Inside the small foyer a dim lamp had been left to guide them. There was only one candle left on the table, so the rest of the household had returned and retired by now.

Keeping his voice low, he said, "The Garden of Eden contained Adam, Eve, and a serpent. You, Lady Kiri, are most surely descended from the serpent who is offering temptation in return for Adam's and Eve's souls."

Instead of being insulted, she laughed. "I've read that sexuality was the real temptation the serpent offered, and Adams and Eves ever since have been grabbing that apple with infinite enthusiasm." Her laughter died as she peeled off her gloves, revealing her elegant, long-fingered hands. "Why shouldn't we do the same? Where is the harm?"

The thought of those lovely naked fingers on his body made him swallow and look away. "You are too intelligent not to understand that sexuality is volatile and sometimes dangerous. It can cause great grief and suffering. It almost got me killed."

"I have no mad husband, and unless you've been keeping her hidden, you have no mad wife," she pointed out.

His mouth twisted. "I haven't lain with a woman since Harriet died."

She caught her breath in surprise. "That can't be from lack of opportunity."

"It isn't. The reason is . . . guilt, I suppose." He forced himself to explain why he'd avoided any kind of entanglement with other women. "I was heedless with Harriet, and that triggered a disaster that killed her and injured too many others. It made me . . . wary."

"She was on a doomed course, I think. If Swinnerton hadn't beaten her to death that night, it probably would have happened another time," Kiri said quietly. "Isn't it time you embraced life fully again?"

He looked into her eyes, green even in this light. "You really are a pagan. But you're too intelligent not to know that consequences are real. Even if I'm not shot by your father or your brother, there is always the chance of a child."

"Give me credit for advance planning," she said with a mischievous smile. "When I was considering marriage to Godfrey Hitchcock, I asked Julia Randall how to prevent unwanted pregnancy. It's so useful to know a good midwife! I came to Exeter Street prepared because I want very much to be with you while I can."

"I'm deeply flattered," he said honestly. "But even if you can be casual—I don't know if I can be." Before Harriet Swinnerton, he'd specialized in light affairs, but he was no longer that man.

She brushed her fingers along his jaw in a gossamer caress. "Given that your last affair ended in disaster and you've had three years of lonely celibacy, no new affair can be casual. Or do you intend to live a lifetime of celibacy?"

He shivered at the touch of her fingertips. "Definitely not. But better that I indulge the sins of the flesh with a woman who is older and more experienced so there will be fewer consequences."

"There need be no consequences between us, other than a proper amount of regret when the time comes to part." She removed her bonnet, revealing that their impassioned kissing in the carriage had left her shining hair in charming disarray. "Don't you think the pleasure we can share before we part will be worth that?"

He wasn't sure whether to laugh or weep. "You are unlike any woman I've ever known. If I have a lick of sense, I'll run upstairs and lock my bedroom door behind me."

In the dim light, her dark beauty had an exotic cast. "You think of me as English because that is the side you see, but I am also a daughter of India. My mind does not always work the way you might expect."

"That I've noticed." He tried not to stare as she removed her cloak, revealing bare skin and curves. "Are all Hindu women dangerous seductresses?"

"Very few." She smiled wickedly. "You're just lucky."

The foyer was small and there was no room to dodge when she linked her arms around his neck. Her voice, her scent, her lovely lithe body, flooded his senses.

Softly she said, "You also think of me as an innocent maiden who needs protection. But I am no innocent." She proved it with a kiss that seared to the marrow.

"You've removed the last shred of my conscience, Kiri," he said unevenly after he came up for breath. "I almost believe we can be lovers without triggering another disaster. And even if we can't—right now I don't care."

"We can be together without destroying each other." Kiri stepped back and caught his hand. "I promise you that. Now come."

He lit a candle from the night lamp and let her lead him up the stairs. The flame flickered wildly in the drafty stairwell, making her look more dream than real. An incredible, beautiful woman unlike any other. One who was strong, not needy. One who could give without demanding his soul in return.

She was too good to be true. But for tonight, he wanted rather desperately to believe.

* * *

Caught between exhilaration and terror at her boldness, Kiri towed Mackenzie up to her room. She'd considered the bedchamber spacious, but his broad shoulders and height made the room seem smaller.

As soon as the door closed behind them, he set the candle on the desk and enveloped her in an intoxicating embrace. He'd fascinated her when he was trying so valiantly to hold back. Now that he'd freed his desire, he was irresistible.

With only a single candle to light the room, she experienced him more through scent and touch than sight. He was delicious and she wanted to inhale him. To taste, to devour. To take him into her very being.

His long, clever fingers massaged her back. They felt so good she didn't realize he'd unfastened her gown until he stepped away and the cool green silk slithered down to pool at her feet. Her shift and corset covered her as thoroughly as the gown had, but his gaze was rapt. "Why are undergarments so wickedly enticing?" he asked in wonder as he traced the edge of her corset across her breasts.

"Because they're forbidden," she replied huskily, her skin singing to life under his touch. "But now it's your turn."

She stepped close and untied his cravat, stripping it away to bare his throat. When she leaned in for a kiss, his pulse beat against her lips. She also tasted a trace of salt overlaying the mysterious essence of who he was. "Hold still," she ordered. "I wish to drive you to madness."

"You already have," he groaned, but he stood statue-still as she peeled off his coat, tugged his shirt from his pantaloons, and ran teasing hands across skin taut over underlying muscle. She loved the pattern of hair on his chest, and the way it caught red-gold glints in the candlelight.

Giddily she yanked his shirt up over his head, then removed the padded vest he wore to look heavier. In the process, her fingers brushed his back, and she felt surprising roughness. Curious, she circled around to investigate more closely.

She caught her breath. His back was a scarred mass of irregular ridges. As an army daughter, she recognized the cause. Gently she laid her hand in the middle of his back. "The results of Swinnerton's flogging, I assume. It's a wonder you weren't killed."

"I damn near was," he said, voice flat. "He ordered twelve hundred lashes, the maximum allowed, but I collapsed somewhere around five hundred. Swinnerton wanted me to endure the full number before the hanging, so I was dragged off and locked up. A surgeon came to patch the damage enough that I could receive the rest of the lashes."

"That's when Randall arrived? You said if it weren't for Swinnerton wanting the flogging, you'd have been hanged before help could reach you."

Mackenzie's broad chest expanded as he drew a deep breath. "I had just enough consciousness left to tell Randall what happened. He'd encountered Swinnerton before, which helped. By the time Will and Wellington arrived, I was coherent again."

She struggled to suppress the tears that wanted to fall. "Then I'm glad for the scars, because if not for the flogging, you would have died before I ever met you."

"You would have been better off if that had happened, my warrior lass," he said bleakly. "I can do you no good."

"Nonsense," she retorted. "You are so magnificently unboring. Not to have known you would have been a sad loss."

"It wouldn't be a loss if you'd never known I existed," he said, his voice dry as desert bones. "But if I'd been

hanged, I'd be remembered as a rapist and murderer.
I wouldn't have wanted to curse Will with that."

"Understandably." Even a man as calm as Will Masterson would be upset by that kind of notoriety. She stroked
his back with both hands. "But you committed no crime."

"Not legally, but the scars are a mark of criminal foolishness. Harriet Swinnerton cast out lures to other officers.
Would Will have accepted her advances? Randall? Even
when they were junior officers, they had more sense."

She realized that he saw the scars not only as a badge of
foolishness, but of shame. She circled his waist with her
arms and laid her cheek against his ruined back. "The
scars are also a sign of injustice," she said softly. "You
almost died for a crime you didn't commit, and because of
that, you developed a passion for justice, didn't you? That's
part of why you work with Kirkland. You changed and
became a better man."

After the space of a dozen heartbeats, he said reluctantly, "I suppose so."

She continued to hold him, feeling the beating of his
heart, the expansion and relaxation of his lungs. He was
strong and masculine and *alive*. Yet he might not have been,
and she would never have known what she had missed.

"Is it better to be born wise?" he asked. "Or to achieve
wisdom only through catastrophic stupidity?"

Kiri considered. "Being born wise would be easier. My
sister, Lucia, inherited sense from her father and was
always a wise child." Unlike Kiri. "But from a theological
view, I think it's preferable to struggle and overcome one's
weakness to become a better person." She laughed suddenly. "It's certainly more interesting."

Mackenzie turned and crushed her against his chest,
burying his face in her hair. "I'm sure Lucia is a lovely and
admirable young lady. Definitely lovely if she looks like
you. But not enchanting. Not able to rearrange my mind

and memories through a mixture of intelligence and beauty."

"Men so seldom mention my intelligence, and never before my beauty," she said approvingly. "This is why you are too much man for me to waste."

But not too much man to be embraced. She loved the power in his broad shoulders and muscular body. Loved the way he kissed and caressed her, as if she was the center of his universe. Loved the way every fiber of her being responded to him, wanting to lure and yield and join.

His nimble fingers unlaced her corset, then massaged the tightness from her sides. His hands moved up to cup her breasts. Gently he kneaded her yearning flesh through the thin cotton of her shift, teasing her nipples to tautness with his thumbs as her back arched with pleasure. She barely managed to gasp, "I need to make one quick detour behind that screen so I can prepare myself. I'd very much like to come back to find a fire burning on the hearth, and you naked."

He grinned. "Your wish is my command, my warrior queen."

She broke away and didn't look back, knowing she couldn't leave him even for a minute if she could see him.

Ever the optimist, she'd set out the sponge and the vinegar earlier. It took only a moment to insert them. She'd been less than truthful when she told Mackenzie there would be no consequences from their intimacy. His name would be engraved on her heart in letters of fire until she died.

But she would do her best to ensure that there would be no disastrous physical consequences. If she became with child, he was gentleman enough to marry her, but she didn't want an unwilling husband.

Coal rattled as he built a fire. Then clothing and boots rustled as he stripped. The knowledge of what he was doing was wickedly exciting. She pulled off her corset, shift, and stockings, balling up the garments and tossing them over the screen one at a time.

"You know how to add fuel to the flames, don't you?" he said admiringly.

"I try." With sudden absurd shyness, she released her thick, dark hair and shook it out to fall to her waist in a shining mass.

After drawing a deep breath, she stepped from behind the screen. She had been told she was beautiful since she was a willful child. Here was the ultimate test.

From Mackenzie's stunned expression, she passed the test. "Oh, my lady," he breathed. "How can you look as innocent as Eve and as desirable as Aphrodite at the same time?"

"I am neither Eve nor Aphrodite, though I'm glad you think so." Her eyes narrowed as she studied every splendid inch of him, from the thick waves of his brown hair to his broad shoulders and chest and down to narrow hips and muscular legs. And most certainly she saw the evidence of how much he desired her.

He could have modeled for a Greek sculptor, but living flesh was far more moving. "You are also beautiful, Damian, but not, I think, innocent."

"Definitely not innocent." He moved forward to take her hand. "But tonight I feel reborn. As if this is my first time." He linked his fingers through hers and rested her hand above his heart.

The motion drew them together so only inches separated them. She was close enough to feel the heat of his body. Their hands were not too dissimilar in color, but she was tan all over in contrast to the English paleness of his torso.

She moved forward and pressed her softer body against his firm muscles and angles. Male and female, designed to mate. Their arms slid around each other as they kissed with sweet exploration.

It took only a dozen breaths for that sweetness to blaze into hot tongues, eager hands, and wildfire. It was time to suggest they not waste this nakedness standing up when it would be even more useful when they were lying down.

Before she spoke, he scooped her up. One powerful arm curved around her ribs while the other supported her bare thighs, causing liquid heat to flow in hidden places.

While depositing her on the bed, he managed to sweep the covers back so she lay on the softly worn sheets. She tried to draw him down, but he pushed her arms away. "I'm ravenous," he said, his gaze intense. "So I will dine on you before the final course."

He braced himself above her so his chest and thighs and . . . and *maleness* were just barely touching her, with insanely erotic results. Then he licked her ear as she'd done to him earlier. As she gasped, his mouth moved to her throat. She writhed against him, half mad with wanting more.

His mouth moved down her body, suckling her breasts. She buried her fingers in his softly waving hair. She hardly noticed the slow stroke of his hand up her thigh until his fingers slipped into moist, secret welcome.

As she teetered on the verge of shattering, he trailed kisses down her torso. His tongue lapping her navel, his lips across her belly . . .

Merciful heaven! When the heat of his skilled mouth and tongue covered the incredibly sensitive center of sensation between her legs, she exploded uncontrollably. Her hips thrashed and her nails bit against his skull. He stifled her shriek by locking a hard hand over her mouth as she splintered into mindless rapture.

As awareness gradually returned, he raised himself and moved between her knees. Entering her was a smooth act of possession, apart from a sharp moment of resistance before they were united in the ultimate intimacy. She opened dazed eyes to see surprise in his face. That vanished when she rocked against him, driving him deeper, filling her and creating wholly new sensations.

Her movement triggered a climax as swift and rapturous as hers had been, and brought her to another culmination. He groaned helplessly, thrusting again and again until their mutual paroxysms faded. She squeezed her eyes shut, reveling in the rich scents of sex and the peace that lay beyond the storm.

She had dreamed of this, and Damian Mackenzie had surpassed her dreams.

Chapter 24

Shaken in every particle of his being, Mac barely managed to roll onto his side so he wouldn't crush Kiri. Even allowing for his three years of celibacy, this was passion and fulfillment beyond his imagination.

They were sharing a pillow, allowing him to admire the elegant line of her profile. His heart clutched when he saw slow tears seeping from her closed eyes. Dear God, had he made another disastrous mistake where a woman was concerned? She'd seemed to want this as much as he.

Concerned, he asked, "Kiri, what's wrong? Did I hurt you?"

That triggered a thought that he put aside when she opened her eyes and gave him a glorious smile. "Not sad tears. Happy tears."

"I'm glad to hear that. Even so, they're unnerving." He propped his head on his hand and studied her as he drew the covers over them. The fire wasn't enough to warm the room now that they no longer created their own heat.

He returned to that earlier thought, mentally replaying every vivid instant of their encounter. Disbelieving, he said, "I'm no expert on such things, but . . . I would have thought you were a virgin. But you said you weren't?"

"I said I wasn't an innocent." She held his gaze steadily. "But technically I was a virgin, I suppose."

"Damnation!" he exclaimed, his lazy well-being vanishing. "If I'd known that, I would have managed to hang on to my conscience and keep my distance!"

"Which is why I misled you, Damian. I'm sorry I was less than honest, but I can't be sorry for the results." She offered a tentative smile.

A chill was sinking deeper and deeper into his bones. "I would appreciate an explanation. I won't believe it if you say that you have fallen madly, irrevocably in love and decided to seduce me into marriage. I'm not that much of a prize."

Her expression turned wistful. "I know you're not the marrying kind, and while I was willing to mislead you into my bed, I would not trick you to the altar."

"Then why?" he asked, baffled. "Straightforward lust? That's powerful." Incredibly, mind-meltingly powerful. "But in the case of a strong-minded young lady like you, not bclicvablc."

"The answer is complicated." Her gaze moved away to the ceiling.

"Then pray enlighten me so I'll know whether I should be angry," he said dryly.

"I hope you aren't, though you have the right." Still not looking at him, she continued, "In India, I fell in love with one of my father's young officers. It was the head-over-heels love of youth and first passion. Charles was honorable and refused to ruin me, but we were very young and craved each other desperately. We found ways to meet privately when we could."

The vulnerability on her face was very different from her usual blithe confidence. Beginning to see where this was going, he said quietly, "So together you explored all the varieties of passion short of actual intercourse?"

She nodded, biting her lip. "It was wonderful. Intoxicating."

"Did he change his mind?" He hoped her Charles hadn't condemned her for her mixed blood! If that had happened, he'd hunt the young devil down and wring his neck.

She gave a humorless laugh. "I wish he had. Instead, the blasted man got himself killed. He was leading a patrol in the mountains up a narrow track that crumbled away, dropping half of his men into a rough river below. He was a strong swimmer and went into the water again and again and managed to save all but one. He was going after that last man when he ran out of strength and . . . didn't survive."

"Oh, my dear," he said softly. "I'm so sorry. But a good officer looks after his men, and he was clearly a good officer. He died a hero."

"I know." She blinked back tears. "But I wish his duty hadn't killed him."

Mac pulled her close. "I don't think lying with a man you don't love is the answer, my dear girl. I wish I could be what you need."

"But you are." She gazed up, her face only inches away. "Losing Charles left a hole in my heart, and also . . . anger. I wished we'd been lovers so I would have had that."

"I'm not him. Not even close." He smiled wryly. "Heroism is not among my limited list of virtues. Nor do I like the idea of being a . . . a substitute Charles."

Kiri gave a quick shake of her head. "That's not it. You are very unlike. But you make me laugh the way he did." She frowned. "And . . . I desire you as I haven't any man since Charles died. Perhaps even more than I did him, though saying so seems disloyal."

It was hard to stay irritated when an amazingly beautiful woman said she desired him so much. "Now you know what you were missing." His voice softened. "Though with Charles you would have had love as well as desire, and that would have added a whole new dimension."

"Likely you are right, but . . . time has passed. I am not who I was then. At least after tonight, I can finally move beyond that terrible loss." She stroked her hand over his chest. "You and I will be together now while we can, and then go our separate paths. When I am a staid old lady, I will remember you with a wistful smile and no regrets."

He laughed. "You will never be staid, Lady Kiri."

"If I can't be staid, I shall be an eccentric old lady instead," she said calmly. "With cats, like the one that has materialized on the foot of the bed."

He looked down and saw a tabby curled up on the corner of the bed as if it had been there all night. "Where the devil did that cat come from?"

"I'm not sure. I think Puss has a secret way in and out of this room."

He shook his head. "I think you've already achieved eccentricity, but that's all right. Aristocrats can get away with things lesser folk can't." He sat up, the air cool against his skin as the covers fell away. "I can't undo what we just did, but I can prevent it from happening again. You have the completion you wanted and can now find a man more worthy of you when you return to your real life."

She caressed his thigh. "As you say, we can't undo what we've done, so what is the point of denying what we both want so much? We will have a fortnight or two to share pleasure. Later on, won't you regret being noble now?"

"Yes," he said firmly, "but regret is better than behaving like a scoundrel."

He was about to get out of the bed when her hand slid over his thigh to cup his genitals. He froze. A minute before, he would have said he was sexually drained and incapable of performing for at least a few hours.

He would have been wrong.

"Kiri," he said helplessly, unable to think, no longer sure what was right and what was wrong. "Every time we come together, we increase the risk of damaging each other."

"No. We won't." As he hardened under her hand, she pulled him into a kiss.

It was nearly dawn before he returned to his own room.

On this night, the Powells' kitchen produced an excellent joint of mutton and sliced potatoes baked with cheese. Mac concentrated on his food, afraid to look at Kiri for fear of what might show in his face. She sat demurely on the other side of the table, not looking at him.

He was still torn between sense and lust. Those big green eyes were very convincing when she claimed continuing as lovers wouldn't ruin her any more than the night they'd already spent together. His instincts were screaming at him that he should never touch her again, yet she undermined his willpower as no woman ever had.

He must master himself before anything more happened. Good Lord, what would Lady Agnes say if she knew he was sleeping with Ashton's sister? He shuddered.

Kirkland entered, looking drawn and tired. He didn't object when Cassie filled a plate for him and added a glass of wine. "Mac, after getting your note earlier, there's now a watch on Rupert Swinnerton. Cassie, have you and Rob learned anything interesting?"

She nodded. "We've identified the boxer who died. He was a Dublin prizefighter who went by the name Ruffian O'Rourke. He came to London to make his fortune but wasn't good enough to be really successful, so he drifted into doing less legal work."

Kirkland grimaced. "Then it's time to plan Mac's funeral. If it were held in London, too many people would want to attend, which will complicate matters when he returns to life. I'll put a notice in the paper that the funeral will be out of town. O'Rourke's body will be sent back to Dublin, where he can be buried under his own name."

"You wrote Will?" Mac asked. He could deal with the complications of other people thinking he was dead, but not Will, the only real family he had.

"The morning after your alleged death," Kirkland assured him. "He should have my letter before any London newspapers reach Spain." He glanced at Cassie and Carmichael. "Did you learn enough about O'Rourke's associates to provide a lead to the kidnappers?"

"We should know more in a day or two," Carmichael said.

Kirkland nodded, and discussion became general. When the meal was done and the investigators were leaving to prepare for another evening of work, Kirkland said, "Mackenzie, will you stay a moment? I need to speak with you."

Being called Mackenzie wasn't good. Warily Mac obeyed, wondering what Kirkland had to say that the others didn't need to hear.

The other man waited till the door to the dining room closed and the two of them were alone before he said in an edged voice, "I do hope I won't have to explain to Ashton that it's my fault you seduced his sister."

Mac felt the blood drain from his face. "What gave you a notion like that?"

"I'm not a fool," Kirkland said in a clipped voice. "You're both practically radiating lust, and the work you're doing throws you together entirely too much. She's an innocent girl, so I suppose it's not surprising that she's intrigued by a dashing rogue, but you damned well know better than to play games with her."

If Kirkland thought Kiri was innocent, he clearly didn't know what she was really like. Nor did he seem to know what had happened the night before, which was a relief. Kirkland usually knew everything.

"I know what Lady Kiri is," Mac retorted. "If we truly respected her youth and position, we wouldn't have allowed her to take part in this investigation."

Kirkland's mouth tightened. "I regret that it was necessary."

"Nonetheless, you were willing to take her on," Mac pointed out. "Duty is a hard taskmaster. To be honest, I'm glad I didn't have to choose between taking advantage of her bloodhound talents and keeping her safely in her own world. But don't blame me because she's here."

"It wasn't an easy decision, but the stakes were high." Kirkland's eyes showed his weariness. He'd made too many difficult decisions in his years of hidden service.

Mac's sympathy ended when Kirkland added, "Save your seductions for the worldly women at Damian's. You'll be back there in a few weeks. Surely you can go that long without a woman."

Even if Mac hadn't been celibate for several years, the remark ignited his temper. "We can't all be happy living like monks," he snapped.

Without moving a muscle, Kirkland's expression changed to white rage.

Kicking himself for having trespassed on the unmentionable past, Mac said, "Sorry. That was uncalled for."

"An understatement," Kirkland growled.

"Give Lady Kiri credit for knowing her own mind," Mac said, trying to sound conciliatory. "She's intelligent, worldly, and not all that young. Most women her age are married with children."

"I know you're right." Kirkland sighed. "But she isn't just any intrepid young woman. She's special."

"She is." Thinking of what had happened the night before, Mac continued, "If it makes you feel better, I promise not to seduce her." It had been quite the other way around. "My job is to protect her, not ruin her."

Kirkland collected his hat in preparation for leaving. "I'm sorry for not trusting you on this. I know better, but it's been a demanding week."

"For all of us. Now if that's all, I'll be off to some more gambling hells with the lady in question."

Kirkland nodded, and Mac left the room. He'd been upset the night before when Kiri had chosen her words carefully to imply something different from the truth. A lie in intent if not words. Now he'd just done the same thing with Kirkland.

Starkly he faced his abominable behavior. He had succumbed to Kiri's delicious self the night before, but he must not let that happen again.

He knew what the right thing was. He just wasn't sure if he could do it.

Chapter 25

As they headed upstairs, Kiri said to Cassie, "We're going to a place called Madame Blanche's tonight, and Mac said I should ask you for help with a disguise. Should I be a doxy or a lady?"

Cassie pursed her lips. "More of a lady. Blanche's house is something like Damian's in that she attracts the well born who want their pleasures with refinement. So you might find your Alejandro man there, but it's also more likely that you could be recognized by someone who has seen you at *ton* events."

"I've been in England only since spring and am not well known," Kiri protested.

"But your appearance is distinctive. You must look more ordinary. I'll collect some things for your disguise and meet you in your room." As she turned toward her room, Cassie added, "Wear the gold gown. It's more respectable than the green one."

"Not by much!"

The other woman grinned. "Respectable enough for Madame Blanche. Now to make sure that no one recognizes you as a duke's daughter."

The gold evening gown had a higher neckline than the

green silk, but it was definitely not the sort of dress worn by young maidens. That was fine with Kiri, since white muslin was boring.

Cassie appeared in time to help Kiri into the garment. "This makes you look older and more worldly, which is good," she said as she fastened a tie. "You also need a wig to change your coloring. I brought a couple with me."

She held both up. One that was medium brown with a sprinkling of gray hairs. The other was lighter brown and cut in a short, curly style.

"This one." Kiri took the curly wig. "I've always wondered how I'd look with short hair."

"No one with hair like yours should cut it, but you'll need to pin it tightly to wear a wig." Cassie produced a handful of hairpins.

After the hair was pinned and the wig settled in place, Cassie said, "I'm going to powder your face heavily. That will lighten your skin to match the wig. It will also make you look like mutton trying to disguise yourself as lamb."

"When instead I'm lamb disguising myself as mutton." Kiri patted her curly head. "I've even got lamb's curls."

Cassie opened her cosmetics box and went to work. When she was satisfied, she said, "Look at yourself in the mirror."

Kiri obeyed, and gave a gasp of astonishment. She literally did not recognize the pale Englishwoman in the mirror. Cassie had drawn dark lines around her mouth and in the corners of her eyes, then powdered over them to give the effect of poorly disguised wrinkles. Something had also been done to make her eyes less vividly green. "I look at least ten years older and English. My own mother would have trouble recognizing me."

Cassie gave a nod of satisfaction. "That's the point."

Kiri opened her perfume case and took out a bottle. "This is my own modest contribution to changing my appearance. The fragrance is light and flowery, quite different from what I usually wear. Scent is part of how we recognize people, though not everyone is aware of that." She applied some of the scent, then offered it to Cassie.

The other woman sniffed. "Very pleasant and it goes with those curls, but I see what you mean. You don't smell like you." She trailed her fingers hesitantly over other bottles in the case. "I didn't realize how little I knew about scents."

Recognizing yearning, Kiri pulled out one of her finished perfumes. "Try this. It might suit you."

The scent was complex, with frangipani laid over darker notes of cedar and frankincense that hinted at unknown depths of character. Cassie's face lit up when she smelled it. "This is marvelous! May I wear some tonight?"

"You may have the bottle. I call it Wood Song."

"It's lovely." Cassie dabbed some on the base of her throat. "It reminds me of . . ." Her face shuttered. "Thank you. I shall cherish it."

"I'd like to make a custom perfume just for you," Kiri said.

"Perhaps someday. But first we must save England." Cassie's voice had a hint of self-mockery.

It was sobering to think that the fate of the nation might rest in Kiri's inexperienced hands. Or rather, her highly trained nose. "I'm only useful here because I happened to witness the attempted kidnapping. You and the other agents I've met are true heroes even though your work is done behind the scenes."

"You make agents sound more romantic than we are." Cassie's mouth twisted. "It's dreary, often sordid work. The kind that grinds away youth and optimism."

"Working as a scullery maid will do the same, and to less purpose." Kiri draped her cloak over her arm. "Time to go. Good hunting."

"The same to you."

Kiri descended to the ground floor and headed for the front parlor, where she was to meet Mackenzie. She opened the door to see a tired old gentleman sitting by the fire reading a newspaper.

Knowing better than to accept anyone in the house at face value, she asked brightly, "Are you my escort for the evening, sir? I was told that a handsome, virile young man would take me to Madame Blanche's house this evening. It appears I've been deceived."

Mackenzie glanced over his newspaper, letting his own grin show. "And I was told I'd be taking a choice young wench," he said in a raspy voice. "Did you see her upstairs? Rather tall and dark-haired and elegant?"

"No such wench here," she said as she admired Mackenzie's disguise. He set aside the newspaper and got to his feet. His hair was mostly gray and his back was hunched with age. No eye patch tonight, but spectacles obscured his eyes so that his mismatched eyes weren't noticeable. And he leaned on a cane. Dropping into her own voice, she said, "People will think I'm your daughter."

"As long as they don't recognize either of us." He took her cloak and set it on her shoulders. "Will you give an old man an evening of pleasure?"

"Only if you promise not to die of a heart seizure at the end." She took his arm and they left the parlor. Respectable life had never been so enjoyable as this.

Kiri was surprised to find that Madame Blanche's exclusive salon was on the edge of fashionable Mayfair. As they climbed the steps, Mackenzie said under his breath, "Blanche is a widow who had to fend for herself and her children after her husband's death. She's done a better job of supporting her family than the late lamented ever did.

Patrons of Damian's often come here as well, which is why I took special pains with my appearance. You might meet people here from your family's social circle."

"If so, they won't recognize me," she said in a flat Midlands accent. "But it sounds like you know the lady fairly well. Will she recognize you?"

"Possibly. If she does, she won't say anything. Very discreet is Madame Blanche." He wielded the heavy door knocker.

They were admitted by a footman, who accepted a swiftly passed entrance payment and took Kiri's cloak and Mackenzie's greatcoat. As they moved into a large gaming room full of laughing, talking people, Madame Blanche greeted them.

The gaming house proprietress was of indeterminate age, and she had the shrewd eyes that Kiri was learning were the mark of the breed. Her casual glance as she introduced herself was stilled when she looked at Mackenzie. A spark showed in her eyes, but her expression gave nothing away. She treated them like new customers, gave them an idea of the delights within, and sent them on to enjoy themselves.

They moved off, Mackenzie using his cane with one hand while Kiri held his other arm. She whispered, "Good that Madame is discreet."

"Indeed." Raising his voice, he said, "Shall we look around before settling down to a game, my dear?"

"I'd like that. This is such a lovely house."

He slanted an amused glance from behind his spectacles and they set off to explore. There were almost as many women as men present and the crowd was lively, making enough noise that Kiri and Mackenzie could talk if they kept their voices down.

Kiri was able to get close enough to other guests to

identify their colognes and perfumes. She attracted some glances, but only a few, and they were more casual than when she was her usual self. She had become safely unmemorable.

When they entered the first card room, she caught a whiff of Alejandro. Her senses went on full alert. The smell didn't seem quite right for the man she sought, but she still moved toward the table where the scent originated. Using her best brainless voice, she said, "What is this game, darling?"

"Baccarat. It's a French game. Do you wish to try it?" He used the indulgent tone of a man who knew his woman was not very intelligent, and who preferred it that way.

"Oh, no. I was just curious." She started walking again.

As they moved away, he asked, "What did you sense?"

"Alejandro, though not on the right person." She shrugged. "That woman with the gray hair wore it. There is no law saying a woman can't wear a man's scent."

She batted her lashes at him. "Can we watch the dancing for a while?"

"Very well." He sighed. "Sorry I'm too decrepit to dance, lass."

"That doesn't matter." But it did matter, Kiri realized wistfully as they entered the ballroom. She found herself marking time to the music with her free hand. A pity she and Mackenzie couldn't join the quadrille, for they might never have another chance. But given Mackenzie's apparent infirmity, they must remain on the sidelines.

They promenaded around the ballroom, staying close to the walls to keep out of the way of the dancers. Most were fairly young and energetic, but a few older couples had joined in. As she looked at a white-haired couple, she wondered what it would be like to be that old and still dancing together.

That wouldn't happen for her and Mackenzie. He

belonged to another world, and he wasn't the marrying kind. But he was hers for now. That was enough.

They were halfway around the ballroom when she caught a scent that turned her rigid. Feeling the change in her touch, he asked, "What?"

"That group of men we just passed," she said softly. "Let's move back a few steps and pause. She sniffed carefully, watching the men out of the corner of her eye. When she was sure, she took Mackenzie's arm and began walking again.

When they were a safe distance away, he asked, "Could you determine more?"

She frowned. "One of those men wore Alejandro, and the scent was almost exactly right. But . . . not quite. I don't think he's the right man. Also, he isn't tall enough. The one in the dark blue coat with his back turned to the dancing."

"I know him," Mackenzie murmured. "Lord Fendall. He's on our suspect list. He's a regular at Damian's and a friend of my manager, Baptiste, but I don't know much about him except that he's a gambling man who wins and loses large sums of money. Kirkland is the one who put him on our suspect list. I'm not sure why."

"If he's a friend of your manager, he might know the back passages of Damian's," Kiri speculated. "But he's still not tall enough. He's also too broad."

"Like Rupert Swinnerton, he needs to be watched closely. Too many coincidences." Mackenzie frowned. "Do individual scents change enough day to day that at another time, he might smell as you remember?"

Kiri hesitated. "Perhaps. But he's still not tall enough, and he just doesn't feel right. I don't think he was one of the kidnappers. But perhaps he associates with them."

"The trouble with being dead is that I can't talk to

Baptiste about Fendall," Mac muttered. "Kirkland will
have to do it."

"We seem to be making progress, so you won't be dead
much longer." That would be good for Mackenzie, but not
so good for Kiri, who would have to return to her normal
routine. Life in the country would be very tame after this.

Enough people were coming and going at Madame
Blanche's that they stayed till after midnight so Kiri could
check out all the guests. She found no other possibilities.

They were leaving the house at the same time as several
other groups when she caught one of the scents she'd been
looking for. Garlic, Frenchness, a perfume she couldn't
name but clearly remembered.

Her nails bit into Mackenzie's arm as they descended
the steps to street level and her eyes darted about as she
tried to identify the source of the scent. Mackenzie said
quietly, "Who?"

Her gaze fastened on a pair of broad shoulders belonging to a man heading down the street on his own. "Him,"
she whispered. "He smells exactly like the Frenchman who
was at Damian's."

"I think it's Paul Clement, from our suspect list. Convenient that he's heading toward our carriage." Though he
still used his cane, Mackenzie's pace quickened.

They passed their hackney at a fast walk, and Kiri saw
their driver come alert as they followed their man around the
corner into an empty side street. "I'll talk to him," she said
under her breath. Raising her voice, she said, "Sir? Sir? I do
believe we've met, haven't we? At Almack's, perhaps?"

The man ahead hesitated, then turned. Warily he said in
fluent but French-accented English, "I do not believe I've
had that pleasure, madame." He bowed gracefully. "I

would never have forgotten so lovely a lady. Now if you'll excuse me . . ."

By this time, they were close enough that Kiri could catch his scent. *Yes!* And he had the scar on his left cheek. Compact and conservatively dressed, he didn't look like a French agent, but she had learned that being unmemorable was part of an agent's stock in trade. "He's the one," she told Mackenzie. "I have no doubts."

Hearing the hard note in her voice, the Frenchman sprang into action. He whipped a pistol out from under his coat and cocked it. "I don't know who you think I am, but I assure you that I am of no interest. If your aim is robbery, I suggest you find an easier victim, because I will not hesitate to shoot."

Before Clement had finished speaking, Mackenzie swung his cane like a club. The weighted end smashed into the Frenchman's hand, damaging flesh and bone and sending the pistol skittering along the street.

Kiri dived for the weapon while Mackenzie went for Clement, all traces of age and infirmity gone. Swearing in French, Clement fought to escape, but Mackenzie used his cane to block the other man's furious blows.

The fight ended when Mackenzie twisted the other man's arms behind his back and Kiri cocked the gun and pointed it at Clement's heart. "Be still," she ordered. "Or you will never move again."

Clement stopped fighting, his expression flat. Mackenzie snapped something metallic behind the Frenchman's back, then moved away. "He's handcuffed, but keep a close eye while I search him."

"You were carrying handcuffs?" Kiri said, startled.

"One never knows when they'll be useful," Mackenzie said as he searched Clement. Kiri grinned. Someday she would like to go through all the pockets of his greatcoat. Heaven only knew what she'd find.

Mackenzie removed a knife and some papers, then gestured toward their carriage, which had followed them into the side street. The driver held the reins in one hand and a shotgun in the other. A useful man, as Mackenzie had said.

Opening the carriage door, Mackenzie said, "Get in. Is Paul Clement your real name? Or is that a *nom de l'espionage*?"

"I am Paul Clement, but I have no idea what you're talking about," the Frenchman said coldly. He appeared to be in his forties, and Kiri guessed he had nerves of hammered steel.

Temper flaring, Kiri stepped forward and jabbed the barrel of the pistol into his midriff. The scar, the scent, the build—this was the man. "Don't try to lie your way out of this!" she said. "I saw you at Damian's."

A flicker showed in his eyes, but his face remained blank. "It is a place I frequent, madame, as do many others. I didn't realize that was a crime."

"It isn't," she said softly. "But kidnapping and murder are."

"He won't talk to you," Mackenzie said. "But we have associates who are very persuasive. They will be able to find out what he knows. If Monsieur Clement is cooperative, he won't even lose any body parts."

She wasn't sure if Mackenzie was serious, or if his aim was to intimidate their prisoner. It would take more than words to frighten Clement. She stepped back and lowered the gun, though she kept it cocked.

Mackenzie bundled the Frenchman into the carriage and gave an address to their driver. Kiri climbed in, keeping the pistol aimed at the spy. He said dryly, "I hope that Madame won't accidentally shoot me if we hit a bump in the street."

"When I shoot men, it's never an accident. One of your kidnappers at Damian's learned that." Not that Kiri had done any shooting, but she liked sounding ruthless. "Were you at Madame Blanche's to speak with Lord Fendall? Or was it someone else?"

Ignoring her question, he gazed out into the darkness. "I always knew the end would come," he said in a distant voice. "I just did not know that it would come tonight."

He said no more. The carriage took them to an anonymous building near Whitehall. Mackenzie helped Clement out of the hackney and took him inside. As she waited for Mackenzie to return, Kiri wondered what would happen to the Frenchman. With an urgent need for information, interrogation methods would also be urgent.

Knowing the man would probably be tortured turned her stomach. But if torture was required, she hoped that at least they'd get the information needed to stop the plot.

Chapter 26

Kiri was yawning when Mac returned to the carriage. As they started back to Exeter Street, she asked, "What happens to Clement now?"

"He was locked in a cell. As soon as Kirkland arrives, the interrogation will begin." Which meant Kirkland would have another night without sleep. Mac knew from experience that his friend's endurance was impressive. But every man had his limits.

After a long pause, Kiri asked, "Torture? Thumbscrews, the rack, hot irons on the soles of the feet?"

"Certainly not as a first resort." Mac frowned. "Torture probably wouldn't do much good. Clement seemed aware of the hazards of his occupation. I don't think he would break easily."

"That was my impression. "

"I'll join the interrogation in the morning." He looked at her, unable to see her expression in the darkness of the carriage. "Do you wish to come also?"

"Am I needed?"

"No. You've provided the identification. No more is required of you. Unless you want to come?"

"I think I will stay inside and write letters and make

perfume until we venture out tomorrow evening." She sighed. "Tonight brought home that this is not a game. Because of me, a man is imprisoned and might die. It's . . . sobering. Very cold-blooded compared to injuring or killing in self-defense."

"It's the nature of this work. The enemy seeks intelligence about us, we seek to counter them. It's a great chess game."

"I think assassination is in another category," she said. "Stealing information is one thing. Stealing lives another."

"I agree." Though stolen information could end up costing many lives. "Particularly the lives of sixteen-year-old girls."

"Which is where we come in." She took his hand.

Mac interlaced his fingers with hers, glad for her touch. "If Clement tells us who the other conspirators are, this could be over in a day or two." And then Lady Kiri Lawford could go back to her life, and he could return to his. Alone.

When they reached Exeter Street, Kiri kept hold of Mackenzie's hand as they went inside. After the night's excitement, she yearned to go into his arms, but thought she could just about manage discretion until they were safe and private in her room.

At the top of the stairs, she glanced toward the front of the house and saw a shadowed man scratch at Cassie's door. Rob Carmichael. Cassie opened the door and went into his arms. They kissed urgently, then moved into her room.

As the door closed behind them, Kiri whispered, "Are they having an affair?"

"They are friends and comrades." Mackenzie took her arm and guided her down the hall to her own room. "What they do behind closed doors is their business."

"Yes, but it's *interesting!*" As he guided her into her room and shut the door behind them, Kiri tried to imagine the laconic Carmichael and Cassie together. "Despite the evidence, it's hard to see them as lovers. They both seem so serious."

"There are many kinds of lover." He moved to the hearth and laid a fire. As slow flames caught, he stood, a tall, dark shadow etched by light. "Both have survived things that would destroy lesser souls. If they find comfort in each other's arms for now, it's a gift not to be wasted."

Kiri interpreted that to mean that Cassie and Carmichael shared a bed, but not a lifetime commitment. She supposed the same could be said of her and Mackenzie. This sweetness and passion might be brief, but it was very real. Before last night, she hadn't really understood the power of desire. Now she wished the other agents joy for however long they could find it together.

If catching Clement broke up the conspiracy, she and Mackenzie would have only a few more nights together. Desperate not to waste a single moment, she slid an arm around his waist, raising her face for a kiss. "Then let us not waste this gift."

He gave her the lightest of kisses, then broke away, putting a yard of distance between them. "You're going to bed alone, Kiri."

Her mouth dropped. "But I thought you'd agreed we would be lovers for now!"

"Actually, I didn't agree," he said ruefully. "It's just that I was unable to resist you last night. But my misgivings didn't go away. They got worse. It doesn't help that Kirkland sensed something between us and tore a few strips from my hide. Thank God he didn't know what really happened."

"Kirkland is not my father or brother!" she exclaimed,

not believing Mackenzie would walk away from what they'd shared. "He has no right to condemn me."

"He's not condemning you, but me," Mackenzie said dryly. "You are the injured innocent, I the heedless seducer."

Her jaw dropped. "You know better than that!"

"Indeed I do. You are a strong, independent woman, sure of your own mind." He frowned, searching for words. "But when Kirkland accepted your aid in this hunt, he also pledged your family that he would protect you as if you were under your father's roof. He trusted me not to ruin you, and I failed. But I will not fail again."

"I felt no dishonor last night." She caught his hands, sure she could change his mind. "Did you?"

He hesitated. "Passion clouds the judgment. Last night I wasn't thinking about honor. Either yours or mine. Tonight I have no such excuse."

She wrapped herself around him, pressing into his beautiful, hard male body. He wanted her as much as she wanted him; the evidence was right there. "How can another night ruin me any more than I have already been ruined?"

"No!" He jerked away, his breathing ragged. "Imagine that our genders were reversed. If you were male and I was female and you were pressuring me to lie with you even though it was against my conscience and honor—what would you call that?"

She jerked as if he'd slapped her. After a long, shaky moment, she admitted, "I would say that . . . that my behavior is not that of a gentleman."

"And you'd be right," he said softly. "You must know that I want you as much as you want me. But not like this."

"What is honor?" she asked helplessly. "How can it be wrong to desire each other so much?"

"The desire isn't wrong. Acting on that desire is." He ran stiff fingers through his hair. "Men define honor in different ways, and by most standards, I haven't much of it. I don't have an honorable family name, I left the army in dishonorable circumstances, I live my life in the demimonde. I dare not throw away what little honor I have left."

She realized that she could probably change his mind. His desire showed in every line of his body. If she drew on the allure her womenfolk were famous for, she could fracture his resistance and soon they'd be lying naked in her bed, mindless with passion and fulfillment.

But that would damage him deeply. Mackenzie had hammered out his own hard-won code of honor, and it would be utterly wrong of her to deprive him of that. Hands clenched, she said, "Very well. I shall not injure your honor further."

He exhaled roughly with relief. "Thank God. Because I really can't resist you."

"I know." Her mouth twisted. "It is equally hard for me to resist you. Tonight I shall sleep alone and ponder the meanings of honor. But first, please unfasten this gown. I can't get out of it without help." She turned and presented her rigid back, which gave her the advantage of concealing her eyes. Her instinct told her that he would be very susceptible to tears. They could keep apart only if neither of them weakened.

"Thank you for understanding," he said quietly. He unfastened ties and removed the pins quickly. Though he touched her as little as possible, the brush of his fingertips sent shivers down her spine. She wondered if the process was as hard for him as it was for her. Very likely.

"Good night, my lady," he said as the bodice loosened and slid down her shoulders. Before she could turn around, she heard the door close behind him.

Kiri finished undressing and donned the embroidered

cotton nightgown that she hadn't bothered with the night before. Even with the fire, the room was very cold now that Mackenzie was gone.

She slid between the chilly sheets, feeling bleak. She had always been good at getting what she wanted, but she was also generous by nature. She loved giving things to others, whether gifts or kind words. That generosity had disguised her basic selfishness. Now she'd been forced to recognize that some of the things she wanted, she should not be allowed to have. Not when the cost was too high for someone else.

She was staring at the ceiling, telling herself that she must not cry. Tears would do no good, and a night of them would leave her with a red nose in the morning. She had wanted to make love with a man she cared about as a way of having what she'd never shared with Charles. She had achieved that. To want more was greedy and selfish and destructive. *Wrong.*

A small thump on the bed was followed by steps that moved to Kiri's side. Once more Puss had managed to join her. The cat curled up under her left arm, purring robustly. Kiri smiled and some of her tension faded as she scratched the cat's neck.

At least she didn't have to sleep alone.

Chapter 27

Mac and Kirkland arrived at the nondescript building at the same time. "You had a busy night," Kirkland said as they went inside, out of the dripping rain. "You found one prospect for heightened surveillance, and one capture."

"What do you know about Clement?" Mac asked as he removed his coat and shook water off before hanging it up. He followed Kirkland into his friend's office.

"He's lived in London for years. He claimed to be a fugitive from the French Republicans, and he supports himself with a tailor shop. No family, few if any close friends, but he sometimes socialized at a couple of the émigré taverns."

"Have you found any suggestion that he's been a spy all along?"

Kirkland gave a knife-edged hunter's smile. "I have some evidence that he was acquiring information from a source at Whitehall. I imagine that was his main work, but since he's here in London, he was probably recruited to help with the kidnapping and assassination plot. Can you tell me anything about him?"

"Only that he's tough and controlled and won't give up information easily."

"The ones who do it for money are so much easier," Kirkland muttered. "All you need do is offer a higher price. Patriots are much more difficult."

He rang a bell, and a few moments later a silent servant brought in a coffee tray with a steaming pot, three pewter mugs, a plate of buns, and cream and sugar containers.

"Mac, will you carry the tray down? I want to be free to break a bone or two if Clement tries to escape."

Mac lifted the tray. He was good at bone breaking, but Kirkland, despite his sleek, civilized appearance, was better.

The small building was the headquarters of Kirkland's very secret intelligence agency. He reported to a high member of the government. Even Mac didn't know who. Nor did he want to know. He helped when needed, but it was Kirkland who had the cool, calculating spymaster brain.

Lantern in hand, Kirkland led the way down to the cellar, which contained two very solid cells with the best available locks and doors. No prisoner had ever escaped. Kirkland nodded to the guard, then used his key to open the right-hand door.

The cell was small and dark, but not actually wet, and a sliver of light came from a window high on the wall. Clement had been lying on the cot, but he came swiftly to his feet, his face wary. "The executioner arrives."

"Being French doesn't mean you have to be melodramatic," Kirkland said acerbically. "Would you like some coffee?"

"Anything hot would be welcome."

Mac set the tray on one end of the cot and poured three mugs, glad to have one himself. Several minutes were spent as they all prepared their coffee.

Clement drank a whole mug in several swallows, then poured more. "Good coffee, for an Englishman."

"It was made by a French émigré. The real kind, not the false sort who are spies," Kirkland said.

Clement's face shuttered. "Now that I am fortified, you will begin beating me for answers?"

"Inflicting pain isn't my first preference," Kirkland said. "Though as you see, I brought my torturer with me."

Mac almost choked on his coffee to hear himself described in such a way, but he managed to conceal his surprise. He narrowed his eyes and tried to look ruthless.

It didn't work. Clement had paid him no attention at first, but now he studied Mac closely. "Ah, the gentleman who captured me and is no longer feeble. You are a torturer? I would have thought your lady friend more dangerous."

"She is," Mac said. "Be grateful I came instead."

Kirkland continued, "You are a professional agent, Monsieur Clement. You have always known that to be captured is to face near-certain death."

Clement took a bun from the tray, trying to look casual, but his hand had a tremor. "I know. Since you will kill me anyhow, I prefer it be done quickly. I will not betray France, and given a choice, I would rather avoid pointless pain."

"Wouldn't we all?" Kirkland murmured. "I respect your loyalty to your country. That makes you harder to deal with than a man who wants only money, but easier to admire. I would rather not have you killed, so perhaps we can work something out."

Clement's brows arched, but he couldn't conceal a flicker of hope. "Since I won't betray my country, what grounds do we have to negotiate?"

"Countries at war regularly steal information from each other. It's part of the game," Kirkland said. "Do you think the game should also include murder and kidnapping? Particularly if one of the victims is a sixteen-year-old girl?"

Clement's mouth tightened. "That was not my plan. I was only a liaison."

"A liaison," Kirkland said thoughtfully. "So there is a

French end to this plan, and an English end, and you were the go-between."

Clement frowned when he realized that he had given that away, but he didn't speak. Kirkland continued, "So going after the British royal family wasn't your plan. Nonetheless, you condoned it. How does that square with your conscience? Surely you've lived in England long enough to know that this plan won't bring us to the peace table. Quite the contrary."

"Britain would be better off without the prince regent and his wastrel brothers. The girl was not supposed to be harmed," Clement said defensively. "I would have made sure of that."

"But you can no longer do that since I have removed you from the game board," Kirkland pointed out. "Do you trust your comrades to be equally careful? Or might they decide that if they can't kidnap her, assassination will do?"

The Frenchman looked away, his discomfort visible. "If you are concerned for her safety, release me so I can protect her if future attempts are made."

"You know that won't happen." Kirkland surveyed the other man's expression. "I have a proposition for you."

Clement's gaze returned to Kirkland. "Yes?"

"I won't ask you to betray your country, but you might ponder on whether it would be betrayal to give up your murderous associates in this particular plot. They are dangerous fools, more likely to harm France than to aid her."

"If I decide I agree with your viewpoint, what do I gain? An easier death?"

"Your freedom, though not right away. You would be sent to a more pleasant prison until the war is over. That will surely come in a year or two. Your emperor is already on the run. When he surrenders, you can go home to France." Kirkland smiled gently. "You can even stay in London if you choose. Good tailors are hard to find."

"How can I believe that you will fulfill your end of the bargain?" Clement asked after a long pause.

"You will have my word."

The Frenchman's lips twisted. "Would a fine gentleman like you feel bound to honor a promise to the son of a tailor?"

"Would the son of a tailor feel bound to honor a promise to a gentleman?" Kirkland offered his hand. "Trust has nothing to do with station in life."

"It is . . . ironic that I feel I can trust an English enemy more than my English allies," Clement said slowly. "I do not know if I can do what you ask. But I shall consider it. And . . . I believe that you are a man of your word." He took Kirkland's hand.

After they shook hands, Kirkland said, "Provide me with some useful information, and I will transfer you to a less dismal prison. But time is not unlimited. If one of the royal family is killed or kidnapped, my offer is withdrawn."

"Understood." Clement's mouth twisted. "Thumbscrews might have been easier."

"Neither of us were put on this earth to make life easier for the other." Kirkland glanced at Mac. "Leave him one mug and the buns."

In other words, nothing the prisoner could use for a weapon. In theory, a pewter mug could be made into a knife, but it would take time and tools. Mac poured the last of the coffee into Clement's mug, then gathered the tray and other mugs.

They left the cell, Kirkland carefully locking it behind him. He said to the guard, "I left a mug with the prisoner. Be sure it's collected later."

They headed upstairs. When they were back in Kirkland's office, Mac said, "Think he'll tell you something useful?"

"He might. It's clear he doesn't like being part of an assassination plot, and he might decide that killing princesses is not in France's best interest." Kirkland shrugged. "Reason seemed a better policy than force."

"If he decides to accept your offer, I hope he does it soon," Mac said. "With their liaison vanished, the other plotters will go to ground and be harder to locate."

"Perhaps they will be alarmed enough to give up their plotting."

Mac's brows arched. "Surely you don't believe that."

"It's unlikely." Kirkland gave a rare smile. "But hope springs eternal."

Chapter 28

The next morning was gray, wet, and autumnal, which suited Kiri's mood. She wondered how she and Mackenzie would react when they met again. It would not be easy. Warily she descended to the dining room, but only Cassie was there. The other woman looked a little tired, but with a slight smile on her face. She must have enjoyed having Carmichael share her bed the night before.

Remembering that Mackenzie had been going to join Kirkland to question the Frenchman, Kiri greeted Cassie and helped herself to beans and bacon and toast, along with lots of steaming-hot tea.

Cassie asked, "Did you have any success at Madame Blanche's?"

Between bites of breakfast, Kiri told her about Lord Fendall, who smelled almost but not quite right, and their capture of the Frenchman. She was just finishing when Mackenzie entered the room.

Her nerves tensed and she wondered if he'd slept as badly as she had. Her hand less than steady, she poured herself more tea. Having Cassie present helped her maintain her composure. "Did you have any luck interrogating Clement?"

"It's too soon to tell." He set a pile of letters on the table. "These were just delivered by a footman."

Seeing the general's handwriting on the top letter, Kiri shuffled through the pile. "I wrote everyone in my family so they wouldn't think anything dreadful had happened to me. Maybe there's also something for you, Cassie."

The other woman didn't look up from her plate. "I never get letters."

"Do you mind if I join you for breakfast?" Mackenzie asked. "I had buns and coffee with Kirkland and the French spy, but a cold day requires more fuel."

"By all means, help yourself and tell us about the interrogation," Cassie said.

"Kirkland handled Clement beautifully." Mac piled the remaining bacon and toast on the plate containing beans, then poured himself tea and sat down. Between bites, he described Kirkland's strategy.

Cassie nodded approvingly at the end. "Offering respect and pointing out the dishonorable side of the current plot was wise. I hope Clement can clear it with his conscience to tell us who the other conspirators are."

Kiri nodded as she flipped through the letters to see who had written. "I'm glad torture isn't being used. I don't think I'm ruthless enough to be a proper agent."

"Torture isn't usually that helpful," Mac said. "Someone in pain will tell you anything he thinks you want to hear."

"That makes sense." Curious, Kiri lifted a letter with unfamiliar handwriting on expensive cream-colored paper "Good heavens! Is this a royal seal?" She held up the letter to show the others the wax seal.

"Looks royal to me," Cassie said with interest. "Open it!"

Kiri broke the seal and found a formal note from Her

Royal Highness Charlotte Augusta requesting the presence
of Lady Kiri Lawford for tea at Warwick House.

The invitation was written in the beautiful flowing hand
of a secretary, but underneath. in young, unformed writing, was a note from the princess herself.

> *Dear Lady Kiri,*
>   *I would so like to see you before I leave for Windsor!*
> *When you come, could you wear a sari gown in the*
> *style of the ladies of India? I would like to see one.*
>   *Yrs affectionately,*
>   *HRH Princess Charlotte Augusta*

Dazed, Kiri passed the letter to Cassie, who read it out
loud. "I'm impressed, Kiri. Did you notice that the date
she set was this afternoon?"

"*What?*" Kiri grabbed the letter and read it again. "This
was sent to my parents, so it took an extra day. This afternoon? I'll need a carriage!"

Mackenzie took it from her hand. "I'll send Kirkland a
note and he can send his best carriage over. There's not
much time to spare. Do you have a sari with you?"

"Actually, I do." Kiri bit her lip nervously. "I'll probably freeze, though. Saris aren't designed for English
weather."

"Wear a cloak, and remember that you've already met
the girl," Mackenzie said soothingly. "She's issuing the invitation, so she'll be happy to see you."

"I'll go as your maid," Cassie volunteered. "I will add
to your consequence."

"The daughter of a duke certainly needs her maid,"
Mackenzie agreed. "I'll ride on the coach as your footman."

Grateful she'd have friends with her, Kiri stood. "Send
for the carriage. I'll change now."

"Do you need help?" Cassie offered. "I've never seen a sari."

"No help required. Saris are easier to put on than English gowns," Kiri said. "Join me when you've transformed into a maid and I'll show you how a sari is worn."

They scattered in different directions, Mackenzie to summon a suitably grand carriage and Kiri and Cassie to dress. Kiri had added the sari to her baggage on impulse, since she had no idea what she would be doing while on this mission.

When she reached her room, she retrieved the sari ensemble from her luggage. There were three pieces: a seven-yard length of scarlet silk decorated with bands of gold embroidery, a matching ankle-length underskirt, and a matching blouse, called a *choli.* She didn't have the proper sandals, but evening slippers and silk stockings would do.

She donned stockings, underskirt, and *choli* and brushed out her hair, which she parted in the middle. Then she coiled the dark mass in a knot at the nape of her neck. Her cosmetics case contained the red paste needed for a bindi, so she carefully painted the red circle on her forehead.

There was a tap on the door. "Kiri? It's me, Cassie."

After Kiri called permission to enter, Cassie appeared in a severely cut brown gown and a maid's expression. The other woman eyed the skimpy *choli,* which was short-sleeved, cut low at the top, and ended several inches above the waist. "That bodice is pretty, but I see what you mean about being chilly."

"It's not much worse than a really fashionable English evening gown, but that's not saying much." Kiri lifted the rolled silk of the sari. "You're just in time for the grand event. This is one of my best saris. There are different styles of draping the fabric. My family is from the north, as any Indian will recognize by how I wear my sari."

Deftly she collected the plain end of the sari and wrapped it around herself, tucking it into the waist of the underskirt. Cassie watched with fascination as Kiri gathered and pleated and draped the decorated end of the material over her left shoulder so that it fell to the back of her knees.

"Properly speaking, I should let my navel show since that's the source of creativity and life." Kiri studied how the fabric fell as she looked in the mirror. "But that might be too provocative for England."

"It would be too much for Mackenzie," Cassie said with amusement. "I've seen how he looks at you. Show much more skin and he'll have a heart seizure."

Kiri glanced up swiftly. "I beg your pardon?"

"And you look back the same way." Cassie sighed. "It's understandable. You are young and share an exciting mission. But remember the future and don't get too close. You have a life beyond this work. You don't want to throw that away."

In other words, beware ruination. Irritated by how everyone felt qualified to offer unwanted advice, Kiri asked, "Does Mr. Carmichael look at you the same way?"

Cassie's brows arched, but she didn't look embarrassed. "You saw? No, we don't look at each other like that, but we are old and jaded. Friends, nothing more."

"Neither of you are that old, and you seemed rather more than friends."

"Old in spirit if not body." Cassie studied the perfume box. "And yes, more than friends. Rob and I are comrades. We have faced danger together."

Deciding that the nuances of Cassie and Rob's relationship were beyond her understanding and certainly none of her business, Kiri opened her jewelry case and selected elaborate dangling earrings with tiny chains of gold ending in sparkling chips of garnet that fell halfway to her shoulders. A sumptuous necklace of gold chains, a dozen bangle bracelets for each wrist. She would give Princess Charlotte a very good show.

Lastly, she reached inside herself for the core of her Hindu nature. Kiri could never match her mother's gentle acceptance, but she released that side of her that would never be English. Looking in the mirror, she made a final adjustment to the drape of the fabric over her shoulder, then turned to Cassie. "Do I look ready for royalty?"

"You look magnificent," Cassie said. "And very, very different. Your features and coloring may be the same, but you are no longer the same woman."

"No. I am not." Seeing herself like this was a powerful reminder of just how much separated her from Mackenzie. Not only the differences in class and birth, but also her dual nature. Could any Englishman understand that?

She thought of Mariah, Adam's wife. No one could be more golden and English in appearance, but she had an understanding heart. Godfrey Hitchcock had not.

If Kiri was ever to find a true mate, it must be a man of understanding and tolerance. The general understood India, and in Lakshmi, he had married the embodiment of the land where he'd spent over half his life. But men like him were rare.

Enough philosophy for now. "I want to take the princess a gift of perfume. There is no time to make a custom blend, but I thought she might like this." Kiri selected a bottle and offered it to Cassie. "What do you think?"

Cassie sniffed thoughtfully. "It is lovely. A young girl's perfume. It smells of innocence and hope."

"Which is not quite right for a girl whose parents fight over her like a bone, and who one day may rule England." Kiri surveyed her perfume box, wishing she had the resources of her full laboratory. Choosing a bottle of her own chypre blend, she said, "This might help."

She poured the young girl's perfume into her prettiest decorative bottle, a graceful spire of scarlet glass. Then she added a very small drop of chypre. After stoppering, she shook it, then took the stopper off. Better. "What do you think, Cassie?"

The other woman took a sniff and blinked. "Remarkable. The smell is more complex and there's an undertone of earthiness and . . . haunting sadness is the closest I can come to describing it."

"That's the effect I wanted." Kiri looked at the other bottles. Perhaps a trace of *fougère*—no, best quit now before she ruined it.

She had several lengths of narrow ribbon in the case, so she pulled out a silver one and tied it jauntily around the neck of the glass bottle. Then she wrapped the bottle in a square of white satin. A good thing she had come prepared. She even had a small embroidered silk bag with inset mirrors that she could use as a Hindu reticule. Tucking the perfume into the bag, she said, "Time to go and wait for the carriage."

"Let me carry my lady's cloak." Cassie fell instantly into servant mode, invisible and competent as she folded the blue cloak over her arm.

Amused, Kiri said, "You look more servantlike than any servant I've ever seen."

"I stand corrected." Cassie allowed herself a sliver of a smile and became slightly less invisible.

"You could have been an actress," Kiri said as she walked toward the door.

"I have been on occasion." Cassie opened the door for her temporary mistress.

Thinking graceful thoughts, Kiri left her room and glided downstairs, enjoying the cool slide of silk over her skin even though goose pimples were rising on her mostly bare arms and shoulders.

Mackenzie waited in the foyer. Hearing her footsteps, he said, "Good timing. The carriage just arrived." He glanced up at Kiri, and froze, looking as if he'd been clubbed. If he weren't healthy as a horse, she would worry that he might be having the heart seizure Cassie had jokingly suggested.

At the bottom of the steps, Kiri sank into a curtsey, at the same time pressing her open hands together in front of her breasts and bowing her head. *"Namaste, sahib."*

He swallowed hard and gave her a deep bow. "You are dangerous, my lady."

She laughed. "A sari is perhaps the most graceful garment ever invented. I trust that Princess Charlotte will enjoy the sight."

"She will." Mackenzie took the cloak from Cassie and placed it around Kiri's shoulders, sending tingles through her when his fingertips brushed her bare neck. "Now we must be off if you are to reach Warwick House at the appointed hour."

Kiri swept outside as he held the door for her. Life had certainly become much more interesting since she ran away from Godfrey Hitchcock.

Chapter 29

"Oh, my," Princess Charlotte breathed as Kiri entered her private drawing room. "You look splendid! Like a princess from an oriental fairy tale." The princess's height and full figure made her look older than sixteen, but the innocent enthusiasm in her eyes showed her true age. She was a girl who yearned to know more of the world.

Kiri curtsied, her sari shimmering fluidly around her. "Your Highness is most gracious. I thank you for your invitation."

"I wished to see you before moving my household to Windsor tomorrow." Charlotte made a face. "Life in the Lower Lodge there is even more boring than at Warwick House."

At least there would be no gambling clubs for the girl to sneak off to. And with luck, the Lower Lodge at Windsor would be in better repair than Warwick House. Kiri was shocked by how run-down this royal residence was.

The prince regent spent staggering amounts of money on his own palaces while condemning the heiress presumptive of England to a house the same size as 11 Exeter Street, and nowhere near as well kept. Keeping her opinion to herself, Kiri said, "At least you will be in the country, Your Highness. I understand you are a bruising rider?"

The princess grinned at the rather racy description. "Indeed I am. But I forget my manners. I'll ring for tea. Please, have a seat."

Kiri waited for the princess to sit first, then offered the silk-wrapped package. "I brought you a small gift. One of my perfumes."

Charlotte's eyes lit with pleasure as she unwrapped the bottle. She opened it immediately and sniffed. "Thank you so much! This smells lovely. What is it called?"

The princess was probably not a perfume connoisseur, but her appreciation was genuine. Kiri thought fast. "I call it Principessa, and I blended it just for you."

Her expression blissful, Charlotte applied some to her throat and wrists. "Will you make more when this is gone? I shall appoint you my official royal perfumer!"

Kiri smiled. "It will be my pleasure, but I am not a professional perfumer, so better that I don't have a title. This is just a small gift from one of your future subjects."

"Of course a woman of your rank can't be in trade," Charlotte agreed.

The conversation was interrupted as a maid entered with a tea tray. It took several minutes to pour the tea and set out a plate of mixed cakes. When they were alone again, the princess said, "I want to thank you for saving me the other night, but I also want to ask if you know what that kidnapping attempt was about. It wasn't random."

"No one explained?" Kiri asked, startled.

Charlotte's lips tightened into a thin line. "I was scolded ferociously by my father and told I must go to Windsor, but there were no explanations." After a simmering moment, she added, "How can I become a fit ruler when everyone treats me as a *child?*"

Kiri was appalled all over again. Charlotte might be

badly raised and ill-educated, but she was not stupid. She needed, and deserved, to be treated as an adult.

Though Kiri knew it would be the height of foolishness to come between the often petulant prince regent and his daughter, at the moment she was too angry to be careful. For her own safety, Charlotte needed to know of the threat. "This is very, very secret. You must speak of it to no one."

"You have my word." Charlotte looked older as she made her pledge.

"You were the target of a French plot against the British royal family," Kiri said succinctly. "They wanted to kidnap you and assassinate your father and his brothers. With the king unable to rule and the heir to the throne in captivity, there would be great confusion, and perhaps an opportunity to make peace on terms agreeable to France."

Charlotte gasped, her face turning pale. "It's . . . it's outrageous! How dare Napoleon do such a thing!"

"We don't know that the plot originated with Napoleon. However, I do know there has been an attempt on your father's life since the incident at Damian's." Reminding herself that she really must not criticize the prince regent, Kiri continued, "This is why you're being sent to Windsor. Your life is too precious to risk."

"Why didn't my father explain?" Charlotte asked plaintively.

Seeking a charitable interpretation, Kiri said, "My stepfather has said often that children grow more quickly than a father realizes, or really wants. The prince regent is a man like any other, and he must have wanted to avoid upsetting you."

Charlotte looked unconvinced. "I appreciate your telling me the truth, Lady Kiri." She looked wistful. "If I was allowed to have ladies-in-waiting, I'd appoint you."

"You are gracious indeed," Kiri said, glad that for the

time being, she was safe from the boredom of court life. If she had to attend the princess, whose existence was so narrow, she'd go mad. "When the time comes, there will be many worthy candidates eager for the honor."

"I would like to have my dear friend, Miss Elphinstone. But not yet." Charlotte frowned. "I do hope the conspirators are caught soon. I am to attend the state opening of Parliament in a fortnight."

Good heavens, did Kirkland know that? "It is not my place to say this, but surely it is not wise to attend so public an event. There will be great crowds, which kidnappers or assassins could take advantage of."

Charlotte lifted her chin. "This will be my first time in attendance. I will not cancel my appearance."

"You may not be safe," Kiri said bluntly. "If they can't kidnap you, they might choose assassination."

Charlotte looked frightened, but also stubborn and very royal. "A coward is not fit to rule England."

"That's hard to disagree with." Especially since Kiri did not want to treat Princess Charlotte as a child. She must be groomed to carry the great responsibilities likely to fall on her in the future. "There are very capable people dedicated to keeping you safe, but you must also be alert and aware of what's going on around you."

Charlotte's brows knit together. "If I hadn't responded to the kidnappers when I was called 'Your Highness,' they wouldn't have found me. Do you mean things like that?"

"Exactly. Our own good sense is our first defense." Kiri sipped on her tea, wondering how long she should stay. The protocol was a short visit, she thought. "Listen to your intuition. If a situation or a person seems not quite right, the chances are your mind has noticed something wrong even if you aren't quite conscious of it."

Charlotte sighed. "Because I'm a royal princess, most

people act oddly around me, so it can be hard to tell. But I shall attempt to follow your advice." Changing the subject, she said, "Your sari is so beautiful. How does it stay up?"

"There are pleats and folds, though it takes practice to wear one," Kiri replied. Discussing Indian clothing was a safely neutral topic. She stood and demonstrated how the sari was wrapped and tucked. After she judged twenty minutes had passed, she said, "I must be going, Your Highness. I'm sure you have much to do before leaving."

Charlotte sighed. "Indeed I do. Thank you for coming on short notice." As she got to her feet, she asked, "May I feel the silk of your sari? It looks so light."

"Of course." Kiri pulled the drape from behind her so the princess could touch it. "Some saris are so delicate they can be drawn through a ring. This one is a little heavier since England is cooler." Though not heavy enough.

Charlotte lifted a handful of the silk admiringly, releasing it to float down again. "When I am queen, I shall have a costume from each country I rule."

"That would be very gracious, Your Highness." Kiri curtsied. "Let me know when you need more perfume."

"I hope you will call again when I return to London." As Kiri took hold of the doorknob, Charlotte asked wistfully, "Will I be free and happy someday?"

"No one is entirely free unless they have nothing to lose, and few of us want to live that way." Kiri hesitated as she felt a swift flash of certainty. "But you will find love and happiness. I'm sure of it."

Charlotte's face lit up. "Thank you for that, Lady Kiri."

Kiri inclined her head and left the drawing room. Her flash of insight did indeed say Charlotte would find happiness, but also that it would be brief.

But at least she would have some happiness. That was an experience no sovereign was guaranteed.

* * *

Given the deteriorating weather, Mac was glad the royal visit was short. When Kiri emerged from Warwick House, the hood of her cloak was pulled up, obscuring her face. Cassie walked a demure two steps behind.

Mac wanted to ask if Kiri had learned anything interesting, but this was not a place to step outside his role of footman. He opened the door to the carriage and flipped down the steps so they could get out of the misty rain quickly.

Once the ladies were safely stowed, he climbed on his perch at the back of the carriage. The November evening was cold and wet and it was well after dark by the time they reached Exeter Street. The rain was coming down harder, too.

Glad he wasn't a real footman, Mac helped Kiri and Cassie from the carriage. Kiri wore gloves and didn't look at him, but he still felt a tingle of awareness as he took her hand. "Kirkland was going to try to join us for dinner again. I don't suppose you learned anything interesting from Princess Charlotte."

"Actually, I did." Kiri started up the steps. "She's planning on attending the state opening of Parliament in a fortnight."

Mac winced internally as he thought of the crowds. "Not good. Could you persuade her to change her mind?" He opened the front door to the house.

"I had no luck. She's pure stubborn Hanover, and sees this as her duty." Kiri flashed him a quick glance as she entered the house. "It's hard to argue against duty."

"Very true." Cassie entered the house at Kiri's heels and headed for the stairs. "I shall see you both at dinner."

Which left Mac alone in the foyer with Kiri. He moved behind her to take the dripping cloak from her shoulders.

As he lifted it away, he first saw the shining dark coil of her thick hair, then the curve of her breasts, and finally the bare skin below her scarlet bodice. The silken swath of the sari emphasized her superb figure.

She glanced over her shoulder with a provocative shimmer of scarlet silk and heady perfume. He stiffened, his hands clenching the heavy wool of the cloak. She was a fever dream of beauty and allure, and he wanted to wrap his arms around her. He wanted to unwind her silk sari to reveal the even more silken skin beneath.

"Why do you stare so?" she asked, her voice a rich strum across his senses.

His control snapped and he wrapped his arms around her, drawing her back and perfect round rump tight against him. Heart pounding, he said, "Please don't flirt, Kiri. It's hard enough keeping my hands off when you're dressed in European clothing. That sari is designed for provocation."

He held her for a moment, feeling the warm pulse of her body through thin silk. He wanted so much to raise the bright fabric and caress her sumptuous curves. . . .

He kissed the side of her throat and she gave a choked gasp. Glad of proof that she was not indifferent to him, he released her and stepped back, cursing himself for a fool for touching her in the first place.

She turned in a swirl of silk, her color high. "Saris are designed to be comfortable in killingly hot weather. Provocation is merely a side benefit."

"A powerful benefit," he said feelingly. "In that outfit, you are every man's fantasy of the sensual, exotic Orient."

Her green eyes narrowed like an angry cat's. "And you are one of those men who thinks Oriental women are toys for European men to play with?"

"You know better than that." Though he understood why she was sensitive on the subject. "You are beautiful and alluring in all times and in all styles of dress because you are a unique blend of East and West. Take away either part of your heritage and you would not be as irresistible as you are. You are lovely now, and will be even lovelier in fifty years when you've gained a lifetime of experience and wisdom."

She gave him an apologetic smile. "Well said, Mackenzie. You have seen my many faces. But since a sari is most inappropriate here, I shall change to something European and boring before dinner." She caught her skirts and climbed the steps, one hand sliding along the railing.

"You cannot possibly be boring under any circumstances," he said softly. She didn't acknowledge his words. He watched her ascend, knowing that as beautiful as she was in a sari, she was even more beautiful wearing not a single stitch.

Life would be easier if he didn't know exactly how beautiful she looked that way.

Dinner was a bubbling-hot shepherd's pie, perfect for a cold, wet night. Mac noted that Kiri now wore a plain, high-necked gown that showed not an inch of skin between neck and ankles. She still looked even more delectable than the shepherd's pie.

As Kirkland poured a rather good claret for the others at the table, he asked, "Does anyone have anything to report?"

Cassie said, "Rob and I have heard a few whispers among the émigré community that something is in the wind, but nothing concrete. There is talk of Clement's mysterious disappearance, but no one has suggested that they knew about his spying."

"So none of them are likely to show up with a writ of habeas corpus and demand Clement's release since he's being held without being charged." Kirkland shook his head. "I'm not doing well by English jurisprudence."

"Don't worry about it too much," Carmichael advised. "Clement must know that if he was charged, it would be with a capital crime and his future would be very short."

"There is that." Kirkland frowned. "I hope he can bring himself to give more information. I would rather not see the fellow hanged."

Kiri sipped her wine. "In other news, I had tea with Princess Charlotte today."

That caught Kirkland's full attention. "She's supposed to be in Windsor!"

"She's moving there tomorrow and wanted to thank me for my help at Damian's." Kiri explained. "I took her a bottle of perfume, and she told me that she planned to attend the opening of Parliament in two weeks."

Kirkland swore under his breath with a vehemence that startled Mac. The other man was known for his even temper, especially in front of two ladies.

Mac said, "From your reaction, it sounds like her attendance could be even more dangerous than I thought."

Kirkland pushed back in his chair, looking weary. "Clement's spy conscience still doesn't allow him to name names, but he doesn't approve of assassinating members of the royal family. The one piece of information he gave today was advising that we be very watchful for the safety of the royals who attend the opening of Parliament."

Cassie frowned. "I wonder if the conspirators are planning to set off an explosion in the Palace of Westminster. Barrels of gunpowder like Guy Fawkes stashed under the House of Lords?"

"You can be sure that the building will be searched from top to bottom and in every closet and cranny," Kirkland said. "But individual assassins could easily get close to the carriages of the royals, or even enter the building."

"We're all worried most about Princess Charlotte," Cassie said slowly. "What if Kiri is one of her attendants? It wouldn't be surprising to include the daughter of a duke, and she'll be an extra line of defense if necessary."

Mac tensed. "If there's trouble, she'll be right in the line of fire. Ashton wouldn't like that." Nor would Mac.

"That's what I'm here for." Kiri gave him a steady gaze. "There's not likely to be much risk."

"It could be dangerous," Kirkland said bluntly. "This afternoon, someone tried to shoot the Duke of York as he was leaving Horse Guards. Luckily it was a long-distance shot and missed him."

Silence fell over the room. The Duke of York, next brother in age to the prince regent, was in line for the throne after Charlotte. "So the conspiracy is still attempting to kill off royals," Carmichael said. "I rather hoped that what we've done already would be enough to drive them underground like rats in the sewer."

"Unfortunately, no." Kirkland's face looked carved from granite. "We need to find the plotters and do it without setting off a public panic."

"In that case," Mac said as he opened another bottle of claret and topped up all their glasses, "we need to drink to our success."

He thought that his frivolity might cause Kirkland to throw the wine over Mac's unworthy self. Then his friend relaxed and raised his glass. "To success."

They clinked their glasses together, then drank. As Mac swallowed the claret, he tried not to think of the gladiators' salute to the Emperor Claudius: *Ave, Caesar, morituri te salutamus*.

We who are about to die salute you.

Chapter 30

Major William Lord Masterson got the news when he was in Oporto, Portugal, visiting his old school friend Justin Ballard. With the army in winter quarters, Will had decided to go home for a few months. Partly on general principles, but also from a gnawing sense of uneasiness. Soldier's intuition, and not best ignored.

Having arrived late the night before at Ballard's home, he slept heavily and entered the breakfast room the next morning with a yawn. Ignoring the food, he crossed to look out the window at the shining path of the Douro River below. "I like your new house, Justin. Last night was too dark to appreciate the view."

"Plus, you were so tired you were reeling." Ballard poured a mug of hot, strong coffee, added cream and sugar, and handed it to Will. "I'm glad you stopped by for a few days before heading home."

Will took the mug and swallowed a long, scalding mouthful, feeling more relaxed than he had in months. "I'd be a fool to head back to November weather in England when I can visit a man who makes the best port in Portugal."

Ballard laughed. "I can't swear that it's the best, but you

can drink all you like for free. The port-making business is in disarray after all the fighting, but give me time."

Will transferred his gaze from the river, which bustled with small boats, to his friend. Dark-haired, part Portuguese, and completely bilingual, Ballard could easily pass as a native. "Do you think you'll ever move back to England?"

"Of course. All that fog and greenery are in the blood. But I love Portugal, too." Ballard sipped his coffee. "Every man would be improved by living for at least a year in another country."

"Especially if he can do it without being shot at," Will said dryly. "I have the feeling that I haven't experienced the best of Portugal and Spain."

"You'll have to come for a long stay when peace finally arrives." Ballard moved away from the window. "Have some breakfast. The eggs are scrambled with onion and chorizo sausage, and they make a good start to the day. Plus, I have some London newspapers fresh off the boat and not much more than a week old."

"The packet must have caught a good wind." Will helped himself to a double serving of eggs and two slices of fresh baked bread. Then he settled at the table opposite Ballard, poured himself more coffee, and took the London paper on the top of the stack that had just been delivered. A nice thing about visiting with old friends was that no conversation was required.

He leafed through the pages idly, reading articles that caught his attention. Then he hit the obituary section, and stopped. A chill went through him.

He must have made a sound, because Ballard's head snapped up from his own newspaper. "Something wrong?"

"It appears that my brother is dead." Will took a deep breath, trying to wrap his head around the idea that the irrepressible Mackenzie was gone. "According to this, he tried to stop a burglary at his club and was shot."

Ballard took the paper and read through the piece, his expression shocked. "It's hard to believe. Mackenzie always seemed indestructible."

"Maybe the report isn't true," Will said, not wanting to believe. "He worked with Kirkland, and that often means things are not as they appear."

"Maybe," Ballard said quietly. "But . . . the odds are against that."

"I know." Will got to this feet, appetite gone. "I'll take the next boat home rather than lingering."

"There's a packet returning to London this afternoon." Ballard also stood. "I'll send my secretary to see if there's a cabin available."

"I'll sleep on the deck if necessary, but I will be on that boat," Will said tersely.

"The deck in November? Not a wise idea. You're an officer, a gentleman, and a baron of England. They should be able to do better than the deck for you." Ballard laid his hand briefly on Will's shoulder before leaving to dispatch his secretary.

Will looked through the other newspapers but didn't find any articles with more details. Damian Mackenzie. Dead in an alley outside his club. He couldn't bring the mental image into focus.

Instead, he remembered Mac as a small boy when they'd first met. His mother just dead, now tossed among strangers, Mac had been terrified and determined not to show it.

Their mutual father had been away, and the servants hadn't known what to do about this strange boy who had been sent by his late mother's maid. The maid herself had vanished, but she'd paid Mac's coach fare to his father's house, with papers that verified his identity.

The butler had been all for shipping the cuckoo in the nest off to the nearest workhouse, but Will had refused to allow that. He was usually an easygoing child, good-natured and cooperative, but on that day he'd discovered his latent aristocrat arrogance. The steward said Will couldn't just adopt a strange boy like a pet, but he'd done exactly that.

He'd always wanted a brother, or even a sister, but no such luck. Then this brother miraculously appeared, looking too much like Will not to be family.

Mac's defiance had crumbled easily. All it had taken was for Will to be nice to him. He'd taken his new little brother up to the nursery, introduced him to his nurse, and given him some of his toys. By the time Lord Masterson had returned, Mac was part of the household, and Will made it very clear that he would not allow his brother to be shipped off to some uncertain future.

Lord Masterson, like Will, didn't like unpleasantness. He also felt some responsibility for his bastard son, so Mac stayed on, treated almost like a legitimate son of the house. Almost, but not quite. Only Will accepted him completely, as if his bastardy hadn't mattered.

It was why they'd both ended up at the Westerfield Academy. Lord Masterson had given up trying to separate the boys, but he didn't want to send his bastard to Eton. So Will had gone off to Lady Agnes and Mac had boarded with a vicar in Westerfield village. The vicar had tutored Mac until his erratic education was up to Lady Agnes's standards, and then he'd joined the school in a class behind Will.

After leaving Westerfield, they'd stayed close despite the distances that often separated them. Mac had gone into the army. Will had wanted to do that, but as the heir, he really couldn't. When tragedy had set Will free from life in England, it had been his turn to go into the army, and Mac's turn to come home.

But they'd written each other. Over the years, there had been masses of letters. Mac's were witty and often wickedly funny.

Will knew his letters were less interesting. Well, Will himself was less interesting. But the letters had kept their bond alive. If one of them was going to die, Will was the likely candidate since he was an active officer in wartime. But no, he'd survived years of warfare with no major wounds and only one serious bout with fever.

Mac should have been safe. If there was any justice in the world, his humor and zest for life should have made him immortal.

After so many years as a soldier, one would think that Will would be less of an optimist.

He wasn't sure how long he stared down at the silver surface of the Douro River, but his reverie ended when Ballard returned. "You have a cabin in the packet that leaves in three hours," his friend said. "It's small and you're sharing it with a large wine merchant, but he owes me a favor, so he agreed. It's going to be so tight that you'll have to take turns breathing."

"We'll manage. Thanks, Justin." Will smiled crookedly. "Just as well I hadn't unpacked."

He'd be glad to get back to London. And the first thing he was going to do was find Kirkland and ask what the devil had happened to Will's only brother.

Chapter 31

Kiri yawned her way down the stairs to breakfast. Though she enjoyed social gatherings and people of all sorts, ten days of clubs, gamblers, and sipping alcoholic beverages she didn't really want had left her yearning for a quiet evening on Exeter Street. Even better would be a quiet evening with her family, but they had all gone north to her brother's estate. She liked it better when everyone she loved was nearby.

Far worse than missing her family was knowing that only a week remained before the opening of Parliament, and they'd made no more progress in breaking the conspiracy. There hadn't been any assassination attempts, but that might only mean that the plotters were waiting for a big strike.

Kiri hadn't been in London long enough to attend a Parliamentary opening, but Mackenzie had explained that it was a very grand affair, with crowds of Londoners watching as members of the royal family and government ministers arrived. There was much pomp and tradition to demonstrate the power and grandeur of the kingdom. That also meant opportunities for the wicked.

Cassie and Mackenzie were eating breakfast. He glanced

up and gave her a warm smile. They had both managed to be businesslike and honorable for the last several days, to Kiri's regret.

Every time she looked at him, she remembered how his arms felt when he'd asked her not to flirt. One arm clasped around her waist, the other above her breasts, fitting her against him perfectly.

For a joyous instant, she'd thought he'd changed his mind about what constituted honor, but then the damned man had let her go. Not happily, but he'd done it. She told herself that she wouldn't want a man with no self-discipline, but she wasn't sure she believed that.

Covering another yawn, she investigated the warming dish that held their hot breakfast. Eggs scrambled with onions and potatoes with bacon on the side. Good fuel for a bright but frosty morning.

Carmichael entered the breakfast room with a purposeful expression. Cassie glanced up. "Good news?" she asked. "Conspirators captured?"

"Not yet, but at least a change of pace," Carmichael replied. "There's going to be a boxing match this afternoon. Not one of the big championships, but a smaller one that will draw Londoners and lower members of the Fancy."

Kiri came alert. "Like the kidnapper who was at Damian's."

"Exactly," the Runner said. "Do you think you can recognize him, Kiri?"

"I might," she said cautiously. "He wasn't wearing a particular cologne, but I got a good look at his build and movements, and a good sniff."

"Certainly worth a try," Mackenzie said. "The clock is ticking, and we're not making any progress."

"Kirkland has other irons in the fire beside us." Carmichael grimaced. "Unfortunately, they aren't heating up either."

"That could change at any moment." Mackenzie glanced at Kiri. "Wear something subdued. We don't want to start a riot."

"Besides, it's cold out today," Cassie pointed out. "Who are the fighters?"

"Two young boxers called McKee and Cullen. They're both considered promising, so they should draw well."

"Poor damned fools," Cassie muttered. "You won't enjoy this, Kiri."

"Probably not," Kiri said, thinking of what she'd heard about bare-knuckle boxing. "But it will be a new experience."

She'd been having lots of new experiences ever since she came to England. She studied Mackenzie as he served himself breakfast. And there was one new experience she very much wanted to repeat. . . .

There had been a hard frost in the night, so the day was bright and cold. The match had drawn a large crowd to a field behind a riverside tavern. Kiri held onto Mackenzie's arm, a little wary of the excited mood. Most of the onlookers were working men, with a sprinkling of well-dressed gentlemen.

The four of them arrived at the match in a dingy but sizable carriage, which the driver parked on one side of the field. Some carriage owners sat on top of their vehicles for a clear view, but the Exeter Street group joined the crowd. There were only a few other women, and none of them were ladies.

In the center of the field, an eight-foot square had been roped off using four stakes. A pair of shirtless men stood in opposite corners glaring at each other as supporters called comments to their favorites.

Mackenzie, who was solidly in his role of northern

merchant, explained, "Each fighter has a couple of attendants who provide water and oranges and towels to sponge off blood and sweat. A round is fought until one man is knocked down. Then there's a thirty-second break for them to recover. Then another round. They fight until one of them can't anymore."

She made a face, though probably he couldn't tell because of the deep bonnet she wore. "They look cold without their shirts."

"They'll warm up quickly when the fight starts," Mackenzie said.

Knowing that many gentlemen studied boxing at Gentleman Jackson's salon, she asked, "Do you box?"

"And ruin my handsome face? Not for me, lass!" He wiggled his brows comically. "They're about to start. The blond fellow is Cullen, and the dark one is McKee."

Within three minutes, Kiri knew that she didn't ever want to attend another boxing match. She winced and looked away as the two men hammered away at each other. "This is horrible! They look like they're trying to do murder."

"That's not the aim, but boxers do die from the beating with some regularity," Mackenzie admitted. "But skill is more important than brute strength. McKee is the better boxer and he's holding his own even though he's smaller. Look at his quick footwork as he moves in to hit, then dances back out of the way of Cullen's fist."

Wryly she realized that her escort had been sucked into the contest, like all the other men around. "Remember why we're here," she said, keeping her voice low, though the crowd was noisy enough to cover a conversation. "You can watch the match, but can we wander around on the edges while I look for suspects?"

He gave her a rueful smile. "Sorry. It's a good match, but you're right that duty comes first."

He began strolling around the edge of the crowd, Kiri clinging to his arm as if she found the rough crowd alarming. The concealment afforded by her bonnet allowed her to study the men. A fair number looked like boxers themselves, with muscular bodies and battered faces, but she didn't see one who looked like the third kidnapper.

Impossible to check scents in this crowd, especially since the third kidnapper had used no cologne or scented soap. These items were the province of the well-off. In a mass of not very well-washed humanity, identifying one man by his personal scent would be almost impossible unless she was right on top of him. But she had seen the man fairly closely, and perhaps that would enable her to spot him.

They passed Carmichael and Cassie, who were staying in one place and keeping a sharp eye on the crowd. Although Carmichael, like Mackenzie, seemed to sometimes get distracted by the fight. Men!

Peddlers moved through the crowd, too, selling hot pies and beer from the tavern that sponsored the match. Mackenzie bought a pair of the pies. Kiri ate hers with relish.

They paused in their perambulations as they ate. Kiri looked at the boxing ring again and shuddered at the sight of the fighters, both of whom had blood streaming down their chests from blows to the face. "Isn't it done yet?"

"They're both still standing and willing to fight. I think McKee will end it soon, though. His greater skill is starting to show."

Kiri looked away, unable to watch more. Even with the noise of the crowd, she could hear the thud of fists smashing into flesh. She and Mackenzie had halted by the parked carriages, so she studied them. Better to look at horses than human brutality.

Her gaze sharpened. Between two of the carriages, a broad, muscular fellow who looked like the boxer-kidnapper was accosted by several other men. They cornered him, and it looked like a heated argument was taking place.

Her boxer tried to escape, but the others pursued and began to beat him. Though he fought back, he was outnumbered and quickly knocked to the ground. Kiri's fingers bit into Mackenzie's arm. "A man has been attacked, and he might be the one we're looking for! There, between the carriages."

Then she darted toward the fight.

Yanked out of watching the match, Mac swung around. The parked carriages were behind them, and he saw that murder was being attempted between a phaeton and a high-perch curricle. The victim was down and being kicked viciously by his attackers.

Mac bolted after Kiri. She moved amazingly fast despite her skirts, but he was able to overtake her. When they were close enough to be heard about the noise of the crowd, he called out, "Eh, there! What's going on?"

"Stay out of this!" one of the attackers snarled. "Ollie here is gettin' what he deserves!"

"Doesn't look like a fair fight to me." Mac was close enough now to swing his cane. He smashed the heavy brass head across the throat of the man who'd spoken. Not with killing force, just aiming to drive the attackers off.

No such luck. Suddenly three men were attacking Mac. He used the cane like a quarterstaff, blocking blows and clubbing his assailants.

Kiri had stayed with him, damn it, and despite her skills, he winced when he saw her go after the man holding Ollie down. She tossed the fellow into a carriage wheel. He didn't even know what hit him as he landed on the frozen ground.

Wishing that this fight was more visible so the attackers

would see the advantage of retreat, Mac smashed the head of his cane between the second man's legs. His target gave a strange, agonized wail and fell, clutching himself.

The third man brought out a knife and held it like an expert. An advantage of the cane was it allowed Mac to keep his distance. Properly directed, it could smash a knife from a villain's hand. Like *now*.

Yells came from behind, and men from the crowd poured into the space between the carriages. The fight exploded as beer-soaked boxing fans joined in, some of them supporters of McKee going after those who favored Cullen.

Mac kicked into serious fighting mode, using the skills and instincts of a lifetime. Cane, fist, feet, elbows, knees—but where the devil was Kiri? No matter how good a fighter she was, this free-for-all was no place for a woman. He spun around, swinging his cane to keep others away while he scanned the brawling bodies.

Then his frantic gaze moved behind the phaeton, and he saw Kiri lying in a pool of blood.

Chapter 32

Kiri! The horrific images seared in his brain flared to appalling life. His heart seemed to stop and he swayed as blackness closed in on him.

No! He damned well would not faint. *Could* not. Not this time.

Fighting off dizziness, he stumbled toward her, more terrified than he'd ever been in his life. She might be above his touch, but he needed to know she was alive and happy somewhere in the world. He needed her. . . .

Clutching the edge of the phaeton to keep himself upright and swinging his club in his other hand, he forced his way through the melee.

He was half a dozen feet away when Kiri scrambled to her feet, then hauled up the battered Ollie. There was blood on her cheek and splashed heavily across her cloak, but she didn't move like she'd been injured.

But so much blood! Hoarsely he asked, "Kiri, where are you hurt?"

His panic must have been visible, because her voice was reassuring when she replied, "I'm fine, the blood isn't mine. Our kidnapper here fell against the carriage and cut his head, and he bled like a stuck pig." As Ollie struggled to escape, she grabbed at his coat. "Don't let him get away!"

The boxer was large, but not as large as Mac. He grabbed the fellow's arms and wrestled the wrists together, then hauled out his handcuffs and snapped them in place. He still felt unsteady, but it helped if he didn't look at Kiri. Didn't think of the sight of her lying on the ground with blood all around her. The scarlet terror of blood across her beautiful face. He almost retched before he managed to suppress the image again.

Carmichael and Cassie appeared, having made their way through the brawl from the other side of the field. They both showed some scuffs and rumples, but no real damage. Kiri said, "This is our kidnapper."

"A good thing we have a large carriage," Carmichael said tersely. "We'll take him to join his fellow kidnapper." He caught Ollie by the arm and frog-marched him away toward where their carriage waited at the back of the group of vehicles. Cassie walked on Ollie's other side.

Rather than follow immediately, Kiri took Mac's arm. "You look ready to fall over. Were you hurt?"

"No more than a few bruises." He tried without much success to keep his voice light. "You know I can't stand the sight of blood."

"At least the blood isn't yours this time." Still holding his arm, she got him started walking after the others.

"Thought . . . it was yours." He screwed his eyes closed, trying to block out the horrific images. "A bloodied woman is . . . worse."

"I see."

From her thoughtful voice, he suspected she saw too damned much. He did his best to pull himself together.

By the time they reached the carriage, Cassie and Carmichael and their prisoner were inside. Mac thought he was composed enough to fool anyone except Kiri.

Ollie sat in the middle of the backward-facing seat with Rob beside him. His shoulders trembled as he stared at his handcuffed wrists. An improvised bandage covered his head wound, but there was bloody evidence of the laceration all over the man.

Mac would have sat on Ollie's other side, but Kiri took that seat. Maybe she wanted to smell the man. She also took up less space than Mac. The seat would have been very crowded with three men jammed together on it.

After the carriage set off toward Kirkland's office, Ollie said in a Newcastle accent, "What you goin' to do to me? I swore I wouldn't talk about the kidnapping!"

Carmichael glanced at Mac, silently turning the interrogation over to him. Mac didn't know if it was because he sat directly opposite the prisoner, or if Rob realized that Mac needed a job to focus on so he wouldn't fall apart.

Ollie had pretty much proved he was their man by his confession. Mac glanced at Kiri, who gave a nod of confirmation. They had their kidnapper. Returning his gaze to their prisoner, he ordered, "Look at me."

Reluctantly Ollie lifted his head, and Mac immediately saw two things. First, he was young, more boy than man. Second, from the slackness of his expression, he'd suffered brain damage in the ring. Guessing that patient questions would work better than intimidation, he asked, "What's your full name?"

"Oliver Brown," he muttered. "Ollie."

"Of Newcastle?"

"Aye," the boy said, looking surprised that Mac knew that.

"Who attacked you?"

"They were sent by the flash cove." Ollie looked puzzled and uncertain. "They like to kill me. Why'd you stop 'em? What you goin' to do with me?"

"I want to find out what you know about the kidnappers

so we can catch them," Mac explained, his gaze locked on Ollie's. "How did you get involved with them?"

Ollie looked from one face to the other. The presence of two women and two strange men must have convinced him that they hadn't come from the flash cove, and that he would benefit by talking. He said haltingly, "My friend Ruffian O'Rourke knew I was trying to earn enough money to get to Newcastle."

"You wanted to go home?"

Ollie nodded. "Thought I'd come to London and be a champion prizefighter." His smile was bitter. "Instead I got my brains scrambled. My pa's a blacksmith and I never should've left the forge. Since I needed money to go home, Ruff said I could join him on a job where they wanted another man."

"What kind of job?" Mac prodded.

Ollie looked frightened. "This flash cove needed some muscle. Ruff said it weren't a robbery, so I figured it was all right. I'd earn enough in one night to go home. I didn't know anyone would get hurt! Didn't know they were tryin' to snatch a girl, either." His lips started to tremble. "Ruff was killed. He was my best friend in London."

"What did you do then?"

"The flash cove was furious and wavin' a pistol around. The Frenchie who wasn't shot tried to calm him down, but I figgered I best disappear while I could. Decided to stay hid while I earned a couple of pounds, and then I'd walk my way home."

Walking north all the way to Newcastle with winter setting in was a sign of desperation. Mac asked, "Why did you come to the fight today?"

Ollie looked down at his feet. "Sometime if a match ends too quick, they ask for volunteers for another fight. If I done that, I'd have me enough for a coach ticket home."

And possibly scrambled what wits the poor devil had

left. "Instead, the flash cove guessed you might come to this match, and he sent his men to take care of you."

Ollie shrunk back in his seat. "What you goin' to do with me?"

"I don't know," Mac said. "That's not my decision. But we won't beat you and leave you for dead in the street."

Ollie tried a sneer. "Don't s'pose you'd want to do that in front of the ladies."

"Don't underestimate the ladies," Mac said coolly. "Either of them is capable of killing you with her bare hands. Cooperate, and you may live to see Newcastle again."

His words made Ollie look warily at Kiri, who was squeezed against him in the seat. "I won't be transported?"

"Probably not, if you help us," Mac said. "Now tell me about the flash cove. What did he look like? Do you know his name?"

"Tall fellow. Only saw him with a mask." Ollie pondered. "Brown hair. Might ha' been in the army from the way he stood. Fancy clothes and a fancy smell."

Mac saw Kiri come alert at that, but she knew better than to think someone as inarticulate as Ollie could describe a cologne accurately. Mac continued to ask questions during the ride, but wasn't able to elicit any useful details.

When they reached the office, Carmichael said, "I'll take Mr. Brown in. I've a few more questions to ask."

Ollie looked terrified as Carmichael hauled him off the carriage. Once they started toward Exeter Street, Kiri asked, "What will happen to poor Ollie? He looked frightened out of his limited wits."

"And well he should. After so many years as a Bow Street Runner, Rob could scare the wings off a fly with a single scowl," Mac said dryly.

Cassie laughed. "A good description. My guess is that

Kirkland will get as much information as he can from young Mr. Brown, put him in the cell next to Clement until the conspiracy is broken, then buy him a coach ticket to Newcastle."

"He won't be thrown into Newgate or transported?" Kiri asked.

"No need," Mac said. "He's not a hardened criminal. Just a poor fool of a lad who had built up his strength in his father's forge and thought that would make him a champion in London."

"Since Kirkland often works outside the law," Cassie murmured, "he is sometimes in a position to offer unusual justice."

The rest of the ride was silent. Mac was glad the early dusk of November darkened the carriage enough that he couldn't see the blood sullying Kiri's lovely face. He was equally glad that the darkness obscured his own features, and his knotted fists.

As the carriage pulled up at 11 Exeter Street, Cassie said, "You've done well, Kiri. Finding two of the kidnappers was remarkable."

"But I haven't found the most important one," Kiri said glumly. "We still don't know who Ollie's flash cove is, and he's the one who matters."

"Even he might not be the man behind the plot," Cassie pointed out. "This sort of work takes time and patience, like putting together a dissected map, piece by piece. Rob and Kirkland may be able to deduce more pieces by putting Ollie and Clement together."

It was a hope, Mac knew, though a slim one.

For his part, he would pray that he could hold his shattered nerves together long enough to reach Exeter Street before he fell into screaming pieces.

* * *

Ollie was thoroughly cowed when confronted by both Kirkland and Carmichael. Clutching his mug of hot, sweet tea, he said nervously, "The other fellow, the one with the eye patch, said if I cooperated it would go easier on me."

"It will." Kirkland let the silence stretch until the young boxer was ready to jump out of his skin before he said coolly, "Did you know that your kidnapping attempt was not only a hanging offense, but treason against the Crown?"

Ollie's face turned white under the dirt and blood and his hands shook so badly that tea slopped from his mug. "No, sir! I didna' know that! I'm no traitor!"

"Then tell us everything you remember about the kidnapping."

"Yes, sir! Anything, sir!"

Kirkland and Carmichael both asked questions. Ollie did his best, but he knew little more than he'd already revealed. After a frustrating hour, Kirkland decided to bring him face-to-face with Paul Clement, though he didn't expect much to come of it. "I'm going to take you to another kidnapper. Perhaps that will jar loose more memories."

He and Carmichael escorted Ollie down to the cells and unlocked Clement's door. Carmichael stood in the doorway, the regular guard just beyond him, but it was unlikely that Ollie would try to escape when he had food and relative warmth, and he was safe from the men who'd tried to beat him to death. Though Clement would jump at the chance to be free, he was too intelligent to think he could escape here and now.

"I believe you two are acquainted," Kirkland said as he took Ollie into the cell.

"Aye, that's the Frenchie," Ollie said, pleased that he could finally answer a question. "He was with the flash cove that night. The cove even listened to him."

Clement had been lying on his bunk, but he stood when

company arrived. "Indeed, the young man and I met on that ill-fated night, though I didn't learn his name."

"It's Oliver Brown," Ollie said belligerently. "And I ain't no traitor."

"Nor am I, to France." Clement looked amused. "I saw my work here as serving my country in the same way a soldier does."

"Damned spy!" Ollie swung a fist at the Frenchman.

Kirkland caught his wrist before the blow connected. Oliver Brown might not be very bright, but his patriotism was real. "Does meeting inspire any more thoughts?"

Clement shrugged. "Mr. Brown was the muscle. We did not engage."

Ollie frowned. "The Frenchie called the flash cove 'Captain.' Mebbe he was army, like I thought?"

From the flicker in Clement's eyes, Kirkland guessed that Ollie was right: the leader was a military officer. One more piece of information that might or might not be useful. "The captain wasn't French?"

Ollie shook his head. "He was as English as me and you."

Kirkland was inclined to believe that since Ollie was the sort to be instantly suspicious of foreigners, as he was of Clement. "That's enough for tonight. Pleasant dreams, Monsieur Clement."

He escorted Ollie from the cell, locking the door and checking it as he left. "You'll be in this cell, Mr. Brown. A meal will be sent down soon. And a towel and washbasin so you can remove the worst of the bloodstains."

The guard opened the door to the other cell and Ollie walked in. "Better than sleeping under a bridge," the boy said. He looked hopefully at Kirkland. "'Ave I been cooperative enough, sir?"

Despite his size and muscles, Ollie was still a painfully vulnerable boy. Sometimes Kirkland really hated his work. "You've been helpful. If you think of anything else that might help find the flash cove, tell the guard and he'll summon me."

"Yes, sir."

Silently Kirkland and Carmichael headed up the steps When they reached Kirkland's office, Carmichael said, "I feel like I've been kicking a puppy."

Kirkland smiled crookedly. "The boy is an innocent fool."

"I'd say the only safe place for him is in the protection of his own family." Carmichael cocked an inquisitive brow.

"When this is over, I'll put him on a coach and send him home," Kirkland said. "Throwing him in prison would just add to government expense."

Carmichael gave a nod of satisfaction. The two of them were both capable of doing what must be done. But neither of them liked kicking puppies.

Chapter 33

Mackenzie was a good actor, but not good enough to convince Kiri that he was all right. Even in the dark of the carriage, she could feel how tightly strung he was. Something had happened at the boxing match, and she guessed it was the sight of her gore-splashed body. He must have thought she was dead or mortally injured, and that had triggered a fierce reaction that had shaken him to the breaking point.

She wondered if Cassie could also feel the brittleness under Mackenzie's casual manner. Perhaps—the other woman was very perceptive. But she hadn't slept with Mackenzie. Even though they'd been together only once, Kiri was sensitized to the man. He was in pain, and she hurt.

When they reached Exeter Street, Mackenzie helped the two females out of the carriage as if nothing was wrong. Ever the gentleman, except that Kiri could feel his vibrating tension even through her glove.

Once they were inside, he said, "I have a bit of the headache, so I'll rest now and not join you for dinner." He bowed politely, avoiding Kiri's eyes, and headed upstairs.

Still worried, she took off her cloak and examined the condition. "The blood should brush off when it's completely dry, but my gown will need a complete wash. I hope it doesn't stain."

"Give both to Mrs. Powell. She's a wizard at getting bloodstains out of clothes." Cassie's mouth quirked up. "Housing Kirkland's agents has given her much experience."

"What an alarming thought." Suddenly tired, Kiri headed for the stairs. "I need a bath after rolling around in that field. Can I get a tray and eat in my room?"

"The Powells will provide food as well as hot water for your bath." Cassie covered a yawn. "I think I'll do the same. Brawling makes me tired."

Kiri turned back on the steps, her brows arched. "This happens to you often?"

"It's not unknown." Cassie pulled out her hairpins and shook out her hair, then ran her fingers through as if she was on the verge of headache herself.

"If you're going to bathe, I have fragrant oils with me," Kiri said. "Would you like lemon verbena or rose?"

"Bath oil!" Cassie's face lit up. "It's been so long. . . . Rose, please."

"I'll bring it to your room." Kiri was glad that the prospect of rose oil could bring such a smile to Cassie's face. The smile made her look years younger. What kind of life had she lived before she was engulfed in war and drawn into being an agent? It was none of Kiri's business, of course. But she couldn't help wanting to know.

Since Kiri was on the steps, she could look down on Cassie's head. Surprised, she leaned over the railing for a closer look. "Your hair appears to have red roots."

Cassie made a face. "Time to dye it again. My natural red is too conspicuous, and the whole focus of my existence for years has been to pass unnoticed. The dye I use gives a boring brown, but it wears off in time, and the roots must be covered regularly."

"You're good at making yourself forgettable," Kiri said

as she tried to visualize the other woman as a redhead.
That would make her skin look almost translucently white.
"I should like to see you someday when you aren't trying
for invisibility."

"I'm no beauty even at my best," Cassie assured her.

Perhaps not, Kiri thought as she resumed her climb of
the stairs. But Cassie would surely be striking.

Mr. Powell and a servant brought Kiri supper, which she
ate while they heated water. Then they brought up a hip
bath and canisters of blessedly hot water. In return, they
carried off her cloak and gown for cleaning.

Having taken the rose oil to Cassie, Kiri added the
lemon verbena to her own tub. The lovely tangy scent was
intoxicating, and the hip bath large enough for her to sink
in to her shoulders if she scrunched up. The hot water
soothed her numerous bruises. She'd been knocked about
more than she realized at the time.

She stayed in the tub until the water had cooled and her
skin was wrinkly, then dried herself off and donned her
nightgown and robe. She considered reading or writing
letters, or even going to bed.

But she couldn't stop thinking about Mackenzie. Perhaps rest had cured his shattered nerves—but she didn't
believe that. She would not sleep easy until she'd seen
herself how he was.

Kiri didn't plan to seduce Mackenzie. Upset as he was,
he needed his honor even more. In her ankle-length nightgown and robe, she was completely covered and shapeless.
Her heavy knit socks were good for keeping feet warm
on cold floors, but they were as unprovocative as any
garment could possibly be.

Even so, she took the precautions against pregnancy
that Julia Randall had taught her. The attraction between

her and Mackenzie made it impossible to predict what might happen.

As she walked silently down the hall, she swore to herself that she would not encourage him to behavior he'd regret. He had troubles enough, from the way he'd looked when he withdrew to his room.

She knocked gently on his door. No answer. Might he have gone out? Her instinct said no, that he was inside and ignoring the knock. She turned the knob.

The door opened quietly under her hand. The only light came from the small coal fire, but it was enough to illuminate the bleak figure standing at the window and looking out into the wintry night. Mackenzie had shed coat and boots and eye patch, but whatever devils had seized him were still present.

"A pity these doors don't have locks," he said wearily. "I knew you'd come, Kiri. Now turn around quietly and leave, closing the door behind you."

She crossed the room on silent feet. "If you knew I'd come, you must also know that I don't obey orders well."

"I've noticed," he said dryly. Even though he wouldn't look at her, she sensed that he was glad he was no longer alone.

She mustn't touch him. That would cause complications and solve nothing. She moved to his side and gazed out the window at the barely visible rooftops of London. "Blood and women are the key to your own private chamber of horrors, aren't they?"

He didn't answer, but she saw his jaw tighten. He looked beautiful and doomed, like an archangel cast out of heaven, falling helplessly toward his inevitable end.

"From the intensity of your reaction, I'm not the first woman you saw like that. I must have triggered something that was already burned on your soul." She hesitated for a moment, not wanting to believe that he could have murdered his mistress. But if he'd been drunk and betrayed, if the woman had provoked him—anything was possible. "Were you remembering Harriet Swinnerton?"

He drew a harsh breath. "Yes, but not because I killed her. After Rupert returned and supposedly heard her name me murderer with her dying breath, he and several of his troops dragged me from my bed and took me to the scene of the crime. He screamed his accusations at me while I had to see her lying there broken, bleeding. . . ."

An image that haunted him still. Kiri locked her hands together to prevent herself from reaching out to him.

"It might not have been a great love affair, but I cared for her," he said haltingly. "Harry could be demanding, but also playful and generous. I liked pleasing her. Certainly I would have tried to protect her. Instead, I brought about her death."

Kiri frowned as she visualized the scene. "Is it possible her husband isn't the one who killed her? If he truly believed you were the murderer, he might have felt it only just to confront you with the evidence."

Mackenzie shook his head. "No, Swinnerton was the murderer. Maybe he wanted me to see her body as a form of revenge, or maybe in his twisted way he was boasting. Whatever his reason—seeing Harriet dead haunts my nightmares."

"He must have wanted that. Not that you would have had nightmares for long if he'd succeeded in hanging you," she said gravely. "Bad enough to know she was murdered, but seeing her body had to have been far worse."

"Seeing and knowing my guilt."

"Those two were locked in a dance of death," she said firmly. "You had only a small role in their drama. Small but nearly fatal."

"I don't disagree," he said, voice bleak. "But it doesn't make me feel any better."

"A conscience is a great nuisance."

His mouth twisted. "I don't have much of one, except when it comes to destroying women."

There was something in his voice. . . . Abandoning her resolve not to touch him, she rested her hand on his wrist. "You're thinking of another woman who died, aren't you?" In a flash of certainty, she knew. "Your mother."

He jerked away from Kiri. "How did you know, damn it?" he said fiercely. "Are you some kind of witch?"

"Of course not," she said quietly. "I am only a woman who loves you, so I watch you very closely."

He pivoted, staring. "You love me? Is that supposed to make me feel better?"

She smiled ruefully. "That's not supposed to make you feel either better or worse. It simply *is*. I have no expectations of you, though I would appreciate honesty." Not only for her own sake, but because she thought honesty might purge his wounded soul.

She took his hand and pulled him down beside her on the edge of the bed. "Tell me, Damian. You were only a child when your mother died. How could you be responsible for her death?"

He gazed blindly at the fire. "Antoinette Mackenzie was an actress to the bone. Brilliant, beautiful, volatile, and ambitious. Sometimes she doted on me, telling me I was her beautiful little boy and how glad she was that I looked so much like my father. Other times she could barely stand the sight of me. I became adept at judging her mood and vanishing when expedient."

Kiri frowned, thinking that she would not have liked his mother. "Was Antoinette Mackenzie her real name?"

"I think it was a stage name, but if so, I never knew her real name." He seemed unaware when his hand tightened on Kiri's. "She wanted to be a lady and she thought Lord Masterson was the way to achieve that. His wife was frail.

Apparently that's why his lordship took a mistress, so as not to burden his wife with marital demands."

When he fell silent, Kiri asked, "Did your mother think he'd marry her after he was widowed?"

"She was sure of it." His lips tightened. "We were staying at an inn in Grantham on the road north to Yorkshire when she read in a newspaper that Lady Masterson had died. She was ecstatic and sent a letter off, probably saying imprudent things like how much she looked forward to them being together. He wrote back immediately saying he would never marry her, though naturally he would fulfill his responsibilities to the child."

Kiri winced. "Did that upset her to the point of suicide?"

Mackenzie's grip was so tight on Kiri's hand that she was going to have bruises. "She had always been prone to tantrums. This time she exploded like a nest of Congreve rockets. She screamed at me that the only reason I'd been born was to give her a hold on Lord Masterson. If she bore his child, she thought it more likely he'd marry her, but no, all the pain and nuisance of bearing a brat had come to nothing."

"Oh, Damian," Kiri said, agonized, unable to imagine how a mother could say such a thing to her child. "She couldn't have really meant that. She was just angry."

"Angry, yes, but she also meant it. Sometimes she seemed to enjoy having a child, but most of the time she handed me over to her maid, who became my nurse. On this particular day"—he stopped for the space of a dozen heartbeats, drawing in ragged breaths—"she said that she'd make his bloody lordship sorry. First she'd kill me, then herself."

As Kiri gasped, he continued inexorably, "And being a woman of her word, my mother then slit my throat."

Chapter 34

Mackenzie's words were stark, unbelievable, yet impossible to disbelieve. Kiri turned to face him. His cravat was off, so she gently unbuttoned his shirt and tugged the fabric away from his throat. There, just above his collarbone, was the thin, ragged line of a long-healed scar. "I'm so very glad she didn't know how to do it right," she said in a choked whisper as she traced the scar with gossamer tenderness.

"I was squirming and trying to get away, so she didn't cut deeply enough," he said, his voice remote. "But there was plenty of blood, so she thought her knifework would suffice. Then she used her best suicidal Juliet voice to cry out, 'This will show his filthy lordship!' and drove the dagger into her heart."

"And you were right there watching?" She wanted to weep for the child he'd been, but she could not allow tears. Her pain on hearing this was only a pale shadow of the pain he'd lived with most of his life.

He nodded. "After she stabbed herself, she had the strangest expression, as if she hadn't expected the pain or the blood to be real. She'd been in the theater so long that she couldn't always tell the difference between the stage and reality. She gasped, then quietly folded onto the floor and . . . bled."

Leaving her son with the indelible image of his mother dying in a lake of blood. God *damn* woman for her selfishness! Kiri swallowed hard and managed to say with credible calm, "She must have been mad."

"A little, I think." He sighed. "I was lucky to have inherited enough of the Masterson steadiness to stay out of Bedlam. Not enough to be really respectable, but enough to be sane." After another long silence, he said, "You can see why Will became the most important person in the world to me."

"Stability, affection, acceptance," she said, wishing that she knew Lord Masterson better. She'd met him because he was one of Adam's closest friends, but only in passing. Masterson was a large, calm man who looked much like Mackenzie, but with a more relaxed disposition.

The next time they met, she might fall to her knees and kiss Will's feet for what he'd done for his terrorized little bastard brother. He could so easily have turned his back. "You were very lucky to have him."

"If not for Will, I would have ended up apprenticed to a tradesman or slaving in a workhouse. I hated when he joined the army. I'm the expendable one, not Will."

"You are not expendable!" She leaned forward and kissed the scar left by his mother's dagger, touching the hard line of tissue with her tongue. "When I think that I might never have met you . . ."

He caught his breath and she felt his pulse accelerate under her lips. "You would have been better off not knowing me, my warrior queen," he whispered, but his hands settled on her waist.

She raised her head to glare at him. "It may be difficult to value yourself when your mother dismissed your worth, but I will have none of that! You have the strength and honor of your father's people, the charm and wit of your mother, and those qualities together make you a remarkable man, Damian Mackenzie. "

His expression softened. "You give me too much credit, my lady."

"And you give yourself too little." She cupped his face in her hands, holding his gaze with hers. "I do not wish to damage your honor. But I very much wish to offer comfort." She tilted her head back and kissed him with love, suppressing passion.

Passion would not stay suppressed. Desire blazed between them, melting her good intentions, and his as well. His arms crushed around her. "Dear God, Kiri," he breathed. "You are so whole and alive."

And her lifeblood beat hotly in her veins, not poured out in death. She leaned into him hard and they fell backward on the bed. As she kissed him again, his hands roved over her. "You smell so good," he murmured. "Lemon and something else. Fresh. Piquant. Delicious."

"Verbena. You have a good nose." She pushed herself up, bracing her arms on each side of him. The room was too dark to show the difference in his eyes, but the strong, handsome bones of his face were sculpted in firelight. "You do not wish to take advantage of my youth and relative innocence. But surely it's a different matter if I take advantage of your maturity and most wonderful experience?"

For a moment he looked startled. That dissolved into laughter and he wrapped his arms around her waist. "How can I resist you?" His voice became husky. "You offer joy and sanity, and . . . I need both so much."

"They are yours for the taking, my darling Damian."

His mouth twisted. "Disreputable Damian comes closer."

"And that is so much a part of your charm!" She dived forward to kiss his throat while she buried her fingers in his thick hair.

Their legs had been over the edge of the bed, but in one expert motion, he rolled them so they were both on the mattress and he was above her. That put her in a position to tug his shirt loose so she could caress the warm skin of his back.

He jumped when she touched bare skin. "You have cold fingers!"

"You are warming them nicely," she said with a throaty chuckle just before she yanked at his shirt, trying to pull it over his head.

He had to cooperate to get the shirt off. By the time he'd fought his way clear of the billowing linen, she'd undone the buttons. He turned rigid when she slipped her hand inside his breeches. Any lingering coolness in her fingers was burned away when she took hold of him.

"Not. So. Fast!" he panted, moving to one side so that her hand slipped away.

In this position, he was able to lift the hems of her robe and nightgown all the way to her shoulders. She hardly noticed the cool air, not when his mouth descended on her breast. "Since I didn't have supper, I find myself very hungry," he said, his breath warming her nipple.

She whimpered as he kissed his way down her body. Dimly she wondered when the initiative had slipped from her to him, but she didn't really care. Not when he was doing such marvelous, provocative things.

"I smell a hint of vinegar," he said with interest. "Did you come here with seduction in mind?"

"I swear I did not," she gasped, writhing as his fingers stroked between her thighs. "But I was raised by a general, you recall. He said one must . . . always be prepared."

"I would rather not think of the general just now, since he would surely pull out his horsewhip. With justice. But the damned man also raised an irresistible daughter."

"The credit for that goes to my mother, who incarnates

the goddess of desire." Then language deserted Kiri entirely as his skilled mouth descended to a shockingly sensitive part of her body. Waves of sensation emanated through her, separating body and soul and whirling her into mindless bliss.

As she began to float to earth again, he sheathed himself in her heated flesh. To her amazement, sensation began building again, engaging her so profoundly that she could not tell where she ended and he began. She felt powerful and empowered, protected and worshipped.

As she convulsed around him, she knew it had been worth traveling halfway around the world to find this man and this time of utter rightness.

Mac gasped for breath, Kiri secure in his arms. He'd recovered from the horror of thinking her dead, but at what price?

"I hope you don't feel dishonored," she whispered against his shoulder.

"For accepting the gift of your honorable and generous spirit?" He pressed a kiss between her lovely breasts. "Not to mention your magnificent body. But I'm having trouble defining honor now. Even if my intentions are honorable, in the eyes of society I've failed utterly."

She sighed. "'Honorable intentions' is a code for marriage, isn't it? That is what the world sees. I do not see marriage as the only honorable estate." After a silence she added, "It's respectable, but that's not the same thing."

"At the moment, neither of us is anywhere near respectable." His lips twisted. "And the hell of it is that even if I proposed marriage, that wouldn't really change matters."

"Pardon?" She raised her startled face to him. "I thought you were not the marrying kind."

"You make me think impossible thoughts, Kiri." He

toyed with her hair, twining a glossy strand around his forefinger. "There is a romantic tradition that declares the world well lost for love, but that's fantasy. If you were foolish enough to marry me, how would you feel if your family cut you off?"

She looked appalled. "My mother would never do that!"

"But your stepfather might," he pointed out. "General Stillwell is one of Britain's great military heroes, but generals tend to see truth as black and white. I'm a middlin' shade of gray at best. He'd see me as black and you as white."

She laid her hand on his arm to show the contrasting tones of their skin. "I'm a pleasant shade of tan, while you look a trifle undercooked."

"You're right, I was taken out of the oven too soon," he said with a laugh. His brief humor faded. "Marriage joins not only two people, but two families. You are an heiress and the daughter of a duke. I'm the bastard son of an actress. The disparity between us is enormous, and horrifying to anyone who believes that there is a natural order to society. And most people do believe that."

Reluctantly she said, "In India, the caste system is a social order much more rigid than here. One thing I like about England is that it's freer."

"But far from completely free." He searched for an example. "If you and my brother fell in love and wished to marry, there would be general approval. You might be seen as marrying a bit beneath your rank since you're the daughter of a duke. Will is merely a baron, but that's close enough because he's a peer, so a marriage would be quite acceptable. Your family would welcome him gladly. I'm quite a different matter."

"You and Adam are friends, are you not? Surely that would help."

"We're friendly and we went to the same school, but

we're not close friends like he and Will." He hesitated before admitting, "I've always felt that Will was most of the reason I was accepted among Westerfield students. Everyone liked and respected him, so I was accepted on sufferance."

"Nonsense," she said flatly. "The Westerfield Academy is famously accepting. Just about every boy who's ever gone there has had good reason to believe that he was an outcast. You might have had to overcome more than most, but you succeeded and were accepted for yourself. You are very well liked."

He shrugged. "More liked than respected. It's one thing to banter with the owner of a gambling club. Quite another to let him marry your daughter."

"Again you mention marriage." Her eyes were narrowed like a cat's. "Is this only philosophy or are you thinking more personally? Marriage would solve your worries about your tarnished honor."

Wondering what was going on behind that lovely face, he retorted, "I'm no philosopher. I like the idea of marrying you, but think, Kiri! No matter how much we care for each other"— he stroked a slow hand from her shoulder to her knee—"and desire each other, would you choose me over your whole family? If you say yes, I won't believe you. Passion is powerful, but it cools over time. That's why marriage needs a broader foundation."

"Which is where family and friends come in."

He nodded. "I would be . . . very upset if Will cut me off. Which he might do if he felt I'd ruined Ashton's sister." Mac would be more than upset if he lost Will. He'd be devastated. "You have a larger family, so you have more to lose. You can't throw them away for passing passion, no matter how intense it is now."

She sighed, her eyes closing. "I have known this all along. Hindus are very fatalistic and accepting, and that part of me knows that marriage between us is unthinkable. That is why I have wanted what few nights we can have." Her eyes opened again, blazing with intensity. "But the Englishwoman in me wants to break rules and *make* it possible for us to be together openly in the eyes of the world."

"A warrior queen in truth." He put his arm around her shoulders and drew her close against his heart. Though wise beyond her years, she was young and privileged, and that made her optimistic that they would find a way to overcome the disapproval of family and society and be accepted.

Mac wasn't optimistic at all. He'd experienced too much of the world's dark side.

And he didn't believe in miracles.

Chapter 35

No rest for the wicked. Though the plot against Britain's royals was at the top of Kirkland's priority list, he had other investigations almost as urgent, other agents who needed to be answered and cared for. And large numbers of papers that must be read, pondered, and answered.

It was near midnight when he finished. He swayed a little when he got to his feet. Fatigue? He analyzed how he felt, and came up with the description "wretched." He was developing a cold or some such ailment. Minor, but enough to multiply his fatigue.

He left the building that housed his small, secret organization and headed for Damian's. He tried to stop by most evenings since he was now the nominal owner. Plus, the club had been the site of the attempted kidnapping, and perhaps he'd see someone or learn something.

His breath showed in white puffs in the frosty night air. It was unusually cold for mid-November, but he guessed it would warm up again by the time Parliament opened.

He dozed off as his carriage carried him to Damian's. He really must try a full night's sleep to remind him what it was like. But not tonight. He had far too much to do.

He dismissed his carriage when he reached the club

since he wasn't sure how long he'd stay. He would have Damian's porter summon a hire carriage when he was ready to leave.

The club was fairly busy, though perhaps quieter than it would have been before Mackenzie's reported death. Baptiste wasn't visible, and a footman directed Kirkland to his office in the back of the building.

The club manager got to his feet when Kirkland entered. Baptiste seemed to have lost ten pounds and gained ten years since the night of the shootings. "My lord." He gave a half bow. "I trust all is well."

"As well as can be expected." Since Mackenzie's death must seem authentic, Kirkland had cleared his desk and office of all personal items. The room seemed very empty with the only signs of the late owner being a neat stack of unopened letters on Mac's desk. Baptiste left them there for Kirkland, since he was Mac's executor.

Kirkland ruffled through the stack. A perfumed note from a lady who must not have heard of the death, a few business letters, probably invoices. "I'll take care of these. How are the supplies of wine and spirits holding up?"

"Luckily we received a shipment just before . . . before . . ." Baptiste swallowed, unable to finish the sentence. "I will go down to Kent soon to talk to our suppliers."

Naturally the word "smugglers" wasn't mentioned. "You know the way to the suppliers' headquarters?"

Baptiste nodded. "He took me there once and introduced me to their . . . man of business so that I would be prepared in case anything . . ." His voice trailed off.

"That was foresighted. See if you can get more of that new claret."

"I shall try." Baptiste frowned. "You look less than well, my lord. You should get some rest."

"That's next on my agenda. Good night." Kirkland

tucked the letters inside his coat and left, going out through the main gaming hall.

As he headed toward the door, a man rose from the roulette wheel and came to greet him. It was Lord Fendall, one of their "persons of interest" in the assassination plot. Kirkland's wandering attention snapped into focus. "Good evening, Fendall. Glad to see you here."

"Town is filling up as gentlemen arrive for the opening of Parliament," Fendall explained. "Will there be some kind of memorial service for Mr. Mackenzie? If so, I should like to attend."

"I'm awaiting instructions from his brother, who is in Spain," Kirkland replied. It was bad enough to declare Mac dead, but he really did not want to go through a false memorial service. "My guess is that Lord Masterson will choose to have Mackenzie buried at the family estate."

"Put him amongst all those Mastersons despite the bar sinister?" Fendall's brows arched. "His brother is generous."

"They were close," Kirkland said briefly. Which was why he'd written Will the morning after the kidnapping and sent the letter to Spain by fast government courier.

Fendall sighed as his gaze moved across the room. "Damian's is not the same without Mr. Mackenzie. Baptiste is my friend, but he is not so good at creating a welcoming atmosphere. Do you know if the club will be sold or closed?"

"That hasn't been decided yet." Kirkland inclined his head. "I wish you a good evening of play. But not so good as to break the bank."

Fendall laughed. "The evening has been amusing so far. The play is the thing. Winning is a pleasant bonus when it occurs."

A good thing his lordship had that attitude, because he'd dropped a small fortune at Damian's. Kirkland bid him good night and headed to the exit at a quick pace, not wanting to catch anyone else's eye and have to talk.

The fresh air cleared his head a little. He turned right and walked next door to Mac's house. Personal letters were delivered there and must also be checked. Then he could finally go home.

He used his key to enter. The house was silent. Not really empty, but the two servants had gone to bed. They were used to Kirkland's comings and goings and wouldn't panic if they heard him.

He headed to Mac's study and lit a lamp, discovering more letters on the desk. Two were from Will Masterson. Kirkland hoped that his own letter of veiled explanation had arrived before the news of Mackenzie's death. Though Kirkland had done his best, communications to the Peninsula could be unreliable.

Another letter stood out because of the coarse paper and unschooled handwriting. It had been forwarded from a mail drop Mac used rather than coming directly to the house. Curious, Kirkland slit the seal. *Got a strange shipment from France you should know about. Best you come down here. Nightfall at the new moon. Hawk.*

Kirkland's brows arched. Mac's smuggler chief thought it necessary to write? Very interesting. This must go to Mac first thing in the morning.

Feeling dizzy, he stacked the letters on the desk. He needed to skim through them, but he was so weary he could barely read handwriting. He also felt wobbly from whatever he was coming down with.

He *hated* being sick.

But there were limits to willpower. He'd go up to the guest room and lie down for a few minutes. Or maybe longer than that since he barely had the strength to make it up the stairs.

In the guest room he was hit by chills, and abruptly

realized that he wasn't coming down with a cold, but a flare-up of malaria. He hadn't thought of that because he hadn't suffered an attack in years.

Or maybe he'd preferred to deny the possibility. So much for being a tough-minded spymaster. On the verge of collapse, he crawled under the covers, boots and all.

Kirkland gave up the struggle to think and sank into merciful darkness.

Kiri came down to breakfast with demurely downcast eyes, though she suspected that with a house full of spies, it would be almost impossible to hide an affair. At least spies were used to keeping secrets.

Mackenzie hadn't come down yet, though Cassie was reading a newspaper while she ate. She glanced up. "The rose bath oil was *wonderful.* I slept so well after."

"Rose oil is good for many things, including calming emotions when one is stressed." Kiri caught a waft of rose scent as she passed the other woman.

"Then everyone in the house can use some," Cassie said. "Do you think we could convince Mackenzie and Carmichael to bathe with rose oil?"

Kiri grinned. "They would probably rather die." Though men used cologne, rose would be considered much too feminine.

A letter from the general had been waiting for her in the foyer. She hadn't noticed the night before, having been distracted by concern for Mackenzie. After serving breakfast, she broke the seal and started reading. His first sentence produced an involuntary, "Oh, lovely!"

Cassie glanced up. "Good news? We can use some."

"Very good news, though nothing to do with saving England from the ungodly. My family has been staying with my brother at the Ashton estate, and my stepfather has decided to buy a manor that shares a boundary with it. So we'll all be close and able to see each other often. I only met Adam this past spring, and we have years to catch up on. He and my mother can't get enough of each other."

Cassie smiled wistfully. "It sounds wonderful. You are fortunate in your family."

"I am indeed." She continued reading the news as she ate, and was halfway through her breakfast when Mackenzie joined them. She glanced up, and for one searing moment, she felt as connected with him as she had the night before when their bodies had been joined. She saw a matching blaze in his eyes before he forced his gaze away.

"I smell roses," he said cheerfully. "Since they can't be in season, it must be one of you ladies."

"Kiri gave me some rose bath oil, which she says is very calming," Cassie explained. "Would you like to try some tonight?"

He looked horrified. "I'd rather die."

Kiri and Cassie broke into laughter.

"What am I missing?" he asked warily.

Kiri shook her head, refusing to explain their amusement, but she was grateful for the change in subject. By the time Mackenzie had served himself breakfast and taken a chair at the far end of the table, Kiri had her emotions under control again.

Or at least, she could keep them from showing. She'd thought herself resigned to the fact that her affair with Mackenzie must be short. Yet since he'd mentioned marriage the night before, she found she was no longer so fatalistic. The situation hadn't changed, all the barriers still existed—but might there be a way?

Hope was cruel.

Chapter 36

Kiri was on her second cup of tea when Rob Carmichael entered the breakfast room, expression grim. Cassie smiled at him. "I see that the lure of a good breakfast has drawn you from your lair."

"I won't turn that down, but it's not why I'm here." Carmichael belatedly removed his hat. "I got a message this morning from one of your servants, Mac. They found Kirkland fully dressed and burning with fever in your guest room."

Mackenzie swore under his breath. "A flare-up of marsh fever?"

"Probably," Carmichael said. "A bad one."

"Did the servants send for a physician?" Mackenzie asked.

"I hope so." Carmichael poured himself a mug of tea and added a serious amount of sugar. "I haven't seen him yet. Thought I should stop here and let you all know."

Cassie drained the last of her tea and got to her feet. "I'll go with you, Rob. It sounds like Kirkland will need nursing, preferably by someone who can be trusted with his secrets if he talks when he's feverish."

"Are you a nurse, Cassie?" Carmichael asked with mild surprise.

"Aren't all women sooner or later?" she replied dryly.

"Marsh fever? That's malaria, isn't it?" Kiri hadn't thought that anything could bring down the tireless Kirkland. "Do physicians here use Jesuit bark?"

Carmichael looked blank. "I have no idea. What is it?"

"The bark of the cinchona tree, which grows in South America. The Jesuits learned from the natives about its use to cure fever. There are many fevers in India, so my parents always keep a supply on hand. I don't know if it's as well known in England, since there are fewer fevers here than in hot countries."

It was a fever that had killed Kiri's father before she was born. The general had learned about Jesuit bark from an army friend who had visited Peru, and he had procured it for his household. Unfortunately, the word "Jesuit" usually horrified Protestant Englishmen. The bark needed to be renamed. "I know an apothecary that usually has Jesuit bark. I'll buy some and take it to Kirkland."

"Good. You can show me how to dose him," Cassie said.

"A cup of boiling water poured over a pinch of bark." Kiri used her fingers to demonstrate about how much. "Let it steep for ten minutes or so, then strain and pour it down him. Give him four or five cups a day. I'll prepare the first dose to show you."

"I wish I could go," Mackenzie said with frustration. "But I really can't appear somewhere I'm known so well when I'm dead."

"You won't be dead much longer," Carmichael said with macabre humor. "After the State Opening of Parliament, we'll either have succeeded or failed. Either way, you should be able to return to life."

"How will you do that, Mackenzie?" Kiri asked. "Just

reappear and tell the truth, that you were pretending to be dead while you helped the government look for spies?"

"The truth?" He looked scandalized. "How tedious that would be. Not to mention ruining any possibility of helping Kirkland in the future."

"So what *will* you do?"

"I'll emerge from St. Bart's hospital claiming that I sustained a head wound while pursuing the thieves from Damian's, and hadn't known who I was for several weeks," he explained. "It will be realized that someone else was wrongly identified as me, and my continued existence will be received with cries of joy from all sides. Business will boom at Damian's as people come to see the nine days' wonder."

Kiri laughed. "What about the fact that Kirkland found your ring on the dead man's finger?"

"He must have stolen it from my hand," Mackenzie replied promptly. "Kirkland will claim that the combination of ring and his shock led to the incorrect identification."

Carmichael looked intrigued. "I can help by saying that I wasn't convinced you were dead, so I did some investigating."

"Excellent! You can find me at St. Bart's. With a head injury, I should be able to get away with much outrageousness for months to come." He grinned at Kiri, and she felt her insides melt. Why did he make every other man look boring?

"This is all wonderfully clever," Cassie said impatiently. "But we need to get moving if we want Kirkland to be around for the great discovery."

Her words sent people scattering to collect coats and hats. Kiri hoped the apothecary her parents used would have the cinchona bark in stock. Otherwise, she might have a long search to find some. She'd feel a lot better if Kirkland was dosed with the bark; malaria could be fatal.

Even if it wasn't—and given Kirkland's general state of robust good health, he should pull through—they needed him to recover as quickly as possible. She suspected that no one else could do the job that he did. He was like a great clever spider sitting in the middle of a web of agents high and low. His ability to call on the prince regent or the prime minister and be received was invaluable.

Without him, their chances of success dropped sharply.

Endless nightmares of crawling through burning sands, sliding over ice, frantic to stop assassins. An eternity of aching and tossing and desperate frustration . . .

Kirkland's return to consciousness was a slow process. First he became aware of a ceiling, looking much as ceilings usually did. Eventually it occurred to him to turn his head—which turned out to be damnably more uncomfortable than it should have been.

He was in a bed piled high with covers despite a fire burning merrily across the room. He blinked to bring his surroundings into focus. He was at Mackenzie's house, he realized. In the guest room, where he'd stayed several times before. But why?

"So you've decided to rejoin the living." A cool hand rested on his forehead. "The fever has finally broken. If you're hungry, I might find some chicken broth for you if you ask nicely."

"Cassie?" He blinked up at her. She had circles under her eyes. He had a vague memory of thrashing around in the bed, of being forced to drink a bitter tea, of throwing blankets off when he was feverish and dragging them back on when he was racked with chills. "How long was I out of my head?"

"Three days. A flare-up of marsh fever. Apparently you came here to Mackenzie's late one night and pretty much collapsed. His servants didn't find you passed out here until the next morning."

"Three days!" He struggled to sit up, only to melt back onto his pillow, so exhausted he couldn't lift his head again.

"Behave, James," she said, as sternly as a schoolroom nurse. "You were playing dice with St. Peter for a while because you take such poor care of yourself. You're not leaving this bed until you get your strength back."

He hadn't realized she even knew his Christian name. "I was that ill?"

"Yes."

"I'll behave," he said meekly.

She grinned. "Only because you're too weak to do anything else."

She knew him well. Refusing to dignify her comment with an answer, he asked, "Have you been soothing my fevered brow this whole time?"

"I've been alternating with your valet, and Kiri has come several times. She brought some Jesuit bark and showed us all how to make tea from it, which is probably why you aren't still raving. Plus, all of us can be trusted with your secrets. You have some interesting ones, Kirkland."

He groaned, wondering how much he'd said. "You will, of course, keep silent in return for an annuity that will keep you comfortable for the rest of your life." Then he wished he hadn't said that, because every time she returned to France, there was a good chance she wouldn't survive to come back to England.

But Cassie just smiled. "That will persuade me to hold my tongue until I get a better offer."

Too tired for more banter, he asked, "What about the plot?" He struggled for breath. "The State Opening?"

"No one has been assassinated yet," she said soothingly. "There haven't even been any more attempts. Rob

Carmichael has been coordinating information from your office, which hasn't been hard because not much has happened despite the best efforts of every agent you put to work on this. Maybe the villains have given up."

"No." Kirkland was sure of that with the sixth sense that made him so good in the secret world of intelligence gathering. "A damned heavy sword is waiting to drop."

"That's what I'm afraid of." Cassie also had excellent instincts. "But it's like a ball of yarn. If we can't find the loose end, it's impossible to unravel."

He closed his eyes, knowing that she was right. Much of an investigation like this was pure luck. But hard work created more chances for luck to appear.

Something tickled at the back of his mind. The night he came here, before the fever knocked him endwise . . . Clumsily he searched his memory. "Letters for Mackenzie. I had some in his study. One in particular. His smuggler captain in Kent. Sounded serious."

"I'll collect the mail and get it to Mac today." She smiled a little. "He would have been here if he weren't dead. But for you, it's time to rest again."

Despite the fact that disaster was hovering over the British royals, he was embarrassingly eager to close his eyes and sleep.

Cassie showed up for supper that night looking tired but no longer anxious. Mac asked, "Kirkland is better?"

"The fever has broken and he's rational again, though he's weak as a half-drowned kitten."

"Fever does that," Kiri observed, "but at least he pulled through."

Mac forced his gaze back to Cassie because he had a bad tendency to stare at Kiri like a moon calf if he wasn't careful. They'd spent the last three nights together, and the more he was with her, the more of her he wanted.

"With the help of your Jesuit bark. His attack was a bad one. Very bad." Cassie didn't need to elaborate further. "Mac, I brought some letters that were at your house. Kirkland was collecting them when the fever struck. Almost the first thing he said when he came around was that there's a letter you must read from your smuggler down in Kent. It made his instincts twitch." She produced a bundle of letters and handed them to him.

"And we all know Kirkland's instincts are powerful and dangerous." Mac took the letters and began shuffling through. "If you'll excuse me for a moment."

He found the letter quickly and read it, frowning. "Hawk, the smuggler captain, is concerned about something, or perhaps someone, that came over from France. He wants me to come down to Kent and meet him at the smugglers' hideout at nightfall tomorrow." Hawk hadn't specified the location, but he'd known Mac would understand.

Kiri's brow furrowed. "Is it plausible that he'd write you like this? He wouldn't have heard of your death?"

"Not likely he reads the London newspapers regularly, and even if he did, he probably assumes that Mackenzie is a false name since it's Scottish and I'm English," Mac said, puzzling it out. "Smuggling is his family business, but he's a loyal Englishman. He has to know that he has transported more than wine and spirits for me. If he learned something he thought should be passed on to the authorities, I'm probably the only person he would know to reach."

Kiri's brow furrowed. "Since I acquired the knife with the Alejandro-scented paper from the smugglers, there must be some connection with the conspirators. But the State Opening is close. Can you get down there, talk to Hawk, and get back in time?"

"There will be time and to spare," he assured her. "But

it wouldn't be a disaster if I'm held up down there. Carmichael and Kirkland are better at organizing protection for the royals and the Palace of Westminster. Socializing with smugglers and other shady characters is my specialty."

"What if Kirkland is still laid up?"

Mac considered that. "I'll be back in time."

"I should go with you," Kiri said. "You suggested before that I might go with you to the smugglers to try to identify the lead kidnapper."

Mac shook his head. "Different circumstances. This time I'm only going to meet with Hawk rather than make a regular business call to the whole band. If I bring a stranger, Hawk might be reluctant to talk."

She bit her lip, looking concerned. "It doesn't feel safe for you to go alone."

"None of what we're doing is particularly safe, but I've been dealing with Hawk for years. If he's worried, I need to talk to him."

She looked unconvinced but let the subject drop. He wondered if her misgivings were related to the fact that they were new lovers. Certainly he didn't like letting her out of his sight, and she might feel the same way. But he wouldn't be gone long, and it was quite possible that Hawk would have useful information. At this point, any promising lead needed to be checked out. Immediately.

The coast of Kent was cold and unforgiving at the end of November. Rather uncanny, too, though Mac had been to the hideaway often enough before. If he were the imaginative sort, he'd be looking for ghosts behind every boulder.

He'd used a post chaise to get to Dover, changing horses at every stage. Then he'd hired a sturdy horse from a stable he'd used before to take him the last few miles to the smugglers' cave.

Despite his best speed, he was late. A new moon meant a dark night, and wind-chased clouds obscured even the starlight. Glad he had a lantern, he made his way down the rocky path to the cave.

He was relieved to smell a fire as he approached the entrance. Hawk was probably still waiting. He entered with the lantern held high, alert and hopeful that there would be benefit to this long ride. "Hawk?"

"Ah, ye made it! I was getting that worried."

But the voice wasn't Hawk's. It was Howard, the angry smuggler who'd wanted Kiri. Mac instantly tried to retreat, but his exit was cut off by two more smugglers who'd been lurking by the entrance. They must have heard him coming and positioned themselves.

They leaped at him with clubs. Mac was fast enough to avoid the worst of their blows, but one grazed his skull hard enough to knock him down and scramble his wits for a few critical moments.

As he fell, Howard barked, "Don't kill 'im. He's worth more alive!"

By the time Mac's head cleared, he'd been stripped and his pockets emptied. Then he was dragged across the cave and chained to the wall. Not with rusted manacles like the one used on Kiri, but two shiny new restraints, one for each wrist. They looked as if they'd been installed just for Mac.

As soon as Mac was secured, Howard came to stand before him, a shotgun ready in his hand as he kept outside of kicking range. "So the fancy London gentleman was stupid enough to believe my handwriting was Hawk's. Mebbe I have a fine career as a forger ahead of me."

Furious with himself for walking into a trap, Mac said coolly, "You've gone to a lot of effort to get me down here,

Howard. Wouldn't it have been easier to wait until my next regular visit?"

"We get a special price for producing you now. Plus, there's no Hawk around at this time of the month to spoil the fun." His eyes narrowed. "Tell me, was that slut you stole from me a good piece? I've been wondering."

Mac's rage was instant and annihilating, but he channeled it into icy contempt. "A man like you cannot even imagine how amazing and special such a woman is."

Howard gave a harsh cackle of amusement. "So you weren't able to get her on her back. You probably prefer molly boys."

That was so absurd Mac had to smile. "Your insults are childish, Howard. Who paid you to lure me down here?"

Howard hesitated as if weighing whether to reply before he said, "An old army friend of yours named Swinnerton. Now that you're caught, I'll send a message to London to bring him down here right away. When he's done with you, he's promised you'll be dead. I'm hoping he'll let me do the honors." Howard's hand tightened on his pistol. "It's like a bonus on top of what he's payin' us to catch you."

Howard continued his taunts, but Mac stopped listening. Rupert Swinnerton. When they'd played cards at the Captain's Club, he must have recognized Mac despite the disguise. He also had to be part of the conspiracy. The mastermind? Probably not—Rupert was no strategist. But he was tough and battle-hardened, and he must have been the leader of the men who had tried to kidnap the princess from Damian's.

It was already night, so it would take two days to get the message to London and for Swinnerton to come down to Kent. It was likely that he wanted to learn how much the government knew of the conspiracy. He'd still have time to get back to London before the State Opening.

Mac surreptitiously tested his manacles. If he had

tools, he could free himself, but he didn't have so much as a diamond ring like Kiri's. Until the situation changed, he was well and truly caught. He drew a deep, slow breath, then settled down against the wall as comfortably as he could.

If he was going to be a prisoner for two days, he hoped they'd at least feed him.

Chapter 37

Mackenzie was in trouble. Kiri knew that in her bones. Over two days had passed, long enough for him to reach the coast and return at the speed he traveled. In theory his business with Hawk might have taken more time, but she didn't believe that. Any discussion with the smuggler captain would have been short, and probably required Mackenzie to head back to London at top speed.

Beyond that, her instincts were screaming that something was wrong. She was not a worrier by nature and she had faith in Mackenzie's competence, so she trusted her intuition on this: Things had not gone as he had planned.

But what could she do about it? She had a good sense of direction and could probably find the smugglers' cave again, but she wasn't sure what she would do when she got there. Too many possibilities, starting with the likelihood that he wouldn't be in the cave. And if he wasn't, she hadn't the least idea where to find him.

Starkly she forced herself to recognize that he could already be dead. This conspiracy had already cost lives. And if he was gone—she might never know how.

The two days he'd been gone felt like two weeks because she'd had so little to do. She could hardly go to gambling clubs and sniff the customers without him. So today she'd come to Mackenzie's house, in theory to help with Kirkland, but mostly to keep herself busy. He was improving and his mind was back to its usual sharpness, but he was still so drained by the fever that he could barely walk from bed to wing chair.

She'd spent most of the morning quietly reading in his room, occasionally talking if he wanted to. Then his protective and unflappable valet had chased her out of the room so he could give Kirkland a bath. That gave Kiri an excuse to wander through the house, which was comfortable with a dash of eccentric. She could almost feel Mackenzie here, though it didn't reduce her anxiety.

She was in the drawing room when the knocker sounded. Wondering if it was Cassie or Carmichael, she moved into the front hall as Mac's footman opened the door.

Silhouetted against the light was a familiar tall, broadshouldered figure. "Mackenzie!" She hurled herself across the hall and into his arms. "I've been so worried!"

As he caught her arms, she froze. Something wasn't right. She pulled away when a surprised voice said, "Lady Kiri? I didn't realize you knew my brother."

She looked up, then swallowed hard as her heart sank. "Lord Masterson. I thought you were in Spain."

"I was already heading home when I read of my brother's death." He dismissed the footman with a glance and took Kiri's arm to lead her into the drawing room. "I headed straight for Kirkland's house when I reached London, and his butler sent me here." Masterson closed the door so they were private. "Things are often complicated where Mac is concerned. You . . . you didn't act as if you thought him dead."

Masterson's tense expression could not conceal the desperate hope in his eyes. "As of two days ago, he was alive and well, Lord Masterson," she said swiftly.

"Thank *God!*" His eyes squeezed shut and Kiri suspected that he was fighting back tears.

When he had regained control, he opened his eyes and asked, "What has been going on? Why are you in my brother's house? Are you and Kirkland . . . ?" His words trailed off as if he couldn't mentally bring them together.

He started again. "If this has anything to do with Kirkland's government work, I'm fully aware of it, and I've sent him information when anything useful came my way."

"In that case, let's both sit down and I'll explain. Kirkland is recovering from a bad bout of fever and tires easily, so better you have a good idea of what's going on before you see him."

"Admirably efficient," Masterson murmured. "I'm all ears, Lady Kiri."

Kiri took a chair, spent a moment organizing her thoughts, and began to talk. She started with her being captured by the kidnappers, moved to Damian's and the attempt to kidnap Princess Charlotte. Then she described what they knew of the conspiracy, and how they were trying to stop it before major damage was done.

Masterson listened without interrupting, absorbing every word. When Kiri was done, he said, "I understand why Mac thought it best to seem dead. I just wish I'd known that he was all right."

"Kirkland wrote you the next day and used a government courier to get the letter to you as quickly as possible," Kiri said.

"The letter is probably waiting for me back with my regiment. I didn't decide to come home for winter until quite recently, so Kirkland's best attempts didn't work out." Masterson got to his feet. "I'd like to see Kirkland now if he's awake."

"You need to check what I've told you against what he has to say," Kiri agreed.

"I'm not testing you," Masterson said swiftly.

"I know. But I am an amateur at spying, and my understanding might be poor."

"Actually, you seem very like Ashton," Masterson said. "Very clear and fair in your thinking."

Kiri almost blushed. "Thank you. That's a high compliment."

"It's meant to be." Masterson paused at the door. "Are you coming up with me to see Kirkland?"

"It will be easier for you to talk without another person present."

He nodded and left. Kiri stayed in the drawing room and . . . plotted.

It wasn't long before Lord Masterson returned. Again Kiri was struck by the general similarity of the brothers. Since they were both tall, broad-shouldered, and powerfully built, it would be easy to confuse them at a distance if a person didn't know them well. Even their features had a similar cast, though Mackenzie had the mismatched eyes and more auburn in his hair.

The real difference was in their personalities. Mackenzie had an irresistible sparkle of mischief and charm, while Masterson had a deep, quiet calm that gave the impression that he could handle anything. She guessed that the two men might have become either enemies who drove each other crazy, or friends who balanced each other. She was glad they had become friends.

Masterson was looking sober, his initial exhilaration at his brother's survival superseded by concern. "Kirkland looks like a herd of horses ran over him. I suffered a similar fever in Spain last year, and it took weeks to get my strength back. His thinking is clear, though, and he confirmed everything you said. I'm glad I came back. If there's going to be trouble at the State Opening of Parliament, I should take my seat in the Lords and be prepared to help if necessary."

"We may need all the help we can get," she said glumly. "We've not had much luck with finding the conspirators, and time is running out."

"Why were you so concerned for Mac that you threw yourself into my arms?" A smile lurked in Masterson's eyes. "Not that I didn't enjoy it, but your reaction did suggest serious anxiety."

"I've been worried ever since he got a letter from the smuggler captain asking him to go down to Kent." She sighed in frustration. "I had no reason to be so concerned. It just felt dangerous from the beginning. Now that he's later than expected, my stomach is tied in knots."

"I've learned not to discount intuition," Masterson said slowly. "I started feeling concerned about my brother in Spain. It was a major reason I decided to return to England when we went into winter quarters. While I'm vastly relieved that Mac wasn't killed at his club, I find that I still feel some concern."

They regarded each other thoughtfully. "You must be tired of traveling, Lord Masterson," Kiri said in her most persuasive voice. "But . . . would you be willing to accompany me down to Kent? I have been wanting to go but wasn't sure I could do anything on my own."

"If we decided to go down to Kent to prove our worries groundless, do you have a chaperone who might travel with us?"

She grinned. "Lord Masterson, I have been living outside the rules for long enough that I see no reason to worry about respectability now. Let's just *go*."

Blessedly imperturbable, he said, "If we're going to run away together, Lady Kiri, you should call me Will."

"And I'm Kiri." She bounced from her chair. "I need to return to the house Kirkland keeps for his agents. 11 Exeter Street, near Covent Garden. I'll change to more practical garments and be ready to go. Is there anything you need to do?"

"I'll leave my gear here, hire a post chaise, and come collect you."

"Done!" Kiri swept from the room to ask the footman to call a carriage for her. She'd always thought well of Will Masterson in their casual meetings at her brother's house. Now she decided that he was *wonderful.*

Mac did get fed, though the cheese, dry bread, and water were barely enough to sustain life. One manacle was undone so that he could eat and take care of sanitation needs, but with his other wrist still chained and an armed man always watching him, there were no opportunities for escape.

The worse part was having nothing to do but listen to the endless sloshing of the waves. Thinking about Kiri helped, because she was never dull even in memory. After the first day ended, he was uneasily aware that she would be starting to worry.

By the time the two days had passed and Rupert Swinnerton arrived, Mac was ready for a confrontation just to end the boredom. Probably it would end with Mac's death—and wouldn't that be an adventure to discover what, if anything, came next! But from what he knew of Swinnerton, the man might want to indulge in some exotic way of killing Mac that would enable him to feel superior. If that meant unchaining Mac from the wall, he might just have a chance.

Howard heard Swinnerton's approach along the path and went out to meet him. Mac mentally prepared himself. After two days of confinement, he was cold and . . . afraid, though he hated to admit it. Since he was officially dead already, he ought to be able to handle the real thing.

No amount of joking could completely eliminate the fear, though. He loved life, loved where he was in it—and he loved Kiri. With the end imminent, he admitted that to himself, for there was no more time for evasion or denial.

Swinnerton entered with the swagger of a man who knew he held a winning hand. That was as Mac expected—but he wasn't prepared for the man who walked beside Swinnerton and carried a lantern.

The man wasn't prepared for him, either. "Mackenzie!" The lantern shook in Baptiste's hand, the flames flaring wildly. "But you were killed! I saw your body. . . ." He stared, his eyes black and incredulous.

Baptiste. Mac had known someone at Damian's must have cooperated with the kidnappers, and told himself that no one was above suspicion. Even so—he had never dreamed it was Baptiste, who had been his friend as well as his most trusted employee.

Swinnerton laughed, and Mac realized that the bastard had been looking forward to Baptiste's shock. He enjoyed pain.

Concealing his own shock, Mac drawled, "You took your time getting here, Rupert. Jean-Claude, I'm disappointed in you. Wasn't I paying you enough?"

Face pale, Baptiste said, "I was told they only wanted to retrieve a runaway girl before she could ruin herself. Nothing criminal, and no one would be hurt. And then"—his face worked—"you and another man died."

"If you're going to let yourself be corrupted, you should be more careful who you allow to do the corrupting." Mac's gaze shifted to Swinnerton. "I assume my disguise wasn't quite as good as I thought the night we played cards."

"You almost fooled me," Swinnerton admitted. "But I wondered why a diamond of the first water would hang on the arm of such a boring man, so I looked more closely. When I saw you spread your cards in a particular way, I realized who you were." His thin lips twisted with anticipation. "Now I will learn what you and your friends know about our plans."

Mac thought swiftly. Swinnerton knew they had some sense of the plot, so there was no point in pretending complete ignorance. It was reasonable that he and "his friends" had figured out that there was a plot aimed at the British royals, but he mustn't give away that they were sure the State Opening would be the focus. If Swinnerton realized that, there would be time for him and his cohorts to change their plans.

Therefore, Mac could admit to some knowledge, but he couldn't reveal that too easily or Swinnerton would be suspicious. "Why would I want to tell you anything?"

"*This* is why!" Swinnerton lifted a short riding whip that hadn't been visible in the shadowy cave and slashed at Mac's eyes,

Acting on pure reflex, Mac jerked away and ducked his head. The lash blazed across his left temple, but the pain was nothing compared to the panic triggered by memories of the near-lethal lashing he'd received in the army. He'd nearly died in agony, and now, as then, his wrists were secured so he couldn't avoid the blows.

Swinnerton slashed at Mac's throat. Again he was only partially successful, but the lash left an arc of choking fire. Since Mac planned to talk anyhow, he let a cry of pain escape. A third lash followed, and he cowered away. "For God's sake. Swinnerton! What do you want to know?"

A fourth stroke followed. "I knew you'd break easily,"

Swinnerton said with vicious satisfaction. "After that army flogging, showing a whip should be enough to make you turn craven." He struck again.

"If you're going to whip me anyhow," Mac gasped, "why the devil should I talk?"

"There is that." Looking regretful, Swinnerton let the whip drop to his side. "Tell me what you know."

"No more whipping?" By telling himself he was playing a role, Mac was able to let go of his pride and cower. Cowering was easy. Letting go of his pride was more difficult. Thank God Kiri wasn't here, or he'd probably let himself be whipped until he died of heart failure. "Your word as a gentleman?"

Swinnerton laughed. "I love to see you grovel. Very well, time is short because I must get back to London, so no more whipping. Tell me what you know of our plans."

"You're targeting the British royals in order to throw the government into disarray," Mac said wearily. "You tried to kidnap Princess Charlotte Augusta"—Baptiste made a strangled sound—"and made unsuccessful attempts to assassinate the prince regent and the Duke of York. I suspect the French goal is to create a situation where Britain will be willing to end the war by treaty, with certain territories under French dominion to be returned to us and France keeping the rest of her conquests."

Swinnerton's brows arched. "You're more intelligent than you look."

"I had help." Blood was trickling down Mac's forehead and into one eye, and with his hands manacled, he couldn't scratch or wipe it away. "Since you're going to kill me anyhow, satisfy my curiosity about what you're planning."

"Why should I satisfy you in anything, you filthy wife-killer?" Swinnerton hissed.

"You know damned well I didn't kill your wife, Rupert," Mac said. "You're the one who beat her to death and tried to pin the crime on me. As for why you should tell me, it's so I can suffer the frustration of knowing and not being able to stop you."

Swinnerton's eyes narrowed. "That actually has merit. But this is for your ears only." He waved the other men back. With the constant sound of waves filling the air, all he had to do was lower his voice to ensure privacy. "We will strike at the State Opening of Parliament. You know the Chancellor's Woolsack, which sits right before the throne in the House of Lords?"

Mac nodded. "Big square red thing filled with wool to remind the lords of the source of England's medieval wealth."

"You know history! I am impressed." Swinnerton gave a smile that showed his teeth. "Princess Charlotte will sit on the Woolsack during the ceremony. A bomb inside will surely kill her, the prince regent, the prime minister, and a good number of England's peers. Clever idea, isn't it?"

Mac gasped, sickened by the knowledge of what would happen. "How are you going to get a bomb into the Palace of Westminster and set it off without being noticed?"

"A cooperative peer of the realm made it easy. Setting it off will be just as easy." Swinnerton's eyes narrowed. "Last question. I'm running out of time and patience."

"Do you wear a cologne called Alejandro?"

Swinnerton's reptilian eyes blinked in surprise. "A strange question for your last on earth. Yes, I have a bottle of the stuff my brother gave me and I wear it sometimes, though it's not my favorite." He turned and beckoned the other men closer. "Good-bye, Mackenzie. Knowing you has been an appalling experience."

So Swinnerton had been the leader of the kidnappers. If he'd worn Alejandro that night at the Captain's Club, Kiri would have been able to give certain identification. They had been so bloody close to cracking the conspiracy.

Swinnerton said to Howard, "You can kill Mackenzie with lingering misery?"

"Aye, sir. There's a tunnel in the back of the cave that goes down to the cove. When the tide is low, we come and go that way. The tunnel floods when the tide comes in." Howard smiled wolfishly. "I drilled a nice new metal hook in a rock below the high-tide level. I'll chain the bastard to that and leave him to wait for the tide to come in."

Swinnerton considered death by slow drowning, with the victim fighting frantically for breath as the water rose higher and higher. "I like that very well," he said with a decisive nod. "Go ahead, then. Baptiste, stay here until you're sure Mackenzie is dead. You know he needs to die, don't you?"

Baptiste nodded mutely. He still looked pale, but resigned.

"I'll see you in London, then." Swinnerton took one of the lanterns. "Enjoy the execution." Then he turned and marched from the cave, arrogant as always.

As well he should be. The corrupt devil had won.

Chapter 38

The wind off the Channel cut to the bone, and Kiri had never been more aware of how far north Britain was. She could use some of India's suffocating heat. At least her divided skirt and riding astride were warmer than a side saddle would have been.

"A nasty night." Will Masterson rode between Kiri and the coast, breaking some of the force of the wind. His enveloping greatcoat was similar to Mackenzie's, and in the dark, they looked unnervingly similar. "Do we have much farther to go?"

"If that's a tactful way of inquiring whether I'm lost, the answer is no, I don't think so." She checked the landmarks. "We have between one and two miles to go."

Will laughed. "It sounds like you have your brother's sense of direction."

"Adam is good at such things?" Having known her big brother only a few months, there was much she didn't know about him.

"Though he's a peaceable sort, he has the talents of a first-rate officer." Will shook his head with mock mournfulness. "All wasted since he's a duke. Actually, you'd make a good officer, too, Kiri, if women were allowed to serve."

"Me?" she asked, startled. "What a strange thought."

"You're decisive and a natural leader. I suspect you also start feeling restless if cooped up in drawing rooms."

"You're very perceptive, Lord Masterson," she said, a little unnerved by the accuracy of his observation. She was only now beginning to realize how ill-suited she was for the drawing-room life. "It's more amusing to ride through a stormy night on what may be a wild-goose chase."

"Maybe it's a wild-goose chase," he said. "But my intuition is still twitching."

"So is mine," she admitted. Not just twitching, but screaming that there was danger and time was running out. "I wish there was moonlight, but it was a dark night on my first ride through this country, too."

"A new moon is good for conducting business at a smuggler's hideaway. Mac and his captain wouldn't be interrupted."

"In theory." Kiri spotted a familiar wind-twisted tree ahead. "Here's our turn."

As Will fell in behind her on the narrow track, she prayed they'd find Mackenzie alive and well at the end of the road.

Howard turned to Mac, his eyes avid. "Tide is just turning now. The perfect time to stake you down there, Mackenzie."

He snapped orders to his two men. They leaped on Mac and immobilized his legs while Howard unlocked the chains from the wall. He removed one manacle and left the other on since it gave him a chain for dragging Mac to his feet. Mac struggled, but he was so chilled and stiff from sitting for two days that he couldn't put up much of a fight.

With the manacle biting into Mac's abraded right wrist, Howard hauled him to the back of the cave. A narrow, irregularly shaped tunnel slanted down toward the cove. With Howard and one of his men ahead and Baptiste and the other man behind, Mac had no chance to escape, and the narrowness of the passage meant he kept banging into the walls and protruding rocks.

The passage ended at a slightly widened area with water boiling up furiously. Each wave splashed a little higher in the tunnel. Howard locked Mac's manacle to the shiny steel hook set into the rocky wall. "I've been waiting for this moment." He stepped back, his expression gloating. "Now I can stand here and watch you drown."

The narrowness of the tunnel concentrated the force of the water. The next wave splashed over Mac's boots. "Good. If you stay, I'll have a light for my final moments."

Baptiste said in a choked voice, "Howard, let's go above rather than wait and watch. This tunnel is too crowded."

Howard laughed. "You mean you're too squeamish to watch a man die. I'm not."

"We can play cards by the fire rather than freeze here," Baptiste pointed out.

Howard's eyes narrowed. "Do you play brag?"

"I know the game," Baptiste said. If Mac hadn't been so bruised and cold, he might have laughed at how Baptiste understated his skill to give Howard confidence.

"I'll play if the stakes are good," Howard said.

Baptiste shrugged. "Set them where you will as long as we don't stay here."

One of Howard's men said, "I'd just as soon take my money and go home and leave you to this."

When the other mumbled agreement, Howard gave them both a couple of gold coins. As they left, he turned to Mac and said in a gloating voice, "You'll die in the dark, Mackenzie. The sea always wins. Water's cold at this season, and it will keep coming. Higher and higher, and no matter how much you struggle, it will rise over your head.

"That'll take time, though. Sometimes you'll be able to grab a breath, then the salt will be in your mouth and you'll be screaming underwater for air until you die."

"You've a gift for description, Howard." Mac was just about able to manage a lazy drawl. "And here I thought your only talents were stupidity and treachery." As insults went, not his best, but he wasn't in his best shape, either.

Howard kicked at him but didn't connect when Mac stepped deeper into the water. "This tunnel isn't used much," the smuggler hissed. "I think I'll leave your body here till the crabs and fish have picked your bones."

Mac shrugged. "Do as you will. I won't care."

Expression furious, Howard turned to climb the tunnel, the lantern swinging in his hand. Baptiste lingered. "I'm sorry, Mac. I never meant for any of this to happen."

"Hell is paved with good intentions," Mac said wearily. "So get the hell out."

As Baptiste turned, he dropped an object to the sandy floor where the water had yet to reach. Then he was gone.

As the last glimmer of lantern light vanished, Mac leaned over and scooped up the object. It was Baptiste's penknife—an ingenious special model that Mac had given the other man as a gift the previous year.

Unlike most penknives, where blade and handle were solid, this knife had two different pieces that folded into the handle. One was a standard blade for sharpening quills, the other was a narrow silver spike for use as a toothpick. And Baptiste had not dropped it by accident.

Holding the penknife in icy hands, Mac managed to latch open the toothpick. By this time the darkness was absolute, but he didn't need light to find the manacle. Though the lock was simple, trying to pick it in the dark as frigid water splashed over him was damnably difficult.

To complicate matters, his right wrist was the one chained and he had to work with his left hand.

He'd almost sprung the lock when the knife slipped from his numb fingers. Panicked, he filled his lungs and knelt, submerged in the ice water as he felt around on the stony floor with his left hand. The force of the current tossed pebbles and small shells along with the tide, and was strong enough to move the knife.

He couldn't find it. *He couldn't find it.* He straightened and gulped in more air, then knelt and resumed searching with fingers that no longer had sensation. Where the devil was it? He filled his lungs once more, then ducked under for the third time.

There! The knife was on the verge of being washed out of his reach, but he managed to grab it. As he stood and gasped for breath, he tucked his left hand under his right arm in the hope he might be able to restore some sensation. But he couldn't wait long to try again. The water was halfway up his chest and rising fast.

Working with excruciating care, he inserted the tooth-pick into the lock and moved it around, trying to strike the pin without breaking the pick. He poked over and over. Howard's prediction of gulping air in the lull between on-rushing waves had come true.

The lock sprang open as a wave washed over his head. Lungs burning, Mac jerked free of the manacle and staggered upward through the churning water. He crashed hard into a wall, but his head broke above the water and he gulped in the blessed air.

He spent a couple of minutes leaning against the wall and marshaling his strength as he analyzed his situation. Though he hadn't drowned, he might freeze to death without warmth and dry clothes. He couldn't stay where he was because they would find him when they came down to verify his death. There was no place to hide between here and the main cavern, where they would be sitting by a fire and playing cards.

One way or another, he would have to get by Howard and Baptiste if he was to survive. Baptiste probably wouldn't attack him, having given him the means to escape drowning, but Howard was armed and dangerous enough to kill both of them.

Rising water splashed his chin, so it was time to get moving. The longer Mac waited, the more his condition would deteriorate. Emerging from the water into the bitterly cold air made him feel even more frozen, and his saturated boots and clothing weighed on him like lead.

He climbed grimly, feeling his way through absolute blackness while trying to avoid crashing into any more rocky walls than was absolutely necessary. The way up seemed much longer than the way down had.

The climb took so long that he was beginning to wonder if Howard and Baptiste had extinguished the fire and left the cave for some more comfortable place. Then he saw a faint light ahead. Rationally he knew he'd be better off if the men had left the cave, but the light was heartening.

Moving as silently as his numb feet could manage, he continued toward the light—and abruptly found himself in the main cave. He'd thought that it was farther ahead because the light wasn't strong, but now he saw that the fire was blocked by the two men sitting at a table in front of it.

He froze, hoping they wouldn't notice, but Howard must have heard his footsteps. The smuggler glanced toward the tunnel and his jaw dropped with shock before he rose from his chair and grabbed his shotgun. "Damn you to hell! Why can't you just *die?*"

"I never had much patience for sitting around." Mac stared at the weapon, wondering his odds for dodging a lethal blast of shot. He could probably avoid being killed right off, but he was bound to be wounded and then he'd become easy prey.

"Rot in hell, Mackenzie!" Howard raised the shotgun to his shoulder and aimed.

As the smuggler's finger tightened on the trigger, Baptiste stood, calmly took aim with a pocket pistol, and shot Howard in the back at point-blank range.

Howard made a gurgling sound and his eyes widened with disbelief. Then he crashed to the floor like a felled tree.

There was absolute silence in the cavern for a dozen heartbeats. Then Mac sighed and walked toward the fire. He spared a glance for Howard and saw that the man wasn't breathing, and good riddance.

Mac tossed the pocketknife to Baptiste and came to a stop as close to the fire as he could get without burning. He was shaking all over with a combination of cold and reaction. As he held his icy hands toward the flames, he asked, "Why, Jean-Claude? For money? Even if Swinnerton claimed they were trying to catch a runaway heiress before she ruined herself, you can't have believed the story or you would have told me about it."

Baptiste barely managed to catch the pocketknife. His shaking hands fumbling, he managed to fold the knife and tuck it away. "I suspected Swinnerton wasn't being truthful, but I didn't see much harm in giving him the information needed to enter the club. I never thought there would be violence."

Mac's eyes narrowed as he studied the face of the man who had been his trusted friend. "How much did they pay you?"

"I didn't do it for money." His mouth twisted. "Their French master promised to send my mother out of France. I haven't seen her since I fled the Reign of Terror."

Mac caught his breath, understanding the power of

that. He would give a great deal to see his mother again, even if only for an hour. "Did they keep their word?"

"They sent a copy of her death certificate." Baptiste's voice broke. "She died over two years ago, and I didn't know it. So it was all for nothing. I betrayed you and England for *nothing!*"

He'd precipitated a disaster in the process, but Mac couldn't help but feel sorry for the other man. God knew that Mac had made monumental errors himself. Sleeping with a fellow officer's wife had been criminally stupid, and it had damned near got him killed. He would have died if Will and Randall hadn't made extraordinary efforts to save him. "Tell me more about the conspiracy. Who is involved, and who is their French connection? Surely not Napoleon."

Baptiste's mouth twisted. "Joseph Fouché."

Mac sucked in his breath. The ruthless French revolutionary had been many things, most notably the commissioner of police. "Isn't he out of power now?"

"Yes, and he wants to regain Napoleon's favor."

"By targeting the British royal family and creating the conditions for a peace treaty." Mac whistled softly. It all made sense now. "Who are his conspirators on this side of the Channel? Surely he didn't contact you directly."

Baptiste shook his head. "Lord Fendall and Rupert Swinnerton are half brothers. Their mother, Marie Therese Croizet, was sister to Fouché's mother."

"Making Swinnerton and Fendall first cousins to Fouché. Perfect tools." Mac frowned. "Didn't you tell me once your family came from the same village as Fouché?"

"Yes, Le Pellerin, near Nantes. He was older and I didn't know him, but I knew his family when I was a boy." Baptiste gave a very Gallic shrug. "That connection was the basis for my friendship with Lord Fendall. He liked hearing tales of the village, which he had visited several times as a child. I liked that we shared some history. It did not occur to me that he was not to be trusted until it was too late."

"I suppose they were after wealth and power."

"Exactly. I don't know the details," Baptiste said, "but great estates in France and vast wealth were promised to both of them."

"Did you know the Frenchman who was killed at the club?"

"I didn't meet the men Swinnerton brought that night. But Fouché would have insisted on having some of his men in the group to look out for his interests."

It sounded as if Baptiste's involvement with the conspiracy had been minor. "The kidnappers included two Frenchmen, and also two boxers. One looked enough like me to play my corpse."

Baptiste blanched again. "When I came out and saw the bodies and Lord Kirkland said you'd been killed . . ."

It sounded as if Baptiste had suffered mightily for his sins. Mac couldn't bring himself to regret that, given the consequences of the other man's mistake. "When you realized that there was trouble afoot, why didn't you report it to the authorities?"

"Who could I have spoken to without getting into even more trouble?" Baptiste asked cynically.

"You could have talked to Kirkland."

"To be honest, I always thought of him as a dilettante who enjoyed having an interest in the club without having to do any real work." Baptiste's brow furrowed. "I underestimated him."

That was an understatement of massive proportions, but Baptiste really couldn't be blamed for taking Kirkland at face value. Kirkland worked hard to appear negligible.

"Besides," Baptiste continued, "though I was appalled

that two men had died, I didn't know until tonight that the girl they were after was Princess Charlotte."

"I certainly never expected her to come to Damian's in disguise," Mac agreed. "Did you know that Swinnerton failed?"

"No, Fendall didn't say anything about that night, and I didn't want to ask. I just wanted them to leave me alone. They did until Swinnerton said I must come down here and speak to some Frenchman who had crossed the Channel."

"He wanted to shock you with my presence." Mac's shivering wasn't quite as bad, though he was still cold right down to his marrow.

Baptiste gave him a level look. "Are you going to have me arrested?"

Mac sighed. "You saved my life twice tonight, so I don't think I should send you to be hanged."

Baptiste looked relieved. "I thought you would be furious."

"I am, but if you're clapped into prison, who will manage the damned club?"

The other man gasped. "You will allow me to keep my position?"

"It's hard to find a good manager I can trust." Mac's eyes narrowed. "I will be able to trust you in the future, won't I?"

"*Oui*. Yes. Always." Baptiste drew a shuddering breath. "England has been my refuge. I would never knowingly have worked against her."

Mac believed that. The bait Fendall had offered would have turned most men's heads. "In another week, I'll either be dead for real or will be able to miraculously return to life. Go back to London and pretend nothing has happened."

Baptiste closed his eyes, shock and relief rippling across his face. "You are . . . generous."

"You made a huge error in judgment, but your betrayal

was not deliberate." And there was the small matter of Baptiste's saving his life. "But for now, get out of my sight."

"I shall." Baptiste handed him a silver flask. "Cognac. Your horse is out in the paddock. Shall I saddle it before I leave?"

"That would be good." Mac was glad that Baptiste had thought about transportation back to Dover, since Mac's concentration was on keeping himself from falling apart until he was alone.

He opened the flask and drank, allowing himself only a mouthful. The spirit burned all the way down his throat, creating at least the illusion of warmth. Feeling too tired to stand any longer, he slumped into one of the chairs beside the card table. From the cards he could see, it looked like Baptiste had been winning.

"Is there anything I can do to stop the conspirators?" Baptiste asked.

"Tell Rupert that I'm dead and my body is food for the fishes. Look normal so he and Fendall won't feel the need to change their plans." Mac took another swig of brandy and debated whether to have Baptiste deliver a message to Kirkland. No, Mac could be there almost as soon, and it would be better not to expose Kirkland's work. "Put more coal on the fire before you leave."

Baptiste obeyed, the coal rattling in the scoop, then an increase in light and heat. "*Merci, mon ami,*" he said quietly, adding a few more words in French that Mac didn't catch. Then the sound of footsteps leaving the cave, and Mac was blessedly alone.

He needed to head back to London and tell Kirkland about the plot, but first he had to recover enough for the journey. Steam was rising gently from his saturated garments. Howard's clothes were dry, except for the blood. Mac's stomach turned at the thought of stripping the smuggler's body.

Telling himself the garments would be too small anyhow, he crossed his arms on the card table and rested his head on them. He'd warm up and get some rest, then off to Dover and London. . . .

Chapter 39

Despite Kiri's clawing anxiety about Mackenzie, she let Will Masterson lead the way down the path to the cave. Not only was he as anxious as she was, but years as a serving officer made him well suited for going into unknown territory.

They left their horses in the small meadow that the smugglers used for a paddock. The presence of another saddled horse suggested that there was at least one person in the hideout, maybe more.

Will had a pistol at the ready while Kiri had her knife. The wind blew spray into their faces from the incoming tide as they covered the last stretch. Kiri's heart pounded like a trip hammer as they entered the cave. Please, God, let Mackenzie be alive!

Light and smoke emerged from the main cave, but no sound. Will made a hand motion for her to stay near the entrance while he moved forward. She ignored that and stayed right behind him.

He cocked his pistol and held it ready as he stepped into the main chamber. The broad, powerful body that was so much like Mackenzie's blocked her view. Limned by firelight, Will turned his head, his gaze raking the cave for possible danger.

"*Damian!*" Will uncocked his pistol and slammed it into his holster as he sprinted across the cavern.

Kiri's heart clenched as she saw the solid figure slumped lifelessly over a table by the fire. Then Mackenzie raised his head, startled into wakefulness.

"Will?" he said incredulously. He lurched to his feet, battered, bruised, and bloody. He looked like a very large, handsome drowned rat. But unmistakably alive.

Will grabbed his brother in a crushing bear hug. "You have *got* to stop getting yourself into these situations!"

"*Damn,* Will." Mackenzie returned the bear hug. "It's good to have a big brother to rescue me."

"Doesn't look like you needed much rescuing."

Kiri followed Will's gaze and saw a crumpled body on the floor. Apparently she and Will had been right to be worried.

Mackenzie grimaced. "Not my handiwork. How the devil did you find me?"

"She brought me here." Will nodded toward Kiri, who had stayed by the entrance during the brothers' reunion.

Mackenzie pivoted and stared at her as if she were an angel descended from on high. "Kiri?" he said huskily. "Is that really you or am I still dreaming?"

"In person." Half a dozen steps brought her into his arms and absurdly close to tears. "I *told* you that you shouldn't come down here alone!"

He was soaking wet and deathly cold, but still strong enough to embrace her so tightly that all the king's horses and all the king's men would have trouble separating them. "It was a near run thing, Kiri. I . . . I didn't think I'd ever see you again."

Thinking they should not expose themselves so thoroughly to Will, Kiri managed to step away. As she did, she got a clearer view of the body. "Howard!" she said with revulsion. "Did he attack you because you helped me escape?"

"That was part of the reason he forged Hawk's handwriting to get me down here, but he was also being paid by the conspirators," Mackenzie said wearily. "Give me a moment to get my thoughts clear and I'll give you the whole story."

"I brought a change of clothing," Will said. "I'll get my saddlebags so you can get into something dry before you freeze to death. Do you want me to dispose of this fellow's body on the way?"

Kiri turned away with a shudder. "If you don't mind. Quite apart from trying to murder your brother, he was in favor of gang raping and killing me."

"I hope he doesn't give the fish indigestion." Will lifted Howard under the arms and dragged him from the cave, efficiently avoiding getting bloodstains on himself.

As soon as he was out of sight, Mackenzie drew Kiri into his arms again. "You have a faint scent of Eau de Fish," she breathed against his throat as she pressed herself full length against him. "Will any other smugglers be coming?"

"It's the wrong phase of the moon for their work. Will you help me warm up?" He kissed her with desperate hunger, his hands roving down her back and over her buttocks. Though his lips were cold, she warmed them quickly.

If not for the knowledge that Will would return in a few minutes, Kiri would rip Mackenzie's cold, wet garments off so she could *really w*arm him up. Relief and passion were a heady mixture.

They managed to separate before Will reappeared. Kiri suspected that he was deliberately making enough noise to warn them.

Will tossed a small saddlebag to Mackenzie. "Lucky we're the same size. I haven't any spare boots, but the sooner you get out of your wet clothes, the better."

"I'll build up the fire and see if I can find the makings for tea," Kiri said. "And I promise I'll keep my back turned." She wouldn't mind seeing Mackenzie naked, but this seemed a good time to maintain the proprieties.

Will reached inside his coat and pulled out a packet. "Tea. I have sugar also. No milk since that's too hard to carry."

She laughed as she caught the tea. "Which of you first came up with the idea of the greatcoat as supply train?"

The brothers looked at each other and grinned. "I did," Mackenzie said. "Then we started competing to find who could carry the most strange and useful items, and we both decided that all the hidden pockets were too useful to forfeit."

Kiri looked hopefully at Will. "Do you have anything to eat?"

He pulled out a flat, paper-wrapped packet. "As a matter of fact, I do have some cheese. It's the easiest and most efficient food to carry around."

Mackenzie seized the packet and swiftly unwrapped it. "I didn't mind so much being fed bread and cheese. The real problem is that they didn't feed me enough of it."

"Eat it all if you like," Will said. "Kiri and I got a quick meal in Dover."

Ostentatiously giving Mackenzie privacy, Kiri tossed more coal on the fire to revive it. Then she investigated an alcove she'd noticed when she was being held prisoner here. As she'd guessed, it was used as a storage area, with crude shelves that held cooking pots of various sizes, a few pieces of cutlery, and chipped plates and mugs. Nothing to eat or drink, but there was a half-full water barrel. No doubt the smugglers had womenfolk who made sure that their men had the basic domestic necessities.

She could hear rustling and squishy wet clothing sounds as she filled a kettle from the water barrel and hung it over the fire. By the time she straightened and brushed her hands off, the men had joined her.

Mackenzie looked considerably better now that he was wearing clean, dry garments. He also had on his brother's greatcoat. On his feet were only heavy wool socks. He set his saturated boots by the fire, then sank into one of the chairs. "You have more domestic skills than I would expect of a duke's daughter."

"I'm also a soldier's daughter, and when we traveled, I was always visiting the soldiers' campfires and learning things that would probably have scandalized the general." The water started to boil, so Kiri used some to warm the chipped brown teapot before adding tea leaves and pouring water on top. "I'm sure my mother knew what I was up to, but she's a practical woman who thinks all skills are worthwhile."

"Amen to that," Mackenzie said. "Will, you're the artillery expert. Is it possible to explode something like a mattress without anyone noticing before it went off?"

Will found a third crude chair and brought it close to the fire so they could all sit as they drank the tea Kiri poured for them. "The bomb itself is easy. Any kind of hard shell, like a cast-iron naval bomb or even a ceramic crock, could be used by filling it with gunpowder. Pieces of sharpened metal could be added if you want to cut people to shreds. The difficult part would be lighting a fuse without having it be noticed."

Kiri sucked in her breath. "A mattress . . . Are you thinking a bomb might be put in the Woolsack, that big red ottoman that sits just below the royal throne in the House of Lords? I saw it when Adam took us on a private tour of the Palace of Westminster."

"The Woolsack is large enough to hold several bombs," Will said. "Princess Charlotte plans to attend the State Opening, and she would probably be seated right on the Woolsack. But it would be difficult for the conspirators to set off the bomb in a chamber full of people who would surely notice a burning fuse."

"I had far too much time to think about this," Mackenzie said grimly. "The fuse could be concealed by drilling holes in the floor underneath the Woolsack. What's underneath in the cellars? Storage rooms and the like?"

"I believe that's all," Will said. "But ever since the Gunpowder Plot, the Beefeaters search the cellars before every State Opening. Wouldn't they notice a fuse?"

"The Gunpowder Plot involved three dozen barrels of gunpowder, which are hard to miss," Mackenzie pointed out. "This is much simpler. Come in at night, move the Woolsack, and drill a hole into the cellar. Insert your bomb into the underside of the Woolsack, thread a long fuse through the hole, and move the Woolsack back into position. Go down into the cellar and pin the fuse along a filthy old beam. Who would notice?"

Will looked stricken. "Then wait until the chamber is filled during the ceremony, light the fuse from below, and escape before anyone realizes what happened."

Kiri asked, "Wouldn't people smell the burning gunpowder of the fuse?"

"Most of the smell would be confined to the cellar," Will said. "In the last moments before the bomb exploded, there might be some of that sharp scent, but in such a crowd, it's not likely anyone would notice in time to act. Clearing a crowded chamber of noblemen and politicians is slow even at the best of times."

"One bomb going off inside the Woolsack would kill

the prince regent, Princess Charlotte, the prime minister, and most of the rest of the government ministers, not to mention half the peerage of England," Mackenzie said soberly.

"Including Adam," Kiri whispered. Her desire to protect the royal princess was powerful, but her brother was *family.*

"Dukes sit right up front. I'd be a little farther away if I take my seat, as I meant to," Will said. "But the plotters will have trouble getting a bomb into the chamber."

"Not if the chief conspirator is a lord." Mackenzie let Kiri empty the last of the tea into his mug. "I'd better back up and explain. Rupert Swinnerton and Lord Fendall are half brothers, and their mother was sister to the mother of Joseph Fouché."

After shocked silence, Will whistled softly. "That explains a great deal."

"Thank heaven we can get to London quickly enough tomorrow to arrest all the conspirators and have them safely locked up before the State Opening."

Kiri bit her lip. "The State Opening *is* tomorrow."

Mackenzie choked on his tea. "Damnation! I lost track of a day while I was here. We need to head for London *now!*"

"Tell us all you've learned while we finish our tea," Will ordered. "Then we'll ride to Dover and hire the fastest post chaise we can find. The main ceremony starts about midday, so we should have enough time."

"But none to spare," Mackenzie said grimly. "Here's what I've learned. . . ."

Chapter 40

They made the trip to London as fast as wheels and horseflesh could take them. Will, who apparently could see in the dark, took over the reins when the postilion that came with the hired horses proved to be too conservative a driver.

Kiri and Mackenzie rode inside the small carriage. Exhausted by his ordeal, Mackenzie was able to sleep even in a vehicle traveling at high speed across a landscape of cold winds and scattered rain.

He ended up folded over with his head and shoulders in Kiri's lap. She stroked his hair tenderly, shaken by how close he'd come to death.

What a strange, wild month she'd had. When she'd visited Godfrey Hitchcock's family, she had been rather restlessly looking for a husband and not finding any satisfaction in her hunt. Now she had discovered service, passion, and adventure. How could she go back to her tame former life? Much as she loved making perfumes, she needed other occupations.

She managed to doze some, one hand holding on to a handle to keep from being tossed from the seat, the other resting on Mackenzie's shoulder. One way or another, soon this would be over. . . .

Mac awoke stiff, bemused, and confused—except for the fact that Kiri was curled into him as they bounced along in a carriage. A gray carriage blanket covered them both, blocking the drafts.

It took him a moment to recall all that had happened. The ride to Dover. Finding a carriage. Almost passing out from exhaustion once he was in the vehicle. He had a vague memory of stopping to change horses at posting houses. He remembered Will telling the postilion that he would take over the driving. Even though he was supremely easygoing, if Will wanted to do something his way, it got done.

Now it was morning, though impossible to guess the time with a heavily overcast sky and a light, spitting rain. Mac stared out the window at a landscape that was moving by fast. They weren't far south of London.

Hard to believe that catastrophe hovered over Britain in general and the royal family in particular. Reality was Kiri resting in his arms, beautiful beyond belief even with circles under her eyes and her dark hair falling in tangles.

She was the most amazing female he'd ever met as well as the loveliest. He had thought he'd drowned and gone to heaven when he woke up to see first Will, then Kiri. Having his big brother ride to his rescue wasn't surprising—Will had always been the best and truest person in Mac's life, and he never, ever let down a friend.

But Kiri was a high-born titled lady. How many such women would come charging halfway across England on a dark and stormy night because a sorry fellow like Mac might be in trouble? And how many would have been able to find a smugglers' hideout that they'd barely seen in the first place? Will was immensely capable, but he'd never been to the cave, and could not have found his way without Kiri to guide him.

He kissed her forehead with gossamer tenderness. It was impossible to imagine living without her—yet even more impossible to imagine how they could be together for always. Though this time-out-of-time was almost over, he would never forget how special Kiri was, nor how lucky he was to have had the chance to love her.

She shifted, then opened her eyes sleepily as she tucked a hand inside his coat with sweet intimacy. "Beds are much, much more comfortable."

He grinned. "Are you saying I'm not as good as a mattress?"

"You are harder and lumpier than a mattress, but you do have your uses," she said, mischief gleaming under her dark lashes. "Where are we?"

She was right about him being harder. "We're coming into London. I'm guessing at the time since my watch was stolen by Howard, but we should reach Westminster a couple of hours before the ceremony begins."

"Good." She stretched hugely, covering a ladylike yawn with one hand. "I wonder if we'll have a chance to change into more respectable clothing."

It would be easier to convince royal officials of the danger if they didn't look like a pack of tinkers, but after a moment of thought, he shook his head. "That would cut the timing too close."

"We can't risk that," she agreed as she looked ruefully at her dirt-spattered cloak and divided riding skirt. "I wonder . . ."

Before she could finish her sentence, catastrophe moved from potential to shatteringly current when Mac heard the unmistakable *crack!* of a breaking axle.

"'Ware!" he cried out as he wrapped himself around

Kiri to prevent her from injury. As the carriage careened off the road and onto its side, he wondered despairingly if the prince regent and his daughter were doomed.

Kiri found out that Mackenzie made a very decent mattress. By protecting her with his body, she survived the carriage crash shaken but undamaged. The vehicle skidded and pitched to the left before smashing down at a severe tilt. As motion stopped, Kiri heard the screaming of frantic horses and the whir of the two wheels that were now up in the air.

She'd landed on top of Mackenzie. When she lifted herself free of his sheltering arms, she was horrified to see blood pouring from a wound where the side of his head had cracked the window frame. "Mackenzie, can you talk? How hurt are you?"

He opened his eyes, blinking dazedly as he brought her face into focus. "Banged my head. Nothing seems broken. You? Will?"

"I'm fine. I'll check on Will as soon as I've bandaged your head wound." She managed a shaky smile. "I don't want you to see your own blood and pass out."

"In that case, I'll close my eyes." Which he did. He looked shaken, but apart from the head wound, he didn't seem badly hurt.

Will's saddlebags were traveling in the carriage, so she opened them and found a clean shirt. She yanked her knife from the leg sheath, tore the shirt into strips, then used the carriage blanket to blot away the blood saturating Mackenzie's hair. She found a laceration that was messy but not deep.

After cleaning away as much blood as she could, she swiftly pressed a pad made of folded shirt over the wound, then secured it with a fabric strip wrapped twice around his head. A scarlet stain showed in the middle of the pristine white linen, but the improvised bandage didn't saturate. "That will do for now. I'll see how Will is doing."

"*Quickly!*" Mackenzie struggled to push himself to a sitting position.

Kiri flattened a hand on his chest and shoved him down again. "Stay still for a few minutes. If you get up now, you might fall over."

"You're probably right." He drew a rough breath. "But please, tell how me how Will is, or I'll be coming out right behind you."

"I shall." The carriage was tilted so severely that the right door was slanted over her. When she pulled herself up on the door frame, the vehicle rocked back onto four wheels again. She clung grimly when it bounced level, the front sagging because of the broken axle. "Are you still all right?"

"Slightly better for sitting upright." Mac started to move cautiously.

"*Please* stay there for a few minutes," she said. "We don't want the bleeding to start again."

"Good point," he muttered.

She grabbed the rest of Will's shirt and swung to the ground. The horses quieted down due to the efforts of the postilion, who had retained his seat on the near leader when the carriage crashed. "Are you and the gentleman all right, miss?" he asked worriedly.

"Well enough." She looked about anxiously. "What about Major Masterson?"

"Over there, miss. I haven't looked at him because I had to settle my team."

She followed his gesture and bit her lip when she spotted Will. He had been thrown from the driver's seat into the muddy field and he lay unmoving on his side. Half a dozen swift steps and she was kneeling by him. "Will, can you talk? Are you hurt?"

He exhaled roughly and rolled onto his back. "Not so bad, lass. The mud cushioned my fall." He gingerly tested his left forearm with his right hand and gasped with pain. "I've cracked or broken a bone in my arm, though."

She raised her voice and called, "Mackenzie, your brother isn't badly hurt." They had been very, very lucky. Letting her voice drop to normal, she continued, "Will, I've already used part of your clean shirt to bandage a scalp wound on your brother, and now I'll use the rest to bind your arm and make a sling. Can you sit up if I help?"

"Maybe." He looked somewhat skeptical, but when she slid an arm under his shoulders, she was able to get him upright. He caught his breath sharply. "You're strong, Lady Kiri."

"Because I'm not much of a lady. Let me slide the coat off your left arm." She began to chat to distract him from what would be a painful process. "Did the axle break because of the speed we were traveling?"

"I didn't think so. We didn't hit any unusual ruts or holes in the road." He winced as she started to ease the coat off his shoulder. "If the axle was already weakened, traveling at high speed might have brought it to the breaking point."

By the time the left arm of the greatcoat was off, Will was sweating and Kiri was ready to have strong hysterics. She didn't like hurting friends, no matter how necessary it was. Not wanting to put him through that again, she bound his left forearm over the sleeve of his regular coat. A proper bonesetter could look at it later. All she could do now was immobilize the bones so they didn't hurt him so much.

"Where did you learn doctoring?" he asked when she helped him slip his arm into the greatcoat. He winced, but it was too cold to forgo the warmth of the coat.

"I was a ghoulish child and always wanted to watch when the regimental surgeons were fixing men up. They'd usually send me out if there was some really appalling injury, but otherwise I was allowed to watch and learn."

She used the last of the shirt fabric to make a sling. "A good thing you're so large. One shirt went a long way."

Mackenzie emerged from the carriage, holding on to the door frame for balance but looking reasonably well. "I'll ride one of the horses to the next posting inn, then come back with two good riding hacks. We can't wait for a blacksmith to repair the axle."

This accident had already cut into the margin of time before the ceremony. Trying not to fidget visibly, Kiri inquired, "Only two hacks?" Did he intend to leave her here for her own safety? If he *dared* suggest that . . . !

"Will can't ride with a broken arm," Mackenzie said. "He can visit a surgeon in the next town while we ride into Westminster."

"I've traveled farther in worse shape," his brother said dryly. "All of us must go. Remember, I'm a peer and have the right to attend the State Opening. If I'm there when this is explained, it will save time. If you can help me get onto a horse, I guarantee I'll be able to stay aboard."

"He's right," Kiri said. "We all hold different pieces of this." As she watched the postilion unharness a horse for Mackenzie to ride, she wondered if they would arrive at the Palace of Westminster just in time to see the bomb go off.

One could have too much adventure.

Chapter 41

They made good time going into the city, but their pace slowed as they neared the Palace of Westminster. "A good thing we're on horseback," Mac said as they slowly worked their horses through the crowded streets.

The State Opening had brought out huge crowds despite the unpleasant weather, and a carriage would have been stopped dead. At least horses commanded respect, so they were able to move faster than they could have on foot. Though not by much.

Kiri rode behind him, a warrior queen in truth, steely and determined. No one could see her and not know she had royal blood. Will brought up the rear, his face gray with pain. Despite his broken arm, he hadn't slowed the pace on their ride into the city.

They turned a corner and were now beside the palace. An honor guard of soldiers lined both sides of the route taken by the sovereign. Will frowned as he looked at the royal standard snapping above the palace in the damp wind. "The royals have arrived and the official ceremony might be under way. Time for me to take the lead."

Moving with care, he urged his horse forward through

the crowd. One of the men shouldered aside shouted, "'Oo the bloody 'ell do you think you are, mate?"

"Aye, we been waiting out 'ere in the rain all mornin'!" another man snarled.

"Ain't that Damian Mackenzie, the one what they said died a few weeks back?"

Kiri raised her voice, cutting through the babble. "We are here on a matter of Princess Charlotte Augusta's safety! Please, let us through! This is truly urgent!"

No man could look at Kiri's lovely face and pleading eyes and not be moved. "Let the lass and 'er friends through," someone said. "Maybe they be chasing frog spies!"

The burst of laughter that followed wasn't particularly respectful, but the crowd parted enough to allow the horses through single file. They reached the entrance to the palace. Military guards completely surrounded the building.

"We are here on a matter of the utmost urgency!" Will barked in a parade-ground voice. "Let us through!"

"Sir, I have my orders," a corporal said uncertainly.

"And I'm countermanding them," Will snapped.

Recognizing authority, the soldiers stepped aside to allow the three riders through. As they swiftly dismounted, Kiri said, "I'll go into the chamber. As a female, I might be able to get closer to the princess."

Mac, who was helping Will from his horse, thought his heart would stop. "Kiri, please don't go in there! The bomb could go off at any second."

"Don't be absurd, Damian." She flashed a reckless smile that made him remember that she was warrior as well as queen. "Why should men be the only ones allowed to die for their country?"

It took only moments for her to be off her horse and climbing the steps, leaving her tired mount for one of the guards to secure. A hard-faced army captain approached, narrow-eyed and suspicious. "What is the meaning of this?"

Will straightened to officer posture. "I am Major Lord Masterson, and we have reason to believe there will be an attempt to blow up the House of Lords at any moment."

The captain looked offended. "The yeoman of the Guard have searched the cellars every year since 1605. There are no barrels of gunpowder hidden there."

"This year, the bomb is in the Woolsack and only a fuse shows in the cellars," Mac snapped. "Can you swear the yeomen would have seen such a thing?"

The captain paled. "Perhaps . . . not."

"We're going into the cellars right now," Will ordered as he headed into the building. "I'm a member of the House of Lords as well as a serving officer, and I have some idea where to look."

"And I know who will be lighting the fuse," Mac said as he walked at his brother's side, uttering every prayer he knew that they weren't too late.

As she approached the Lesser Chamber that housed the Lords, Kiri mentally summoned the arrogance of her royal Hindu ancestors. She was a queen with a life-or-death mission to perform, and she would not be denied.

A colorfully dressed official in front of the massive doors turned his long staff sideways to block her passage. "Halt! No entry to the House of Lords!"

She gave him her fiercest glare. "I am Lady Kiri Lawford, sister to the Duke of Ashton and Princess Charlotte's chosen companion. I have urgent need to speak to Her Royal Highness *and you will let me pass!*"

Before the guard could decide whether to block her passage, Kiri had swept the staff aside with the strength that men never expected her to have. She stepped into the vast hall, seeing the familiar moon-shaped windows near the high ceiling and the great tapestries on the walls.

When Adam had brought his family here, the chamber had been empty except for the ghosts of lords past. Now it was packed to the gills with scarlet- and ermine-robed lords and well-tailored politicians and members of the House of Commons. MP gathered in the Lords to hear the royal speech because by tradition, the sovereign was barred from entering the Commons.

The prince regent was seated at the far end of the chamber, his massive carved and gilded throne no less magnificent than his massive and sumptuously robed self. And damnably, Princess Charlotte was perched below the throne on the scarlet square of the Woolsack, her eager gaze darting around the room as she waited for the ceremony to begin. If the bomb exploded, she and her father would be killed instantly.

Hearing pursuit being organized behind her, Kiri swept down the left aisle that ran the length of the room. Eyes began turning toward her. Lord Liverpool, the prime minister, looked startled. He signaled to guards to stop her. Kiri dodged the first and deftly put the second onto the floor.

As she approached the Woolsack, Princess Charlotte turned and saw her. Face lighting up, the princess rose to her feet. She was wearing the perfume Kiri had made for her. "Lady Kiri! What's wrong?" Charlotte waved the guards off. "Is this about the matter you discussed with me?"

Giving thanks for the princess's quick mind, Kiri said, "It is indeed, Your Highness." Her voice dropped. "This chamber must be evacuated immediately. Please, come with me!"

Before Charlotte could answer, the prime minister and the prince regent himself had converged on her. "What is the meaning of this?" the prince thundered.

Kiri dropped to one knee, looking as humble as she

knew how. Was the prince regent a Highness or a Majesty? Deciding to go with the higher title, she said in a low voice, "Your Majesty, I bring word of a traitorous plot. We believe a bomb has been hidden right in this chamber, and it might explode at any moment."

As the prime minister and prince stared at her, aghast, her brother appeared at her side. She hadn't seen him earlier in the sea of scarlet velvet robes, but as a duke he was seated in the front row only a few steps away.

Adam took Kiri's arm and helped her up, his grip firm. "This is my sister, Lady Kiri Lawford. She has been helping to investigate a treasonous plot. If she says there might be a bomb and the chamber should be evacuated, I believe her."

"Your sister, you say?" The regent's startled gaze moved from Adam, dressed in the full ceremonial garb of a peer of the realm, to Kiri, who was filthy and wore her divided skirt, along with a number of splotches of Mackenzie's blood. "You have the same eyes. Very well, Liverpool, evacuate the chamber until we decide the merit of Lady Kiri's charges. Charlotte, come with me."

Looking more excited than afraid, Princess Charlotte said, "Yes, Papa." She and her father departed by a small door tucked into a corner of the room near the throne.

Kiri's relief was so intense that her knees might have given out, but Adam still held her arm. "How probable is a bomb?" he asked quietly.

"Very, very probable. The chief conspirator is Lord Fendall, so he had access to the House of Lords." She shuddered. "The plan was to put it inside the Woolsack."

Adam stared at the Woolsack, appalled. "Fendall. I scarcely know him, but if I had to pick possible traitors in this house, he'd be on the list. He's a dangerous combination of ambition and malice. But we can talk about that later. For now, we're leaving the chamber."

Kiri scanned the seats where the peeresses sat. "Is Mariah here?"

"No, thank God. She wasn't feeling well." Invoking ducal rank, Adam took a quick look around the churning mass of confused people, then led Kiri toward the same door the prince and princess had used, since it was closest and the least busy.

As they headed away from the Woolsack, Kiri's blood chilled in her veins as she smelled the unmistakable acrid odor of burning gunpowder.

The nightmarish search through the cellars of the Palace of Westminster had Mac's heart beating like a frantic drum. At least they knew the rough location since the fuse had to be below the chamber of the Lords, but it was hard to be sure of the right direction in the dark maze of corridors and dusty rooms stuffed with old furniture, piled documents, and less identifiable objects.

"What are all those piles of wooden sticks?" he asked as he looked in the first room after they'd descended the stairs to the cellar.

An elderly warder had joined them, and he was struggling to keep up with the younger men. "Tally sticks, sir. Used to record accounts for men who can't read or write. Elm wood, you know. Notches are cut in the stick to represent pounds and pence, then the stick is split with half going to the creditor and half to the debtor. A receipt, so to speak." He smiled fondly. "We have tally sticks going back to the Plantagenets."

Mac stared at the huge piles of wood in horror. If any kind of explosion was set off, the whole damned palace would burn like a Guy Fawkes bonfire. "Will, where to?"

"This way." A lantern in his good hand, Will led since he had been down there before and had an excellent sense

of direction. Mac and the captain followed close behind
with the warder farther back holding another lantern.

Moving at a near run, they soon reached a long corridor
lined with drab doors. Will said, "We're right below the
House of Lords now, aren't we?"

"Aye, sir, you're right," the warder confirmed. "There
are a dozen storerooms along here."

"Then we'll have to search all of them," Will said grimly.

The warder and captain set to work methodically at the
near end of the passage. Will leaned against a wall and
closed his eyes, his face damp with sweat.

Frowning, Mac followed his nose to the end of the
corridor. He'd become much more aware of scents since
meeting Kiri, and he thought he detected a faint odor of
burning black powder.

His pace quickened as the scent grew stronger. Directly
overhead, he heard shuffling sounds that might have been
footsteps.

Praying that people were evacuating the chamber, he
reached the last door on the left side of the corridor. The
scent seemed to be coming from the room, and an edge of
light showed under the door. Wishing he was armed, he
flung open the door, standing to one side so he wouldn't
be an easy target.

Swinnerton was inside. Expression avid, he watched
the long fuse that hung from a hole in the ceiling. Slow
flame crept upward along the cord. He must be waiting till
the last possible moment before escaping so he could savor
the imminent disaster.

Hearing the door open, Swinnerton spun around and
reached into his coat for his pistol. "My God, Mackenzie!"
he said incredulously. "Aren't you dead yet?"

Mac threw himself into the room in a rolling dive. He
calculated his trajectory so that he was able to kick the
pistol from Swinnerton's hand as he rolled by.

He halted under the dangling fuse and lunged to his feet, then leaped upward to grab the fuse above the burning section. The weight of his body yanked the fuse from the bomb hidden in the room above.

In an instant, the fuse went from lethal to harmless.

Not entirely harmless. Mac threw the burning fuse into Swinnerton's face. "Like a cat, I have nine lives," he panted. "I'm down to four or five, but I have enough left to take care of you."

Swinnerton stumbled back, swearing furiously, as the burning fuse lashed across his eyes. "God *damn* you! It was a perfect plan! I would have been rich, a duke of France. Except for *you!*"

Mac scooped up the pistol, cocked it, and aimed. "It was a stupid plan. Do you really think blowing up half the government and peerage would make England want to make peace? Quite the contrary. It's over, Swinnerton. You are about to get long-delayed justice for murdering Harriet."

From his expression, Swinnerton knew he'd lost. Eyes mad, he dug into a pocket and drew out a fist-sized explosive grenade. "Maybe so, but you're going to die with me!" He grabbed the burning cord from the floor so he could light the fuse of the grenade. "Rot in hell, you bastard!"

The grenade was only a fraction the size of the one they would have planted in the Woolsack, but it was big enough to kill the two of them in this small room. Mac fired the pistol at Swinnerton, trying to stop him before the grenade was lit.

The pistol misfired. Swearing, he threw it at Swinnerton and bolted out of the room, slamming the door behind him.

As he sprinted down the passage toward Will and the others, the room exploded behind him. Mac was knocked from his feet but automatically tucked his body and rolled so he didn't hit hard enough to break bones.

He was lying on his back, gasping for breath, when Will

reached him, moving faster than the others despite his injury. "What the devil happened?" Will studied the splintered door as he went down on one knee by Mac. "That wasn't a big enough explosion to be a bomb in the Woolsack."

Mac pushed himself to a sitting position, then crossed his arms on his knees and rested his head on them while he shook. God, Kiri was up there! What if he hadn't been in time? A good thing he'd had no chance to think until after disaster was averted.

"Swinnerton was in that storeroom, and he'd lit the fuse running up into the chamber." Mac gulped in more air. "When I yanked the fuse out of the bomb, he produced a nice little grenade to send the two of us to hell."

The captain approached the wrecked door and stared inside. Turning away hastily, he said, "Whoever it is, he won't be setting off any more grenades."

Will stood and offered his good hand to help Mac to his feet. "What about fire?"

The warder trotted up carrying a sand-filled fire bucket. "Here!" He handed it to the captain, who pushed the door aside and threw sand into the room. "Not much to catch fire in here," the captain said, "but more sand wouldn't be a bad idea."

"Let's leave them to it," Mac said to his brother. "I want to get upstairs and make sure that Fendall doesn't escape in the confusion."

Will gave a faint smile as he turned to make his way from the cellar. "After that, can we collapse?"

Mac certainly hoped so.

Chapter 42

The explosion in the cellar was enough to silence the questioning, chattering crowd that had been ushered out of the House of Lords. Kiri's heart was in her throat as she waited to see if the whole chamber would blow up behind them, but it didn't.

"They must have stopped the main explosion," Kirkland said. He'd made it to the opening even though he was far from recovered from his bout of fever. His scarlet robes made his skin look chalk-white. "Ashton, any idea where Lord Fendall might be?"

Narrow-eyed, Adam scanned the mass of excited nobles, then pointed. "There! Near that door." Fendall was some distance away, his expression furious as he tried to fight his way free of the congestion.

"Let's get him!" Kiri hissed, reinvigorated by the prospect of capturing the man whose selfish ambitions had almost caused such destruction.

Moving in perfect harmony, she and her brother cut through the crowd, catching up with Fendall just before he reached a door that led from the building. "My pardon, Lord Fendall, but you are required to bear testimony to this most unfortunate matter," Adam said in a silky voice. "Blowing up the House of Lords just isn't done."

Fendall swung around, his feral expression revealing a resemblance to Swinnerton. Seeing Adam and Kiri closing in on him, he chose Kiri as the weaker target and lunged for her. "You'll not stop me!"

It was his last mistake. With a sweep of her leg and a twist of his arm, Kiri sent Fendall flying toward her brother.

Adam moved too quickly for Kiri to see exactly what happened, but suddenly the baron was lying on the floor with his neck bent at an impossible, deadly angle. His scarlet velvet robes splayed around him like spilled blood.

"You should not have attacked my sister, Fendall," Adam said softly.

Kiri remembered Mackenzie saying that her brother was one of the most dangerous men in England. She hadn't believed it then, but she did now. Perhaps Fendall's death had been an accident—but she wouldn't have bet on it.

The Gentleman Usher of the Black Rod rushed up to them, his eyes a little wild because of the disruption of what should have been a solemn and stately ceremony. "The prince regent wishes to speak with you both. Follow me."

Praying that Mackenzie and Will had escaped the cellar explosion unscathed, Kiri followed Black Rod through the crowd, Adam right behind her. They were taken to a small audience chamber nearby.

The prince regent still wore his magnificent formal robes and he sat in a high-backed carved chair that bore more than a passing resemblance to a throne. Princess Charlotte sat beside him. Her gaze and a smile went immediately to Kiri.

Kirkland was present, presumably to explain what the

devil was going on. As Kiri and Adam entered, Mackenzie and Will came in through an opposite door escorted by a different court official.

Kiri smiled at the brothers, putting all her relief in her eyes since she was pretty sure she shouldn't speak unless spoken to. Mackenzie looked even more battered and disreputable than earlier. She wouldn't have thought it possible. But the weary smile he returned set every fiber of her body on fire.

The regent dismissed the other official but kept Black Rod. Adam murmured to Kiri, "The Gentleman Usher of the Black Rod is responsible for security in the House of Lords. Usually the post is honorary and ceremonial."

But not this time. Based on the prince regent's stormy expression, heads might roll. It was time for Kiri to be very, very quiet and ladylike.

She was tired enough to make that easy.

Mac watched the prince regent warily. The man had visited Damian's a number of times and had demonstrated that he could be volatile, gracious, melodramatic, charming, willful as a spoiled child, and occasionally even kind. Here's hoping that today his better qualities were on display.

The prince took in the disgraceful appearances of Mac, Will, and Kiri. Even Kirkland looked as if he was staying upright by sheer willpower.

Tartly the prince said, "Mackenzie, you're looking remarkably sprightly for a dead man. Kirkland, you and your people are to be commended for stopping this plot short of disaster, though sooner would have been better."

"Intelligence work is a chancy business, sir," Kirkland replied.

The prince scowled. "Have you cut off the serpent's head? I've had quite enough of French assassination attempts."

"The ending came so quickly that I'm unsure of the details myself," Kirkland replied. "Mr. Mackenzie, Lady Kiri Lawford, and Lord Masterson can better supply them." He glanced toward Mac and Will, silently turning the discussion over to them.

"Most of the story belongs to my brother and Lady Kiri," Will said. He looked ready to keel over from the pain of his broken arm, but one didn't sit in the presence of royalty without invitation. "They have spent weeks investigating possible leads to the conspirators, while I returned from the Peninsula only two days ago."

Mac drew a deep breath as he tried to organize a concise explanation. The prince had a notoriously short attention span, and he already knew the basics of the plot.

"Lady Kiri and I started investigating after the attempt on Princess Charlotte," he said. "We are just returned from Kent, where we learned that the kidnappers were led by Lord Fendall and his half brother, Rupert Swinnerton. They are first cousins to Joseph Fouché on their mother's side. Apparently the aim of the plot was to restore Fouché to power by weakening Britain to the point of wanting a peace treaty."

The royal brows shot up. "Fools. Fendall was the mastermind?"

"Yes, with Swinnerton in charge of mayhem. Apparently Fouché promised his cousins great wealth and power if their plot was successful."

"Has Swinnerton been captured?"

"I found him attempting to set off the bomb under the Woolsack," Mac replied. "I removed the fuse. In the ensuing struggle, he died when a small grenade went off."

"That was the explosion heard in the cellar?" Kirkland asked.

Mac nodded. "He wished to share the explosion with me, but succeeded only in killing himself." Kiri and Kirkland winced at his flat words.

"A pity," the prince said coldly. "I should have liked to see the man drawn and quartered for treason. What about Lord Fendall?"

"I don't know his whereabouts," Mac replied. "My guess is that when he realized that his plot had failed, he fled the House of Lords. He can't have gone far, so if a search is set in motion immediately, it should be possible to catch him."

Though it might be hard to prove a case against Fendall. The only evidence Mac had was hearsay. If he was clever and kept a cool head, Fendall might still be in the Palace of Westminster, ready to glibly disclaim all knowledge of the plot. He could blame everything on his brother, who was in no position to dispute that.

Ashton discreetly cleared his throat. He and his sister stood side by side, looking very much like each other: strikingly attractive in a dark-haired, green-eyed way. Contained. Dangerous.

"If I may interject, Your Majesty, Lord Fendall has not escaped," the duke said. "When Lady Kiri told me he was behind the plot, we moved to stop him from fleeing the palace. Unfortunately, he fell while trying to escape and died of his injuries."

"How did that happen?" Will asked with a satirical glint in his eyes.

"The fault is mine," Ashton said, looking misleadingly regretful. "Fendall attacked my sister, and when I yanked him away from her, he fell and broke his neck."

The prince regent gave Ashton a hard glance but didn't

pursue the matter. "Well, that will save scandal. No need for the public to learn how close the French came to assassinating the royal family."

"There is a furnace below the chamber," Black Rod volunteered. "It can be announced that it failed and the evacuation was a precaution taken in case fire took hold. The explosion occurred as the furnace was shut down."

"That will do nicely. The less said, the better. But before I resume the ceremony"—the prince gave Mac a basilisk stare—"it sounds as if Mr. Mackenzie has seriously compromised Lady Kiri. What do you have to say for yourself?"

Mac felt skewered as every gaze in the room—including Kiri's great green eyes—locked onto him. His throat closed. Good God, how could he possibly speak about something so vital and intimate?

After swallowing hard, he said haltingly, "Your Majesty, during the course of this investigation, I have come to have the utmost respect for Lady Kiri's intelligence, loyalty, and courageous service to the Crown."

He flicked a worried glance at Kiri but couldn't read her expression. "I would marry her if the lady would have me, but I realize that the difference in our stations might make such an offer seem an insult. The very last thing I would ever want to do is insult the bravest, most remarkable woman I've ever met."

The room was so silent that a falling pin would have been audible.

"It would hardly be conducive to good order in society for an illegitimate gambler and businessman to marry one of the highest-born young ladies in the land," the prince regent agreed, "but the situation is demmed improper."

"Indeed it is, Your Majesty." Will smiled at Kiri. "But

as head of Mr. Mackenzie's family, I would give such a union my wholehearted blessing."

Mac felt a lump in his throat the size of Tower Bridge. "Lord Masterson has always been the best and most supportive of brothers, and I am grateful beyond words for his approval of my deepest wish." His gaze returned to Kiri. "But my fear is that her family would disapprove, since she is the one who would be accepting far less than she deserves. I . . . I don't want her to be the cause of becoming estranged from her family."

And her family was represented in this room by Ashton, the reserved, enigmatic duke who had just broken the neck of a man who had been fool enough to attack his sister. Though Mac had always liked Ashton, he found the other man more than a little intimidating. He braced himself for Ashton's verdict.

"My sister is very dear to me and I wish for her to find as much happiness in her marriage as I have found in mine," the duke said slowly, his gaze fixed on Mac. "If she wishes to marry Mr. Mackenzie, I will not object. I believe that her mother and stepfather would also accept the marriage, given Mr. Mackenzie's exemplary service to the Crown. But the choice, of course, is Lady Kiri's."

Mac stared at Ashton, shocked speechless. The prince, however, did not suffer such shock. "Still demmed irregular," he said peevishly. "*Demmed* irregular!"

"Papa." Princess Charlotte spoke for the first time. She was enjoying this immensely, her fascinated gaze going from Kiri to Mac and back again. "I believe I know a way to mitigate the disparity in their stations to some extent." She leaned over to her father's chair and whispered something in his ear.

The prince looked first startled, then wickedly amused. "An excellent thought, Charlotte." He got to his feet and fumbled through his layers of robes. "Where the devil is that ceremonial sword? Ah, here it is." Rather awkwardly, he pulled the long, elaborately decorated sword from the sheath on his left hip. "Mr. Mackenzie, kneel before your sovereign."

Mac stiffly knelt before the prince regent. Every muscle in his body protested the abuse he'd suffered in the last few days.

The prince rapped Mac's right shoulder sharply with the flat of the sword. "Damian Mackenzie, in recognition of your honorable service to your country and your sovereign, I bestow on you this knighthood." Another sharp tap, this on his left shoulder. "Arise, Sir Damian Mackenzie."

The back of the sword clipped Mac's ear as the prince lifted it away. Mac could only be grateful it wasn't the sharp edge of the blade.

Dazed, he persuaded his aching muscles to get him to his feet. He was Sir Damian? A knight? "I . . . I thank you, Your Highness. You honor me beyond what I deserve. Any loyal Briton would have done the same in my place."

"But they might not have done it so well." The prince sheathed his sword. "This narrows the gap between you and Lady Kiri. So, will there be a wedding to regularize your behavior?"

Kiri hadn't spoken since entering the room, and her fists were clenched at her sides. "I don't know, Your Majesty. Mr. Mackenzie hasn't asked me." Her eyes narrowed. "The matter would need to be discussed."

"Well, get to it then," the prince said impatiently. "Charlotte, Black Rod, come along. The ceremony must be resumed without further delay." They left the room, Charlotte glancing bright-eyed over her shoulder.

When the royals were gone, Will said with a glint of amusement, "We three peers should also be in attendance for the royal speech, but I'm not dressed for it, so I think I'll go to Mac's house and sleep for a couple of days."

"Maybe you should get that bone set first," Mac suggested. "But otherwise an excellent idea. Kirkland, how about you head for home before you drop in your tracks?"

"What, and show common sense?" Kirkland murmured. "I'll last long enough for the ceremony. Then I'll go home and sleep for a day or two."

"If we leave now, Kiri and Mackenzie will have a chance to settle matters." Ashton laid a hand on his sister's shoulder. "My carriage will take us home to Ashton House after the ceremony. Kiri, you don't have to make a decision today if you're not sure about it."

The three lords left, leaving Mac alone with a green-eyed warrior queen.

Chapter 43

Mackenzie was watching Kiri with a mixture of hope and wariness that would have amused her if she hadn't felt tied in knots. "You should sit down," she said tartly, "before you fall down."

"Can't sit when there's a lady standing," he said with a crooked smile.

Damn that charming smile. She sat in the prince's throne chair and drummed her fingers on the carved walnut arm. "How embarrassing to have your sovereign prod you into making an indirect offer for me. And in front of such an audience!"

Mackenzie dragged the princess's chair so that it faced her and sat down with a speed that barely missed being a collapse. "I certainly hadn't planned on proposing in the midst of chaos, but doing so did produce a surprising amount of support. Your family, my family, the prince regent, and Princess Charlotte. Probably even Black Rod." He frowned. "The only exception seems to be you."

"Our time-out-of-time is over, Mackenzie. You can go back to your club, I can return to my family, and it's like the last weeks never happened." She stared down at her hands.

There was still blood under her nails from bandaging Mackenzie's head. "Isn't that what we both want?"

He took her hand between his and said gently, "It's not what *I* want, Kiri. How about telling me what *you* want?"

She stared at their joined hands. Her tan half-Hindu skin, his bruised and powder-blackened fingers. So different. Too different, apparently.

Her usual confidence had splintered away in slow, agonized pieces when he expressed stuffy admiration for her to the prince regent, then followed up with all the reasons a marriage shouldn't happen. She had thought what was between them was rare and special, but that belief disintegrated as he spoke. She was a mixed-blood slut with too few morals, and he was a dashing gambler with no desire to wed.

She smiled mirthlessly at her self-deception. She had told herself that it would be enough to have him for a little while. Now that the time had come for them to go their separate ways, she felt as if her heart was weeping tears of blood.

"Kiri? What's wrong? Please?" When her hand clenched hard on his, he said coaxingly, "Maybe you could give a hint of what you want from me?"

Saying the words aloud would make her pain even worse, but for her own self-respect, she must be honest to the end. "I want to be loved," she whispered, knowing how weak and foolish this would sound. "I wanted you to . . . to tear down the social barriers and be deliriously romantic and willing to change your life. I didn't want the barriers to tumble and then see you scramble to find a way out."

After a startled moment, he said, "That's easy, then."

Before she could react, Mackenzie scooped her onto his lap with her head on his shoulder. "Damn, every muscle in my body is sore," he muttered as he wrapped his arms around her and rested his chin on top of her head.

"I love you truly, madly, and deeply, my sweet and indomitable lady," he said softly. "I fought that knowledge because I couldn't see how it would be possible to be with you for always. But when the waves were crashing around my knees and rising face, I recognized that you are the most important person in my life. The only woman I've ever felt I could trust completely." He gave a rueful chuckle. "There hasn't been much chance since then to tell you."

She tilted her head up and stared at him with tear-filled emerald eyes as she searched his face. What she saw caused her face to relax into a crooked smile. "I . . . I'm sorry for my foolishness, Damian, but I needed to hear the words. When you spoke to the prince regent, you were so detached and worldly that I thought you . . . didn't want me."

He'd never seen her look younger or more vulnerable. Loving her even more, he said, "I had trouble adjusting my thinking to believe that marriage is possible. Not to mention the difficulty of speaking the most private things in my heart in front of the most terrifying audience imaginable." He thought a moment as he caressed her glossy hair. "No, it would have been worse if General Stillwell was here, too."

She gave a hiccup of laughter, then buried her face against his shoulder and began sobbing. "I *never* cry," she said in a choked voice, and wept even harder.

He was surprised and moved to realize how love made everyone vulnerable. Even this magnificently strong and independent girl needed him as much as he needed her. He'd have to start believing in miracles.

She had made herself vulnerable, and he could do no less. When her sobs abated, he swallowed hard, then tore away every shred of frivolity to say with painful honesty, "I need to hear the words, too, my warrior queen. I need to hear that you love me. I need to hear that a beautiful, well-born lady with the blood of queens in her veins can love an unrespectable bastard gambler whose own mother told him his birth was a mistake." His mouth twisted. "I need to know that . . . that I'm not just your rebellion and that one day you'll regret choosing a man so far from your station."

"Oh, my foolish beloved, haven't you noticed that I'm not terribly respectable myself?" She cupped his unshaven chin and caught his gaze, concealing nothing. "I love you, Damian Mackenzie. Love your wit and good nature and wickedly attractive body. I love that you claim not to be respectable, but I've never met a truer gentleman." She smiled provocatively. "Did I mention the wickedly attractive body? And your wonderful, unique, and utterly male scent drives me *mad!*" She leaned in for a sizzling kiss.

Her kiss melted any lingering doubts. Though they would have a formal wedding and much rejoicing, this was their true marriage. Their vows and commitment were being made now, through word and touch and emotions too powerful to fit into mere words.

"Kiri, my darling," he said huskily, "I never thought I would marry, because I could never imagine a woman as unique and wonderful as you."

"I always assumed I would marry, but I never imagined that I'd be so *happy* about it!" Her brow furrowed. "I hope you won't mind that I'm a considerable heiress. Some men get all prickly about the possibility that the world might think them fortune hunters."

He grinned. "Owning a luxury gaming club may not be respectable, but it's insanely profitable. I've made enough money in the past few years that even high sticklers would be willing to overlook the source." He considered. "Shall I buy us a fine country manor so Sir Damian and Lady Kiri Mackenzie can become country gentry?"

She slanted a glance through her thick lashes. "Actually, I own a fine country manor. As part of my inheritance, Adam signed over a property that marches with his."

Mac groaned. "I am impressed by Ashton's generosity, and terrified that we will be neighbors forevermore."

"I predict you and he will be excellent friends within the year," Kiri said. "After all, you are removing my alarming self from the list of his responsibilities."

"The fact that he countenances our marriage has earned my undying gratitude." Mac considered. "I'm becoming part of a rather large family, aren't I?"

Kiri nodded apologetically. "My parents, two brothers, a sister, Adam's wife, Mariah, and her family, the general's family. The Stillwells are mostly vicars, but not the painfully staid sort. I think they'll all adore you. How could they not?"

"You'd be amazed how many people don't adore me," he said earnestly.

She laughed. "I hope you don't find so many new relatives overwhelming. We don't have to live in my family's pockets, but you were right that it would devastate me to be estranged from them." She looked grave. "I'm very, very glad I don't have to choose between you and them."

He was equally glad that he wouldn't have to see what that choice would be. "I'm delighted that you have so many relatives whom you actually like," he said seriously. "I have very few blood relations. Mostly just Will, along with a few Masterson cousins who find me something of an embarrassment. Will has been my anchor, the best thing in my life until I met you. So the more family, the better."

"They will definitely adore you once you meet, but they'll sometimes drive you mad," she warned.

"From what I've seen, that's part of the fun of family. People who care about you enough to make you miserable." Mac caressed her from shoulder to thigh, slowing on the curves. "I look forward to spending less time at Damian's and more time with you."

"And I look forward to spending more time at the club. I think I might create a perfume boutique for your customers," she said mischievously.

"What a splendid idea," he said enthusiastically. "As long as you don't sniff any of your male clients."

"None of them could possibly smell half as irresistible as you." She nuzzled his throat, which led to another kiss.

"You smell irresistible, too." He slid a hand between her thighs. "Your blasted divided skirts are useful for riding and adventure, but not so good for seduction."

She made a rueful face. "Alas, this isn't a very good time for seduction. When the opening is over, Adam is going to whisk me back to Ashton House. I expect he and my parents will keep me under guard until you and I are safely wed."

Mac grinned, happier than he'd ever been in his life. "Then we'll just have to get married soon, won't we?"

Chapter 44

Kirkland managed to stay upright during the State Opening. The prince regent's speech was extremely well done. When the man was good, he was very, very good.

After, his profoundest desire was to return to his own home and his own bed and sleep like a stunned ox, but duty led him to stop at his office first. He needed to see if there were any other crises that required his attention. He prayed there wouldn't be.

He also had to tie up the last ends of this conspiracy. Descending to the cells, he first visited Ollie Brown. "Mr. Brown, you are free to go. I've instructed my assistant to purchase a coach ticket to Newcastle for you. He'll give you enough money that you can eat along the way."

The young boxer rolled from his cot, eyes alight with happiness. "I can go home? Tomorrow?"

"Indeed you can. If you wish to spend the night here where it's warm, feel free, but your door will be unlocked. In the morning one of my men will take you to the inn where you can catch your coach north."

"Thank you, sir!" The boy said shyly, "I'll be more careful in the future so I won't fall into trouble again, sir. I swear it."

"Stay close to those who love you, and accept their guidance." Oliver Brown's mind might never fully recover from the damage received in the ring, but with a family to look out for him, he should live a good life far from the dangers of London. Kirkland offered his hand. "Safe journey, Mr. Brown."

Ollie pumped his hand. "If I ever have a son, I'll name him after you."

"Do you know my name?" Kirkland inquired.

Ollie's face fell. "No, sir, I don't. But I can call him 'Sir.'"

Kirkland smiled. "Call him James."

Wearily he moved to the cell next door, where Paul Clement lay on his cot, his gaze fixed on nothingness. When Kirkland entered, the Frenchman sat up.

"Something has happened. I see it in your face." His eyes narrowed. "Have you come to commend me to the British justice system as a spy?"

"On the contrary," Kirkland said. "Your warning about the State Opening of Parliament was invaluable. Through the efforts of my agents, we prevented a bomb from going off that would have killed the prince regent, Princess Charlotte, the prime minister, and half the British peerage."

Clement's brows arched. "So that was the plan. I'm glad you were able to prevent such a disaster. Killing the innocent has no place in our work." He cocked his head. "And the fate of the conspirators?"

Clement still wouldn't name names, so Kirkland did. "Lord Fendall and Rupert Swinnerton are dead."

The Frenchman gave a nod of satisfaction. "A fitting end. Have I earned a comfortable imprisonment until the end of the war? If I am truly fortunate, the lovely Parisian widow I was courting might wait for me."

Kirkland leaned tiredly against the door frame. He wasn't just physically exhausted, but weary of destroying lives. Drained to the soul by playing God.

But God could be benevolent, and in this case, perhaps Kirkland could be also. "I have a proposition for you, Monsieur Clement. If you'll give me your word of honor to do no more spying against Britain, I will release you. You can return to your tailor shop and your friends and your Parisian lady. Just promise me that you will never work against my country again."

The Frenchman caught his breath, hope and disbelief in his eyes. "You would free me in return for my word? You'll *accept* my word if I offer it?"

"We settled that when you were first captured, I believe. Are you prepared to go forth and spy no more?"

Clement gave a shaky laugh. "Indeed I will, my lord. And gladly. Spying withers the soul. Will . . . will you take my hand?"

"Indeed I shall, sir." As they shook hands, a thought struck Kirkland. "I never got around to asking this, but a close friend of mine named Wyndham was captured in France when the Peace of Amiens ended. Nothing has been heard from him since. I suppose he's long since dead, but . . . I have to ask."

Clement's eyes narrowed thoughtfully. "As a matter of fact," he said slowly, "I may know where the gentleman is. . . ."

Epilogue

Regular newspaper notices of the wedding were as discreet and formal as one might expect, but a popular woman's magazine ran a longer story with the details their readers loved. Their society reporter wrote:

> *The nuptials of Sir Damian Mackenzie and Lady Kiri Lawford were celebrated at St. George's, Hanover Square, followed by a sumptuous wedding breakfast at the home of the bride's brother, the seventh Duke of Ashton. In an unconventional touch, the bride was given away both by her stepfather, General John Stillwell, the Hero of Hind, and her mother, Princess Lakshmi Lawford Stillwell, the dowager Duchess of Ashton.*
>
> *Standing up with the happy couple were the bride's sister, Miss Lucia Stillwell, and the groom's brother, Major Lord Masterson. His lordship was most dashing in his scarlet regimentals and with his arm in a sling due to injuries suffered on the Peninsula in Noble Service to His Country.*

The elderly widow who supplemented her income by writing such pieces paused to nibble on the end of her

pencil. Since churches were places of public worship, she
was free to attend the weddings, christenings, and funerals
of the beau monde. With her gift for friendly chat, she
could usually glean enough material from those in attendance to make it appear that she was an invited guest.

In this case, she wasn't sure if it was a war wound that
Lord Masterson was suffering from. For all she knew, he
might have fallen off his horse when drunk. But being
wounded in service to his country sounded so much better.

She made a note to learn the name of his regiment later.
Some details could be invented with no harm, but one
must be accurate about military matters.

She wondered whether she should refer to the fact that
the groom's birth had been . . . irregular. She found it
touching that the half brothers were obviously close, but
her editor wouldn't like any references to bastardy.

Best not to discuss the matter of Sir Damian's reported
death, either. She had no idea what the true story was, but
his claim that he'd woken up at St. Bart's some weeks after
a head injury sounded like pure gammon to her.

The Duchess of Ashton, a charming, gracious, and
enceinte young woman with not a trace of haughtiness,
had provided several good nuggets of information. The
widow bent to her work again, writing very small because
paper was expensive.

> *The happy couple met because Sir Damian attended*
> *the Westerfield Academy with the bride's brother,*
> *the Duke of Ashton. Numerous other distinguished*
> *graduates of the school were present. The founder*
> *and headmistress, Lady Agnes Westerfield, traveled*
> *up from Kent as an honored guest.*

The widow worked on the principle that one could
never mention titles too often. In her final draft, she would

reduce most of the titles to initials for discretion's sake, but in this version, she preferred to write them out. Best not to reveal that the Westerfield Academy had been founded for boys of "good birth and bad behavior." That would raise far too many questions in her readers' minds.

> *Other guests included Lord Kirkland; Major Alexander Randall, heir to the Earl of Daventry, and his lovely bride, Lady Julia Randall; the Honorable Charles Clarke-Townsend and his wife and daughter; and the Honorable Robert Carmichael.*

Should she mention the veiled young guest who'd looked remarkably like Princess Charlotte Augusta? Tempting, very tempting, but the princess had obviously been attending in a purely private capacity. It wasn't wise to mention royalty when they thought they were being incognito.

Now for the part the widow liked best, which was describing the bride and groom.

> *The tall and splendidly handsome Sir Damian is a noted leader of fashion, and his military bearing gives evidence of his own Peninsular service.*

Oh, a fine and dashing rogue he was, too! He reminded the widow of her own dear husband. When the officiating cleric had asked if anyone knew any reason the marriage should not take place, she'd been tempted to stand up and object on the grounds that she wanted him for herself. She might have done so if she had been thirty years younger. Not that Sir Damian would look at anyone other than the bride he so clearly adored, and that was as it should be.

> *In a tribute to her mother's royal Hindoo blood, the demure and beautiful bride wore a magnificent*

scarlet silk sari with stunning borders of intricate golden embroidery. Her gold necklaces, earrings, and myriad bangle bracelets were also of Hindoo origin.

The widow had been a little shocked to see what looked like intricate brown tattoos on the bride's slim hands and arms, but the Duchess of Ashton had explained that the designs were temporary and part of Indian wedding tradition.

Nor was the widow convinced of the bride's demureness. She'd been close enough to the altar to hear General Stillwell—such a fine-looking man, even at his age!— tell Sir Damian that he hoped her husband would do a better job of controlling Lady Kiri than her father had. Sir Damian had just laughed and taken firm hold of his bride's hand.

The widow suspected that there hadn't been any surprises on the newlyweds' wedding night. When they'd come laughing down the aisle as man and wife, the widow had the distinct impression that the couple had sampled the goods and were well pleased with what they'd found. Not that she was one to judge—she and her future husband had anticipated their wedding vows with enthusiasm and as much frequency as they'd been able to manage.

The happy couple will be spending the Christmas holidays with family and friends at the Duke of Ashton's seat, Ralston Abbey, in Wiltshire. In future they will reside in London and Wiltshire. The union of Sir Damian and Lady Kiri was a splendid joining of East and West that all may rejoice in.

Pleased with her efforts, the widow set down her pencil with a smile. She knew happily ever after when she saw it.

Historical Note

The real Princess Charlotte was much as I have depicted her—a good-hearted girl who had a horrible upbringing, caught between two parents who despised each other. She seems to have lacked the arrogance that usually goes with royalty, and was known to happily chat with the village baker when on holiday in a seaside town.

Charlotte had a rebellious streak, and sneaking off at night to attend a masked ball is by no means unlikely, based on her track record. She did find happiness briefly in her marriage to Prince Leopold of Saxe-Coburg-Saafield, but sadly, she died in childbirth at the age of twenty-one due to bad medical treatment. If she'd had a good midwife, she probably would have been fine.

The doctor whose incompetence cost the lives of Charlotte and her son later committed suicide. It is known as the "triple obstetrical tragedy."

Since she was the heiress to the throne, her death spurred a frantic rush by her royal uncles to find legitimate wives so they could father heirs to the throne. (Her many uncles preferred mistresses whose children were ineligible to inherit.) Her first cousin, Queen Victoria, would never have been born if Charlotte hadn't died so young.

The State Opening of Parliament is an enormously grand affair of the sort the British do so well. Princess Charlotte did indeed attend her first State Opening in 1812 and she sat on the Woolsack, luckily without my added melodrama. She was cheered as she arrived. Her father was not. The London public had good taste.

There were times when Napoleon would have welcomed a peace treaty with Britain. His on-again, off-again minister of police, Joseph Fouché, never stopped plotting.

Did you miss the first two books in the Lost Lords series? It starts with LOVING A LOST LORD . . .

In the first of a dazzling series, Mary Jo Putney introduces the Lost Lords—maverick childhood friends with a flair for defying convention. Each is about to discover the woman who is his perfect match—but perfection doesn't come easily, even for the noble Duke of Ashton.

Battered by the sea, Adam remembers nothing of his past, his ducal rank, nor of the shipwreck that almost claimed his life. However, he's delighted to hear that the golden-haired vision tending his wounds is his wife. Mariah's name and face may not be familiar, but her touch, her warmth, feel deliciously right.

When Mariah Clarke prayed for a way to deter a bullying suitor, she didn't imagine she'd find the answer washed ashore on a desolate beach. Convincing Adam that he is her husband is surprisingly easy. Resisting the temptation to act his wife, in every way, will prove anything but. And now a passion begun in fantasy has become dangerously real—and completely irresistible.

After an eternity of cold water, numbness, and despair, he was dragged ashore. Emerging from the water pulled him from the deathlike trance that had allowed him to survive in the cold water for so long. Dimly he remembered stumbling along with help, sliding into blackness, and then awaking to—perfection.

The woman bending over him seemed more dream than reality, yet the warmth radiating from her was palpable. Her eyes were warm brown and a cloud of golden hair floated around her perfect oval face. She shimmered in the lamplight. Wondering if he'd drowned and gone to some other realm, he raised an unsteady hand to stroke those finely spun strands. They were gossamer silk against his fingers.

"You're safe now." She pulled her long hair back and tied the shining mass in a loose knot at her nape. Her every movement was grace. "Do you speak English?"

He had to think to answer her question. English. Language. Understanding. He licked his dry lips and whispered, "Y . . . yes."

"Good. That will make things easier." She slid an arm under his shoulders and raised him enough to drink. He swallowed thirstily, thinking it strange how much he craved water since it had almost killed him. And it was humiliating that he was so weak that he couldn't even drink without help.

When he'd had enough, she took the glass away and gently laid him down again. She wore a night robe, and though it covered her thoroughly, her dishabille was deliciously tantalizing. "Such green eyes you have," she observed. "They are striking with your dark complexion."

His eyes were green and the rest of him, dark? He shifted his gaze to his right hand and examined it. The skin was medium tan, a half dozen shades darker than her ivory complexion. He realized that he had no idea what he looked like, beyond tan and bruised. Or what he ought to look like.

She continued, "Can you tell me your name?"

He searched his mind and came up with—nothing. No name, no place, no past, just as he had no sense of his own body. That had to be *wrong*. Panic surged through him, more terrifying than the cold sea that had nearly drowned him. He was nothing, nobody, torn from his past and thrust into an unknown present. The horror of that echoed through every fiber of his being. Struggling to master his fear, he choked out, "I . . . I don't know."

Seeing his fear, she caught his cold hand between her warm palms. "You've endured a considerable ordeal. After you rest and recover, you will surely remember." She frowned uncertainly. "Can you have forgotten that I'm your wife, Mariah Clarke?"

"My . . . my *wife*?" He stared, incredulous. How could he possibly forget being wed to a woman like this? But even though he didn't remember their marriage, his fears diminished as he compulsively clenched her hand. "Then . . . I am a most fortunate man."

She smiled warmly. "Rest while I go for tea and broth. I've sent for someone who will know how to treat that blow to your head. With luck, she'll be here soon. By tomorrow, you will likely remember everything about yourself."

He raised unsteady fingers to the ragged gash that ran down the left side of his skull. He had so many aches and bruises that he hadn't noticed any in particular, but now that she mentioned it, his head throbbed like the very devil. "Tea would be . . . welcome."

"I'll only be gone a few minutes," she promised as she whisked away.

He stared at the ceiling after she left. He had a *wife*. He hated that he remembered nothing about that vision of loveliness who had saved his life, nor about being married. It was easy to imagine kissing her, and a good deal more. But of actual memories he had none. It seemed damned unfair.

He spent time during her absence searching his mind and memory and trying not to knot the sheets with nervous fingers. He recognized objects around him. Bed. Blanket. Fire. Pinkness in the sky outside. That would be . . . dawn. Oddly, a second set of words shadowed the first. *Palang. Kambal. Aag.* He was quite sure the words meant the same as the English ones that came to mind, so he probably knew a different language, though he had no idea what it might be.

But he had no personal memories. Again he fought the rising fear. The emotion was a screaming, vulnerable awareness that he was alone and so helpless that he didn't even know what might threaten him.

Strangely, deep inside he sensed that this was not the first time he had been torn away from himself. Perhaps that was why his fear was so great. But he couldn't remember anything about that other situation, whatever it might be.

He had survived that earlier loss. This time he had a wife who told him he was safe. Surely she would look out for him until he was strong enough to look out for her.

For now, he remembered the most basic fact of all: that he was male and Mariah Clarke was female.

. . . and continues with NEVER LESS THAN A LADY.

New York Times bestselling author Mary Jo Putney continues her stunning Lost Lords series with this stirring, sensual story of a rebellious nobleman drawn to a lovely widow with a shocking past.

As the sole remaining heir to the Earl of Daventry, Alexander Randall knows his duty: find a wife and sire a son of his own. The perfect bride for a man in his position would be a biddable young girl of good breeding. But the woman who haunts his imagination is Julia Bancroft—a village midwife with a dark secret that thrusts her into Randall's protection.

Within the space of a day, Julia has been abducted by her first husband's cronies, rescued, and proposed to by a man she scarcely knows. Stranger still is her urge to say yes. A union with Alexander Randall could benefit them both, but Julia doubts she can ever trust her heart again, or the fervent desire Randall ignites. Yet perhaps only a Lost Lord can show a woman like Julia everything a true marriage can be.

"Mrs. Bancroft?" a light female voice called as the bells on the cottage door rang to indicate a visitor. "It's me, Ellie Flynn."

"Good afternoon, Ellie." Julia moved from the kitchen into her examining room, taking the young woman's toddler into her arms. "How is Master Alfred feeling today?"

"Much better, Mrs. Bancroft." The woman smiled fondly at her redheaded son, who was reaching for Julia's cat. "That horehound and honey tea you gave me helped his cough right smartly."

"The Duchess of Ashton's cough remedy." Julia looked the little boy over. He grinned back at her. "The name alone is halfway to being a cure."

The tea was a recipe she'd learned from her friend Mariah, who hadn't been a duchess then. Mariah had been raised by a grandmother who was a village healer not unlike Julia, but more knowledgeable about herbs. Julia had learned a few simple remedies from the midwife who had trained her, but Mariah knew many more, and her recipes had been a good addition to Julia's store of treatments.

She handed the little boy back to his mother. "He's flourishing. You're doing a fine job raising him, Ellie."

"I couldn't have done it without your help. When he was born, I hardly knew which end was which!" Ellie, also redheaded and no more than nineteen, shyly offered a worn canvas bag. "I've some nice fresh eggs for you, if you'd like them."

"Lovely! I've been wanting an egg for my tea." Julia accepted the bag and moved to the kitchen of her cottage, removing the eggs from their straw packing so she could return the bag. She never turned away a mother or child in need, so while many of her patients couldn't afford to pay in cash, Julia and her household ate well.

After Mrs. Flynn and her little boy left, Julia sat at her desk and wrote notes about patients she'd seen that day. Whiskers, her tabby cat, snoozed beside her. After finishing her notes, Julia sat back and petted the cat as she surveyed her kingdom.

Rose Cottage had two reception rooms at the front of the house. She used this one as an office for treating patients and storing remedies. The other front chamber was her sitting room. Kitchen, pantry, and a bedroom ran across the back of the cottage. A slant-roofed but spacious second bedroom was up the narrow stairs.

Behind the cottage was a stable for her placid pony, and a garden that produced herbs and vegetables. The flowers in front of the cottage were there simply because she believed that everyone needed flowers.

Rose Cottage was not what she'd been raised to live in, but that life had turned out very badly. This life was so much better. She had her own home, friends, and she provided a vital service for this remote community. With no physicians nearby, she had become more than a midwife. She set bones and treated wounds and minor illnesses.

Some claimed she was better than the doctors in Carlisle. Certainly she was cheaper.

Though her trip to London several months earlier as Mariah's chaperone had left her restless, she was mostly content in Hartley. She would never have a child of her own, but she had many children in her life, as well as the respect of the community. She took pride in the fact that she'd built this life for herself with her own hard work.

The front door opened and a young woman bustled in, a toddler on one hip and a canvas bag slung over her shoulder. Julia smiled at the other two members of her household. "You're back early, Jenny. How are Mrs. Wolf and Annie?"

Jenny Watson beamed. "Happy and healthy. Since I delivered Annie myself, whenever I see her I'm as proud as if I'd invented babies."

Julia laughed. "I know the feeling. Helping a baby into the world is a joy."

Jenny reached into her bag. "Mr. Wolf sent along a nice bit of bacon."

"That will go well with Ellie Flynn's eggs."

"I'll fix us our tea then." Jenny headed into the kitchen and set her daughter in a cradle by the hearth. Molly, fourteen months old, yawned hugely and curled up for a nap.

Julia watched the child fondly. Jenny was not the first desperate pregnant girl who had shown up on Julia's doorstep, but she was the only one to become part of the household. Jenny had married a man against her family's wishes. Her family had turned their backs when he abandoned her, saying that she'd made her bed and must lie in it.

Near starvation, Jenny had offered to work as Julia's servant for no wages, only food and a roof over her head. The girl had proved to be clever and a hard worker, and after Molly's birth, she became Julia's apprentice. She was well on her way to becoming a fine midwife, and she and her child had become Julia's family.

Jenny had just called, "Our tea is ready!" when the string of bells that hung on the front door jangled.

Julia made a face. "I wish I had a shilling for every time I've been interrupted during a meal!"

She stood—then froze with horror at the sight of the three men who entered her home. Two were strangers, but the burly, scar-faced leader, was familiar. Joseph Crockett, the vilest man she'd ever known, had found her.

"Well, well, well. So Lady Julia really is alive," he said menacingly as he pulled a glittering knife from a sheath under his coat. "That can be fixed."

Whiskers hissed and dashed into the kitchen while Julia backed away, numb with panic.

After years of quiet hiding, she was a dead woman.